Take Back Tomorrow

Other Books by Richard Levesque

Strictly Analog
Dead Man's Hand
Unfinished Business
The Girl at the End of the World
The Devil You Know
Foundlings

Take Back Tomorrow

RICHARD LEVESQUE

This is a work of fiction. Any resemblance to people living or dead is purely coincidental.

ACKNOWLEDGMENTS

I owe several people thanks for their help with this book in its various stages. My friends Bruce Henderson and Tamara Trujillo read early versions of the manuscript and provided valuable feedback (and even more valuable encouragement). Brandi Bowles, my literary agent at the time, provided extensive notes and was a great sounding board as the book continued to take shape. Finally, my wife, Kari, read through early versions as well, offering valuable insight along the way and helping me keep my focus throughout the whole process. I honestly don't think the book would have come together without her in my corner.

CHAPTER ONE

Eddie Royce sat in Whistler's office on the sixth floor of the Meteor building and waited patiently for the editor to look up from the galleys he studied, a smoldering cigar held between his thick lips and a look of quiet disgust on his face as he read. The muffled clack and ding of a typewriter made its way into the office from somewhere beyond Whistler's closed door, and Eddie tried hard not to let it distract him. He sat in one of the mismatched chairs that faced Whistler's enormous, scarred desk and thumbed nervously through the March 1940 issue of *Stupendous*, silently going over the pitch he had been formulating for days and hoping Whistler would not notice his anxiety. The magazine had hit the newsstands only three days ago, and Eddie had already read it cover to cover, focusing most of his scrutiny on one story—"Dark Hearts of Mars" by Edward Royce. It was his second publication in *Stupendous*, his second publication anywhere, really, but he already had two more stories and a serial accepted. After finally seeing his name in print following months of trying and failing, he had quickly come to believe in his success as a writer in spite of what he knew to be true—that he was at best unoriginal and at worst a plagiarist.

As with every issue of *Stupendous*, the cover of the magazine in Eddie's hands was a work of art that no doubt accounted for a large portion of sales each month. The covers were always sensational, and this one featured a beautiful female space explorer watching in exaggerated alarm as her space ship exploded in the background, apparently leaving her stranded as she floated in space, her skin tight suit accentuating her curvaceous figure. Eddie knew from having carefully studied "Castaways in Space" in this issue that the story featured no such character or scene, but that did not matter. The *Stupendous* covers pulled readers in, and the stories kept them there until next month. Dozens of recent issues were scattered around Whistler's office, each with its brightly lurid variation of the barely clad female warrior, seductive villainess or imperiled princess to draw the eye. With the first installment of his serial to appear in the May issue, Eddie knew that promoting it with a cover illustration would ensure reader interest and secure his position in the stable of *Stupendous* authors, and he had phoned to make an appointment with Whistler this morning to try to convince the editor of the same thing.

That Whistler had largely ignored him after having him seen into the office had not helped Eddie's nerves any. He was made even more agitated when Whistler looked up from the desk for a moment and mumbled around his cigar, "Blackwood's coming in this morning. I mentioned you'd be here. Says he wants to meet you." He paused, an eyebrow rising to make deeper wrinkles in the editor's already craggy forehead, before adding "Can't imagine why" and returning to ponder the galleys before him.

Eddie did not know how to respond. Chester Blackwood was the most famous, most successful writer of science fiction in the last fifteen years. His stories and novels had been among the most inspirational things Eddie had ever read, and meeting his idol was something he had been hoping for since he had first begun getting published in *Stupendous*.

"I assume you don't mind," Whistler said, pulling the cigar out of his mouth and holding it over the galleys like a pen.

"About Blackwood?"

"Yep." The editor set the galleys down now and stared at Eddie with more scrutiny than Eddie would have liked.

"No," Eddie said a bit too quickly. "I don't mind at all." He paused. "Why would I mind?"

Whistler shrugged. "Star struck maybe. A writer like you. A writer like him. Some guys get antsy."

"No, no," he said. "It's fine. What time's he coming in?" He realized he might not get his chance to bring up the cover illustration if he didn't say something about it quickly.

Whistler glanced at his wristwatch. "Should be here now. SOB's always late, though."

Eddie barely had time to register shock at the epithet when the door to Whistler's office swung violently open behind him, slamming against a wall and half bouncing closed again before Eddie could turn in surprise. He heard before he saw the woman in the doorway shouting, "Whistler, goddammit, I've had it!" Twisted around in the chair, Eddie beheld a beautiful woman whose anger practically bubbled out of her. With platinum hair hanging to her shoulders and bright, gaudy makeup exaggerating otherwise stunning lips and eyes, she stood in a tattered green terry cloth robe, her chest heaving, her face red and her eyes brimming with tears of rage. She looked to be about 25, perhaps a year or two younger than Eddie.

Whistler stood up behind the desk and calmly said, "Now look, sweetie."

"Don't sweetie me, you son of a bitch!" she shouted, stepping all the way into the room, only two feet away from Eddie but oblivious to his presence. "I'm not doing it. Not this time. Not anymore."

"All right, all right. Just calm down and catch your breath for a second." When she remained silent, Whistler continued. "This is Mr. Royce, by the way. You may be modeling for one of his stories next month if he gets his way." Eddie turned again to look at Whistler, stunned at what appeared to be Whistler's amazing intuition. The editor really did know writers. But probably not women, Eddie thought.

The woman barely glanced in Eddie's direction and then said, more calmly now, "Not a chance. You either need to get Klaus another model or you need to get me another artist. I've had it, I tell you."

"Let's not go overboard here, Roxie." Whistler was beginning to take a patronizing tone with her. Eddie doubted that it would do any good. "Now tell me what the problem is, and we'll see what we can work out."

"This is the problem," the woman said, her voice rising again as she quickly undid the terry cloth belt and pulled open the robe. Eddie felt his face grow red, and he glanced quickly at the floor before finding himself compelled to look up again and stare. She stood in an outfit that would have been perfectly suited to one of the women on the covers of *Stupendous*: gold boots that went to just above the knee, fish net stockings covering her thighs, gold short pants that went only to the tops of the thighs and wide, gold suspenders that crisscrossed her bare chest, leaving her breasts almost completely exposed. They swayed slightly from the motion of her arms having yanked the robe open, and Eddie found himself wondering what kept the suspenders in place. It was the same question he would have asked if he had seen her on the cover of the magazine.

Whistler cleared his throat. "A little too much skin, huh?"

"Yeah," she responded sharply, her eyes growing wide, challenging.

"You know he'll change your face on the final drawing. It's not like you'll be walking down the street and people will recognize you from the cover. They never have before."

"That's not it, and you know it. He's a pervert! You should see the way he stares."

"He's an artist, Roxie. He's got to look if he wants to paint you."

"But do I have to be dressed like this while he does it? Couldn't I just strike the pose?"

Whistler sighed as though he had been through this with her before. "You know he's got his limitations. He needs his models in costume, or he can't capture the feeling of the scene."

"He can change my face but not the outfit? You know that's not it. You know it as well as I do. Even you can see that, can't you?" This last was addressed to Eddie, and he felt himself grow redder, both at having been acknowledged by her and at having been caught so obviously staring at her breasts.

He self-consciously looked up into her eyes. They were deep and blue and stared right back at him. "I . . ." he began, but she waved her hand dismissively at him, glared once more at Whistler, then turned on her heel and strode out of the office, the robe still open and fanning out behind her as she walked past a tall, gray haired man outside Whistler's door.

"Hi, Daddy," she said and kept walking.

Behind Eddie, Whistler let out a long sigh and then said, "Eddie Royce, meet Chester Blackwood." Eddie spun quickly to look at Whistler, then turned again as he got out of the chair to face the door. "You've actually met the whole Blackwood family now," Whistler added, sounding quite amused.

Blackwood stepped into the office, a mischievous look on his face. He was taller than Eddie had imagined and looked considerably older than the pictures on the backs of his books. He wore a wide brimmed fedora, which he took off almost immediately to reveal a head of thinning gray hair. He had a full, thick mustache that drooped down past the corners of his mouth, hiding his smile almost entirely. His eyes were the same deep blue as his daughter's but with deep crow's feet around them. When he smiled, the wrinkles lifted and were more expressive than his mostly hidden mouth, but when the smile faded, the wrinkles made his eyes appear heavy, weary and empty. He smiled now as he gave Eddie a firm handshake while Whistler formally introduced them.

"Roxanne can be a bit volatile," Blackwood said as he released Eddie's hand and looked back at the door his daughter had just stormed out of. Eddie could only grin in embarrassment. Painfully beautiful, Roxanne's presence alone would have been enough to shake Eddie, but her outburst and her costume had left him in a spin, and immediately meeting the writer he most wanted to be like after Roxanne's tempestuous departure had caused Eddie to feel almost numb and self-consciously foolish. It was not the professional meeting of peers he had fantasized about. After a few moments of exchanged pleasantries, Whistler left them, clearly feeling the need to find a pretense to leave the two writers alone. His departure was so awkward and obvious that it made Eddie even more nervous, as though Blackwood had made it known ahead of time that he wanted to be alone with the younger writer, something Eddie had not been prepared for. Under any other circumstances, he would have been thrilled, but now it made him uneasy.

When the door clicked shut after Whistler, Eddie smiled unsteadily and Blackwood, who had remained standing since entering the office, now walked around Whistler's desk and sat in the editor's swivel rocker, making it squeak loudly. He pushed himself back from the desk a bit and crossed his long legs, his elbows on the arm rests and the fingertips of each hand meeting lightly in front of his chest. He nodded toward Eddie and then directed his eyes downward toward the chair Eddie had hopped out of when Blackwood had walked in the room. Taking the cue, Eddie sat, continuing to smile at the older writer, not knowing what else to say or do. Blackwood had seemed pleasant enough when being introduced to Eddie, the deep lines around his eyes making him appear open and inviting. But he was not smiling now as he quietly asked, "Did you think no one would figure it out?"

Eddie hesitated. The blush he had felt at Roxanne's presence returned tenfold. He knew there should be a dozen ways to respond, had thought out this moment a hundred times and planned all the possible ways out of it. But he had never thought it would be Chester Blackwood asking the question, and he couldn't think of a single thing to say. His mouth instantly dry and his heart pounding fiercely, he could see in a straight line six months back to September 1939, could see the direct cause and effect chain that had gotten him here and how it had started with his decision to cheat the system rather than beat it.

****

He had been sitting on the uncarpeted floor of his apartment during the hottest part of the day in the middle of the hottest month of the year. Eddie had only been in L.A. a short time but had learned that September in Southern California was always the worst, and he had the windows open and a cheap electric fan blowing right on him. It didn't do any good, just moved the hot air around, reminding him there was no way out of it. The air wasn't the only thing weighing on him. He sat with his back to the wall, the apartment's single door to his right, dressed in faded dungarees and a worn undershirt, sweat beading on his forehead and dripping from his dark, unkempt hair. On the floor next to him lay a small pile of envelopes, most of them still sealed. The one that mattered had been torn open in haste, and the letter it contained now rested on the floor next to Eddie's thigh. He had learned from experience to look for the first negative word. It always jumped out—words like "sorry" or "unfortunately" or "regret"; phrases like "cannot use" or "does not fit our needs" or "unable to place at this time." This one was no different. As much as typewriters or time alone, rejection letters made up the life of the professional writer, or the person trying to become one. Eddie knew this as well as anyone and had been stoic about it, patient about it, but the steady stream of rejection and the barely polite, insincere encouragement of "perhaps another time" or "we wish you success" that came at the ends of the letters was beginning to get to him.

He had been sitting there for half an hour, his gaze shifting from the letter to other spots around the room—to the rickety second-hand desk with the big black Underwood perched on its edge, to the single bed with its dingy pillow and lone sheet, to the wall heater that had barely functioned when he first moved in and which he had not needed to use for several months, to his shelves packed floor to ceiling with books and boxes of pulp magazines. And as he sat, he really hadn't been reading the letter or taking in any of what he looked at. Instead, he had just been thinking, a litany of phrases going through his head repeatedly, variations on "I'm not good enough," "I'm not original enough," and "I should just give up." Eventually, it was originality that he began to fixate on, to worry about, to grow frustrated and angry over. Since the time he had gotten his first rejection letter, he had been plagued by the question of what other writers had that he lacked. This had driven him to read and study not only the work of geniuses but also the successful, well-paid hacks, trying to find their secret. He knew the works of Wells and Verne inside out. He admired Edgar Rice Burroughs' originality and success, his slick craftsmanship. He didn't aspire to their greatness. He just wanted to be published. And there were so many possibilities; his shelves were a testament to this with their carefully catalogued collections of *Amazing Stories, Weird Tales, Astounding, Stupendous, Startling Stories, Thrilling Wonder Stories* and dozens of other lesser pulps. He bought, read, studied and preserved his collection, perusing old issues in the middle of the night, becoming truly amazed and astounded at the work being produced in the last several years by people like C.L. Moore, Stanley Weinbaum, and Chester Blackwood.

And that, he realized, had been his problem. The thought struck him with an almost physical impact, and he let his head fall back against the wall with a thud, his eyes now brighter and more alert than they had been since he had opened the letter. *I've been trying to be original,* he thought, *but I've just been crowding my head with other people's ideas.* What was worse, he knew, was that the process was probably irreversible, that there could be no unique plots when the outlandishness of Burroughs crept into his subconscious imagination whenever he began mapping out a story, that there could be no unique aliens when Moore's Shambleau or Weinbaum's Martians held their constant influence over his creations. He had learned from experience that the more he tried to break away from the ideas of others, the less interesting his work had become. *I haven't got an original idea in my head*, he thought and felt almost freed by the realization. *I can write, but I can't create. So now what do I do?* The temptation to stride across the room and toss the big black Underwood out the second story window to the street was momentarily overwhelming, but another thought, even more radical, popped into his head almost immediately. He had been trying so hard, too hard, to be original, and the attempt had failed him. What if he tried deliberately to be unoriginal, to copy blatantly, unashamedly? He smiled at the thought. But who to copy? Borrowing from other science fiction writers hadn't gotten him anywhere, even when he didn't know he was doing it. So why not borrow from elsewhere, take someone else's plot and set in space?

The possibilities were endless and exhilarating. He sat down at the typewriter, rolled a fresh sheet of paper into it, and began thinking, looking at the shelves across the room on which he kept the few works of literature that were not science fiction. He laughed out loud as he began to ponder Hemingway's Lost Generation set in space, a galactic Jake Barnes running with horrifying beasts through the streets of an alien city, desperately in love with an aloof space princess but filled with doubt and anxiety over his emasculating injury from a recent interplanetary war. Or Faulkner: generations of psychologically repressed space colonists on a distant moon whose interactions with each other were all colored by the past and the faded glory their families had known before a great war had relegated them to this sad and tragic existence. Or the Bible: a space messiah, oppressed people, a betrayal, an execution, a resurrection, a revolution. There were so many ideas, so many possibilities, and none of them had ever been tried in science fiction. He could churn out novels for the rest of his life and never run out of ideas—because he wouldn't have to think of any in the first place. The work had all been done for him already.

He had finally settled on Shakespeare and began rewriting *Hamlet* as a space opera. His hero, whom he named Rider, was an alienated prince who had just returned to his home world after his father's death. Rider was informed of his father's murder and his uncle's treachery not by a ghost but rather by a faithful pet that communicated with the dead king through psychic and telepathic abilities. Rider swore revenge and decided to affect not insanity but shell shock. Here, Eddie had to go back and revise, having Rider return from a war rather than from an intergalactic university. Seemingly deadened to his existence and oblivious to the attempts of friends and the seductive Princess Euphonia to interest him in life at court, Rider successfully presented himself as harmless to his dangerous uncle while developing a plan to avenge his father. Realizing that the suicides and murders of almost all the principle characters was not as suitable for the pulp market as it had been for Shakespeare's stage, Eddie rewrote the end to have Prince Rider kill his uncle in a duel, banish his mother to a penal colony on the planet's moon and take Euphonia as his wife after rescuing her from space pirates loyal to the dead uncle.

It took Eddie three days of constant writing and revising to finish the sixty page manuscript of "Rider's Revenge," three days and nights of banging away at the Underwood with only breaks of an hour or two to sleep or wander down the hallway to the bathroom and down the stairs and out to the street to get a sandwich at the Terminal Café, the small restaurant built into the corner of the Southern Pacific station a block away. Finally finished with the manuscript and actually satisfied with it after reading it with pencil in hand a dozen times, Eddie pushed himself away from his desk and walked around the room. His hands shook, and although it was two o'clock in the morning, sweat beaded on his brow. He knew the story was good, better than anything he had done before, because he had never had such a physical reaction to anything he had ever written. Surprised, he found that he was afraid of what he had done, not because it was Shakespeare plagiarized but because he knew with absolute certainty that it would change his life. He looked around the apartment, at the shelves, the hot plate, the bed and the litter of discarded pages around the floor, and knew the manuscript in his hands was his ticket out.

After finally allowing himself to fall asleep for a few hours, Eddie woke up, ran down to the Terminal for a cup of coffee, and spent the rest of the morning perusing the most recent issues of *Amazing, Astounding, Fantastic* and *Stupendous* to determine which would be the best place to submit "Rider's Revenge" to. He finally decided on *Stupendous* for a handful of reasons and started the four-block walk to the drug store for an envelope and stamps.

As a twelve-year-old boy in 1926, Eddie had been initiated into the world of space ships, aliens and time travel when his eye had been drawn to the third issue of *Stupendous* on a drugstore rack, and the magazine had held a special place in his collecting and reading ever since. Back then, the magazine had been titled *Stupendous Stories of the Strange and Supernatural*, and it had been the first pulp to compete with Hugo Gernsback's *Amazing Stories*. The brainchild of its original editor, Augustus Swinburne, *Stupendous* had undergone a lengthy evolution, publishing serialized classics from the last century as well as the pioneers of the new science fiction. By the late 1920s, it had changed its title to *Stupendous Science Stories* when it dropped the supernatural elements, shifting those stories to a new magazine called *Macabre*. By the early 1930s, it had been shortened to just *Stupendous* and had a reputation for publishing the most innovative, creative and artistic stories in the field. While *Amazing* stressed the science in science fiction, and *Weird Tales* focused on the uncanny, *Stupendous* published stories that were character driven. Because of this, Eddie felt that the stories in *Stupendous* always made sense; their characters' choices were always justified and consistent with their personalities and motivations. Explosions, death rays, bug-eyed monsters and the like were not likely to appear at the end to effect an escape for some hapless hero or struggling superman.

And best of all, as far as Eddie was concerned, *Stupendous* was the flagship of a publishing empire; after *Macabre*, Swinburne's company had branched out, and Swinburne had given up editorship of the magazine to form the Meteor publishing company, printing Westerns, Romances and Detective stories in a variety of pulp magazines. What was more, they took the occasional wildly successful serial and reissued it as a hardcover book. Eddie had several of them on his shelf, most by Chester Blackwood, who was unequivocally the star in the Meteor family of authors. He thought about the books as he walked to the drug store with the manuscript for "Rider's Revenge" in his hands—the dust jackets, the excerpts from book reviews, the "About the Author" paragraph on the back cover. He imagined his name on the spine instead of Blackwood's, and he started to shake again.

When the letter had come, he hadn't needed to look for the negative words. Pulling the letter from its envelope, he had felt his heart all but stop as a check slipped out with it and fluttered to the floor like a sick bird. He had stood as if entranced, not even thinking to read the acceptance letter signed by Whistler himself rather than by the generic "editorial staff" that typically closed the rejections. Instead, he had looked at the check lying face up on the floor, the sum of $30 clearly visible in blue ink, already thinking about *Troilus and Cressida* set on Mars.

****

Now he sat in Whistler's office a changed man. The dungarees and sweat stained undershirt had been replaced with a decent suit to cover his wiry frame, still bargain basement but respectable. He shaved every day now when he wasn't in the middle of a writing frenzy, and he wore cheap cologne and convinced himself that it didn't smell cheap at all. He kept his dark hair cut and combed, and when he looked in the mirror every morning, he imagined his face on the back of a book, telling himself it was the face of a writer—angular features, dark eyes, a nose maybe a bit too pointed and a bit too big but overall an attractive package. It was not that he had grown conceited but rather that he simply had confidence. "Rider's Revenge" was long passed, having seen publication three issues ago and, according to Whistler, having generated quite a bit of reader mail although Eddie had never seen any of it. "Dark Hearts of Mars"—the *Troilus and Cressida* story—would be followed by Eddie's version of *The Tempest*, or rather the first installment of his first serial. His versions of *Othello* and *Measure for Measure* had already been accepted for publication, and he had spent the last several days reading *Richard III* and *Macbeth* trying to decide which could be more suitably adapted with ray guns and robots.

But now he found himself wondering how to respond to the first person to hint that he had figured out where Eddie's story ideas had come from. If it had been Whistler asking if he had thought anyone would figure out his deception, Eddie would have explained that it wasn't really plagiarism, that there were no original ideas, that his stories were nothing more than adaptations and really no different from the adapting that Shakespeare himself had engaged in when borrowing his plots from older stories. But it was not Whistler asking. It was another writer, one whom Eddie had deep respect for, one whom he idolized. He could not so easily justify to Chester Blackwood what he had done to get himself published.

13

Blackwood just raised an eyebrow and waited. Finally, Eddie simply said, "No."

"No?"

"No. No, I knew someone would figure it out at some point, but . . ." He felt a mixture of shame, embarrassment and indignation. He didn't know how to proceed.

"But you figured it would get your foot in the door," Blackwood finished for him. Eddie nodded. "Figured once they knew you were good, maybe even once you had some fans out there," he waved his hand towards Whistler's filmy window, "they'd have to keep you on, keep printing you, maybe even take seriously all the stories they hadn't bothered with before."

"All true," Eddie said. He felt diminished, childlike, as though he would be walking out of the office a different man than the one who had walked in, as though he had never received an acceptance letter or seen his name in print.

"And besides," Blackwood went on, "Whistler wouldn't expose you, as that would just embarrass the magazine. At worst, he could give your original work a shot, and if it didn't work, didn't live up to Shakespeare," he raised an eyebrow again, "he could just let you fade away, a writer who couldn't maintain the quality of his original output. Happens all the time."

Eddie nodded. "Does he know?"

"Whistler?" Eddie nodded again. "No. Well, at least not from me. He's smart, though. Just not that well read in the classics. But he keeps up on this and that, and if there's fan mail that's made the point, you can bet he's been thinking about it. Probably got some flunky in the mailroom reading the collected works and writing up a synopsis so he can figure out what to do. If it hasn't happened yet, it will."

A new thought occurred to Eddie. "And what's this to you, Mr. Blackwood?"

Blackwood smiled. "Chester. Please." He drummed his fingers together. "You intrigue me, Eddie. You remind me a lot of myself when I was starting out." He paused, a little too long, Eddie thought, but he could not fathom what the pause was meant to reveal. "You also worry me. Perhaps for the same reason."

Eddie smiled uncertainly, thinking that Blackwood was perhaps putting him on. Blackwood did not return the smile. "Worry?" Eddie finally asked.

"You underestimate Whistler and the people he works for. More so them than Whistler. He's shrewd, but he is just the editor. His superior, though . . . I don't think would take kindly to being fooled. You're just lucky you settled on Shakespeare to borrow from and not someone alive. With a lawyer. Even so, our friend on the top floor might feel as though you owe him something. And he's not good people to owe."

Eddie felt himself begin to sweat. "I'm not sure I understand."

"I'm not sure you want to understand." Blackwood stood up. He did it quickly, spryly. He was a tall man and looked like he had been muscular once, but in his late fifties now he seemed on the verge of frailty, and his sudden movement caught Eddie off guard. "If you really understood, it would probably scare the shit out of you. Let me ask you this—have you ever stolen anything before?"

"Stolen?"

"Yes. Like you're stealing from Shakespeare. Like you're technically stealing from this magazine when you cash those checks for half a cent per word. The Shakespeare is harmless, I suppose, since it's so old, but someone who steals even something harmless usually has a propensity for theft in general. Wouldn't you say? And if you haven't stolen before, you're bound to steal more now that you've seen how easy it is—easier than writing on your own."

Eddie told himself he should feel insulted, but he knew Blackwood was right. Still, he did not think of himself as a thief and never had. "I've never stolen anything," he said. "I mean, kids steal things. Penny candy and things. But no, nothing like this ever before."

"And what drove you to it? Money? Fame?"

"Desperation."

"For?"

He hesitated. Blackwood was asking him to reveal a truth he was not even comfortable admitting to himself. There was no point in hiding it, though, and he said with a shrug, "The dream." Blackwood just raised an eyebrow in response, and Eddie continued. "I wanted to see my name in print. I wanted people to read me. I wanted to be able to say I was a writer."

"Anyone can write," Blackwood said, leaning now on Whistler's desk.

"But only the people who get published and paid for it can call themselves writers."

Blackwood smiled, the crow's feet around his eyes crinkling up. "True enough. So you'd steal to realize the dream." The crow's feet faded with the smile, and Blackwood looked coldly serious as he said, "What else would you do?"

For reasons he did not understand, Eddie found the question frightening. Perhaps it was the way it had been asked. All he could say in response was, "I don't understand."

"You don't understand a lot, Eddie. For a smart guy . . . What else would you do for the dream? Would you kill for it?"

"No."

"You're sure?"

"Of course."

"Would you defy the laws of the universe?"

"Excuse me?"

Blackwood's smile returned, his lips actually parting below the moustache to reveal yellowed teeth. He spoke matter-of-factly. "If you had to defy the laws of the universe in order to realize your dreams, would you do it?"

Eddie hesitated and watched Blackwood's eyes, his mouth. They betrayed nothing. The older man was like a teacher who had just asked the biggest question of the day and had no intention of offering help or hints. "Theoretically," he began, but Blackwood's eyes immediately shifted away and his droopy moustache swallowed up the smile. "Yes," Eddie said quickly. "Not just theoretically. Yes."

Blackwood's smile returned. He raised an eyebrow. "You're sure?"

"Yes."

"Then we do have a lot in common." He walked around the desk, reaching into the inside pocket of his coat as he did. He pulled out a business card and stopped in front of Eddie, took a pencil off of Whistler's desk and stooped to write on the back of the card. He handed it to Eddie, who stood up to accept it. "You may need this. I can't say for sure."

"How so?" Eddie glanced at Blackwood's business card. It had his name, but the address and phone number were for the offices at *Stupendous*. On the back of the card, he had penciled in a Pasadena address and a phone number.

Blackwood held up a hand to stop him. "Enough questions. I want to talk to you more about this later. Today if we can."

Eddie slipped the card into this shirt pocket. He felt confused and was responding more automatically than anything else when he said, "Okay. When?"

Blackwood looked at his watch. "Let's say five. At a little bar at Sixth and Los Angeles. Called the Reno Lounge for some reason. One of my haunts. Good?"

"Sure." Eddie met Blackwood's offered hand and shook it for the second time that day. He hoped his voice did not betray his confusion or his doubts about himself and everything that had just been said. "I'll see you at five."

"If I'm late, wait. I have a lot to do this afternoon, and time has a way of slipping away from me. Now get out of here, would you?" he said good-naturedly, "And let Whistler know he can have his office back. I need to kick his ass over what he wants to do to my next story."

Eddie walked to the door and then turned back to face Blackwood. "Just one other thing," he said, his hand on the knob. "Your daughter . . ."

Blackwood nodded. "She's trouble, kid. You don't want to be interested."

"No, it's . . . How long has she been modeling for the covers?"

"Long time," Blackwood said, clearly not happy about it. "Quite a long time."

Eddie took the hint and did not pursue the subject further. He turned to the door. Outside the office, Whistler sat at his secretary's desk, looking agitated as Eddie came out. He waved Eddie over and ignored him when Eddie told him Blackwood was waiting for him. Whistler spoke in a low voice, just above a whisper, and tapped a legal looking document on the desk with a pen as he said, "I just got a call from Swinburne while you were in there with Blackwood. He wants to put you on a three-story contract."

Eddie was dumbfounded. He had never met Augustus Swinburne but knew of the publisher's reputation as a shrewd businessman who never let a penny go unless absolutely necessary. Eddie knew that some writers got contracts. It kept them focused while guaranteeing that their work would go to one of the Meteor publications. It also kept them too busy to submit stories anywhere else. But those kinds of deals only went to the sure bets, the established writers with proven track records—not to hacks with only a few stories to their credit.

"You're kidding," Eddie said.

"I wish I was. I don't get it, and I don't like it. You're good, Eddie, but you're just getting started. I don't mind telling you this doesn't make any sense."

"How much is the contract for?"

"It's not for a money amount. It's for three more stories. At a bit more than half a cent per word. But the final money will depend on how much you write. Still you've got a guaranteed sale for the next three stories. If you want to sign it."

"You got a pen?"

Whistler reluctantly handed the pen to Eddie while glancing at the door to his office. "What did Blackwood want with you?"

"Just to see what I was going to do next. I guess he's a fan," Eddie said without hesitation as he signed the contract. He surprised himself by being able to lie with such facility.

Whistler pulled a carbon copy from the back of the contract. He glanced at Eddie's signature. "Been practicing your autograph?"

Eddie blushed. Whistler really did know writers.

"You got a safety deposit box?" Eddie told him he did not. "Get one," Whistler said.

"Why?"

Whistler sighed heavily, glanced at his office door again, and actually began to whisper, causing Eddie to lean closer to hear. "You're going to take this the wrong way, but you've got to trust me on this. You don't deserve this." He tapped the contract. "Swinburne and Blackwood taking an interest in you . . . there's something odd about it. Swinburne's smart. Too smart sometimes. One thing I've learned is that he doesn't waste money. And when he figures out this contract is unnecessary, he's going to want to go back on it."

"It looks plenty legal," Eddie said, his own voice lowered now though not as far as Whistler's.

"It is. But that won't stop him from trying to get around it. If you want to cash in on it, keep it in a safe place."

"My apartment's not safe enough?"

Whistler sighed again. He appeared to be growing increasingly exasperated. "Look, I'm taking a risk here doing you a favor. I'm offering you advice. Swinburne doesn't always play fair. That's all I'm going to say."

Eddie nodded and straightened up again. He felt the editor was being paranoid, but he also had to agree that there was something odd in the coincidence of Blackwood and Swinburne suddenly finding him worthy of attention. "All right, then," he said, no longer whispering. "I'll take care of it." He was not sure he meant it as he shook Whistler's hand and walked quickly out of the office, certain that Whistler had stood up to watch him go.

the floor that made her heels click conspicuously as she made her way from the elevator to the doors of Swinburne's office.

In less than a minute, she had covered the distance and had her hand on the knob of one of the double doors at the end of the hallway. Taking a deep breath and looking down at the floor, she knocked twice. "Come," was the response she heard from within the office. Her eyes still on the floor, she nodded to herself and turned the knob. She had quickly changed back into her own clothes before leaving the dressing room and so was wearing a conservative floral patterned skirt and white blouse. Rather than meet Swinburne with her hair unflatteringly bobby pinned down, she had kept on the wig and so still felt ridiculous but not as self-conscious as she would have if fully dressed in the costume she had worn when confronting Whistler.

Swinburne's office was large—as big as three or four offices the size of Whistler's—and had been converted into a high ceilinged open space with skylights above and four more large windows opening onto views of the city around the Meteor building. Behind a broad oak desk, Augustus Swinburne sat in a thickly padded, high backed leather chair. A pudgy man in his late fifties with graying hair combed straight back off his forehead and glasses rimmed with thick black plastic, he looked at Roxanne with a thin-lipped smile. The moment she was through the door, she wished she had defied Whistler and the summons to come upstairs. It was bad enough that she was expected to come at Swinburne's beck and call, but far more humiliating to find that the man was not alone in his office.

Roxanne saw that two other women sat in leather chairs facing the publisher's desk, and they both turned to look in her direction as she approached. She could feel her cheeks beginning to turn red as the women appraised her. Before she was halfway across the room, one of them had stood to wait for her. The woman looked to be in her mid-thirties and was tall and mannish in her appearance with extremely short black hair parted on the side and a thick, square jaw. Wearing only the slightest bit of make-up and dressed in slacks and a button-up shirt, she smiled at Roxanne's approach and kept her eyes locked on Roxanne's, making her feel so uncomfortable that she had to look away almost immediately. The second woman stayed seated, but Roxanne could see that she was younger than the woman who had stood; her red hair hung past her shoulders and curled at the ends, and her make-up accentuated full lips and large, bright eyes.

"Miss Blackwood," Swinburne said before she had reached the desk, "I'm glad you were able to join us for a moment."

Roxanne stopped a few feet away from the desk and the standing woman. She nodded politely.

"Roxanne Blackwood, I'd like you to meet Vivian Parker,"

Feeling as though she had no choice, Roxanne leaned forward and extended her hand to the woman whose eyes had not left hers once as she had made her way across the room. Vivian Parker took Roxanne's fingers gingerly and gave them the lightest of squeezes between her thumb and forefinger.

Swinburne continued. "And Miss Parker's protégé, Rebecca Le Blanc," he said, nodding toward the second woman. She stood now and stepped out from behind the chair. A petite woman with a nice figure, she wore an expensive looking dress of bright green material and reached out for Roxanne's hand without saying a word and only barely making eye contact. Her grip was firm but brief. Again, Roxanne nodded and smiled politely while hating every second of being in this room. "Miss Le Blanc is Meteor's latest discovery," Swinburne added. "Her first novel hits the stores on Saturday."

A book rested on the blotter in front of him, and Swinburne slid it slowly, calculatingly across the desk toward Roxanne. He clearly intended that she pick it up, which she did while hoping her shaking hands did not show. The book was titled *Last Stand on Venus* and had a cover illustration showing a space suited warrior firing a ray gun over the parapet of a fortress, aiming it at an army of countless red aliens whose numbers streamed back to the horizon. Behind the hero, shielded by the arm that did not hold the ray gun, was a woman in an extremely tight, form fitting space suit; inside her helmet, her face showed a mixture of horror and ecstasy. Roxanne remembered having held this pose in a tight suit but had had no idea what the rest of the image would eventually look like. Trembling and knowing that her ears and cheeks were burning red, she set the book back on the desk without a word.

"We have Miss Parker to thank for discovering Miss Le Blanc," Swinburne said. "She brought me the manuscript, and I knew it would be the next big thing."

"How nice," Roxanne said.

"Indeed." Swinburne was eyeing her carefully. "In fact, I'm hosting a party in Miss Le Blanc's honor this coming Friday. At my house in Hollywood." He paused, a smile creeping over his face. "Miss Parker, Miss Le Blanc and I would like to have you there as our guest."

Roxanne raised an eyebrow. She felt suddenly as if she were in the middle of a chess match, one in which Swinburne had been able to make several moves before she even knew she was in the game. "Thank you," she said after a moment's hesitation. "I'll check my engagements and let you know if I'll be able to make it."

Swinburne stood slowly, keeping his hands on the top of his desk as though he was leaning on it. He looked directly at Roxanne and said, "I'm sure you'll be able to join us, Miss Blackwood. The celebration would not be the same without you, what with your gracing the cover and all." He paused a moment. "If you have concerns that we will draw attention to your role in our enterprise, please rest assured that I intend to respect your desire for anonymity." The unspoken threat was that Roxanne's anonymity would not last if she failed to come to the party. Swinburne went on, saying, "Whatever plans you may have for Friday, I'm sure you'll be able to adapt them to include us. Bring along any young man you may have your eye on." There was nothing welcoming about the invitation; Roxanne felt as though she was being invited by a reptile.

Still, she quietly said, "Well, then. I'll see you Friday."

"Outstanding," Swinburne said.

Roxanne turned to the two standing women and nodded. "Nice to have met you," she said with a nod and was about turn and leave when Vivian Parker raised a hand, gesturing that Roxanne should stop.

"Miss Blackwood," she said, "I just want to say how pleased I am to have met you." Her voice was cool, and she sounded quite refined, but the expression on her face was disturbing. Where Swinburne seemed like a lizard in his dealings with her, Roxanne got the sense that she was looking into the eyes of a hungry leopard when Miss Parker spoke to her. It was a look not unlike those she had been on the receiving end of countless times, but until now it had always been a man looking at her this way—with raw, barely contained desire. She had become hardened to the look over the years when it came from men, but now she found herself unnerved as Vivian Parker stared at her, making no effort to hide from Roxanne the fact that she wanted her intensely.

Feeling suddenly flushed and sure that her cheeks were turning red again, Roxanne glanced nervously away from the woman's gaze and caught the expression of Rebecca Le Blanc where she stood behind Vivian. Although the younger woman was unable to see the predatory look on Vivian's face, Roxanne noticed with some alarm that Rebecca's expression changed from one of disinterested passivity to sudden alarm and confusion once she made eye contact with Roxanne. It was a look of jealousy; of that, Roxanne had no doubt. Rebecca had not needed to see the look on her companion's face. Instead, Roxanne's reaction to Vivian's leer had been as a mirror for Rebecca, and in an instant, Roxanne knew that the pretty redhead in front of her had just gone from feeling like a princess to a beggar. And the expression on Rebecca's face as she glared at the back of Vivian's head made Roxanne feel suddenly and inexplicably weak, vulnerable and endangered.

It was all she could do to say, "Thank you," and turn on her heels to leave. Behind her, she heard the creak of leather as Swinburne sat in his chair again. Trying to keep her composure, she kept moving, walking quickly out of the office and toward the elevator. She needed a cigarette and could not wait to be out of the building and on her way home. Klaus Frehling would have to do without his model for the rest of the day.

CHAPTER THREE

Normally, Eddie would have taken a bus east to Central Avenue and then walked the rest of the way to his apartment, but today he walked north toward downtown a few blocks, turned left and went into the bank where he had his savings account and normally cashed his checks. Whistler's advice about a safety deposit box had struck him as paranoid, but there was something to be said for the editor's wisdom and experience. Eddie had not felt anything malevolent in Blackwood's interest in him, but he had to agree that the contract seemed out of the ordinary, especially coming from someone with Swinburne's reputation for penny pinching. The contract gave Eddie some security, but it still might not be enough if there was truth to Blackwood's warning about Swinburne being extremely unhappy upon learning the sources of Eddie's stories. At the very least, it would not hurt to see how much a safety deposit box would cost for a few months until he could write three stories and get the money he had been promised.

Half an hour later with his contract safely tucked away in the vault and a receipt for his safety deposit box in his wallet, Eddie decided to walk the whole way home. He told himself he needed time to think but found it hard to concentrate for long on anything. Thoughts about Whistler's warning were quickly chased out of his mind by exhilaration over the contract itself, which soon gave way to thoughts of Blackwood. Eddie wondered what the older writer had been driving at about the laws of the universe and what more he could possibly want to talk to Eddie about that he hadn't already said in Whistler's office. Finally, though, everything in his head was overridden by the image of Roxanne Blackwood pulling open her robe in Whistler's office and the fire in her voice as she tore into the editor.

It was March, and a breeze was blowing lightly, carrying just a bit of a chill from the leftovers of the mild L.A. winter that had just passed. Traffic was light, and the sidewalks were crowded with commerce, but Eddie paid no attention, just followed his feet down to Eighth Street, over to Central and then down toward Olympic. When he reached the door at 845 1/2 Central, the intersection at Olympic just a dozen yards away, he stopped and went inside.

The building that housed his apartment was a strange setup. Though he thought of it as an office building, it would have been more accurate to describe it as former offices that had been converted into single apartments. Inside the front door were mailboxes, and Eddie fished his keys out of his pocket to open the one marked "5." A larger communal box for packages was below the other mailboxes, and Eddie checked this, too; he was not expecting a package but always checked regardless. Mail in hand, he walked up the long flight of stairs that went straight to a landing with a skylight above. The landing opened onto a large reception area and a walkway that led along the banister and down a hallway. Windows opened out from the reception area into the hallway, and on the other side of the reception area was a bathroom that would originally have been intended for the public but was now shared by the tenants. The bathroom had a toilet and a sink. If Eddie wanted a bath, he had to go down the hallway, past his own room and into an adjoining hallway that led to the back entrance. There, just before the door that led to a flimsy wooden exterior staircase and a barely used alley, a bathtub had been installed in the utility room that housed the water heater.

He walked along the hallway, glancing into the empty reception area. There were two old sofas against the walls and a battered dining table with mismatched chairs. The apartments had no kitchens; had there been a common kitchen off the reception area, the whole affair would have been more like a dormitory with this as the common room. As it was, tenants either cooked on hot plates in their rooms or ate out, and the couches and tables went largely unoccupied. For all its inconveniences, the building suited Eddie well as it cost less to live here than it would have in other apartments nearby.

Like Eddie, most of the tenants kept to themselves, and Eddie knew only a few by sight and only one by name, a private detective in his late thirties named Will Pence who had moved earlier in the year into a converted office across the hall and one door down from Eddie's apartment; Eddie's faced the street and Pence's the alley. If pressed, Eddie would have admitted that Pence was his only real friend in Los Angeles. Their relationship had started late one night when Eddie had come up the stairs to find Pence drinking alone at the table in the reception area. Already inebriated, the private eye had called Eddie over for a drink, and Eddie had reluctantly accepted. This had turned into a regular event with Pence inviting Eddie at least once a week down to the reception area for drinks straight from the bottle. Eddie usually felt obligated to reciprocate, so a few nights later he would spring for a bottle he could not afford and drink again with Pence. The detective did not read science fiction but was interested in what Eddie was doing, and the two talked about their work, their pasts, and women.

Noncommittal about his past, Pence told Eddie only that he worked for the movie studios. He was on retainer to at least two and did contract jobs for others. It was not unusual for him to disappear for days at a time, and upon his return he would make vague reference to a case he had been working; after these absences, Pence's drinking was always worse for a few days, somehow more desperate. Hesitant to appear as though he were prying but curious about his friend and neighbor, Eddie asked late one night what a movie studio needed private detectives for. Pence had just laughed and then said, "You can't be that naïve, kid." When Eddie had not replied, Pence opened up, the whiskey no doubt helping to ease his inhibitions. "The thing about the movies," he said, "is that they attract so many people, some of them not good. And all these industries make their bread and butter off the movies. You got your set designers and costume designers and all that, but beyond them you've got lumber companies that just supply the studios for building sets, and fabric companies that just supply for costumes. There's probably a dairyman out in the San Fernando Valley who's making a living doing nothing but supplying cream for the pies that the Three Stooges take in the face. You ever thought about it like that?"

"No," Eddie had said.

"And every one of these people thinks they've got an in, got a friend in the business, so when little Susie or Sally or whatever her name is gets off the bus in big ol' L.A. and tries to break into the movies, she can't turn around without bumping into somebody who says they can give her a break. The only problem is that sometimes it's a son of a bitch with a camera or a little dungeon built in below his bungalow or Christ knows what else. And little Susie's talked into doing all kinds of things she never would've dreamed of, never even knew people did back in Iowa. You're from Iowa, ain't you?"

"Yes."

"So when five years go by and little Susie actually does end up on the red carpet with Clark Gable, then the perverts come out of the woodwork with their blackmail. And that's why the studios need me."

Eddie was fascinated. He had heard scandalous stories about unruly actors and actresses, but he had never heard about anything like the depravity Pence described. Pence made it seem like it was happening all around them. At the same time, Eddie was wary of the alcohol and the possibility that his friend was exaggerating or fabricating altogether. "So what do you do?" he asked, his curiosity getting the better of him.

"Find the pervert. Usually pay him off a little and scare the shit out of him. Let him know if the negatives ever show up or if the starlet gets another nasty letter, no amount of money is going to make the pain worth his while." He shrugged and took another drink. Pence clearly found his work distasteful, which was probably why he drank, but he also admitted pathetically that it was all he was good at. He was not needed by the studios on a daily basis, or even weekly in most cases, but he received steady paychecks, which kept him supplied in liquor. He would have been a good looking man if he shaved and didn't drink and if he ate and slept a bit more. As it was, he always looked haggard when he was home, with bloodshot eyes and several days' worth of stubble. When he looked cleaned up, he was working, and he did not drink.

"One of these days, though," he said, "it's going to end."

"What do you mean?"

"The wrong girl is going to spread her legs for the wrong guy. Maybe a studio head's daughter, or a star who's so big they can't stand the risk of knowing that I know what she did. So I'll be done in Hollywood. But I've got insurance so I don't get myself killed." Eddie asked what kind of insurance, and Pence smiled evasively. After another sip from the bottle, he said, "I've kept some pictures. Some of the better ones. When they come for me, I'll show them what I've got. Tell 'em there's more, copies stuffed in a safe deposit box and a little old aunt who'll go straight to the press if I don't call once a week with the password."

"Smart," Eddie said.

"You got to stay ahead of them," Pence had said.

Occasionally, Eddie would hear a woman's laughter from Pence's room in the middle of the night, and four or five times he had bumped into one of Pence's companions in the hallway; never the same girl twice, always drunk and always pretty. Pence picked them up at the jazz clubs down on Central. Eddie had not been lucky with women since moving to California. He had dated one of the secretaries at *Stupendous* a few times, and there was a girl who cashiered at the drugstore who he had gone dancing with once, but neither situation had lead anywhere. Before his success at writing, he had tried to build up the nerve to ask Pence to take him to the jazz clubs, but never did. Now that he was actually publishing, he did not think about women so much and wished he could get out of the habit of drinking so often with Pence as it distracted him from his work. There would be plenty of time for such things after his career was firmly established.

As he approached Pence's room, Eddie decided he should stop and ask him about the contract and if he knew anything about what Eddie should do to protect his interests. With Pence's precautions against potential strong-arm tactics from the studios, Eddie knew his neighbor would have some advice for him. Pence was used to keeping two steps ahead of people with power who did not mind using it. Eddie knocked and after a few moments' silence heard movement beyond the door, and then the lock clicked. Pence opened the door a crack, as was his habit. When he saw that it was Eddie, he smiled and opened it all the way.

Eddie could smell the liquor on his breath. He had not talked to Pence in two or three days, had not been invited down to the reception area for drinks, and so he had assumed Pence was working a case. But if that was so, the job was finished, and Pence was in the first stages of drinking his paycheck. He still wore a decent shirt, and there was no stubble on his face, so Eddie knew he could not have been at it for long. He was glad to be catching Pence at a reasonably lucid moment.

"What's up, Eddie?" Pence asked, no slur yet in his voice.

"Nothing much. I just wanted to get your opinion of something. You got a minute?"

By way of answering, Pence swung the door open farther and stepped aside, silently inviting Eddie in. As he stepped through the doorway, Eddie realized he had never actually been inside his friend's apartment, all their socializing having occurred down the hall and any other conversations over the months they had known each other having taken place here at the threshold or two doors down in front of Eddie's room. Eddie knew that Pence was not neat, nor was he a reader; there was nothing about him that would have suggested that Pence's apartment would bear any resemblance to Eddie's almost library-like quarters with its book-lined shelves, desk, typewriter and relative organization. For some reason, though, Eddie had imagined Pence living in completely opposite conditions—slovenly disarray characterized by dirty clothes strewn about amidst empty liquor bottles, half-read newspapers and trash. Instead, the room was purely Spartan, with a neatly made bed, a small table and chair that could have served as a writing desk, an end table with a radio on it, a small filing cabinet, and virtually nothing else. There were no photographs, no reading material, and no bottles—empty or otherwise. Eddie could not have been more surprised.

Pence offered Eddie the single chair and sat on the bed to face him, but not before restoring one of Eddie's illusions by opening the bottom drawer of the filing cabinet and pulling out a bottle and two shot glasses. When Eddie declined, Pence closed the drawer, leaving the bottle unassaulted. As Eddie sat down, Pence met his gaze with a single raised eyebrow, inviting him to speak. Eddie quickly explained about the contract he had signed and Whistler's admonitions about Swinburne. He saw no need to mention anything about Blackwood.

Pence listened attentively but without a word until Eddie had finished, saying that he had taken Whistler's advice and put the contract in the bank vault. He thought about what Pence had told him about his own secret file kept in a safety deposit box as insurance against his bosses. "That's good," Pence said when Eddie stopped talking. He sat silently for a moment and then asked, "This guy Swinburne. He sign your checks?"

"No. It's always Whistler."

"His name on the masthead of the magazine, or anywhere public?"

Eddie thought about it. At some point in the late 1920s, Swinburne's name had disappeared from the pages of *Stupendous* and his other publications. He was not like Hugo Gernsback and other publishers who felt the need to put their names on their magazines. "No," he said.

Pence nodded. "Okay. I know his type. You've got your rich people, Eddie, and then you've got the ones who tell the rich people what to do. The rich ones, the ones with names you've heard in the newsreels and the papers, they're pretty easy to deal with. The thing that concerns them is their reputations—whether they're good or they're bad. The thing they want is to keep what they've got and to get more of it, and it's keeping their reputations intact that'll do the trick—they think. Once you figure out what their reputation is, you can handle them pretty well. But these other types . . ." He sighed and looked at the floor for a moment. "They're a lot less predictable. They don't want anything, don't need anything. They've literally got it all."

"But Swinburne's got a reputation as a penny pincher," Eddie interrupted.

Pence shook his head. "Doesn't matter. He maybe loves his money too much, but money's not the thing that excites guys like these. It's beneath them to have their names in the papers. They get their thrills by telling the other rich people what to do. In the movie business, it's the ones who tell the Mayers and the Cohns and the Warners what to do. It's the same in politics, industry. They're old money. They dabble in power the way other rich pricks dabble in polo ponies or blondes or airplanes. They don't care about adoration. Is that the right word?"

"Do you mean adulation?"

"That's it. They don't care about adulation. They care about making someone who only seems powerful shit himself when they call him on the phone and tell him what to do. Sounds like that's what this guy Swinburne is like. Never heard of him, though. Which isn't surprising since I don't move in publishing circles. But still. I might be able to find something out about him. Let me look into it."

Eddie was taken aback. He had not intended to enlist Pence's services but had only wanted advice. "I didn't mean to make it seem like I wanted to hire you," he said quickly, shaking his head.

"No, no. Don't worry about it. I could use a little something to keep me busy for a couple days. I got a job coming up next week. And I just finished up another thing. If I don't want to stay pickled in between, this will be the perfect thing."

"Thanks," Eddie said. "Are you sure I can't give you a few bucks for your trouble?" As he said it, he was wondering just how much he could afford and knew the answer involved a very small amount. He hoped Pence would not take him up on the offer.

"Forget it," Pence said. "Buy the next bottle." They shook hands, and Eddie got up to leave. "Check with me tomorrow morning," Pence said as he saw Eddie to the door. Eddie thanked him again and walked down to his own room. Along with everything he had gleaned from Blackwood and Whistler, the perspective he had gained from Pence gave him a lot to think about. It had not, however, made him feel any better. With another meeting with Blackwood looming in a few hours, he told himself he needed to at least try to sort through his thoughts and go into the meeting with a clear head. The first thing to do would be to try to figure out Blackwood as best as he could.

****

The door to his apartment squeaked open as he pulled his key from the lock, exhaled sharply through tight lips, and then went straight to the bookshelf with Blackwood's books on it, a mixture of novels and collections of short stories and novellas. He pulled the dozen books off the shelf, carried them in a stack to the bed, sat down on it and began to flip through the pages of the one on top. Eddie's apartment had changed little in the year he had lived there, and the modest success of the last six months had not had much effect. The checks from *Stupendous* were nice, but he was still living off his inheritance and had not done anything extravagant since he was published, save buying some new clothes. The furniture was still the same rickety second hand bed, desk, bureau and a single end table that was not placed at the end of anything but rested between the bed and bureau. A couple of framed photos of himself and friends from Iowa were on the bureau, and in one of its drawers was a loaf of bread, a jar of peanut butter, some cans of soup and a few plates, bowls and utensils. He still ate in his room when he did not feel like paying for meals at the Terminal Cafe, pushing the Underwood aside on the desk and staring out the window at traffic rolling by on Central Avenue.

The first book he looked at as he sat on his sagging mattress was *Nelphi*, the story that had been Blackwood's most popular. The cover illustration was nowhere near as lurid as the covers of *Stupendous* typically were; rather, it showed a young man with thick, curly hair drawing a ray gun and pointing it at some unknown pursuer who was not pictured. Eddie flipped the pages, past the 1936 copyright, and began skimming. He had read it several times already, always careful not to dog-ear or mark the pages, and he enjoyed the story of young Sater Moss, a hunted orphan and later a valiant champion of his people, a new race of humans called Nelphi. With thick wormy tentacles in place of hair and telepathic powers that could be relied on to get Sater and his band of underground Nelphi out of trouble, the new race Blackwood had created had caught the imagination of science fiction readers across the country.

After reading random passages, Eddie set *Nelphi* down and picked up another one, and then another, not really paying attention to what he read but looking for Blackwood in the text, trying to hear the voice of the man he had met this morning and wondering what he could possibly have meant about defying the laws of the universe. He was also bothered by what Blackwood had said about Eddie reminding him of himself in younger days. Reading the genius of Blackwood—not just in style but in plot and character development that made the work as much literature as science fiction—Eddie could see nothing of himself and could only continue to wonder what the older writer had meant. Oddly enough, he couldn't find much of Blackwood in the books either; where the books were graceful and provocative, Blackwood had seemed hard around the edges, cynical. Still, the incongruity pushed Eddie on, and when he had finished pondering the stack of books, he turned to the boxes of carefully organized and preserved magazines for Blackwood's uncollected stories and serials.

First he pulled out the May 1939 issue of *Stupendous*. It had Blackwood's story "Sundown" in it, the story featured on the cover. Eddie remembered having bought the magazine shortly after arriving in Los Angeles and studying it carefully; as much as anything else, the story of people on a far-off planet with several suns about to face the darkness of night for the first time had inspired him to strive for success as a science fiction writer. Now, he did not even bother opening the magazine. Instead, he stared at the cover, at the image of a beautiful woman dressed in a long, tightly fitting gown with a plunging neckline. She looked in horror out a window at a darkening sky, a huge moon filling the horizon. It was Roxanne. The face was slightly different, but the likeness was still uncanny. Unable to pull his eyes off the picture, Eddie thought about the real Roxanne, thought too about the dozens of times he had looked at this issue without thinking that the woman on the cover was real. Until today, she had just been a fantasy.

He finally set the magazine down and turned back to the boxes on the shelves, taking down the one labeled "Stupendous 1938-1939" that he had just pulled the May issue from. He began flipping through the covers. Roxanne was on every one. The faces on all the covers varied a bit;

cheekbones, noses, and eyes changed shape from cover to cover; some of the women were blondes, brunettes, redheads; most were white but occasionally they had an exotic and alien skin color such as green or light blue. Sometimes the artist had cast her as the aggressor—as the whip-wielding princess or ray gun toting maul of some space mercenary. On most of the covers, though, she was in need of rescue—either from some villain with a ray gun of his own or else from a horrifying bug-eyed monster. One of the most famous, and one of Eddie's favorites, was the January 1938 cover in which the woman in distress was being embraced by the multiple tentacles of a menacing creature. The tentacles were strategically placed—one between her breasts, another with its tip reaching under the hem of her skirt, another coming up from behind and between her legs. The look on her face was enigmatic—sheer horror combined with a strange hint of joy and anticipation. Like all the other covers, it had the artist's unobtrusive signature in the lower left corner— "Frehling." When he came across this issue, Eddie stared in fascination for a long time.

Before the afternoon had passed, he had dug through box after box, carefully considering Roxanne on the cover of each and in some of the interior illustrations as well. They stopped with the March 1933 issue. The covers by Frehling continued for a few issues more going sporadically back into 1932, but they lacked the intensity and artistry of the covers with Roxanne. *She must be his muse,* Eddie thought, *must have been for the last seven years.* That was the answer Blackwood had not wanted to give him.

CHAPTER FOUR

The Reno Lounge was a dive. There were no windows, and the interior was dark and dank. Yellowed photos of boxers and football players lined the walls along with some collegiate pennants. There was no jukebox but instead a tinny radio behind the bar that played equal parts of big band music and static. When Eddie walked in, he saw a few other patrons in booths along the wall and at the bar. The place smelled of beer and cigarettes, and he noted that the floor was sticky. A fat bartender in his fifties leaned against the bar. He looked like the kind of man who kept a gun behind the bar and knew how to use it. There was nothing malevolent about him, though, as he rested with his elbows on the bar in front of him, seemingly looking at nothing in particular, just staring into the open space of the lounge and waiting for someone to need his services. Eddie doubted he would move quickly when called upon.

After standing in the doorway for a few seconds to let his eyes adjust to the light, Eddie walked in and headed for the bar. Before he could reach it, a figure stood up in the back of the room and waved him over. Eddie saw that it was Blackwood. He had been sitting at a booth in the back corner of the barroom facing the doorway. When Eddie changed directions and began making his way to the back of the room, Blackwood sat down again. Eddie glanced at his wristwatch and saw that it was twenty after five. He had left his apartment with plenty of time, not wanting to be late, and had been glad to find the Reno Lounge easily and ahead of schedule so that he could collect his thoughts before Blackwood showed up. Now, with Blackwood here ahead of him, he was not going to get the chance. He had dozens of questions for the older writer, mostly about how he had broken into the book publishing market and how he had gotten his ideas. Now that Eddie had the contract with *Stupendous*, he had been feeling more confident about talking to Blackwood about the business of writing. Still, when he got to the booth, he found himself just as nervous as he had been this morning in Whistler's office.

"Have a seat," Blackwood said, pointing to the padded bench opposite him. "Glad to see you found the place all right. Drink?"

"Sure," Eddie said as he sat down. He found himself staring at Blackwood. Something was markedly different about him from the way he had looked this morning. As far as Eddie could tell, he still wore the same clothes—an expensive looking tan suit—but it appeared rumpled now, and Eddie could clearly make out stains on the lapels even in the dim light of the Reno Lounge. The older writer's face also looked haggard and pale as though he had not slept well for days. Eddie was worried that he was ill. He thought for a moment that he might simply be drunk, that he had been waiting for Eddie in the bar for a long time, but he dismissed the thought immediately. Not only were there no empty glasses on the table, but when he looked at Blackwood's eyes Eddie saw that they were not bloodshot or glassy. Instead, his eyes looked piercingly back at Eddie in strange contrast to the worn look that marked every other aspect of his appearance.

Blackwood waved his hand in the direction of the bartender and said in a voice a bit too loud for the Reno Lounge, "Two whiskeys. The best you've got, Jimmy." Eddie rotated in his seat to see the bartender nod and turn to his stock. He was surprised that Blackwood had gotten any movement at all out of the man.

When he turned back, Eddie saw that Blackwood was looking intensely at him. He reached a hand across the table, clearly not in an invitation to shake hands, and put a finger up to Eddie's collar, plucking at his undershirt. "In the future," Blackwood said, "young men like yourself, and young women too, will walk around wearing undershirts with nothing over them." Eddie smiled, entertained by the idea that Blackwood was giving him a taste of what a genius science fiction writer thought of the future. But as Blackwood continued matter-of-factly, Eddie's smile faded, and he began to sense that Blackwood was not being creative or building up to a punch line. "So they won't really be undershirts anymore, and even though there is no remote connection between these shirts and tea, for some reason people will call them tea shirts. These people will feel no qualms about walking around in their underwear, and it will be the height of popular fashion to have slogans on these shirts. Like a stew bum wearing a sandwich board all day in exchange for a bowl of soup, these people will wear the slogans and brand names of all manner of companies." He pulled a folded piece of paper from the inside pocket of his coat. "I've written some of them down here. Need to convince Roxanne to invest when she hears about them so she can be a rich old lady." He tucked the paper away again as the bartender appeared beside their table and unceremoniously placed the glasses of whiskey in front of them. "But aside from slogans, there will be clever sayings on these tea shirts. And one of these will read, 'Life Is Too Short to Drink Cheap Liquor.'" With that, he finally smiled and then reached for his glass, tipping the whiskey back in one swallow.

Eddie did the same. It was good whiskey, better than anything he had drunk with Pence. He set his glass down and was about to offer to buy another round. But before he could say a word, Blackwood began scooting across the booth to the edge of the seat as though he were about to get up. "Are we leaving?" Eddie asked, surprised.

"If you don't mind," Blackwood said. "Now that we've met up and the time is right, I need to get a few things accomplished. It is five-thirty, isn't it?"

Eddie looked at his watch. "It is now. Why?"

"Not important. I'll explain in a bit. I need you to come with me to get my car back and then we'll head to your place. There are some things I need to explain to you, and then I've got to get moving."

Eddie was confused but stood up regardless and followed Blackwood toward the bar. He almost bumped into him as Blackwood made a sudden stop and turned to put his face close to Eddie's ear and whisper, "Say, I hate to do this, but would you mind taking care of the tab? My resources are a bit depleted at the moment."

Eddie raised an eyebrow in surprise but said, "Sure." There was nothing else he could say.

After paying the bill, he followed Blackwood outside. It was almost dark now, and the air had gotten cold with a light breeze blowing through the canyons of tall buildings around them. Neon lights above myriad businesses—even dentists' offices—had begun to burn, and cars rolling past all had their headlights on. "Come on," Blackwood said, pulling the suit jacket tight against his body, clearly feeling the cold more than Eddie did. "We'll get a cab."

Irritated, Eddie told himself he would be paying for this, too. Blackwood must be a millionaire, and why he was out at a bar without money or his car left Eddie feeling puzzled, but he was also definitely beginning to feel taken advantage of. He wondered what else Blackwood had in mind that he would need Eddie to pay for. After the drinks in the Reno Lounge, he only had about twelve dollars in his wallet, enough to cover a cab and a bit more, but not enough for a night on the town, and at some point he would have to say something about it.

Blackwood quickly hailed a cab and climbed into the back seat, Eddie sliding in beside him. Eddie listened as Blackwood gave the driver instructions to take them to a parking lot on Eighth Street, and he realized that this was the lot across the street from the Meteor building. Blackwood leaned back as the cab pulled away from the curb and entered traffic. He looked at Eddie and said, "How long have you been in L.A., Eddie?"

"About a year now."

"From where?"

"Iowa."

"You and everyone else." He paused for a moment and then said, "What did you do in Iowa?"

Eddie felt like he was being interviewed but did not see any reason to object to Blackwood's questions. He had a few of his own he wanted to ask and hoped Blackwood would be more amenable to answering them if his own questions about Eddie's past were answered openly. "My father had a machine shop. He mostly fixed farm equipment. He taught me the trade, and I ran the business for my mother after my father died. Fixed tractor engines by day and read Robert E. Howard by night."

Blackwood smiled. "Sounds pretty good. Kept you afloat through the Depression?"

Eddie nodded. "Even if the farms were owned by the banks, tractors and threshers and harvesters still needed fixing."

"And you came out here?"

"To write. About a year ago. After my mother died, I sold everything and gave myself a year to make it."

"And have you? Made it?"

Eddie smiled, thinking about the contract in the safety deposit box and the serial that would begin in *Stupendous* next month. "It's looking that way," he said.

Blackwood nodded. "I've been here since 1913," he said. "Seen it change an awful lot since then. Came here from Frisco. Came to write."

"I didn't know you've been writing that long," Eddie said as the cab made a right turn. The earliest Blackwood stories he had found dated from 1926. They were all good, all innovative, almost revolutionary. It was as though Blackwood had just sat down at a typewriter one day and let the genius pour out of him without ever having tried before.

"Oh, yes. Since then and before. But not fiction. Newspapers. I wanted to write fiction, science fiction—even though we didn't call it that back then—but I couldn't get a foot in the door, so I fell back on the newspapers. There was one housed right around here, down on Wall Street. Called the *Record*. Wrote freelance for them all through the early 20s. Wrote for the movie magazines, too. They were why I came here in the first place."

"Movie magazines?"

Blackwood chuckled. "No, the movies. I had thought I might be able to write scenarios for the movies. Knew some people in New York who were making a decent living with Biograph. Anyway, Ince and Sennett and others were setting up shop here, and a lot of artistic types came down from Frisco to get in on it. All kinds of hangers on, no-talent dreamers, get rich quick types—dozens of them for every one person with real talent. You know which type I was."

"Not so talented?" Eddie was thinking about Pence's description of Hollywood today. It sounded virtually the same as the Hollywood of twenty-five years ago that Blackwood was describing.

"Indeed." The cab slowed and pulled up to the curb in front of a small parking lot tucked between two large office buildings. The Meteor building was across the street. As Eddie reached for his wallet, Blackwood stopped him with a hand on his elbow. "I've got it," he said as he handed a five-dollar bill up to the driver and told him to keep the change.

"I thought you were broke," Eddie said once they were out of the car and on the sidewalk. He did not feel awkward about saying it. The more he had been around Blackwood, the less awed he had felt.

"No," Blackwood said, "not broke. Just that my resources were depleted. Jimmy's a friend. I didn't want to stick him with one of these." He pulled out his wallet as he began leading the way into the rows of cars and handed Eddie another five-dollar bill. He looked at it in the dim light from the street lamps but did not notice anything odd about it. "Look at the date," Blackwood said.

Eddie held the bill up closer and saw that the date read 1984. He did not know what to think but handed the bill back to Blackwood. "Counterfeit?" he asked.

Blackwood chuckled. "It would be a pretty lousy counterfeiter to make a mistake that stupid, don't you think?"

"I suppose."

"So. Not counterfeit. Just a bit ahead of its time."

"You're saying this money is from the future." Eddie was beginning to wonder if Blackwood was losing his mind. The disheveled clothes, the evasive statements, and now claiming to have money from the future all pointed toward some sort of delirium.

"You could say that," Blackwood said. "Although my notion of what's future and what's present may not be the same as yours any more." He had led the way to a white Packard convertible parked toward the back of the lot. Now he got his keys out of his pants pocket and unlocked the driver's door.

"I don't understand," Eddie said as he got into the car and Blackwood started the engine.

"You will. I'll explain it all in just a bit. Let's get out of here first." At the exit, Blackwood rolled down his window, handed the attendant his ticket and paid for the time the car had been there, no doubt using more anachronistic currency. "We should head to your place and talk a bit," he said as he pulled the big car into traffic and gunned the engine. "Central and Olympic, right?"

Eddie was taken aback. He looked suspiciously at Blackwood for a moment. Blackwood looked back, clearly expecting the stare Eddie now gave him. "Don't get so bothered. I asked Whistler to pull your file. Just to see where I could find you if I missed our date at the Reno Lounge."

Eddie nodded. Blackwood was right about him being bothered, but he saw that there was not much point in it. "Why were you expecting to miss it?" he asked.

"Wasn't expecting it so much as I knew it was possible. I had a few things to take care of . . . today, and I knew there was a chance they would get out of hand. Turns out I was right. Still, I managed to make it there ahead of you."

They rode in silence for a few minutes, Eddie's thoughts racing. If he had had a dozen questions for Blackwood before walking into the Reno Lounge, he had ten times that many now, and he did not know where to begin. If Blackwood were out of his mind, as Eddie was seriously beginning to suspect, asking anything would be pointless. If he was not crazy, Eddie did not know what anything meant anymore. And Blackwood seemed in no hurry to resume their conversation. He just drove intently, caressing the wheel as though he had missed the car, letting Eddie's questions fester.

Finally, Eddie said, "So how did you get money from the future?"

Blackwood stayed silent for a moment. Then he said, "We're getting ahead of things. That's the future. I was telling you about the past."

"And being a no talent screenwriter?"

"That's right." They were on Olympic approaching Central. Blackwood slowed the Packard and turned left. He pulled over to the curb and parked, leaving the car idling for a moment as he said, "This your place?"

"Up there." Eddie pointed. For the first time since he had lived there, Eddie found himself not liking the look of the building. No lights were on yet in any of the windows on the second floor, and the building looked quiet, dark and unwelcoming. Blackwood shut off the engine, and they got out of the car. They jaywalked across the street and Eddie led the way into the building and up the stairs. Blackwood talked as they went.

"They say people have a hard time breaking into the movies these days, but you should have seen it back then," Blackwood said on the stairs behind him as Eddie approached the landing, no moonlight shining through the skylight above. "There were guys I would have expected could cut your throat if you got in their way, and all over the chance to get a scenario looked at by Griffith or de Mille. And women, too. My God. The women."

They had stopped in front of Eddie's door, and he took his keys out of his pocket.

"And me just trying to keep my head above water," Blackwood said, smiling to indicate this was an understatement. "It's tough to write and compete in a town like this when you're a morphine addict."

Eddie had been listening passively to Blackwood's reminiscences, wondering when he was going to get to his point and start putting together the puzzle pieces he had been laying out for Eddie since the Reno Lounge. Now he was stunned. He stood still in front of his open door as Blackwood, still smiling, stepped past him and into the apartment. It was dark inside, and Blackwood felt for the light switch, turning on the bare overhead bulb as though he lived here. He began walking around the room, glancing at the neatly labeled boxes on the shelves, the typewriter and papers on the desk, the stack of his own hardbacks on the office chair next to the bed. "Quite a collection," he said, nodding his approval as he appraised the shelves from the center of the room. Eddie still stood in the open doorway. "Come in, Eddie. It's your place, after all. And shut the door." Eddie complied. "Don't be so shocked. L.A. drew a pretty rough crowd back then. Always has, I suppose."

He pulled a pen from the inside pocket of his jacket and picked up one of the books on the chair. He flipped it open to the title page and, without asking, scribbled an inscription and signed it. He set it down on the desk and did the same to the next, working his way to the bottom of the stack as Eddie just watched. "*Nelphi*," Blackwood said when he got to the last one. "This one is going to be special, I think. This will be the one people look at as far reaching and profound." He signed the book. "Not sure why, though. Mind if I sit?"

"No." Eddie indicated the single chair and then sat on the bed as Blackwood turned the chair and sat on it to face him. Eddie realized they were in the same positions he and Pence had occupied in his neighbor's apartment a few hours earlier.

"You a college man, Eddie?"

Eddie shook his head. "I barely made it out of high school." He nodded toward the shelves. "I always wanted to read what I wanted, not what the teachers told me I should read."

"I see." Blackwood surveyed the shelves as well. "Been collecting a long time?"

"Since I was about twelve. I walked into the corner drugstore and picked up a copy of *Stupendous* and I was hooked."

"Mm-hmm." Blackwood paused. "I figured you for a college man with the Shakespeare and all. So not much background in science?"

"Just what I've picked up here and there."

"I see . . . Have you ever thought about time travel, Eddie?"

Eddie hesitated. "You mean like Wells? I've thought—"

"No, not like Wells. You need to get your head out of the past. That's your problem. You're too heavily influenced by what's come before, what others have said. For no-talent writers like us, that's death."

"Like us?"

49

"Sure. I'm no different from you. I couldn't come up with an original idea to save my life. Or I was too focused on being Edgar Rice Burroughs to let myself really discover what I had to say. The difference between you and me, though, is that you're content to steal from the past." He paused and then added, "And I've been stealing from the future."

He looked squarely at Eddie as he said it, no hint of a smile. He wore the same serious expression he had affected at the Reno Lounge when talking about tea shirts. Eddie still expected a punch line. None came. "The future?" he finally said.

"That's right. You remember what I asked you about defying the laws of the universe?"

"Sure."

"Well, I found a way to do it. Accidentally of course."

"How?"

"You sure you want to know?"

"I'm sure."

"We'll see," said Blackwood. He paused and looked again around the room. "You want it bad, don't you? Not just a few stories stolen from Shakespeare in *Stupendous* but the real thing, the big deal."

Eddie just nodded.

"I wanted it, too. Only I wasn't quite as focused as you are. Twenty-five years ago, I was juggling writing for whoever would pay me for slice of life stories with keeping my drug connections and trying to support a wife and daughter. Crazy. Roxanne's mother was one of those no-talent starlets who swarmed into L.A. as soon as the cameras started rolling. We were made for each other. Two self-destructive losers. To try to make ends meet, I made myself available to a Chinaman who had his fingers in most of the drug trade moving through here. There was this country club in Vernon where the Hollywood types went—the ones who were actually in the movies and the ones who just wanted to be. By the end of the war, you could have found me on any given day standing at the bar in the clubhouse with two or three other fellas. Enough morphine, heroin and cocaine stashed away to kill a horse. My Chinaman—called himself Johnny Woo—knew I was smart enough not to sample too much of the wares, and he was mostly right. All the big stars came through there, and you'd be surprised how many were steady customers or else had their flunkies do business with me. Barbara La Marr. Mabel Normand. Wallace Reid had a trick golf club with a hypodermic he could slip out of the handle, take a shot right on the ninth hole, and then finish out his game. You even know who I'm talking about?"

Eddie shook his head. "Not really."

"No matter. They're all gone now. The point is, it was a living, sort of a desperate one, but it kept the wolf from the door. Also kept me from really doing what I wanted to do. But then things started falling apart. Between Fatty Arbuckle and William Desmond Taylor taking turns making headlines, and then Reid dying after he tried to kick his habit, things got a bit too hot for Mr. Woo. He used me here and there, but I was mostly out of a job and had to go back to the typewriter. I had made enough connections around the peripheries of Hollywood to be able to find this and that to write about for the movie magazines. Even managed to have the occasional bout of sobriety. But every time Edgar Rice Burroughs had a new book come out, I'd get so damned depressed that I'd go right back to it, which was about the least productive thing I could have done, I suppose. But still, that's what I did."

Blackwood shrugged and turned his palms upward in a gesture that indicated his complete surrender. Eddie understood that at some level he was ashamed of his actions but not enough to say so directly. He continued talking.

"So one night in 1925, there's a knock on the door. Roxanne's mother was long gone by this point. I had set us up in a little bungalow in the Hollywood

Hills. Wasn't like it is now up there—lots of little spots hidden up in ravines and such, not so high rent. Woo had come by once with a little delivery right after my wife left me and Roxanne. Must have had a hell of a good memory because a couple years later, there he is on my front porch—at two o'clock in the morning with a bullet wound in his side. He comes staggering in when I open the door, bleeding all over the floor. He's mumbling in Chinese, completely incoherent it seemed. I mean to say, I don't speak Chinese, but it seemed like he was raving, repeating the same phrases and looking around the room like he saw things that weren't there. About the only phrase in English he said that I could make out was 'Dragon's Tears.' And not long after, he's stone cold dead.

"If it had been five years earlier, I would have known what to do, who to call. But as it was, I was so out of that life that I didn't have the first idea of who he dealt with in Chinatown anymore. Making the wrong call to one of his enemies, maybe even the one who had shot him up so good, could easily have meant the same treatment for myself and probably worse for Roxanne. So after Woo'd been dead for an hour or so and me just sitting there staring at him, I went through his pockets, wrapped him up in the rug he'd bled all over, and dragged him out the back door and onto the floor in the back of my Ford. I bundled Roxanne up out of bed, tossed her in the car, and drove up Angeles Crest. Dumped him off the side of the road up there. Far as I know the body's still there."

"Did you ever find out who did it?" Eddie asked.

Blackwood shook his head. "No. At the time, I figured he was probably making a deal somewhere in my neighborhood, and it went bad. I figured soon enough it was best not to know. Regardless, his dying on me that way changed my life."

"How so?"

"Well, for starters, he had two thousand dollars on him. That was two thousand more than I had had that evening and two thousand more than I knew what to do with for a while. Ended up keeping Roxanne and me afloat for quite some time. Let me off the hook where the hack work was concerned, let me follow my muse."

"That's how you wrote your first book?"

"Not exactly. But it led me to inspiration. See, Woo had that two thousand and he also had a little vial in his breast pocket. And that's what made all the difference."

Eddie's rising emotion at the thought that he was hearing the genesis of Blackwood's career crashed again as his hero worship turned once more to disillusion. "More drugs?"

"Sort of. Not the kind I was hoping for. In this vial was just a little bit of this amber fluid. Hadn't seen anything like it before. Had no odor to it. No idea what it was or what it would do. I just stuck it up high on a shelf for a long time and let it work on my imagination. And then one night, when the desperation had crept back in and Roxanne was asleep and that two thousand was on its way to being two hundred, I put just one drop on my tongue. And the whole world changed."

"How?"

"I saw things that weren't there. Things that weren't there yet, anyway."

"It let you see the future?"

Blackwood shook his head. "No. More like it showed me where the future was. And the past. Turns out that Dragon's Tears is a drug used by a very tiny sect of monks in Tibet and India as part of a ritual. Puts them in touch with the transcendent nature of reality. That's how they see it, anyway. There are things, Eddie, that are around us everyday that we just can't perceive. This substance opens up one's perceptions. The effect lasts for about a day, and then you're back to perceiving only what the five senses can normally pick up.

The thing the monks work towards, apparently, is being able to perceive without the drug, but it takes a lifetime of work for them to do it."

Eddie knew about meditation and had heard stories of Buddhist monks able to defy the laws of physics and human endurance, but still he was skeptical. "So what exactly did it let you see?" he asked.

"Bridges. Bridges to the future and the past. Like little openings that you can see through, some of them. And others big enough to walk through. And on the other side of the opening, it's the same room only two days in the future, or six months, or thirty years. Or else it's the past."

"And how do you know it's not just a hallucination?"

"Because I've been through some of the ones big enough to step through. And I've brought things back."

"Like five-dollar bills?"

Blackwood nodded. "Like five-dollar bills," he repeated.

Eddie looked hard into Blackwood's smiling eyes, trying to determine how much of what he said was truth, how much was alcohol, and how much was madness. He was telling himself that he should be alarmed, that he should be considering Blackwood insane, but the older writer's sincerity and good humor disarmed him. If Blackwood was crazy, listening to his story wouldn't hurt anything. But a surreal, nagging sense told him Blackwood was telling the truth. The five-dollar bill had looked awfully authentic, after all.

"Tell me more," Eddie said.

"Intrigued. That's good. What do you want to know?"

"What's the future like?"

"Well, for one thing, I haven't gone that far. The longest bridges only go about fifty years either way. And long and short bridges in combination can still only get you about fifty years away from where you started. You can find other bridges from there, but they all seem to go the opposite direction, so it's not possible to go back and stop the Lincoln assassination or anything.

McKinley maybe, but why bother? It's like you can't perceive of bridges that go further once you've taken them a certain distance, like your body is somehow always tethered to the time you belong in, and you just can't get that far away from it. And not much changes in fifty years. Cars go faster, planes go higher, skirts get shorter, and everything is louder. But everything else is pretty much the same."

Now Eddie raised an eyebrow.

"Skeptical? Don't get me wrong. There are wars, advances, tragedies. I don't understand it all, haven't been able to. You see, when you cross over, you can't stay too long. If you're in a different time more than a day or so and the Dragon's Tears wears off, then you're stuck there until you take more. And, like I said, Johnny Woo didn't leave me that much to start with, so I had to conserve."

"How many times have you done it?"

Blackwood eyed him carefully for a moment before saying, "You sound like you believe me."

Eddie did not respond right away. Unsure of whether he believed Blackwood or not, he could only say for sure that he wanted to hear more of the story. "I might."

"Good enough. I don't know how many times I've crossed over. Quite a few times at first. Not at all for the last several years until . . . today. It's a nerve-wracking sort of thing. Had to be sure I didn't get lost."

"How so?"

"Let's say there's a bridge in this room. Here it's—what time is it?"

Eddie looked at his watch. For the first time, he noticed that Blackwood was not wearing one. "Six-forty," he said.

"Okay. Six-forty on March 19, 1940. On the other side of that bridge, it might be three in the morning on September 12, 1963. I cross over, walk around for a while, step through another bridge to nine at night on August

20, 1980. Bridges to the east are into the past, and to the west are into the future. I keep moving around. These bridges in time usually appear in clusters, so you can move around pretty good once you find one to go through. When I decide it's time to come back, I have to take the same bridges, retrace my steps exactly from bridge to bridge. If I've been gone three hours, I come back at nine-forty on the nineteenth, and everything is fine. If I'm not careful, though, I lose my time, miss the exact bridges I used the first time and maybe lose a day or two or come back a day before I left."

"What would be wrong with that?"

"If I come back to March 18, 1940, then for a day there's two of me, and I have to stay out of my own way until I know the original me has gone over the bridge. I don't want to run into myself and mess up the sequence of events. If I come back on March 20, it's not so bad, but I've lost a day, and if there was something I needed to do—like meet a plagiarist at the Reno Lounge—there's no way I can get back to that time."

"You're saying you were time traveling today?"

Blackwood nodded. "Wasn't exactly planned. I had a feeling I might be in some trouble, so I took a dose as a precaution. Turns out I was right. I was in a situation I had to get out of and couldn't retrace my steps. Had to do a lot of trial and error to get back here. Back to the time I needed to get back to. Which is actually just about impossible. Left me with some time on my hands."

"Meaning?"

"Meaning the closest I could get was two weeks ago. I've been holed up in a downtown hotel since then, waiting until today rolled around again. That's how I ended up a bit financially embarrassed."

Eddie felt baffled. "Wait a minute," he said. "How could you have been gone for two weeks? I saw you this morning in Whistler's office."

"That's right. In the sequence of things, I met you late in the morning on March 19th. At about three-thirty in the afternoon, I stepped through a bridge in time. Went into the past, then found another bridge into the future and so on. I couldn't go back the way I had come, so I had to find another bridge that would get me to March 1940. The best I could do was March 5th. When I came through and figured out where I was, or when I was, I knew there was another version of myself walking around doing all the things I had done between the 5th and the 19th. So I had to lay low and not let any of those events get altered. Once three-thirty on the 19th came and went, I knew it was safe for me to go out."

Eddie was trying to take it all in, but he was skeptical. "If you were in such a bad spot, why couldn't you just contact yourself and warn yourself not to go to wherever you were today?"

"Because then the original me wouldn't have gone through the time bridge. Theoretically, there'd have been two of me permanently, and I don't want to think about that. Maybe the version of myself that you see here would have ceased to exist. I really don't want to find out."

Eddie nodded. "I think I get it."

"Good."

"So what happened at three-thirty that made you have to get out of 1940?"

Blackwood did not answer right away but rather smiled for a moment, ironically, Eddie thought. "I'm not sure I'm ready to say just yet. I will tell you I was up in Hollywood, though. You know, funny thing is that everywhere I've been, I've never seen a greater concentration of time bridges than there are in Hollywood. It's like the place is goddamn Swiss cheese, there are so many holes in it. And no one really knows about it. Except you, now." He nodded, looking as though he had just given Eddie a gift and expected to be thanked.

Eddie felt not the least bit grateful. "It's your story that sounds like it has a lot of holes in it."

"Don't believe me?" Blackwood asked. "How do you explain the five?"

"It's a gag. A novelty bill. Or, like you said, the product of a stupid counterfeiter."

Blackwood shook his head. "I got that money in 1986. Sold my watch at a pawnshop for two hundred bucks."

"Why?"

"Because I didn't know how long I was going to be gone. Needed to eat and get a place to sleep. I didn't want to take any more Dragon's Tears, so I made sure I got back as close as I could to March 1940 before the dose I took had worn off. So I had two-hundred dollars cash that won't be printed for forty-four years, and I've been passing it on the sly for the last two weeks, hoping no one bothers to look at the date before I can get away."

The story, Eddie realized, did not have as many holes in it as logic told him it should. It certainly accounted for Blackwood's disheveled appearance. Eddie decided that the older writer definitely looked like he had been living in the same clothes for two weeks, and his pale skin suggested that he had been indoors for about that length of time. After hesitating a moment, he said, "If these holes in time are all over the place, why don't people accidentally step through them?"

Blackwood smiled and nodded. "Maybe they do. People disappear sometimes, after all. Or have déjà vu. Or think they see something out of the corner of their eye that just isn't there. But it's doubtful. Some of the bridges are in inaccessible spots. The ones that are accessible are usually a foot or two off the ground, and you have to get your whole body through, not just an arm or a leg or your head. Crossing over the bridges big enough for a whole person to fit through is a rather deliberate act, not something I could imagine happening accidentally."

"Who else knows about this?"

"Some monks, I suppose. Probably people Johnny Woo was working with or for, but that was fifteen years ago. The more I've thought about it, I realize I shouldn't just have been concerned with where he got shot but when also."

"You think he was time traveling?"

"Sure of it. It has a rather disorienting effect on you when you come back to your time. The look in his eyes I've seen in my own when I've come back. It wasn't just pain or fear or loss of blood. He could have gotten shot in 1890 or 1950 for all I know."

"But who else knows about you?"

"No one. Except you. A couple others have an idea, but they don't know the particulars. Roxanne has no idea."

"Whistler?"

Blackwood snorted. "Whistler doesn't know anything beyond what's right in front of him. He's a great manager, but he's no visionary."

"And you are?"

"No. No more than you are. In many respects, you could say I squandered what I found. If I'd been smarter about it, I could have had more than just a list of companies for Roxanne to invest in. I should have thought small— gone ahead a few days and then come back and invested in the stock market or the horses. But I suppose you could say whatever character defects I have that led me into drug addiction and crime also steered me as a time traveler. The first dozen or so times I went into the future, I used it to find more drugs. That's something else that does get better in the future. And sex. Attitudes get a bit more relaxed in another thirty years or so. After a while, though, I had the revelation that I could be the greatest science fiction writer since Wells. I could accurately predict the future. So I made a few more trips and really looked at technology, but I couldn't understand half of it. Got so damn depressed. You'd have laughed, Eddie. It was pathetic. All I had wanted my whole life was to be the next Wells or Jules Verne, and here I had the tool that could let me do it, and I couldn't figure out what to do. But then one day in 1980, I was walking past a bookstore and had a revelation. Same one you had, I suppose."

"Using what had already been written."

"That's right. Sort of like playing the horses or the stock market, only with publishing. I could find out what would be a great book in 1930 and write it myself in 1929. It was practically a guarantee. Only I found a way to do the great book even greater."

"How?"

Blackwood shook his head. "Some things I'm going to keep to myself for the moment. Let's just say it was pretty much foolproof."

Eddie leaned forward. "So you're saying someone else wrote *Nelphi* and *Empire* and all the others and you just beat them to the publishers with the same stories?" He continually had to remind himself to question Blackwood's sanity but believed every word regardless. Now he found himself fascinated, angry and amused. If Blackwood had actually done this, it was maddening to think that the writer Eddie had been so devoted to was a charlatan, but at the same time it was a brilliant and audacious trick. Deep inside, Eddie knew he would have done the same thing if he had been able to.

"Not exactly," Blackwood answered. "As I said, I found a way to improve on the originals. But my method had its limits. And now," he said, sighing, "I've found myself once again the victim of my own lack of vision. I was too limited in my thinking." He looked Eddie in the eye. "To put it plainly, I've run out of ideas."

"How's that possible? Can't you just go back and get more?"

"I could. But it's not that simple. I only had a small amount of Dragon's Tears from Johnny Woo. And at one drop on the tongue for each journey, it went fast. Before today—which actually was two weeks ago for me—I had abstained for ten years. There's very little left now. A couple of drops at the most. So I'm faced with a choice. Take a trip to the future, gather up enough . . . shall we say, inspiration? Gather up enough inspiration to sustain me for another ten years or so. That's one option. The other is to just go into the future and not come back."

"Why would you do that?"

"Because sometimes the devil you know is worse than the devil you don't."

"Isn't that the other way around?"

"No. Not for me. I've made some people here pretty unhappy lately. People you'll find out soon enough are best kept happy, Eddie."

"Swinburne?"

Blackwood looked sharply at Eddie, clearly surprised to hear him use the name. "What do you know about Swinburne?"

"Nothing. Well, almost nothing. I know he runs Meteor. I know he's got a reputation for being difficult."

"He hasn't contacted you?"

Eddie thought about the contract, the safety deposit receipt in his wallet, and wondered if he should tell Blackwood about it. Whistler's warnings echoed in his head, and he thought it better to keep quiet about it for now. "No," he answered. "Will he?"

Blackwood stroked his mustache. "I expect so. Keep your eyes open."

Eddie nodded. This made two times in one day that Swinburne's name had come up, and both times he had been warned to watch out for the man who was essentially his boss. He hoped Pence would be able to come up with some information about Swinburne that would be of help. "Is Swinburne the reason you're running?" he asked.

Blackwood answered indirectly. "Even if I hadn't ruffled feathers, I still probably won't live another ten years if I stay in 1940. I doubt I'll live two."

Eddie raised an eyebrow, questioningly. Blackwood continued. "Cancer. They haven't cured it by 1990. That's one of the things I looked into in my little unscheduled trip to the future. But they can treat it. Help you get a few more years than you'd have otherwise."

Taken aback, Eddie said, "I'm sorry to hear that."

"Don't be. All the abuse I've put myself through, it's a wonder my body didn't give out on me a long time ago. One way or another, I'll be all right. I've been lucky up to this point. And since I got the Dragon's Tears . . . Well, I finally got what I wanted. What I have to figure out now, though, is what to do about you."

"Me?"

"Yes. I've managed to get you involved in my little adventure without your knowing it. Not seriously involved, but I'm afraid it's going to get serious. How's your health, Eddie?"

"My health? Fine. Why?"

"Nothing. Let me ask you this. Have you believed any of what I've been telling you?"

Just as Eddie had felt like a pupil before a professor this morning when Blackwood had asked him about the laws of the universe, so now did Eddie feel that he was being examined, that there was a right answer Blackwood was looking for and it wasn't necessarily the answer that Eddie would have considered the truth. And taking too long to fathom the right answer over the real one would give away what he really thought regardless. "Yes," he said after a few seconds' hesitation. He watched Blackwood's face, his eyes. They did not betray anything, not satisfaction, disappointment, nor relief. He continued. "It's hard to believe. You've got to give me that." Blackwood nodded silently in response. "But I believe it. And if the way you're explaining it isn't the absolute truth of it, then I still believe something happened to you and that this is what you believe it was."

Blackwood smiled. "Good enough," he said. He stood up from the chair, towering over Eddie for a moment before stepping back and giving him room to stand as well. "We'll put an end to this for now. All of a sudden, I feel the intense need to sleep in my own bed."

Eddie felt panic begin to rise in his chest at the thought of Blackwood leaving without explaining everything to him. "When will we talk again?" he asked as he involuntarily made way for Blackwood to get to the apartment door.

"Soon enough," Blackwood said. "I've got a few things to work out first." He opened the door and seemed about to walk unceremoniously out without really saying goodbye.

"I'll walk you down," Eddie said.

"No need."

"It's fine," Eddie insisted, not ready to let the older writer go. They walked silently down the hallway and to the landing beneath the skylight.

"Interesting place," Blackwood said as he glanced through the interior windows into the common room with its couch and table.

"True." Eddie hit the light switch on the wall, and the dim bulb above the door at the bottom of the stairs lit up. He and Blackwood began their descent. A few seconds later the door below them opened, and Pence stepped through. Eddie saw him glance up the stairs, hesitating a moment at seeing two others coming down, and then he began to climb, keeping to one side of the stairs to be able to pass.

Eddie smiled at him and was about to say "Evening" when he saw that Pence and Blackwood had both paused on the stairs a few feet from each other. It lasted only a second, but Eddie could not mistake the slight hesitation in both men's progress up and down. He also saw a quick look of surprise on Pence's face, a look that shifted rapidly to confusion, alarm and then the cool detachment Eddie was used to seeing on the detective's face when he was not drinking.

The encounter left Eddie feeling even more unsettled than he had been in his apartment listening to Blackwood, so when Pence passed Blackwood and was for a moment on the same level as Eddie, all he could manage was a brief nod to Pence, which his neighbor silently returned. When Eddie and Blackwood reached the bottom of the stairs, Eddie turned to glance upward before following Blackwood onto the sidewalk; Pence stood at the banister below the skylight and stoically watched them leave. Eddie did not nod again but went through the door and closed it behind him.

The second it had latched, Blackwood turned on his heel and looked Eddie in the eye, his face only inches away from Eddie's. "Who was that?" he asked, just loud enough to be heard above the traffic rolling by only a few feet away.

"My neighbor," Eddie said. "You know him?"

Blackwood shook his head and took a step back. "No. Looks like someone I used to know, though. Neighbor got a name?"

"Pence," Eddie said. "Will Pence." If the information meant something to Blackwood, his features did not betray it. If anything, the seriousness of his expression faded a bit. "Ring a bell?" Eddie asked.

"No," Blackwood repeated. "Couldn't be who I thought, anyway. A bit like seeing a ghost." He half turned toward the street and his car parked on the other side of it. Then he said, "Thanks for meeting me tonight, Eddie. I think everything's going to be just fine now. I'm going to let you think on this for a while. Not too long. And then I'll give you a bit more information. Let you make your own decision."

"About what?"

"About what to do with the rest of your life. About how long you want it to be." He took a step toward the curb.

Without thinking about it, Eddie put a hand on Blackwood's shoulder, half turning Blackwood and then quickly moving to stand between Blackwood and the street as he took his arm off the older man's shoulder. "Are you saying I'm in danger?" He felt a surge of adrenaline.

Blackwood sighed and looked at the sidewalk for a moment. "I suppose I am. It's not immediate, and I can't say how much of it I've caused, but I can say that things are going to get interesting for you before too long. You're going to need to figure out what to do."

Growing angry now, Eddie said, "How can I do that if you won't tell me what it's about? You've seen the future. What's going to happen to me?"

"I've seen the future, Eddie. You're right there. But I haven't seen your future. And I know enough about the future and the past to know it's changeable, so even if I did know what was going to happen to you, it doesn't mean it really would. And the other thing, Eddie, is—to be blunt—I don't know if you're worth saving." Now it was his turn to put his hand on Eddie's shoulder, both in a gesture of comfort and with a slight shove to move Eddie out of his way. "Don't get me wrong. I know you're not a bad guy. But if you can't figure out what to do on your own, well, I don't need you monkeying around in my future. You might just be an unscrupulous writer with a lucky streak that's about to end. Or you might be a smart guy who can play against the house and win. And maybe fix some other mistakes along the way." He moved around Eddie and toward the street, then turned and offered Eddie his hand. Eddie shook it. "I'll be in touch," Blackwood said. "Soon. Just not in the way you might expect. Keep your eyes open. For more than just me." He smiled, sadly, Eddie thought, and stepped off the curb, offering a slight nod as he did so.

Back upstairs and heading to his apartment, Eddie was surprised by Pence, who opened his own door as Eddie was walking past it. Eddie stopped short, catching his neighbor's serious expression, and was about to ask what was wrong when Pence spoke first. "Who was that guy?" he asked.

Eddie furrowed his brow. "You know him?"

Pence shook his head but said, "Might. Who was he?"

Seeing no reason to lie, Eddie said, "That's Chester Blackwood." If the name meant anything to Pence, his expression betrayed nothing. "He's a writer. Pretty famous, really."

"Did he say anything about me?"

With half a shrug, Eddie said, "He asked the same kind of question—thought he knew you from somewhere. But then he said he couldn't have."

"Why?"

Eddie shrugged. "He didn't say . . . just said it was like looking at a ghost." Pence nodded, thoughtful. "What's it all about?" Eddie asked. "Do you know him or not?"

Pence shook his head. "No." He moved to step back into his apartment.

Eddie spoke quickly. "Wait. What's this all about? Two guys who both think they know each other but don't? Seems unlikely."

Pence raised an eyebrow and half smiled. "Unlikely things happen, Eddie. You'd be surprised. Just take my word for it. That guy you were talking to doesn't mean anything to me. Not now, not ever. Okay?"

"Okay," Eddie said. He wanted to believe Pence but could not entirely. Even so, he knew there was no point in pushing Pence any further. He repeated, "Okay" and stepped back from his neighbor's door.

"Good," Pence said, turning into his apartment. Then as Eddie took a few steps toward his own door, Pence added, "Your man Swinburne?" Eddie stopped and looked at him. "You're right to be cautious."

"What did you find out?"

"Nothing concrete yet. But what I'm hearing doesn't make him sound like someone you want to mess around with. Watch yourself."

Eddied nodded. "Thanks, Pence." He paused, then added, "'Night."

Pence nodded his response and shut his door. Eddie turned and walked the last few feet to his room. He felt exhausted. Inside his apartment, he told himself he should get some sleep right away even though it was still early. But his eyes were drawn to the stack of books on the corner of the desk that Blackwood had flipped through and signed, and Eddie had no choice but to pick each one up and ponder the title pages. They were identically marked: "To Eddie Royce, a writer after my own heart. Chester Blackwood." Like a pilgrim handling a sacred relic, Eddie found himself touching the dried ink of the inscriptions on the books, feeling more reverence for them than he had for the man who had written them.

CHAPTER FIVE

The Blackwood mansion was impressive, but it was not the lavish estate Eddie had been expecting. With so many books and stories under his belt, and more than ten years of phenomenal popularity, Blackwood should easily have been able to afford a gated villa with vast expanses of lawn, circular driveways and servants' quarters. This was what Eddie had imagined when Blackwood had handed him the business card the morning before in Whistler's office, and it was the sort of house he had expected finding when he had set out this morning from his apartment and taken a Red Car from downtown Los Angeles to Pasadena. When the taxi he had taken from the Pasadena station had pulled onto this street and stopped in front of this house, Eddie had asked the driver if he was sure it was the right address. After receiving an indignant grunt in the affirmative, Eddie had paid his fare and gotten out. He stood at the curb for a moment looking at the house before walking toward it.

It was large, to be sure, bigger than anything Eddie had ever imagined himself being able to afford, but it was not gaudy or expansive, not baronial in the least. Instead, Blackwood's house was a white two-story affair with a modest entryway, oak double doors beneath a small cupola, a single column on either side, and rows of four windows spreading out across the face of the house. There was a circular driveway, but instead of running across a huge lawn with croquet sets and Afghan hounds lounging in the shade, it was modest and covered the short distance between the house and street. As Eddie walked up it, he noticed several cracks and small potholes in it, and there were weeds in the lawn. Blackwood's Packard was not in the driveway, but a large black Lincoln and a red Cord convertible were; there was a garage off to the side of the house, and Eddie assumed the Packard would be parked there.

Standing before the double doors, Eddie took a deep breath and exhaled before ringing the bell. Blackwood had told him to wait to be contacted the evening before, and now Eddie was at his door, drawn there not because of defiance but rather because Blackwood's cryptic tale and his intimation that Eddie might be in some danger had driven Eddie into a state of anxiety. He had managed to sleep the night before, but only fitfully, and had decided after waking up and showering that he would go to Pasadena and do his best to convince Blackwood to tell him everything he had left out the night before.

Expecting a servant to answer, Eddie anticipated handing over Blackwood's card and being ushered in, shown a seat and asked to wait. He grew more nervous the longer it took for the door to be answered, and when it was, it was not by a servant. The door cracked open about a foot, and Eddie found himself staring again at Roxanne Blackwood. It took him a second to realize it was her. The shoulder length platinum hair, exaggerated makeup and outlandish costume were gone. The wig had been replaced by honey colored hair that framed her face and curled gracefully about her neck. Her pink lips and blue eyes were bright but not from an overdose of cosmetics. Eddie did not know much about make-up, but he knew enough to tell she was wearing very little and that she did not need much at all to appear gorgeous. She wore a white dress with small red polka dots on it and a wide red belt. Seeing as little of her as he could with the door only partially opened, Eddie could still tell that her outfit accentuated her figure as much as any space princess costume could. When she asked, "Can I help you?" Eddie was speechless for a moment.

"Yes," he finally said, fumbling in his pockets for Blackwood's card. "Miss Blackwood, we met yesterday in Whistler's office. I'm Eddie Royce." He smiled awkwardly, half expecting her to remember. Her face betrayed no recognition as she took the card, glanced at it, and handed it back. "I spoke with your father yesterday, and I wondered if I could see him again for just a minute. He left me with some—"

"My father's not in, Mr. Royce," she said, cutting him off.

"Oh." Eddie felt dumbfounded. "Of course. I'm sorry, Miss Blackwood. Sorry for the inconvenience. Do you know when he might be available?" Eddie felt himself beginning to sweat and was irritated with himself. He hadn't been this nervous about meeting Blackwood. And Roxanne Blackwood was not the first beautiful woman he had ever spoken to. Even so, there was still something about her.

"I'm sorry," she said. "I don't know when he'll be back. And this . . ." She glanced behind her, into the house. "This just isn't a good time right now. If he comes home, I'll tell him you were here."

"All right," Eddie said. "Thank you." He smiled as she shut the door. She did not return the smile. Then he turned and began walking back toward the street. He did not think about where Blackwood might be but instead found himself wondering about Roxanne and the nervous manner she had had at the door. The Blackwood house was on a narrow residential street off of Lake that rose up on a slight incline from Colorado Boulevard, a section of Route 66. Eddie had not thought about getting home, had not even considered asking the cab driver to wait, and he did not entertain for a moment the prospect of going back to the house and asking Blackwood's daughter to call him a cab. So now he was faced with the walk back down Lake. He would get his bearings when he got to Colorado and find a bus or cab to take him back to the Red Car and then home again.

Before he could reach the end of the street, though, and start walking down the hill, he heard the rumble of a car behind him and turned to see the red Cord that had been in Blackwood's driveway. It pulled up to the curb beside him and Roxanne rolled down the window. She wore a pair of sunglasses now and appeared even more flustered and nervous than she had been at the door. "Excuse me, Mr. Royce," she said. Eddie had stopped walking and stood, hands in his pockets, looking at her. "This is going to sound awfully forward of me, but would you mind taking a short ride with me? I could offer you a lift to wherever you're going if you like."

Eddie hesitated only a moment, narrowing his eyes to study her. After her aloof behavior at the door of her house, getting a ride from Roxanne was the last thing Eddie had expected. Her nervous demeanor had made him curious, as it seemed the complete opposite of the fire she had possessed when dealing with Whistler the day before. He guessed that something had disturbed her badly, and he could not guess why she should have changed her demeanor with him so radically. Thinking of what her father had said about Roxanne being trouble, he asked himself if he really wanted to get mixed up in whatever had upset her. Still, a ride was a ride, and all those images from *Stupendous* covers still haunted him. Her smile might have been forced, but he told himself that only an idiot would turn her down.

"Sure, that would be fine," he said a few seconds later and walked around the front of the car, opening the passenger door and sliding into the white interior. As he closed the car door with a firm click, he thought of the damsels in distress Roxanne had portrayed so perfectly on Frehling's *Stupendous* covers along with the tough-as-nails, laser toting heroines. It seemed he had now seen two parts of her personality that Frehling had tapped into beautifully and perfectly. Eddie thought about the other type she had played on the covers—the seductress—and wondered a bit guiltily how close to the real Roxanne those images had been.

71

Roxanne glanced over her shoulder, saying, "Thank you. I didn't mean to sound so abrupt with you back there," as she pulled away from the curb and then turned onto Lake.

"No, no. That's all right. Your father probably gets his share of fans knocking at the door at all hours."

"Some. What did you need to see him about?"

"Oh, it's nothing really. I spoke to him last night and—"

"Last night?" She sounded surprised. "When?"

"About five-thirty or so. He stayed at my place until a little after seven."

The car was almost to the intersection of Lake and Colorado. She slowed down and said, "Would you mind terribly if you told me about it?"

Eddie heard worry in her voice. "No. Is there something wrong, Miss Blackwood?"

"Please. Call me Roxanne. It's just that my father's gone missing."

"Ah." Eddie felt surprised by the news and a bit alarmed. He began thinking about the things Blackwood had said the night before about being in trouble, probably with Swinburne.

"Which is nothing new, of course. I'm not really worried about him. He's likely to show up in a day or two with a few bruises and no memory of where he's been." She paused, looking at Eddie for a moment, sizing him up, it seemed, before continuing. "Or else we'll find him in an opium den in Chinatown. Or laid up with a whore in Hollywood."

Eddie smiled at her candor. Roxanne clearly knew more about her father's misdeeds than he did, but Eddie realized that Blackwood may have been telling the truth the night before when he said that Roxanne knew nothing about his supposed time traveling. He also realized that by letting her talk more about her father, it was possible that Roxanne would enlighten him a bit more about her father's veracity, albeit unintentionally. "I see," he said. "I thought he had gone on the straight and narrow."

She laughed briefly. "My father? Never. When he's writing, he's usually sober, but whenever he dots the last i, it's back to his current favorite vice." She looked at Eddie for a moment and then back at the road. "Am I shattering your illusions, Mr. Royce?"

"No. He pretty well took care of that last night. And you can call me Eddie if you like."

"Eddie," she repeated.

"So it's true that he's not writing anymore?"

"Is that what he told you?"

"Yes."

Roxanne did not say anything for a moment. She watched the traffic in front of her and slowed the Cord. Before long, she said, "Is there somewhere you need to be, Eddie? Somewhere I should drop you?"

"Just at a bus stop if you like." He did not want the conversation to end. "I don't have anything pressing at the moment, though. If you'd rather talk for a bit, you can take me as far as Central and Olympic, downtown."

She turned the car onto Colorado and started heading west. "We can end up there. Would you mind just driving for a bit, though? I need to be away from the house for a while. My father's associates are going through his papers with a fine tooth comb trying to find out where he's gotten to."

"Have you called the police?"

"No. It's not like that. I'm really not worried about him. It's everyone else who seems bothered."

"His agents, I suppose?"

"Daddy doesn't have an agent. He's been exclusive to Meteor for ten years now. Which partially explains why he's so cash poor. You've been publishing there now?"

"Yes, for *Stupendous*."

"Have you met Mr. Swinburne yet?"

Eddie shook his head. "No."

"Avoid it if you can. It's his goons who are going through my father's papers right now."

"Goons?"

She flashed him a nervous smile. "Accountants, really. Lawyers. You know. The type who panic when the cash cow looks like it's dried up."

Eddie thought she was lying. "How long since he's written anything?"

"I haven't asked him about it. We're not exactly close, Eddie." She gave him a glance over her sunglasses and shrugged. "So what did he tell you last night? Have you any idea where he's gone?"

They had been traveling along Colorado through light traffic. Near the Suicide Bridge, Roxanne turned the Cord onto another road, taking a northerly route through streets Eddie was not familiar with. He decided to offer her a bit of her father's story to see how she would react.

"This is going to sound absurd," he began, "but he told me that he's been traveling in . . . well, traveling in time."

Roxanne laughed loudly.

It was not the reaction he had expected. "I'm serious. That's what he told me last night."

She glanced at Eddie. His face must have conveyed how serious he was, as she said, "And he convinced you that he was telling the truth?"

Eddie smiled in mild embarrassment. "Well, in the light of day everything seems more far fetched. That's what I came to talk to him about today."

"Don't you realize how good my father is at telling stories?"

"Of course. It's just that—"

"My father is an inveterate liar, Eddie. He lies about everything. To himself most of all. He does it religiously. The truth is distasteful to him. So much so that he doesn't know what it is anymore."

"It's not like I believe him. I'm just . . . He told me some things that just seemed like they could be true. He made it seem like I was somehow mixed up in it. And . . . this may be another fabrication, but he also told me that he's very ill."

After a moment, Roxanne said, "How so?"

"Cancer. Has he told you about it?"

She looked serious, as though she was shaken by the news. Then she shook her head and said, "No, but that doesn't mean anything. We're not exactly forthcoming with each other about the minutia of our lives. But even so, I wouldn't put too much stock in it. He's made up maladies before." She watched the road for a moment but appeared to be thinking about something else. "What else did he tell you about time travel?"

Not entirely confident about giving away too much information, but at the same time not used to having to think on his feet to keep a deception going, Eddie decided he should just answer her questions for as long as it seemed wise. "Well, he explained that he hadn't done it in a long time, that he did a lot of it back in the twenties and then used it . . . ." Eddie smiled nervously. Roxanne glanced at him, encouragingly. "He said he used it to help his writing."

"How?"

Eddie shrugged, trying to show her that he had not entirely believed a story that sounded more and more crazy the more distance he got from it. "He made it sound as though somehow he found a book before he started publishing, and it opened things up for him. I think he was trying to tell me it helped him steal other writers' ideas from the future."

"That," she said after moment, "would explain a lot."

"I know it sounds crazy."

She seemed to ignore the comment. "And did he say where this book was, or what it was?"

"No. He was pretty evasive about it."

"And what about how he traveled through time?"

"It was a drug. He said he got it off a dead Chinaman."

"Did he say what it was called?"

She said it eagerly, almost anxiously, with none of the skepticism he had heard in her voice before. Talk of her father's drug use and fabrications should have made her scoff, but she did not. Eddie had no reason to distrust Roxanne, but her fervor over the drug her father had used made him nervous. Just as he had decided not to be forthcoming with Blackwood about the contract from Swinburne, now he decided not to add any more details about the story of Johnny Woo. Roxanne glanced at him again, raising an eyebrow, and Eddie said, "No. He said he got it back in the twenties, but that was all."

Roxanne nodded. She drove in silence for a moment, heading the car up toward the foothills. It was a clear day, and it had grown warm. Finally, she said, "Eddie, would you mind if I stop and call my home for a moment?"

"No. Not at all."

"I just want to see if Swinburne's people are still there. If they've heard from my father yet."

After a few more blocks, she pulled the Cord up in front of a small diner. "There's a payphone inside," she said, putting on the brake and opening her door. She had a large red purse and took it with her. "I'll just be a minute."

Eddie exhaled and sank back into the leather seat as he watched her walk away, his eyes focusing on her hips and the way they were accentuated by her belt as she walked. He realized he had been holding himself tense for most of the time they had been in the car. Roxanne was hard to read. She came off as fiercely independent, hardened to her father's shenanigans and irresponsibility, yet at the same time she appeared deeply concerned about his well being. She was clearly able to hold her own with Whistler, and probably Swinburne, too, and with her looks could easily get modeling jobs with any magazine, but at the same time she continued working for *Stupendous*, obviously unhappy with conditions there. Given the car, the house, her looks and her father's success, Roxanne Blackwood did not strike Eddie as the kind of woman who needed to work. She would have done just fine making the rounds at the parties of the elite in Pasadena and Beverly Hills, could easily have landed a young millionaire and been set for life. But instead, she spent her days, as far as Eddie could tell, trying to keep her father out of trouble and dressing up as Venusian princesses and sexy space pirates for the lecherous Klaus Frehling.

It didn't add up.

CHAPTER SIX

Roxanne walked out of the diner feeling sick to her stomach. She carried in her hands two white paper sacks, one with sandwiches and the other with two bottles of beer inside. The phone call she had just made kept running through her mind as she walked toward her car, making her oblivious to the people around her. So distracted was she that even the click of her heels on the asphalt of the parking lot seemed to be reaching her as through a tunnel. But then as she walked toward the red car where Eddie Royce sat waiting for her, she willed herself to smile. With his dark hair, blue eyes and honest smile, Eddie would at least be easy on the eyes if she had to spend the afternoon with him trying to find out as much as she could about what had happened to her father. That it was not her choice to do so was something Eddie should not know, and a scowl on her face would certainly raise suspicions in him and keep him quiet whereas a smile or two just might do the trick.

Opening her door and sliding in behind the wheel, she said, "I thought you might be hungry," and set the bags and her purse on the seat between them.

"Thanks," Eddie said.

"Things are still topsy turvy at my house. Would you mind just keeping me company for a while?"

"No." He said it quickly, and she saw that he was trying none too well to hide his delight at the prospect.

"There's a place up in the mountains I like to go to sometimes. Just to sit and think and write. We could go up there and eat if you like. The view's beautiful."

Eddie agreed and Roxanne started the car again, turning north at the next corner on a long, straight street that went directly into the foothills. The Cord's powerful engine seemed to growl as the car ascended rapidly, eating up the road eagerly like a predator. Soon, they were above homes and street lights, and the road had begun to twist up into a canyon. "Have you ever been up here before?" Roxanne asked.

"No."

"We'll take Angeles Crest for a bit and then cut over. There's a road that goes up to Mount Wilson, where the observatory is. The view up there is amazing. You don't mind waiting to eat until we get up there?"

"That's fine," Eddie said. They were silent for a while as Roxanne navigated the road that twisted around long curves and then doubled back, drawing them just as steeply up into the mountains as it had on the straightaway below. Occasionally, the view would open up to reveal the distance they had already covered, the city seeming to be a distant, hazy miniature. "Did you say you come up here to write?" Eddie asked after a few minutes.

"Mm-hmm," she said, nodding and grateful that Eddie had broken the silence. She had been replaying the morning's events, leading up to their stop at the diner. At the same time, she was conscious of seeming aloof, which would not help her at all in what she needed to do. She took the opportunity to talk as she drove, glancing occasionally at Eddie as she brought the car out of a curve and finding that his eyes were almost always on her rather than the scenery around them. "Daddy says writing's in my blood, but I'm not sure it's that simple. My maternal grandfather was a playwright, though. Even though most of what he wrote was only put on in bawdy houses. My mother said he was what they called a professor. You know what that is?"

Eddie blushed at the question. "Yes," he said with a slight grin.

"And his father, I'm told, was a rather respected journalist. When I was a kid, we had clippings that went back to the Civil War, but they're long gone now. So maybe it is genetic. All I know is it's all I've really wanted to do since I was about twelve or so."

"What do you write?"

"A bit of everything. Poetry, drama, but mostly stories. You know. The types of things *Stupendous* or the other magazines at Meteor would publish."

"Westerns and romances?"

"And detective stories. I think, like Daddy, the science fiction stories are what I do best."

Sounding surprised, Eddie said, "Have you tried publishing any of them?"

"Mm-hmm." She smiled and raised an eyebrow. "More than tried."

Now she saw Eddie turn completely red. "I'm sorry," he said. "I didn't mean to imply . . ."

"It's all right," she said cheerfully. "Most people don't expect it."

Eddie remained silent for a moment, and Roxanne guessed that he was trying to decide how to respond. Finally, he said, "You mean good looking and smart?"

Roxanne nodded, still smiling. She liked that she had been able to surprise him with the fact that she was also a published writer, but she liked better the fact that he was able to call her good looking and smart. It was what she had been hoping he would say. She replied with, "I can cook, too." Then, feeling a bit cruel, she added, "How many women science fiction writers can you name, Eddie?"

He hesitated, obviously thinking about the question, and at the same time looking embarrassed that he was not able to answer immediately. "C.L.

Moore," he said finally, his tone suggesting that Moore's was only the first name on a list that was about to follow. Roxanne looked at him with one raised eyebrow, then turned her attention back to the road. "Leslie Stone," he added after a long pause and then fell silent again.

"Mary Shelley?" Roxanne offered.

"Of course. There must be others. It's just . . ."

"Hard to think of any? I know. Publishing is generally a man's game, but there are a lot of women who make a success of it. But science fiction? It's a boy's club, Eddie. And my father is the head boy."

"Sort of like Peter Pan?"

The thought made her smile. "Worse. I want into the club, but I don't want to be just another footnote." Without thinking about it, she added, "One more woman writer people have to struggle to remember."

An awkward silence hung in the air for a moment before Eddie opted to change the subject. "I don't recall reading anything of yours."

"Pen name," she said, relieved that she must not have made him too uncomfortable.

"Ah. You don't want to ride your father's coat tails."

"Something like that."

"And what would the pen name be? I mean, if you don't mind saying?"

She smiled coyly. "No, I don't suppose I mind. Have you read anything by Archie Dumont?"

"You're kidding," Eddie said, sounding taken aback. "You're Archie Dumont?"

"In the flesh."

"Wow. But . . . Archie? What about the boys' club?"

Roxanne shrugged. "There's that line about if you can't beat 'em. Archie Dumont was my grandfather. Using his name has been sort of my way to break in. I think of it as practice for one of these days when I'm able to write under my own name."

"Well. That's . . . that's great. I really like your work. I have for years."

She thought he sounded like he meant it. "Thanks," Roxanne said. "I hate to say it, but I can't return the compliment. I haven't had a chance to read your stories."

"That's all right," Eddie said. After a moment's silence, he added, "Okay, this is going to sound like I'm prying." He involuntarily slid a couple inches closer to her as the car took a sharp curve while barely slowing down. "But if you're successful at writing, and your father obviously makes enough money to have a comfortable life for the two of you even if you weren't successful, why do you keep posing for the cover art when it's obvious you don't like doing it?"

Roxanne remained silent, watching the road. She had begun to hold her jaw tightly as he had spoken, feelings of anger and frustration welling up in her. Throughout much of her life, she realized, she had put herself in one situation after another in which she had had to do things she did not want to. Posing for the covers of *Stupendous*, taking care of her father, writing under a pseudonym, agreeing to go to Swinburne's party for Rebecca Le Blanc in a few days, even being here on this mountain road with a man she barely knew and telling herself she was ready to do what was expected of her to get the information she needed: in every instance, she was acting contrary to her own sense of what she knew she should be doing. More than at any other time she could remember, she regarded herself with disgust. At the same time, she knew that Eddie's question hung between them, awaiting an answer—and that she had no choice but to provide it. Finally, she said in a controlled, even tone, "Are you looking to hear a morality tale? Because that's what you're going to get."

Answering quickly, Eddie said, "Don't tell me if you don't want to. I didn't mean to pry. It's just . . ."

"It doesn't make a lot of sense?"

He nodded. "You could put it that way."

"Not a lot of people know I'm the girl behind the covers. And not a lot of people know I'm Archie Dumont. And the people in either group generally don't mix, so the paradox doesn't come up all that often. But if you want to know about it . . . I'll tell you." She paused, taking her eyes off the road and looking at him for a few seconds. "But there's something I have to know. If I'm going to be straight with you, I have to know you've been straight with me. Is there anything else about my father and his little time travel story that you haven't told me?"

Eddie hesitated for a moment, and Roxanne tried hard to read that hesitation, hoping to be able to see the sincerity of whatever answer was about to come. "No," Eddie finally said, and Roxanne knew it was a lie. Now she was faced with a choice—answer Eddie truthfully, purging herself to some degree, or keep the truth to herself and turn their conversation into even more of a game of cat and mouse. The latter, she realized, would do her no good. The former would do no harm. Especially since she would be divulging her past to a total stranger, there was no real risk involved. Telling Eddie the truth would make her no more vulnerable than she already was. And so, a few curves later, she said, "Okay. I hope you don't have too high an opinion of me because it may get a bit tarnished here."

"I'm no angel either," Eddie said.

"We'll see about that." She forced herself to smile at him and then looked back at the road.

"Your father told me you were trouble."

"Wouldn't he like to think so?" Roxanne shook her head and smiled at the thought. "My father has no idea what kind of woman I've become. And he

83

knew even less back then. When I was a teenager, I ran with a pretty wild crowd. Bad girls and worse boys. Where did you grow up?"

"A little city in Iowa you've probably never heard of."

"Ah. Then you probably didn't grow up with those types."

"I can fill in the blanks."

"I'm sure. Anyway, it wasn't like I was a drug addict like my father. Although I suppose I would have headed down that road before long. I'm not trying to make excuses or anything, but growing up with him as a father didn't exactly make virtue seem all that attractive or vice all that forbidding. And I spent a lot of time angry. But that's beside the point." She paused a moment and then went on. "What isn't beside the point is that one of the girls I knew got involved with modeling. And I don't mean the kind of modeling that gets you in the fashion magazines."

"I'm following you."

"Good. So one night when I'm lonely and angry and a little drunk, she introduces me to her boyfriend, who's this thirty-year-old man with a foreign accent—very suave and sophisticated and worldly. And before you know it I'm in the nude in front of his camera." She looked at Eddie for a reaction. He didn't give her one but just nodded for her to continue. She remembered how shocked he had appeared the morning before in Whistler's office and was glad now to see that he wasn't a prude. Continuing, she said, "This went on for a few weeks. The pictures got worse. The situation with the two of them just got creepier, and I eventually turned my back on both of them. Not before I had been paid, of course. I wanted the negatives, but he wouldn't let me have them. Do you have some idea where this is going?"

"Blackmail?" he asked.

"In a manner of speaking. Time passes, I straighten myself out a little, try a few semesters of college and realize I really don't want to waste my life the way my father has. I start writing, start submitting stories to different magazines. At the same time, creepy photographer has tracked me down. He starts sending me letters and flowers. Starts parking outside our house." She shuddered at the memory.

"What did he want?"

"Not what you'd think. He just wanted me to pose for him again. He said I was his muse, that he couldn't do decent work without me."

"Let me guess. Klaus Frehling."

"Bingo." She turned the car off the main road and began following a more narrow, steep and twisting road up and around a tree lined peak. "I fended him off, of course. He's not exactly formidable. And then, miracle of miracles, I get an acceptance letter from *Stupendous*. I didn't use my real name then either—the whole coattail thing—so I was thrilled that I was actually making it on my own. But when they accepted the story, I had to tell them who I really was so I could get paid. I received an invitation to come in to the office to discuss the story and publication, and when I got there, I met our friend Whistler."

"This was how long ago?"

"Seven glorious years," she said with sarcasm. "I sit down across the desk from him, and as soon as pleasantries are finished with, he pulls out a manila envelope that I assumed contained my story. 'Miss Blackwood,' he says, 'I was very sorry to find out that you're the daughter of one of our premiere writers.' My heart sank. I figured he was axing the story because he didn't want competing Blackwoods in the magazine. But then he says, 'Your father's embarrassment is something we're just going to have to put up with. And we're going to have to go to great lengths to keep that embarrassment very private.' I had no idea what he could mean, but then he unclasps the envelope and slides the contents out onto the desktop. And of course it's me in all my glory. Eight by ten glossies *á naturel*. A stack of them. Most I had never seen, of course, and some I didn't even remember taking. Some were pretty bad, and what was worse was a magazine mixed in with all of it. A cheaply put together little thing called *Secret Lives* with yours truly on the cover. There was even a form with what looked like my signature on it stating I was over eighteen, which I don't remember ever signing, but like I said, I wasn't exactly in my right mind the whole time I was with Klaus. I just sat there with these . . . these things spread out on the desk. If Whistler said anything, I couldn't have heard because my heart was pounding so loud in my ears."

"How did he get them?"

"Our boy Whistler wasn't always the editor of *Stupendous*. As it turned out, he had just taken on the post a few months earlier. Before that he had been in charge of smut for Swinburne. *Secret Lives* had been one of his babies."

"Meteor publishes stuff like that?"

"Not Meteor so much as Swinburne. It was a bit of a side project back then. He may still publish those things—not so you'd know about it, though. It's all hush hush. He probably produces stag films for all I know. Anyway, Whistler had brought Frehling along with him when he made the move up to *Stupendous* and had been sympathetic to his need to get me to pose for him again so he could base his magazine covers on me, but he hadn't made the connection between Klaus's Blackwood girl and Chester Blackwood. So when my story crossed Whistler's desk and he put two and two together, he knew he had me."

Painful and humiliating as the memories were, Roxanne found that it actually felt good to tell the story of what had happened to her seven years earlier. And she was also finding in Eddie a sympathetic listener. He seemed intrigued more than just curious, and Roxanne had to wonder if Swinburne was not trying to put Eddie in a bind of his own.

"What did he do?" Eddie asked. "He couldn't print those pictures in *Stupendous*."

"No, but he could see to it that they got published elsewhere, and often. He told me the pictures would ruin me if I really wanted to become a serious writer, to get published the way Daddy had been. An "About the Author" photo on a dust jacket really shouldn't be of one in the buff, after all.""

As the car wound its way around the mountaintop, nearing the observatory, she continued. "So there was a combination of threats and intimidation and deal making. Whistler, and later Swinburne, convinced me that if I tried to publish anything anywhere under my own name or someone else's, they'd know about it and expose me. Swinburne's got spies, it seems, all through the publishing world."

"Spies?"

"Mm-hmm. He's unscrupulous and incredibly competitive. Wants to know exactly what's going to be in next month's *Amazing Stories* two months before the editors even know. Anyway, I believed him. Still do."

"But why pose if you didn't want to? Why not just give up on writing for a while?"

Without hesitating, she replied, "Could you give it up?"

"No." He shook his head, and Roxanne saw him looking at her with real understanding. It told her a lot about him and how he felt about writing. For the first time since they had begun their drive, she felt she was talking to a kindred spirit.

"Me neither," she said. "Whistler promised to let me out of the deal in a few years and to turn over the negatives and everything else. In the meantime, I would pose for Klaus as often as he needed me, and *Stupendous* would publish everything I wrote but under a pen name, just to keep me humble. Which hasn't really worked. I don't care if I'm writing under my grandfather's name. As long as I'm writing."

"And your father couldn't get you out of this? Even with his money and reputation?"

Roxanne shook her head and sighed. "My father has lots of reputations, not all of them good. And as for money, he's been profligate to the extreme. I think every dime he's been paid has gone to the horses, or to women, or into his arm, or up his nose. He couldn't help me to save his life. In fact, I've helped him far more than he's helped me."

"How so?"

The car had reached the top of the mountain, and Roxanne slowed as they crossed a large graded area with no trees. To their left was a tall fence, and through the trees on the other side of the fence, they could see the dome of the Mount Wilson Observatory. "I get paid very well, Eddie," she said as she brought the car to a stop and turned off the engine. "That was part of the deal. Swinburne wants me happy for Klaus, wants me for the covers. Whistler says without them, *Stupendous* wouldn't be *Stupendous*—which I'm not sure of, not sure I appreciate as a writer. But at any rate, Swinburne puts more money into me and Klaus than he does most of the rest of the magazine. This car, Daddy's cars, the house, everything else. It hasn't come from *Nelphi* or anything my father's done. And it hasn't quite come from the half-cent a word I get as Archie Dumont. I'm not proud of how I earned it, but I've been smart with the money Swinburne has paid me. When they let me out of the deal and I burn those goddamned pictures, I'll be set pretty well, and I'll be able to write what I want to write, something that will make their heads spin and they won't have the satisfaction of being able to publish it."

Her voice had risen as she spoke, all of the anger she had felt and kept quiet about for years coming for a moment to the surface. At the same time, she was struck by the absurdity of her situation—with Whistler and Frehling as well as here on the mountaintop with Eddie. She had come this far and needed to take it further, but it would be difficult to do so if she continued coming across as angry. Having said her peace and exorcised some of her demons, she knew she had to change her focus. And so she exhaled deeply and threw her hands into the air with a shrug as she turned in the seat and said, "Until then, it's brass brassieres and short skirts and building up my writing muscles as Archie Dumont." Then, giving Eddie a wry smile, she said, "Do you want to eat?"

CHAPTER SEVEN

E ddie smiled. He felt some compassion for her but did not exactly feel sorry for her. She seemed all right with the situation she was in, resigned to it for the time being. Her story—which he believed entirely—had gotten him wondering more about how unscrupulous Swinburne and Whistler were. It had also brought back the vivid image of her in the revealing outfit she had worn in Whistler's office, and he found himself responding to her smiles and little flirtations. Without hesitation, he said, "Sure. What's on the menu?"

Roxanne reached for the two bags she had brought out of the diner. She handed Eddie one bag and reached into the other one. He began unwrapping two ham sandwiches while she produced two bottles of beer. "They're a bit warm by now. I hope that doesn't bother you." Eddie said it did not, and Roxanne told him there was a bottle opener in the glove compartment. After they had eaten and drank for a few minutes, she said, "So what do you think my father is up to?"

"I don't know. Honestly. You're going to think I'm crazy, but there's part of me that really does believe him. Or wants to believe him. I know what you said about him being such a good liar, and that, plus a bit of natural skepticism, is keeping me from buying the whole story completely. But it's nagging at me. The part about the dying Chinaman, the way he said he wasted the whole thing for most of the time he was traveling in time. It just seems very real."

"Because he didn't make himself out to be the hero?"

"I suppose." Eddie took a long sip of warm beer. He didn't like it at all, but he made a conscious effort not to reveal it.

"And the Chinaman. That's where he got this drug from?"

"That's what he said."

"And you don't remember anything else about it?" She was digging for information again. Some part of her seemed almost desperate to know more about the Dragon's Tears, and Eddie was tempted to tell her. He felt guilty having heard her story about being blackmailed and not being completely honest with her about what Blackwood had told him the night before.

He resisted the temptation, though, saying, "I don't think there's anything else to remember."

Roxanne nodded. She put her sandwich back in the bag half eaten and took another sip of beer. She reached for her purse. "You smoke?" she asked, opening the purse and pulling out a pack of ivory tipped Marlboros and a silver Zippo. She tipped the pack toward him.

"I don't normally," Eddie said, "but I'll indulge this once."

"Let's go outside," she said after Eddie had taken a cigarette from the pack.

"Isn't it a bit cold up here?"

She had already opened her door and was getting out. "Maybe a bit," she said. She walked toward the back of the car. By the time Eddie had gotten out, she had retrieved a plaid wool blanket from the trunk and was walking toward him. The mountain air was crisp and cool, probably in the mid-fifties. It was nothing he hadn't been accustomed to while growing up, but a year in Los Angeles had gotten him used to warm winters. Dressed in shirtsleeves, he did not relish the thought of spending much time outside and was surprised that Roxanne, similarly dressed for a day in the valley below, was so eager to get out of the car. "Come on," she said, beginning to unfold the blanket and leading him around to the hood. Planting a heel on the front bumper, she hopped up and sat on the smooth paint. Eddie joined her, and they draped the blanket around themselves. The warmth from the engine had heated the metal, and it felt good to sit there next to Roxanne, their arms and thighs brushing against each other. Unwrapping her hands from the blanket, she offered him the lighter, and he lit her cigarette and then his own. Not having had a cigarette in years, he held the smoke in his mouth at first, not wanting to inhale and risk coughing. He found himself reveling strangely in the sound of Roxanne inhaling deeply and then blowing smoke luxuriously from her pursed lips.

The view before them was spectacular. She had parked the car at the edge of a clearing, its nose pointed toward the city below. There were some clouds high above them but none below to obscure the sight of Los Angeles spreading out before them, the harbors of Long Beach and San Pedro in the distance and the blue of the Pacific beyond. Roxanne pointed toward the horizon, her burning cigarette between her fingers. "Catalina," she said.

"Nice. So you come up here to write?"

She nodded. "Sometimes. When I'm just looking for inspiration. Trying to get ideas. I like to imagine it all gone."

"The city?"

"Everything. Just a smoldering ruin. That's the book I'll write when I'm through with *Stupendous* and Archie Dumont."

Eddie was surprised. From what he recalled, Archie Dumont stories were good, well written yarns but hardly the serious stuff Roxanne was describing. "When do you think that'll be?"

"I don't know." She sounded sad as she said it, and she deftly bent a knee to put out her cigarette on the sole of her red high-heeled shoe. Eddie could not help looking at her ankle through the silk stockings she wore. She dropped the butt in the dirt, pulled her arm into the blanket and then inched closer to Eddie, snuggling against him for warmth. He took the cue and put his arm around her shoulder, pinching off the burning end of his own cigarette with his other hand.

Roxanne turned to face him, and Eddie kissed her, lightly at first. Then she closed her eyes and put her hand up on his neck and let her fingers run through the hair on the back of his head, and he kissed her harder, touching her cheek lightly with one hand and running the other down the middle of her back, pulling her tightly to him. As he felt her exhale through her nose against his upper lip, he could not believe this was happening. His heart was pounding as she closed her lips, opened her eyes and withdrew a few inches. She looked up at him and smiled. He smiled back and was about to kiss her again when, still looking deeply into his eyes, she said, "God, this is humiliating."

If she had slapped his face, he would not have been more startled. "Excuse me?" he said, hoping she was joking.

She bowed her head, looking at the ground, and he knew she was not. When she looked up again, he could see that she was about to cry. "I'm sorry, Eddie."

"What's wrong?"

"Nothing. I mean . . . Oh, for Christ's sake, Eddie, you're a nice guy, and I actually do sort of like you. Under any other conditions, I'd . . . well, who knows, but now . . ."

"It's your father, isn't it? I understand. It was a pretty lousy thing of me to do, kissing you, but I thought you wanted me to."

"I did," she said, "only not how you think. The thing is, Eddie, that . . . well . . . okay, it's like this. It's not just my father. I mean, it is, but it's more." She exhaled. "When I came after you earlier, it wasn't just because I was looking for some company. Swinburne sent me out after you."

"Swinburne? He was there?"

"Yes. It wasn't just his goons—and that *is* what they are, not accountants and lawyers. He's going through everything of my father's, desperate to find out where he's gone and if he's really traveling in time."

"Swinburne believes it?"

"Apparently. Enough to have me drag you up here and seduce you."

Eddie felt a mixture of hurt, anger and deep curiosity. "You're kidding."

"I wish I was. After I sent you away when you knocked, he asked who it was and got terribly excited when I told him. He said to go find you and get you to tell me everything you knew about my father's little exploits. He already knows about the book, but he doesn't know what it is or where it is or how my father used it. The same goes for the drug. So I stopped at the diner and called him and told him what you'd said. I'm sorry I lied about all that." As she had spoken, her confidence had returned. The hint of tears was gone, and she spoke rapidly, coolly.

"It's okay," Eddie said, not entirely certain that he meant it. Now he was relieved he had kept parts of Blackwood's story to himself. "I'm sure you had your reasons."

She shrugged. "At first it was just obedience. I've been doing what I'm told by these people for a long time now. I guess I'm just used to it. But when I phoned him and didn't tell him anything he didn't already know, he got upset. He feels sure you're lying or hiding something."

"Wait. How does he even know about me? I'm just a guy who published a couple stories in one of his magazines."

"I don't know. He didn't say, and I didn't ask. He was extremely interested in the fact that you saw my father last night. He seems to think Daddy disappeared yesterday afternoon. I suppose that's why he thinks you know more than you're saying. Anyway, he told me to try harder, to seduce you if I had to."

Eddie raised an eyebrow. "What was in it for you?"

"He didn't come right out and say it, but he suggested that if I got the truth out of you, he'd let me out of the modeling deal."

"That's a pretty good offer after being stuck in it for seven years."

"True." She looked around the clearing. "Here we are. Pretty romantic setting, isn't it?"

"Very. What made you change your mind?"

She smiled. "I just realized that I'm a writer, not goddamn Mata Hari. Taking off my clothes in front of Klaus Frehling got me into this mess. It just doesn't make sense that taking them off again because Augustus Swinburne says to will make it any better. It would probably just make it worse. I'm really sorry."

Eddie nodded and said, "It's okay. Really." This time he meant it. He reached a hand out from under the blanket and offered it to her. She shook and then held it for a moment, as he said, "No hard feelings."

"Thanks."

"So does this mean you're done doing what Swinburne tells you to do?"

She nodded. "I'm still stuck career-wise, but he can take a flying leap when it comes to anything beyond that. There's a stupid party he's got me roped into going to this weekend. He can just go to hell if he thinks I'm going to be there. Son of a bitch. And I think I'll go home and tell him that."

Eddie felt himself go red again as she swore and hoped she wouldn't notice. Without thinking about it, he quickly said, "Do you want me to go with you? Moral support?"

"No. It's all right. Besides, you don't want to get any more mixed up in this than you already are."

"I don't know," Eddie said. "To be honest, I'd like to meet him and find out why he's so interested in me."

"You probably don't want to know. It's probably something my father said to him about you."

"Okay, but what? Seriously, if you wouldn't mind, I'd like to go with you to talk to him."

Roxanne agreed but said again that he would be better off just going home, a warning Eddie brushed aside. He was done being warned, and now he had been fooled. Swinburne sounded dangerous, but Eddie knew that sounding dangerous and being dangerous were not the same thing. He thought about Pence and the way he planned on dealing with threats from studio executives when they came. Eddie had decided that he needed to face Swinburne and find out what all of this was about.

They hopped off the hood of the car and got back inside. Roxanne lit another cigarette and started the engine as Eddie rolled up the blanket and tossed it in the back seat. "You can trust me now," she said as she put the car in reverse and backed away from the edge and the view.

"I'm sure I can," Eddie said but still felt no compulsion to tell her any more than he already had. On the way back down the mountain, they talked about writing, life with Chester Blackwood, the idiosyncrasies of Los Angeles, the work Eddie had done in Iowa before he had been able to work up the nerve to come west and try to write for a living. Eddie confessed his plagiarism to her, which she found delightfully amusing, and she promised to read his stories at the first opportunity. And as they drove and talked, the car taking the curves more cautiously on the downhill, Eddie found himself unable to stop himself from stealing glances as Roxanne watched the road. With each pause in the conversation, the memory of the kiss overtook him. He could taste her lips, could smell her skin as he had breathed in her scent while embracing her, could feel her skin on his fingertips and her body pressed against his. It was all he could do to bring himself back to the present and the cadence of her voice. He found himself thinking about what Blackwood had told him the morning before. Although it may not have been in the way he had meant it, Roxanne's father had been right. Eddie had just gotten himself into serious trouble.

CHAPTER EIGHT

"They're gone," Roxanne said as she turned the Cord off the street and into her driveway. It was dusk and the house was heavily covered in darkness already from the sheltering trees that grew all around it. There was no longer a black Lincoln in the driveway. Blackwood's Packard was still obviously absent. "Let me run you home," Roxanne said, slowing before her front door but not stopping.

As much as he had wanted to confront Swinburne, Eddie was more disappointed at the idea of saying goodnight to Roxanne than he was at the fact that Swinburne and his men were gone. Even so, he felt uncomfortable with the idea of Roxanne taxiing him home. "No," he said. "Thanks, but it's okay. You've probably got a thousand things that need doing. I can just call a cab."

She stopped the car, asked him again if he was sure, and then killed the engine after he had politely refused her offer one more time. "All right," she said as she opened her door. "It's just as well. I need to pee."

Eddie smiled as he got out and followed her to the ornate front doors where they had started their day together hours before. Roxanne slid her key into the lock, turned the knob and opened the door. She stepped inside and flicked on the lights in the entryway, then quietly, chillingly said, "Oh my god," before Eddie had a chance to step over the threshold behind her.

Alarmed, he pushed in beside her and saw the source of her distress. He had been expecting to find her father dead on the floor or hanging from a chandelier, but there was no one else there, dead or alive. Instead, he saw scattered books on the entryway floor and from the light fixture directly overhead could make out the dim chaos in the large room that the entryway opened onto. Eddie reached behind Roxanne, who stood in stunned silence for a moment, to turn on a second light switch by the door, revealing the thorough ransacking that Roxanne's house had undergone.

The entryway opened onto an ample room that apparently served as a combination library and living room. Dual staircases wound up on either side of the entryway, framing an arch that led into the main room. Directly across from the entrance was a large fireplace and mantle. The walls leading away from the fireplace in either direction around the room and back to the entryway were lined with built in oak bookcases. These had been filled with books, statuary, vases and framed pictures. All of these were now scattered on the floor. The statues that could be smashed had been; terra cotta arms and legs littered the floor along with pieces of plaster, sections of vases, dried flowers, hundreds of books and torn pictures. A large framed landscape was on the floor in front of the fireplace, partially leaning against the hearth, the canvas slashed diagonally from corner to corner. The overstuffed chairs and sofas in the room had been overturned, their cushions removed and gutted, the fabric lining their bottoms slashed and torn away.

"Oh my god," Roxanne repeated, louder now.

"We'd better call the cops," Eddie said, closing the door behind them and turning to try to determine where a phone might be.

"Bastards!" Roxanne shouted, slamming her handbag to the ground at her feet. She was breathing hard and was clearly about to cry. Eddie edged past her into the wrecked room.

"Where's a phone?" he asked.

She hesitated for a moment, just looking at the devastation, and then said, "No."

"What do you mean, no?"

"Just no." She walked down the three steps from the entryway into the main room. "No cops."

"Why not? You can't let them get away with this."

She shook her head. "It won't matter. Swinburne's got cops on his payroll. Judges too. They'll just whitewash this, make it look like a burglary. There probably isn't even anything missing. And if there is, it's just Daddy's book and his drugs. That's what they were looking for. That's the real reason the son of a bitch wanted me out of the house. I guess I'd feel like a real idiot now if I'd made love to you this afternoon."

"I guess," Eddie repeated quietly. Then he added, "But come on, Roxanne. No one's that powerful. He can't just do something like this at will."

Roxanne surveyed the room. The anger and the tears had both subsided. She just looked defeated now. "Sure he can. He's got so much money . . . He's connected to so many powerful people in this city. You have no idea." He wanted to tell her that he did have an idea, that Pence had characterized Swinburne the same way without having met him, but he did not see that any of this would help Roxanne right now. She sounded completely disgusted, defeated. As she bent to pick up a smashed picture frame, she said, "If I go to him and raise enough hell, he'll just write me a check for a few thousand dollars to have this cleaned up and the broken items replaced. Story of my life."

Eddie moved into the room and stood next to her. He remained unconvinced that keeping the police out of this was the best course of action but at the same time was replaying the things Pence had told him about the super rich and how difficult it could be to deal with them because there was nothing they really needed. Apparently Swinburne did need something from Blackwood, but his own power kept him from worrying about the methods he used to obtain it. Wondering what, if anything, Pence had been able to find out about Swinburne, he put his hand on her back and said, "I'm really sorry, Roxanne."

"None of this is your fault," she said.

"Well, maybe. I actually could have told you a bit more earlier. It might have stopped this."

She turned to face him, anger flaring up momentarily. "You held out on me?"

Eddie could see an outburst coming like he had witnessed in Swinburne's office. Though he knew he deserved it, he spoke quickly to head it off. "Just about the drug. What it's called. I still don't know where it is or the book. Or how it works." He paused for a breath and then added, "You weren't exactly straight with me all day either."

Her jaw had been tightening, and he watched it relax. "I suppose not. And it's just as well. The more I think about it, the more I feel Swinburne is the last person on earth who should know what Daddy's been up to. I'm glad you didn't tell me. I would have just told him, and then who knows what would have happened?"

"You think it's real?"

"Swinburne does. I tend to believe him a lot more than I believe my father. He must have something to base it on if he's going to do this." She looked at the mess surrounding them. "Christ."

Together, they walked around the room for a minute. The destruction was sickening. Finally, Eddie said, "You shouldn't stay here. Get a hotel for the night. We can go to Swinburne's tomorrow, and I'll help you sort this out."

"I don't know, Eddie. I'm starting to think you shouldn't get any more mixed up in this. If you were just an excuse to get me out of the house today, then maybe we should leave it at that. I can handle this on my own."

"I don't like it." Eddie bent to pick up a copy of *Wuthering Heights* that had been splayed open and probably stepped on. "You know . . . If the cops can't help you, then maybe you need to play dirty, too."

"How?"

"I have a friend. He's a private eye."

"You want me to hire a private eye to stop Swinburne?"

"No. It's not like that. He's not that kind of p.i. He works for the film studios, mainly making blackmail cases go away. I could get him to talk to you. He might be able to tell you some things to say that would scare Swinburne into at least leaving you and your father alone."

"Swinburne doesn't scare easily."

"Then maybe Pence—he's the private eye—could line you up with some other people. It would probably cost a bit, but you could go into Swinburne with some muscle."

Roxanne laughed. "You want me to turn to gangsters to get Swinburne off my back? Isn't there that saying about out of the frying pan and into the fire?"

"It wouldn't have to go that far. Pence's a pretty smart guy. I'll bet he could help you."

Roxanne sighed and looked around the room once more. "Well," she said, "I suppose it couldn't hurt to talk to him. Does he owe you a favor or something?"

"Not exactly. I already told him about Swinburne but not how bad he's been. He's like a dog on a scent now. I can tell he's interested in figuring Swinburne out just to be able to do it. Besides, if he wants to keep a drinking buddy, he'll cooperate."

"All right," she said with some hesitation. "Let's see, at least."

Before leaving, they took their time to explore the rest of the house and found it similarly ransacked on both floors and in every room. Several times, Roxanne was overwhelmed with anger and grief as she saw the violation around her. When they got to her father's room on the second floor, Eddie simply stood in the doorway looking in, feeling as though he should not step in. Even though the mystique surrounding Blackwood had been tarnished by his stories of drug use and inspiration that involved theft from the future, the sight of Blackwood's typewriter on an enormous oak desk at the back of the room left Eddie awed. He was compelled to enter, though, when Roxanne said, "Look at this," from her vantage point in the middle of her father's things spread about the floor. Eddie saw that she was pointing at an open safe against one wall, and as he entered the room she went over to it. The safe's contents were dumped on the floor in front of it. There was clearly no money among the scattered papers her father had been keeping safe. "They tried to get me to open it," Roxanne said, kneeling down and closing the safe door, spinning the combination dial. "But Daddy never told me the combination, and we couldn't find it written down anywhere."

"They must have found it somewhere," Eddie said quietly. "Or else they found a way to crack it. Do you think there was any money in it?"

"Who knows?" She shut the door and stood up, walking out of the room without another word.

They continued their survey of the damage in the house. By the time they were done, she had turned to Eddie for a hug more than once. Each time, he felt a surge of desire coupled with self-loathing at his inability to separate lust from compassion. He told himself he was a heel for enjoying the sensation of her body pressed against his, but that did not stop him from feeling it. As they finished their survey of the damage, Roxanne showed him one washroom, went off to use another, and met him at the front door where she pulled a coat from a closet and offered Eddie one of her father's, which he declined. The sun had gone down, and the March air was still brisk, but there seemed something definitely out of order with wearing one of Chester Blackwood's jackets. The old man was either dead or lost in time, and illogical

103

though it was, Eddie was beginning to feel as though any more contact with Blackwood would put him in the same situation.

Roxanne asked Eddie to drive, and even though he had not yet renewed his license in California, he took the keys. He had never driven anything but Fords and tractors before, and at any other time he would have relished the smooth drive and power of the Cord. Tonight, however, he was trying to concentrate on Roxanne, on how much he was wrapped up in her predicament and on how he was going to get her out of it, all the while being distracted by her smell, the glint of oncoming headlights reflecting in her eyes as they glanced at each other on the drive from Pasadena to downtown. They rode mostly in silence, and Eddie did not want to ask what she was thinking about for fear of making her more upset. He guessed that she was thinking about her father more than she would have let on. More than likely, the possibility that he had really disappeared, in time or elsewhere, was beginning to seem increasingly real to her just as it was becoming to Eddie.

He drove the car south along Central and cursed beneath his breath as he saw that there was no parking left on the west side of the street where his building was. He considered parking in the alley behind the building, and if the car had been an old Ford he would have done it, but he did not feel comfortable with the idea of leaving Roxanne's car in such isolation, so he made an illegal U-turn in the middle of the street and parked on the northbound side directly across from the door at 845 1/2.

"Home sweet home," he said, indicating the building and smiling sheepishly at Roxanne.

She smiled and took the keys as Eddie held them out to her. She took her purse and got out of the car, slipping on her coat after she shut the door. The evening had grown cold. They locked the car and then waited for a break in traffic and jaywalked across the street just as Eddie had done with her father the night before. "We need to get you out of here," she said, looking up at the shabby building. "Not exactly befitting a great writer."

Eddie opened the door and, by habit, got out his keys and opened his mailbox at the base of the stairs. "Nice skylight," Roxanne said as he was reaching in for the mail.

"Mm-hmm," he said, looking up at the landing above them as Roxanne started ascending the stairs. "I like it when it rains," he added, closing the mailbox and pulling out his key without looking at the envelopes in his hand. He had been about to check the larger parcel mailbox below the rest of the smaller boxes, but he did not want Roxanne to get too far ahead of him. He began following her up, his eyes drifting from her ankles to her hips as he explained the building's unusual layout and its apparent history as a suite of offices before it was apartments. After pointing out the common room and restroom from the landing, he led her down the hallway. "I'm down there in number 5," he said, indicating one of the doors facing the street. "Pence's here in 3." They stopped before one of the doors on the other side of the hallway, facing the alley side of the building. "You ready to talk to him?"

Roxanne said she was, and Eddie knocked. There was no response. A dim glow came over the transom, so Eddie knew there was at least a light on, but that did not necessarily mean Pence was inside. He knocked again and they waited. Eddie felt embarrassed to have dragged Roxanne all the way downtown for nothing when she clearly had more pressing things to take care of in Pasadena. After a few more moments, he said, "Looks like we're out of luck. The light's on, though, so maybe he just went down to the café. Or the liquor store down Olympic. I can just keep an ear out for him when he comes in and talk to him for you. Or have him call you if you like."

Roxanne just nodded, clearly a bit disappointed. Though he had known her for only a short time, Eddie had the distinct impression that Roxanne was not the type of person who was used to needing help. Earlier, he had thought she was a bit like the damsels in distress she portrayed so beautifully on the covers of *Stupendous*, but now he realized this was out of character for her, that she was in unfamiliar territory now. While she might not have been able to get herself out of trouble with Whistler and Frehling, she seemed to have faced her problems fiercely over the last seven years and had done it without assistance. And now she needed help. Because she did not know Pence, Eddie told himself, she would have no idea if he would be able to help, but she had clearly resigned herself to the idea that she needed someone, which appeared to be a bit of a defeat for her, and Pence's absence now appeared to be magnifying her distress. A bit guiltily, he found himself wondering if he could stand in for Pence and be the one she counted on.

"Or you could wait, too, if you like," he added.

Roxanne looked at her wristwatch and nodded. "I guess I'll wait a few minutes," she said with a slight frown. Then she looked up and smiled, bravely, Eddie thought. "You can show me this great collection of science fiction you've been telling me about in the mean time."

Eddie led the way to his door, put the key in the lock, and opened it. Immediately he knew something was wrong. He felt a slight resistance against the door after opening it only a foot. "Uh-oh," he said, pushing it all the way open and glancing at Roxanne before he reached in to switch on the light.

"What is it?" she asked and then gasped as the room was illuminated.

"Son of a bitch," Eddie said quietly.

They walked into the room. It had received the same treatment as Roxanne's house. Every box of magazines from every shelf had been taken down and dumped on the floor. Books lay strewn among the pulps. Eddie's bed had been stripped and the mattress tipped off the frame. Dresser drawers had been pulled out and emptied, and now his clothes lay strewn across the floor amidst papers, pencils, letters and the rest of his few belongings—photos, a cheap camera, his battered suitcase among them. Scattered among the magazines were several issues face up with pictures of Roxanne on the covers.

"I can't believe they did this to you," Roxanne said, her voice shaking.

"Me neither." He squatted down and fingered some of the magazines at his feet. Just glancing around, it did not look as though any of his treasured collection had been seriously damaged. While several issues looked dog-eared and a few had clearly been stepped on, nothing looked torn or otherwise ruined. He stood up as Roxanne lightly swung the door shut behind them. "You can do what you want about your place, but I think I need to call the cops."

"You can't prove it was them." She said it quietly, defeated.

"Maybe they left prints. Something."

She shook her head. "Swinburne's too smart."

He sighed. "Maybe you're right. But still."

He turned toward the door, and she put her hand on his chest, stopping him. "I'm sorry, Eddie."

"Why?" he said sharply. The growing anger that he had been feeling toward Swinburne quickly turned on Roxanne. He expected another confession from her, as though she had known this was going to happen.

She looked confused for a moment and then said, "I should have just left you alone. If I hadn't listened to Swinburne and gone with you, none of this would have happened. They used me to keep you away from here so they could do this. I'm sorry."

Eddie's anger abated as quickly as it had built. "It's okay," he said, looking around the room. Nothing looked ruined, and he was sure nothing had been stolen. "You couldn't have known. Besides, your place got it worse. I didn't have that much to wreck."

She smiled. Her hand was still on his chest. "If you're going to go call the police, let me come with you. I don't want to be alone here in case . . ."

"In case they come back?"

"Yes."

He took her hand in both of his. She squeezed. They were almost as close as they had been on the hood of her car wrapped in the blanket, and they simply stood looking at each other for a moment before Eddie lowered his head to kiss her. He had been waiting hours to do it in spite of everything that told him he should not, and this was surely among the worst possible times to kiss her, but the way she kissed him back, hungrily opening her mouth against his, told him that she had been waiting, too. Soon, their hands were running up and down each other's backs, pulling each into the other. Roxanne slipped out of her coat, and Eddie let a hand trail lower and lower down her back. When she did nothing to stop him, he squeezed gently and pushed her pelvis against his. She moaned as she kissed him and was soon unfastening the buttons on his shirt. He pulled back and looked greedily at her mouth as she smiled and licked her lips. Without a word, she reached behind herself and unzipped her dress before letting it fall from her shoulders, stepping deftly out of it after undoing her belt.

Eddie quickly and rather awkwardly started taking off his clothes. Amidst brief kisses and caresses, they undressed quickly. Eddie did not think to lead her to the overturned mattress but rather took her hand in his shaking one and pulled her down onto her coat on the floor. Roxanne lay beneath him, pictures of herself on the magazine covers scattered on the floor around her. As he held himself poised above her, her arms on his shoulders, Eddie could not help noticing that Roxanne had the same look in her eyes as she had on the January 1938 cover, a look that was both hunger and resistance. It was as though she were struggling silently with herself as her body took over, and she pulled him down and squeezed the backs of his thighs with her bare ankles. He knew now why Klaus Frehling had been unable to get her out of his head.

****

They had ended up on the mattress eventually, dropping it all the way to the floor from its half overturned position against the bed frame. Now they lay on it together, Eddie on his back with a pillow under his head and Roxanne on her side snuggled up close against him, one leg across his, one arm curled about his shoulder, her other arm on his chest and her head using his bicep as a pillow. They were covered by a sheet only, and Eddie had turned on the gas heater not long ago, so the room had reached a comfortable level of warmth. Roxanne ran her fingers absently through the hair on Eddie's chest as they talked. They had covered a variety of subjects in the last half hour, and now their conversation turned, as it had kept turning all day, to their writing.

"Tell me about the book you want to write," Eddie asked her. "The one where L.A. is gone."

"Everything's gone," she said. "I think I want to call it *The Blighted Land* or something like that."

"What happens?"

She raised herself up on an elbow and leaned more into him so she could turn and look at him as she spoke. Eddie moved his arm and draped it over her back. "There's been a war," she said. "Huge. Lots of countries involved. Like what's happening with Hitler only worse. And at the end of the war, to stop it, they released a secret weapon. No one knows which side released it or even how it worked. It doesn't matter anymore because the weapon worked too well, and now every major city in the world has been wiped out. There's illness and decay and lingering effects of the weapon. The story is about a small band of survivors. Each one is going to have escaped the weapon in some way through total blind luck. Some of them are good and some are bad. And they meet up and decide the only way to survive is to make their way into the Midwest. They assume the damage or the lingering effects aren't as bad there. So they go into the heart of America—literally and figuratively, see?—and they find out a lot of unpleasant things along the way."

"About what?"

"About themselves. About America. About what it was and what it's become and how it all happened."

"Wow. I'm impressed. It doesn't sound like the kind of thing you'd run across as a serial in *Stupendous*."

"No. I want it to be different. I want a real publisher, not Meteor. I don't want it to be looked at as just science fiction."

"What's wrong with science fiction?"

"Nothing. Obviously. It's just the way some people look at it. Like it's disposable. I don't want what I write to be thrown away. Most people who read what we write aren't like you, Eddie. Magazines that sell for a quarter aren't meant to be catalogued and cherished like you do. They're read and forgotten, tossed in the trash."

"I suppose." He rubbed her back for a moment. Then he said, "I have a strange question to ask you." Her eyes glinted, and a raised eyebrow showed she was intrigued. "If you could break the laws of the universe to get your book written, would you do it?"

"You're right. That is a strange question. What kind of laws? Are you talking about time travel again? You don't really think my father has done it, do you?"

"That's beside the point. Would you if you could?"

She did not hesitate but said "No" immediately.

"Why not?"

She dropped her head down onto her hands folded over Eddie's shoulder. He could taste her breath as she spoke so close to his face, and her hair brushed against the skin on his chest. "Because I don't want the help. It's the same reason I tried to use a pen name before the whole Klaus thing got thrown back in my face. I want to write what's in me, and if it gets published it's because it's good, not because I knew someone, not because I cheated the system, and certainly not because I defied the laws of the universe."

Eddie winced a bit at her mention of cheating the system but did not say anything about it. "And time travel? Knowing the future? You wouldn't be tempted to go and see and get it right and be marveled at in twenty years?"

"Who cares? It's not fiction any more then, is it? It's just reporting. I'm not a reporter. And besides, I wouldn't want to be influenced. I don't want to know what happens next year or fifty years from now. I want to be able to make it up. So what if the stories I tell have no bearing on reality or the way the future turns out? Do you think that bothered Stanley Weinbaum? Do you know how long it's going to take humans to get to Mars? And when we do, it's not going to be like anything he imagined. We write to entertain and to get people to think about today, not just to predict what's going to happen tomorrow. Don't you think?"

To answer truthfully, Eddie would have had to admit that he had not thought about it this way at all. Rather than appear shallow, he changed the subject, saying, "You haven't started writing it have you?"

"No. Just in my head. I think about it every day. It's all mapped out—the characters, the settings. Even the dialogue." She turned on her side again, and Eddie kept his arm around her, reaching under the sheet to caress her smooth skin.

"Why not write it down then?"

"Because I'd be tempted to submit it to Whistler, and I don't want to give them the satisfaction of being the first ones to publish it and make money off of it. I'm going to wait until he lets me out of this bind."

"And when will that be?"

She laughed. "Whistler says he'll let me go when my tits start to sag."

Eddie smiled at that but then moved his hand to cup her breast. "No danger of that anytime soon."

"Troublemaker," she said.

He kept his hand there and began to rub her nipple.

She responded by doing the same to him, and in a few moments she rolled over on top of him. She smiled mischievously and started kissing his chest. "You want me to show you how the girls on Mars do it?" she asked.

"The slave girls or the princesses?"

"Mmm. I've been both, you know."

"Yeah. I know."

She kept kissing him. "The slave girls are a lot more fun, but the princesses have a few tricks of their own."

"Do I have to choose?"

"You are in so much trouble," she said. She had been kissing her way lower onto his stomach, and now she kept going.

CHAPTER NINE

Roxanne sat on the floor of Eddie's apartment amidst the scattered mess of books and magazines that Swinburne's men had left. Dressed only in her slip, she had begun sorting through the piles almost an hour ago. On the mattress across the room, Eddie dozed, snoring faintly, and she glanced up from the magazines occasionally to look at his face. It made her feel warm, and she thought about climbing back onto the mattress, but the dozens of pulps strewn around her had kept drawing her attention back to them. She had originally intended to straighten things up for Eddie while he slept, sorting the magazines into piles and organizing them, but she had grown fascinated by the old covers and the stories inside each issue. In all the time she had been posing for Klaus Frehling, she had never seen so many copies of *Stupendous* at one time, each with a variant of herself on its cover; she had found the collection unsettling but had quickly been drawn to the older issues of *Amazing Stories*, *Astounding*, *Startling Stories*, *Wonder Stories*, *Weird Tales* and a dozen others that she had never seen before.

The alarm clock on the floor near the mattress read 11:30 when Eddie began to stir and then blink into wakefulness. "Hey there," she said with a smile.

He sat up. "What are you doing?"

She glanced around the room. "Just straightening up. And getting an education in science fiction history. You have some amazing stuff here. It's like a museum."

"Thanks," he said. He stood up and slipped on a pair of boxers. "You don't have to do that, though."

"It's fine," she said. "I was looking for something to do. Can't sleep in strange beds all that well. I'd say let's go back to my place and I'll make you breakfast, but . . ." She glanced around. "This mess is a bit more manageable." She reached past the stack of magazines in front of her and picked up a thick book with a red cover, Eddie's copy of the collected works of Shakespeare. "I found this pretty interesting, too."

He walked toward her as she flipped through the pages, glancing up teasingly at him as she did. "Your notes on *Hamlet* are eye opening," she said with a smile, thinking about how Eddie had confessed to borrowing from the bard. "I missed the part about the space pirates when I read it in school."

"Very funny." He sat on the floor next to her and rubbed his eyes. He nudged himself closer to her so his bare knee touched hers.

"And then there's this," she said, slipping a finger in between pages where a paperclip had been inserted as a bookmark. The book closed on *Hamlet* and opened on *Macbeth* where a passage had been underlined in pencil.

Eddie cleared his throat. Sounding a bit embarrassed, he said, "I thought about how that speech would work in a time travel story, changed around a bit, of course."

Roxanne tapped the underlined passage and began to read. "Tomorrow and tomorrow and tomorrow, creeps in this petty pace from day to day to the last syllable of recorded time, and all our yesterdays have lighted fools the way to dusty death." She stopped and looked at him, an eyebrow raised. "What if it doesn't creep?" she asked.

Eddie nodded and said, "You mean what if it skips around, back and forth?"

"Mm-hmm. So tomorrow isn't always tomorrow, and it doesn't go from day to day."

"Who knows? Are you saying you're starting to believe what your father told me?"

"No. But I'm awfully intrigued." She looked back at the book again and kept reading. "Out, out, brief candle. Life's but a walking shadow, a poor player that struts and frets his hour upon the stage and then is heard no more. It is a tale told by an idiot, full of sound and fury, signifying nothing." She looked at Eddie again and said, "It might not signify nothing if the player didn't just leave the stage at the end of his scene."

"But what? Disappeared into the future like your father said he would? Do you think he's beaten dusty death?"

"No. But Swinburne thinks he has. That may be why he's so desperate to find the secret."

"It could be," Eddie said. He put his hand on hers over the open pages of Shakespeare and gave it a little squeeze. "We'll try to find out in the morning. Can you find his place?"

"I think so. I've been there a time or two for some of his big parties."

"The literary life I've been missing out on," Eddie said with a grin.

"Believe me, it's nothing to get that excited about." She thought again about the party Swinburne had insisted she attend in a few days. Whenever she thought about how Swinburne had been so sure of his complete control of her, she grew angry all over again, as though she had only just now walked out of the meeting with Swinburne, Vivian Parker and Rebecca Le Blanc. And the thought of Rebecca Le Blanc getting a book deal from Swinburne, maybe based on real talent but more likely because she was sleeping with a woman who seemed to have some influence over the publisher, made Roxanne even more upset.

She closed the book firmly and looked Eddie straight in the eye. "I want out of this mess," she said. "All of it. Swinburne, Klaus, my father. All of it."

"But how? Stop writing? Forget about it?"

She shook her head and sighed, her resolve already fading as her anger transformed itself into resignation. "I don't know." Looking around the room at all the evidence of what she had had to put up with for the last seven years, she saw several of her father's books lying on the floor among the pulp magazines. "My father got us into this, didn't he? And neither one of us really knows how or why."

Eddie nodded. "It's bound to make sense soon."

"When?"

Eddie shook his head. "Your father said he would contact me. He just didn't say when."

"What exactly did he say?"

"That he would contact me. Just not in a way that I might expect."

"What do you think he meant?" Roxanne asked, pleased to note that Eddie had not hesitated to answer her question. If he still doubted her sincerity in the least, unsure of whether she was truly and completely finished being loyal to Swinburne, he would have kept silent. It made her feel good to know that he trusted her, as fully as she now trusted him. She could think of no friends or associates or acquaintances whom she felt she could count on now to help her get out of her bind with Swinburne. Eddie may not be able to help either, but she felt her best chance was in sticking with him and in their working together.

Again, Eddie shook his head. "I don't know. Have to think about it." He looked at the floor for a moment, drumming his fingers on the volume of Shakespeare. "What *would* I expect?"

"A phone call?"

"No phone."

"Him dropping by again? Contacting you through Whistler again?"

"Those would make sense. So what wouldn't I expect?"

Roxanne thought about it for a few seconds. "For him to use me to contact you?"

"Maybe. But you haven't seen him since . . . when? In Whistler's office?" Roxanne nodded. "So I've seen him more recently than you. Maybe he left you a message at your place to bring me."

"In which case," Roxanne said, "Swinburne's men would have found it when they ransacked my place. Besides, I don't think Daddy went home at all yesterday. The only way he could have left me a message would have been to send it in the mail."

Eddie looked up with a start. "The mail!" he said.

Puzzled, Roxanne looked down at the scattered pieces of mail on the floor where Eddie had dropped them upon entering the apartment and finding that Swinburne's men had been here. There was a bill, a letter from Iowa, and two letters from New York magazines. "Nothing here," she said, confused at Eddie's excitement.

"That's not it." He stood up, found his pants on the floor and began pulling them on. "That's not all of it. There's another mailbox for packages." Shirtless and barefoot, he went to the door. "Be right back."

Roxanne stood and went to the door as Eddie went out. She held it open a few inches and stood there, the cool air from the unheated hallway giving her goose bumps all up and down her bare arms. One dim bulb burned in the ceiling halfway between Eddie's apartment and the stairway, and in its light she watched as he practically ran the length of the hallway. For a second as he turned the corner before the stairs, he was out of her view; then the light above the stairway switched on, and she could see him descend the stairs through the spaces in the railing at the end of the hall. The building was silent, and she could hear Eddie's steps on the stairs and the sound of a metallic squeak moments after the footsteps stopped. Seconds later, the sound of steps ascending more rapidly than they had descended were followed by the sight of Eddie coming up the stairs.

Roxanne felt surprised by the sudden flush of warmth she felt at seeing him come back, her goose bumps disappearing. But she did not have time to consider her feelings; Eddie held a small package in his hands, and the look on his face was one of triumph. Roxanne opened the door all the way as he approached and greeted him with a bright smile.

CHAPTER TEN

There was no return address on the package, and the postmark was from Tuesday. It looked to be about the size of a cigar box, and when Eddie had torn the paper away, he saw that that was exactly what it was.

"Does your father smoke these?" he asked before opening the box. Roxanne nodded, clearly nervous. "Well, let's see what he's sent us."

Eddie pulled open the cigar box and found a handwritten note resting on the cover of a book bound in brown cloth. The book was smaller than the box, and a wad of newspaper had been stuffed into the box to fill the space that the book left. Eddie began reading the note out loud without removing it from the box. "Dear Eddie. Based on our conversation tonight, I feel you are the only logical recipient of the contents of this box. Do with it what you will. I can only hope that reading this book does not cause you to become too disappointed in me. We are, after all, kindred spirits, and you will see that there was at least some measure of artistry in what I have written. The bottle's contents I'm sure you can discern. Use it wisely. I apologize deeply for any inconvenience I have caused you or will soon. Perhaps I will see you at a future date. Best, Chester Blackwood."

"What the hell," Roxanne said. Eddie handed her the note, which she looked over for a moment. It was definitely her father's handwriting and signature. Eddie walked past her and into the room, gingerly carrying the box and setting it down on his desk. Roxanne watched as he took the book out of the box. "So that's what Swinburne's been after?" she asked.

"I think so." He held the book up. There was no writing on the cover, but the spine read *The Golden Age of Science Fiction, 1938-1945*. Eddie read the title to her, and the author, Marion Rigby. "Ever heard of her?"

"No."

He flipped the book open and turned the first couple of pages. "Okay," he said. "This is either the real thing or a really good hoax. Is your father a practical joker?"

She shook her head. "Not at all. He has a lousy sense of humor. What does it say?"

Eddie sat down at his desk, setting the book in the spot where his typewriter usually sat. He began turning pages. "There's a copyright date of 1978, and it says it was published by Rutgers University Press."

"It has to be a fake."

Eddie nodded. "I know it has to be, but who prints fake books? I mean the whole thing would have to be typeset and bound. And just to make one copy. Do you know how expensive that would be?" He turned more pages and began reading aloud from the table of contents. "Chapter One, The Astounding Editor. Chapter Two, A.E. van Vogt. Other chapters on Robert Heinlein, Isaac Asimov, Theodore Sturgeon. Have you ever heard of any of these guys?"

"No," Roxanne said. Then she repeated herself, "It has to be a fake."

"But why?"

"To fool Swinburne? To get something out of him or maybe just get him off my father's back? I don't know." She crossed the room and sat on the bed, looking at Eddie's back as he continued thumbing through the first chapter.

"John Campbell," he said.

"What about him?"

"You've read him?"

"Yeah. He's good. What does it say about him?"

Eddie read silently for a minute, skimming paragraphs and turning a few pages. He shook his head and turned to look at Roxanne, holding the book in his lap now. "It doesn't make sense," Eddie said. "I mean, he's a good enough writer. 'Twilight' was an amazing story. And he's been editing *Astounding* for a couple of years, but this says he revolutionized science fiction, turned *Astounding* into the premiere science fiction magazine of the decade and changed the whole face the genre."

"That's crazy. *Astounding* is just a little rag. They barely pay. It's nothing compared to *Stupendous* and *Amazing*."

Skimming through the book again, Eddie nodded his agreement absently and continued flipping pages.

Watching him, Roxanne's arms broke out in goose bumps again, and she nervously rubbed her hands over her upper arms for a few seconds before saying, "Eddie?"

He looked up from the book. Roxanne's eyes were wide and glistening; she looked as though she was about to cry. "What is it?" he asked.

"It's real, isn't it?"

"It can't be." He hesitated, moving his eyes from the book to her face and back again. "You sound like you're sure."

"It's not the book. It's the note. He said 'tonight' like he wrote it after he left your apartment."

"Right."

"But he couldn't have mailed it last night and had it arrive here today. And the postmark is yesterday."

Eddie looked again at the note and then at the postmark on the wrapper he had torn off the cigar box. "Jesus," he said.

"He really did it," Roxanne said, her voice breaking. "He's really gone, isn't he?"

"Jesus," he repeated. Seeing that she was about to cry, he set the book on the desk, leaning forward and taking her hand. "Look, it might not be. It looks like it's real, but . . . he might have written the note and mailed the package after he talked to me in Whistler's office. He might have written 'tonight' knowing we'd meet later and that we'd think exactly what we're thinking."

"That he went back in time to early yesterday after talking to you last night."

"So he could get the package here today."

Roxanne squeezed Eddie's hand and then released it to wipe at her eyes. She shook her head. "He really did it. He wouldn't have mailed you this without actually talking to you about it first. What if you had stood him up at the bar? Your getting the package now wouldn't have made any sense."

"I suppose you're right."

"God, I feel like an idiot," she said, almost laughing as tears finally ran down her cheeks. "I haven't cried over anything he's done since I was fourteen."

"He may not be gone for good," Eddie said, trying to console her though he knew it was not true.

She shook her head and wiped her tears. They had stopped flowing as quickly as they started. "No. The way Swinburne and his men are acting. The way he was acting the last few days. He's not coming back."

"How did he act?"

"Nervous. Distracted. Like he did when he was using drugs, but I could tell he was perfectly sober. Something was going on, and he didn't want to tell me about it."

"Do you think it was the cancer? Had he been to the doctor lately?"

"Not that I know of." She paused and sighed, half smiling as she said, "It's just like him not to say goodbye."

Eddie shrugged. "Maybe he did. Maybe you've got a letter waiting for you, too."

"Maybe," she agreed. "Funny that Swinburne would have torn both of our places up and not thought to check the mailboxes."

"Too obvious."

Not looking at Eddie but still staring at the book on the desk beside him, Roxanne quietly said, "Eddie, where's the bottle?"

He looked startled. The note had mentioned a bottle, but they had been so fixated on the book that neither of them had thought about it until now. Eddie turned quickly in his chair and picked up the cigar box, which now held only the wad of newspaper. After a few seconds of gingerly pulling the newspaper apart now, he held up a small medicine bottle with a drop of amber liquid in it. Made of clear glass, the bottle looked very old. It had a glass dropper attached to the screw top, but there was so little fluid in the bottle that the dropper was useless. The bottle had to be tilted on an angle for the liquid to pool and form a drop.

Eddie set it down on the desk, and they both stared at it. "So that's it?" Roxanne finally said.

Eddie just nodded in response.

"What did he say about it?" she asked, her voice just above a whisper.

Earlier in the day, during their drive into the mountains, when Roxanne had asked Eddie about the Dragon's Tears, she had done so with a hint of desperation in her voice. Suspicious of her at the time, he had withheld information. Now, though, the uncertainty and distrust he had felt for her were gone, nor did the thought even cross his mind that she was not to be trusted with the information. He told her everything he could remember about what Blackwood had said the night before.

"Okay," she said when he had finished. "So now what do we do with it?"

"I don't know. Swinburne's probably not done looking for it."

"And he shouldn't find it."

Eddie nodded. He was trying to figure out what Blackwood had wanted him to do. Was he supposed to use the Dragon's Tears himself? Did Blackwood want him coming into the future with him? It seemed so. But for what reason? Eddie could not begin to guess. "What would happen if he did?" he asked.

"I don't want to think about it. He's dangerous, Eddie. You don't know. If my father could use this stuff to . . . steal science fiction stories?"

"It looks that way."

"Then who knows what Swinburne would do with it?"

"Okay," Eddie said. "But if your father wanted it kept out of Swinburne's hands, why not take it with him? Or dump it down the sink before he left? What does he want me to do with it?"

"Maybe there's something in the book?"

Eddie nodded and picked it up again. "We should read it."

"No." She said it sharply, abruptly, causing him to look quizzically in her direction. "I mean, you read it if you want to. I don't want to know what's in there."

"Why?"

She hesitated and then nodded toward the book in Eddie's hands. "I meant what I said about not wanting to know the future."

"But this looks like a future that's not going to happen. Your father changed it."

"I don't care." She got up from the bed and walked across the room to where her purse was lying on the floor. She began rummaging for cigarettes. "Who knows what bits of information are in there? I don't want to know."

Eddie watched her, a bit surprised. "You're scared of it," he said.

Roxanne lit a cigarette and blew smoke toward the ceiling. There were tears in her eyes again. After another drag, she said, "You're not?"

Eddie knew that this was the closest she would come to admitting fear. He was content to back off from the subject, but her reaction still frustrated him. Realizing not only that time travel appeared to be a reality but also that the man he had met the day before had completely changed the course of science fiction by stealing stories and novels from the future, Eddie felt like a child suddenly thrust into an unfamiliar world, and up to this point it had been a help to be able to talk through his ideas with Roxanne. For the first time, he realized he was afraid of what he was finding out, but he had been approaching the issue automatically up to this point, not allowing himself to feel anything. Now she was abdicating her role, telling him to go on without her, mostly because she, too, was afraid of the truths they were uncovering. Eddie did not want to tell her that he was also afraid and wondered what gave her the luxury to withdraw into herself. Trying to keep irritation out of his voice, he said, "Let me look at this for a few minutes then and see what I can figure out."

He sat on the bed and began poring through the first chapter, quickly glossing through descriptions of John Campbell and the status of *Astounding* before he took control of the magazine, his managerial style, his philosophy of writing and science fiction, his talent for finding promising but untried young authors and grooming them for success, at times feeding them plot lines to guide them in the direction he felt they should go. Meanwhile Roxanne had gone to the window and, after asking Eddie if he minded, cracked it open a few inches before sitting down beside it to smoke her cigarette and blow the smoke out into the cool night air.

Eddie's heartbeat was rapid and his palms were sweaty. He could not believe what he was reading. According to the general information in the first chapter, the authors that were profiled in the rest of the book had written every one of the major works that Chester Blackwood had penned in the last ten years. Titles and character names were different, and there were clear deviations in plot and theme, but the basics were all there. He skipped ahead to the first chapter, one about a writer named A.E. van Vogt. Skimming through it, Eddie found an extensive description of a book called *Slan* that was supposed to come out in 1941. It bore a remarkable similarity to Blackwood's *Nelphi*, which Meteor had published in 1936. There were differences, though. Marion Rigby noted that *Slan* had promise, beginning with the suspense-filled pursuit of Jomy Cross after his mother is killed by authorities; however, the book lacked focus and was ruined by an improbable ending relying entirely on coincidence for which there was no thematic or dramatic preparation anywhere in the book's framework. "Furthermore," Rigby wrote, "the novel's handling of the sensitive themes of alienation and persecution is bungled and lacking in vision and consistency. What could have been a sensitive and timely critique of the Othering of minorities, even in a pre-Holocaust world, is rendered impotent and is clumsily incorporated into a text that tries to weave together too many themes. Still, for all its flaws, *Slan* was one of the most popular science fiction novels of the 1940s, prompting fans to proclaim, 'Fans are Slans.'"

Reading this, Eddie's mind raced. He could see how Blackwood had taken the plot entirely and even stolen the compelling opening scene. But he had then taken the poorly executed themes and reworked them. *Nelphi* had not stopped being discussed in four years, had seen multiple printings and was even being taught in some college courses. It rivaled *Brave New World* in many respects. Eddie could imagine how tantalizing the description of *Slan* must have been for Blackwood and clearly saw now how and why Blackwood had seen Eddie as a kindred spirit when he had discovered Eddie's plagiarism. More than anything, though, he wondered what the Holocaust was, or what it was going to be. He wanted to ask Roxanne what she thought but kept replaying her words about not wanting to know the future, and so he kept silent.

He glanced at his watch. It was after midnight now. He wanted to read the whole book tonight and figure out what to do about it. Now that he knew exactly what Blackwood had done, what he had brought back from the future, he needed to figure out how to use it to get Swinburne off of his and Roxanne's backs. He could just give the publisher the book, but as Roxanne had said, there might be something in the book that Swinburne could use to terrible advantage. Eddie eyed the bottle with the tiny drop of amber fluid in the bottom and told himself that it was the bigger problem, one he could not even begin to think of dealing with. Clearly, Blackwood had wanted him to have the book and the bottle, had even hinted that Eddie should take the Dragon's Tears and travel in time as Blackwood had done. The question was: why?

Turning back to the book, Eddie thought again about the names of important writers he had never heard of. He flipped to the index to see what other names it listed and if any of them were familiar or if Blackwood had changed the face of science fiction one hundred percent. Skimming down the list, Eddie was not surprised to see that there were no Blackwoods—neither Chester nor Roxanne. There was also no Archie Dumont. He would not tell this to Roxanne unless she asked. Some names were familiar—C.L. Moore, Eando Binder, Jack Williamson—but most were not. When he got to the R listings, he felt the blood drain from his face. There was an entry for Edward Royce on page 310.

He instantly flipped to the page, or tried to. It was gone, torn out. "Son of a bitch," he whispered and then looked up at Roxanne to see if she had noticed. She still sat in front of the window, working now on a second cigarette. If she had heard him, she did not indicate it but just exhaled slowly in the direction of the narrowly opened window. Page 310 was the last page of a three-page afterword entitled "Science Fiction After the Golden Age." With it had also gone page 309, so all Eddie had to go on was the first page of the afterword. It revealed very little, spoke in generalizations about the shape the Golden Age authors had left science fiction in by 1945. It gave Eddie no sense of what else Marion Rigby had to say about science fiction after that point or what Eddie Royce had to do with it.

"Eddie," Roxanne said from the other side of the desk, interrupting his thoughts. She sounded cautiously alarmed.

He looked up, still focused on what he had been reading and said, "Your father knows something about what's going to happen to me in the future." Roxanne looked in his direction and blew smoke into the room, one eyebrow raised. "But he's kept it to himself."

"Not surprising. I think I know something else that's going to happen in the future, but probably not so far away." There was a hint of disgust in her voice, almost resignation.

"What are you talking about?"

"Does anybody around here drive a black Lincoln?" she asked, nodding toward the window.

Eddie thought of the car he had seen outside her house earlier in the day and got up quickly, walking to the window and leaning down to look out. "It's not exactly a Lincoln neighborhood," he said. "Is that Swinburne?"

"It's his boys. Hobart and Luna. Swinburne wouldn't be here himself, watching us like that."

"You think they have been?"

"They're waiting for us to come out. Or for me to come out most likely."

"You think they know you're here?"

"They're parked behind my car. It's not exactly a convertible Cord neighborhood either."

Eddie could have taken it as an insult, a reminder of how far away they were from Pasadena culturally if not geographically, but he did not. "True enough," he said. "So what do we do?"

"I've been thinking about it while you looked at Daddy's book. Swinburne can't have it. Or the Dragon's Tears either. He shouldn't even know it really exists or he'll never give up trying to find it. We could sneak out of here, but they'd just find us again." She fingered her Zippo. "I think we should burn it. And dump the Dragon's Tears down the sink."

Surprised, Eddie said, "You can't be serious. Do you know what you're saying?"

"I think I do."

"We can hide it."

"You see what he's done so far to try and find it. Wait until he has Hobart and Luna start breaking your fingers to find out where it is." She nodded toward the window and the black Lincoln at the curb.

Eddie thought about it.

Roxanne continued. "And you know what they'll threaten to do to me. I don't think they'll actually go through with it, though. Swinburne needs me. But I don't think he needs you."

"Your father seems to have made him think he does."

"True. But not necessarily looking the way you do right now anyway."

"There has to be an alternative," Eddie said.

Roxanne put her cigarette out and rubbed her eyes. "There may be. But I think it's a pretty bad idea."

"What?"

"Take the Dragon's Tears. If it works, you can maybe hide the book in the future. Just get rid of it. And if it doesn't work, then at least Swinburne doesn't get it."

The idea scared him. "Why is that a worse idea?" he asked.

"Because it might not work the way my father said. Because it might be poison or opium or who knows what. Because the amount that's in that bottle might kill you in a heartbeat."

"But your father took it."

"You don't know that. You don't know it for sure. I told you what a liar he is. Was." She tightened her jaw. "Damn it, Eddie, I don't know. I think we should just get rid of it."

Eddie took a deep breath. "Okay. I agree we have to do something, but I don't think we should decide in haste. There's a back entrance out into the alley. We should get out of here and just walk away, get a hotel over near Pershing Square and sleep on it."

Roxanne nodded. "Fair enough." She stood up, closed the window, and pulled the shade all the way down before she began to get dressed, stepping away from the window as she pulled down the straps of her slip and began fastening her bra. Eddie was transfixed. She noticed and smiled. "Shirt, Eddie," she said.

He smiled back at her, a bit embarrassed, and went to find his undershirt, shirt, shoes and socks while Roxanne began on her stockings. They were dressed in a few minutes, Eddie zipping her dress for her. He found his coat on the floor where Swinburne's men had tossed it earlier and then picked up the book. "Do you have room for this in your purse?" he asked. Roxanne nodded and took the book, slipping it into her red bag. It was a snug fit but not so tight as to look like she was carrying anything out of the ordinary. "I'll keep this," he said and slipped the bottle of Dragon's Tears into his front pants pocket.

Roxanne stooped to get her lighter from the windowsill where she had left it. Hesitating a moment, she pulled at the edge of the shade and peeked out, and then sharply said, "Shit!"

"What is it?" Eddie moved to her side.

"They're out of the car."

"Are you sure?"

"I could see their silhouettes before from the streetlight. Now they're not there." They both heard the sound of a door being closed somewhere in the building. This late, there was very little traffic on the street and no other noise coming from inside the building. Sound traveled more now than it normally would. "They're coming." She sounded frightened.

Thinking about what she had said about broken fingers and worse, Eddie asked, "Are these guys really that bad?" as he moved to the door. He made sure it was locked and then pressed an ear to it to listen for the sound of feet on the stairs.

"They're bad enough. I can't say. I'm not used to dealing with them like this. Swinburne tries to keep things looking respectable."

Eddie stepped away from the door and moved to the small table where he kept his hot plate plugged in. He picked up his single spoon and reached into his pocket with his other hand for the bottle of Dragon's Tears.

"You're taking it?" Roxanne asked in a sharp whisper.

"Have to," Eddie said quietly, calmly. He felt rushed but resigned. "I don't think your father was trying to kill me, and we know he did something with this stuff that definitely gave him an advantage. Which is what we need right now." As he spoke, he twisted the top off the bottle. The dropper came with it, attached to the top, and he set this down on the table and poured the drop of amber liquid onto the spoon. Picking up the dropper, he dipped it into the solution that had pooled in the bottom of the spoon. The Dragon's Tears clung to the glass rod in a perfectly formed droplet. Holding the dropper over the spoon, Eddie brought it up to his mouth, stuck out his tongue, and touched the dropper to it.

For a second, the room glowed bright white, and he could see nothing. There was the sound of wind blowing fiercely, but also only for a second. The shock made Eddie feel as though he was about to pass out, but the sensation was gone as quickly as it had come. He looked at Roxanne, his eyes wide. She looked back, seemingly afraid to say anything, with just a quizzical look on her face. Sweat broke out on his brow, and he could feel his heart beating rapidly, but in a way he had never felt before. The intensity of all his sensations seemed to have doubled, or more. Looking around the room, everything appeared more vivid, crisper, as though he had needed glasses and then suddenly had twenty-twenty vision. If it was possible, Roxanne looked more beautiful, more vibrant, than she had moments before. Her eyes looked bluer, her lips more pink.

"Are you all right?" she finally asked, just above a whisper. He could hear her perfectly well, though. Her voice, too, was more crisp, the syllables she spoke more distinct.

"I think so," he said. He could clearly hear the sound of two pairs of shoes coming down the hallway. Swinburne's men moved quietly but not quietly enough. He put his finger to her lips and nodded toward the door so Roxanne would know they were almost there. Eddie had a slight burning sensation left on his tongue, and he looked at the spoon. He could clearly see residue of Dragon's Tears left behind from the dropper. "Here," he whispered, handing the spoon to Roxanne.

"What do you want me to do with it?"

"Lick it. I don't know if there's enough residue left on there to do anything, but it might. And I might need your help with whatever happens."

Roxanne looked doubtfully at him. Then she jumped slightly as the doorknob rattled. One of Swinburne's men was trying the door. This was followed by a light knocking. Roxanne took a deep breath and put the spoon in her mouth. Eddie watched as she left it there for a moment and then pulled it through tightly held lips. Her eyes widened, and she looked frightened for a moment. Then she just nodded.

"You okay?" Eddie whispered. She nodded again. He took the empty bottle and the dropper, set them on the floor, and then crushed them with the heel of his shoe. When he stepped away, just the cap and powdered glass remained on the floor. He brushed at the remains of the bottle with the sole of his shoe so it looked like something that had been broken in the earlier ransacking of the room.

There was another knock, louder this time, and then a voice. "Miss Blackwood? Mr. Royce?" the voice asked quietly. "We need to speak with you for a moment." It was a smooth, calm voice, not the voice Eddie would have imagined coming from a thug. He raised an eyebrow at Roxanne and then nodded toward the door, silently asking if she was ready for him to open it. She nodded back, and Eddie reached for the door, unlocking it and opening it.

Two men walked in. The first was short, a bit heavy, dressed in a good suit. He had a pencil thin mustache and dark complexion. The second was taller, more muscular looking in his suit but still on the thin side. His face was angular, and his nose had been broken at some point. Eddie would have made him out as a former boxer, one who had not fared well in the ring but who could easily get work as hired muscle. He stood behind his companion and looked briefly at Eddie, sizing him up Eddie thought, and then stared lasciviously at Roxanne. It was clear he did not care if his stare bothered her.

"Mr. Royce, I presume," the short man said. He was the one who had spoken through the door. Eddie nodded. "I am Alfredo Luna. My partner and I represent Mr. Augustus Swinburne. I'm sure you're aware he is also your employer."

"In a manner of speaking," Eddie said.

"In a manner of speaking," Luna replied, grinning. He turned to Roxanne. "Miss Blackwood. Mr. Swinburne has instructed me to ascertain whether you have obtained the information in question."

Roxanne shook her head and looked nervously at Eddie, who realized there was a bit of acting called for here. "You're kidding," he said, his voice rising in anger. "You've been trying to get information out of me? The whole time?"

Roxanne looked at the floor, ashamed. "I'm sorry, Eddie," she said. "You don't know how it is."

"I know how it is, all right."

"Sure he does," said the ex-boxer. His voice was more highly pitched than his demeanor would have suggested, and he had a slight New York accent. "We know, too. We been sittin' down there for a while watchin' the lights up here go on and off and on again. Figured Roxanne'd either had enough time to get what we needed or else maybe she was gettin' a little more of what she needed."

"You son of a bitch," Eddie said, his anger not feigned. He took a step toward the tall man, but Luna put a hand on his arm to dissuade him. At the same time, Roxanne gasped in alarm and Luna's companion tensed, ready to swing his fists if Eddie followed through. Eddie stopped. He could actually sense the adrenaline pulsing through him, could feel its impact on his heartbeat and his breathing, could feel more blood rushing to his thighs and arms as his primitive brain took over and prepared for fight or flight.

"Enough," Luna said, addressing himself both to his companion and to Eddie. When he saw that his warning was being heeded, he spoke again, his voice as calm as it had been before Eddie's outburst. "In that case, Mr. Swinburne has requested your presence and that of Miss Blackwood at his home this morning. Would you be so kind as to accompany us?"

"Isn't this a bit late for a social call?"

"Business never sleeps, Mr. Royce. Please." Luna stepped aside, indicating that Eddie should go first through the door.

"And if we don't?"

"Then Mr. Hobart will be compelled to convince you," Luna said. He indicated his partner, who smiled at the idea, his grin razor slim. "I would prefer that we not go to those lengths, however. And, I can assure you, you would prefer it also."

Eddie looked questioningly at Roxanne, who just nodded resignedly. Eddie could not be sure if she truly felt beaten or was just playing it up for the benefit of Hobart and Luna. As far as Eddie was concerned, anything they could do to keep Swinburne's men from searching her purse was a good thing. Compliance seemed the best way to go, for now at least. With his jacket in his hand, he walked out the door, glancing again at Roxanne and trying to convey some reassurance. Roxanne, purse and coat in hand, followed, and then Hobart and Luna. They all stood in the hallway for a moment as Eddie locked the door. Then they made their way to the stairs, Hobart shadowing Eddie closely. As they walked past Pence's door, Eddie noticed that the dim light coming over the transom had not changed since he and Roxanne had knocked at the door hours earlier. Pence was almost certainly not home, and even if he had been, Eddie felt it would not have been the right move to call out to him for help. Though he did not like being strong-armed into going to Swinburne's, he also felt that this was the only way he and Roxanne would be able to find out what Swinburne wanted with them. And while he knew that their having taken the Dragon's Tears and possessing Blackwood's book gave him and Roxanne some advantage over Swinburne, he could not help wondering if this would be the last time he would be leaving this building.

CHAPTER ELEVEN

The interior of the Lincoln was padded leather. Eddie sat in back with Hobart while Luna drove with Roxanne in the front seat. As they had pulled away from the curb, Roxanne had turned around to look at Eddie. "I'm sorry, Eddie," she said. He could not be sure if this was more acting for the benefit of Swinburne's men or not. "For getting you into this, I mean. And for lying to you," she added.

Eddie had just nodded and said, "Don't worry about it." He had tried to muster a smile, but the best he could do was a nervous grin. The effects of the Dragon's Tears had intensified once they had gotten outside. Everything from the cold of the night air to the neon sign above the door of the Terminal Café to the rumble of the Lincoln's engine filled his mind more vividly than anything he had ever experienced. He felt almost faint when they began to move, as stationary objects they passed seemed to shimmer with some inner movement. He furrowed his brow at Roxanne, hoping he could silently convey to her that he was feeling out of sorts from the effects of the drug, but she merely raised an eyebrow, paused and then nodded before turning back in the seat. Eddie had no way of knowing if she understood that he was experiencing something odd. On the seat next to him, Hobart had given an amused grunt, clearly putting the exchange between Roxanne and Eddie down as a lover's quarrel.

Not long after the Lincoln turned off of Central, Eddie saw the first of what Chester Blackwood had called bridges through time. He had not been looking for one, and at first it did not occur to him what he was looking at.

About a block ahead, he saw a bright light on the sidewalk in front of a warehouse. It struck him as unusually bright for a street lamp, and it would have been odd for a business to be so lit up at this time of night. Still, the vividness of the light may have simply been another effect of the Dragon's Tears, so Eddie did not think too much of it. But as the car approached, he kept his eye on the light and had to force himself not to sit upright in his seat and stare when he realized what it was. The time bridge looked to be about six feet high and maybe two feet across, coming to points at the top and bottom and spreading out in the middle. Its lowest point was about two feet off the ground. The light it gave off was jagged and bright blue-white. It looked as though a hole had been torn in the air. Nothing looked out of the ordinary inside the bridge; Eddie could clearly see through it to the other side, and it was just the warehouse front that was there—not visions of past or future—and Eddie remembered what Blackwood had said about needing to be deliberate in passing through a bridge. Most likely, a time traveler could not see past or future by merely looking through; a bridge had to be crossed for anything to happen.

As the car passed, Eddie turned in his seat and looked out the back window, allowing himself only a glance so as not to draw Hobart's attention. There was nothing there. The bridge had simply disappeared. He remembered Blackwood's statement about the bridges' directions, that those facing west led to the future and those facing east led to the past. There was apparently only one way in and one way out, and the bridge they had just passed was facing west. Eddie wondered how far into the future it would have taken him if he had been free to step through. He looked at Roxanne, but she had not turned in her seat, so he had to assume she had not seen anything, that the dose of Dragon's Tears she had taken had been too small.

He saw more bridges as the Lincoln rolled on, cutting through downtown Los Angeles and then north before catching Sunset Boulevard and following it west for several miles. The closer they got to Hollywood, the more bridges Eddie saw, which verified one more piece of Blackwood's story; Eddie remembered he had described Hollywood as being so full of holes in time that it was like Swiss cheese.

At this hour, the streets were practically deserted, and a light fog had rolled into the cool L.A. night. At an intersection where the Lincoln halted at a stop sign, Eddie saw a time bridge hanging in mid air not far from the street sign on the corner. It glowed eerily with the fog around it, and Eddie shuddered involuntarily at the sight, as he was now able to observe it steadily for the few seconds the car was stopped. Even though it would have meant getting away from Hobart and Luna, the idea of crossing into the future to do it was suddenly very frightening, perhaps because it was now so real and not just the focus of harmless fantasy in the pages of the pulp magazines.

As the car continued toward Hollywood, Eddie grew increasingly uneasy. He was getting farther and farther from territory he knew, moving more inexorably into the power of Augustus Swinburne, and with every mile that the car covered, Eddie's options were growing more and more limited. Soon enough, the power of the Dragon's Tears would be the only card he had left.

When they got to Hollywood, the car continued along Sunset and soon took a right turn to begin climbing into the Hollywood hills. The road instantly became narrow and wound its way around tight corners, snaking around impossible mansions that loomed out of the dark and fog, climbing steep hills and then twisting along hilltops before plunging back into Byzantine neighborhoods. Frequently, the road would reveal great open spaces above dark, unoccupied hills with the expanse of L.A. and Hollywood below, still lit up past one in the morning, the lights revealing more to Eddie now than he had ever seen before with his perception so artificially heightened. He thought of the view from Mount Wilson he had seen earlier with Roxanne and was amazed to think it had been not much more than twelve hours that they had been together. It seemed impossible, like it had been days instead, or like he had always known her. He looked again at the back of her head, wanting desperately to say something to her but knowing he should not. His feelings for her, he realized, had grown incredibly strong, and the apparent danger they were in seemed only to heighten them. It was possible, he realized, that the Dragon's Tears had also intensified his emotions, but if so, there was no denying that he welcomed the intensity.

Eventually, the car slowed and then pulled into a driveway entrance, stopping in front of an immense double gate, the only opening in a formidable wall that ran along the street. They had passed dozens of time bridges now, and Eddie felt overwhelmed by the immense possibilities they presented. Luna put on the brake and got out of the car, using the headlights to illuminate the gate. Where the two sides of the gate met, there was a lock, and Luna pulled a key ring off his belt and quickly had the gate open. The two sides swung inward, off the street, and from the headlights and his own enhanced perception, Eddie could clearly make out a winding driveway, neatly manicured trees lining it, that led straight to a large house with imposing columns around the entrance and immense wings branching off to the left and right. This was the type of house Eddie had imagined Blackwood living in.

Luna got back in the car, drove it through the gates, then got out to shut and lock them again before taking the car down the driveway and to the house. Eddie could see that the grounds were beautifully kept, but of greater interest were several time bridges glowing with a blue-white light. There was a small outbuilding on the mansion's west side with one of the time bridges right beside it. Eddie looked at Roxanne again but only got the back of her head. During the whole trip over, she had not done anything to signal her awareness of the time bridges they had passed.

Parking in front of the mansion's entrance, Luna killed the engine and turned to Roxanne and Eddie. "Here we are," he said pleasantly, as though he were their chauffeur. Hobart got out of the car without saying anything and stood by the open door, clearly expecting Eddie to slide out on the same side, which he did. Meanwhile, Luna had also gotten out and gone around to open Roxanne's door. Eddie wondered if the gentlemanly approach was an act meant to put Swinburne's "guests" at ease or if this was how Luna always behaved. He assumed that there was a rougher, more violent side to the man that would come out if he were crossed. Eddie also assumed that before the night was over, he would be forced to find out. He had no intention of giving Swinburne what he wanted.

The front doors were not locked. Luna led the way in, Eddie and Roxanne following with Hobart behind them. The doors opened onto a two-story room with banistered walkways on the second level running the lengths of the walls and disappearing into arched doorways. There were high windows that would have lit the room during the day and a chandelier and several lamps that were all burning now, illuminating the room's every detail. Eddie glanced around as they followed Luna through the room, taking in the art on the walls, the expensive furniture, the ostentatious fireplace. It was clear that more money from Blackwood's books had gone into this house than into Blackwood's own. Some movie tycoon had probably built the place in the twenties, Eddie thought, when Hollywood had first really come into its own. He doubted that Swinburne had been in L.A. as long as the mansion had been perched on this hilltop overlooking the city.

Two broad openings led off from either side of the room, leading to long galleries lined with windows that led to other sections of the house. Luna now led them through to the right. Eddie glanced over his shoulder as they turned and saw that halfway down the opposite gallery behind him was another time bridge next to an ornate bookcase. He remembered what Blackwood had said about clusters of time bridges and realized that they must be in the midst of one.

The gallery they walked through opened onto an enormous room, one that could easily have served as a ballroom in the mansion's past, Eddie thought as they entered. High ceilings and chandeliers, a polished hardwood floor, and candelabras built into the walls were a few of its amenities. If Hollywood's elite had danced here in the twenties, however, there was little room for dancing now. Elegant furniture littered the floor, and high bookcases hugged the walls. In the center of the room was what looked oddly like another small structure, as though a small square house with a flat roof had been put into the middle of the ballroom. It took up about a third of the room and rose up to about two-thirds of the room's height. Its walls were white and hung with paintings and small tapestries. Eddie noticed with interest a blue-white glow coming from the opposite side of the odd structure. In the center of the wall of this room within a room, there was a large door, and in front of this rested an enormous mahogany desk on a bearskin rug. Sitting at the desk was Augustus Swinburne.

At least, Eddie assumed it was Swinburne. He looked paunchy, and Eddie guessed that he was short and squat, but he could only guess, as the man did not stand when they entered the room. He wore eyeglasses that reflected heavily off the room's lamps, so Eddie had a hard time seeing Swinburne's eyes. He sat there with his elbows on the desk and hands clasped in front of his mouth, barely hiding a broad, self-satisfied smile. There were no other chairs on this side of the desk, so once they had walked across the ballroom, Eddie and Roxanne simply stood before it as Swinburne studied them before speaking. Hobart and Luna stood silently behind them.

"Miss Blackwood and Mr. Royce," he said, his voice a bit nasal. It was not a voice Eddie liked. Swinburne lowered his hands to the desktop, laid them there self-consciously as though he did not know what to do with them. "Mr.

Royce, I'm sorry we have to meet under these circumstances. I have high hopes for you and sincerely wish that whatever transactions we engage in tonight will not color our future dealings. Are you aware, Mr. Royce, that Miss Blackwood has been trying to get some information from you that I badly need?"

Eddie nodded. "I am." He decided it would be best to continue to affect bitterness at having been duped by Roxanne. Still, he did not want to take it too far and act the wounded lover. He needed Swinburne to see him as independent of Roxanne, not in love with her.

Eddie watched as Swinburne quietly read his face, doubtful that he was able to read much. "My apologies for the deception, such as it was," Swinburne said. He turned to Roxanne. "The fact that the two of you are here tells me that you were not successful in your endeavors, Miss Blackwood." Roxanne simply nodded and looked at the floor. Eddie glanced at her. She looked ashamed of herself, but he could not tell if her shame was meant to be a response to her failure or to her seeming duplicity. Swinburne quietly added, "Too bad for you," before turning his attention back to Eddie. "Mr. Royce, I don't know how much Miss Blackwood has told you about our situation here, so forgive me if this is redundant. Her father has had some dealings with me that he has reneged on, and now he seems to have disappeared. I need you to tell me where he is."

"I don't know where he is," Eddie said.

Swinburne blinked behind the glasses and got a sour look on his face. Eddie could tell it was the answer Swinburne had expected, but he was still unhappy to have received it. "I don't believe you, Mr. Royce. Forgive me for calling you a liar, but it's late. Why should we beat around the bush? If you won't tell me where he is, then I need you to tell me how he's gone there. Miss Blackwood has already informed me that you know about her father's adventures in time travel." He paused before adding, "How does he do it?"

"You believe that's really what he's done?"

Swinburne nodded. "I have my reasons. I also think you believe it as well."

"What makes you think I know anything? I just met the man yesterday." Eddie paused. It was Thursday now. He corrected himself. "Two days ago. We talked twice, and I haven't seen him since. I'm basically a stranger to him. Why would he have told me anything?"

"Because of the kind of man Mr. Blackwood is. Because you went to call on him earlier today. Because of what he's told me about you already."

"Which is?"

Swinburne sighed. "I can see that you're going to make me belabor the point. Alfredo, would you bring our guests some chairs please?" Eddie heard movement behind him as Luna crossed the room. Swinburne spoke as Luna brought chairs over and placed them before the desk for Eddie and Roxanne to sit in. "I'm sure you're aware that Mr. Blackwood has been my proverbial cash cow for some time now. The problem is that the cash cow seems to have dried up. Miss Blackwood's father hasn't written a word for me in two years now."

The news surprised Eddie, and he glanced at Roxanne. She met his gaze, and he could see that she was equally taken aback. They both knew that Blackwood had stopped writing, but Eddie had no idea how long the dry spell had lasted. Their eyes locked for only a moment before Eddie made himself look back at Swinburne. It was really the first time they had looked at each other without playacting since they had pulled away from his apartment in the Lincoln, and even though the circumstances were tense, Eddie could see in her eyes that nothing had changed between them, that the show she had put on for Hobart, Luna and Swinburne had been just that; he had nothing to worry about where her loyalty was concerned.

"The problem is that I have had Mr. Blackwood under contract for quite some time now, not unlike the contract you signed recently, Mr. Royce, only far more extensive than yours. And being unable to write, fresh out of ideas as he put it, Mr. Blackwood has been in a rather delicate position with me. There has been a backlog, of course, of stories and such that he's written over the years, and we've been releasing the material slowly, but the supply is about at its end." He paused dramatically and gave what Eddie assumed was meant to be a benevolent smile, but the effect was the opposite. "So I had to put a bit of pressure on him. Nothing untoward, Miss Blackwood, I can assure you."

He smiled at Roxanne, who gave no reaction. Eddie thought about how volatile her relationship with her father was and wondered whether she was worried about him at all or instead focused solely on getting herself out of one more situation her father had created. Swinburne continued. "Under pressure, then, Mr. Blackwood struck a separate deal with me. He told me that he could get more ideas if I would pay him more, and he also promised to point out the next guaranteed writing sensation that would replace him if, in fact, he proved unable to fulfill his obligations to me. That sensation is you, Mr. Royce."

Eddie felt obliged to smile, was sure that Swinburne expected it. The publisher would have been surprised and alarmed if he knew that Eddie was actually smiling at the absurdity of it all. Whatever was on the missing page 310 of Blackwood's book had no doubt been the thing that prompted Blackwood to give Swinburne Eddie's name. "You're kidding," he said as he thought about things Blackwood had said to him about writing and his future involvement with people in the industry whom he needed to be careful of. He realized now with Luna and Hobart standing behind him what Blackwood had meant and how he had been responsible for Eddie being here.

Swinburne shook his head. "No. Personally, I don't see it. The things you've written for us have been mildly entertaining but not earth shattering by a long shot. You may improve, Mr. Royce, and I sincerely hope that you do, but so far I am not impressed. No offense. But Mr. Blackwood has seen it differently, and that's partially why you're here. Now. What did Chester Blackwood see in you? What secret do you share?"

Eddie's smile had turned nervous. "Honestly," he said, "I have no idea. What makes you think he really knows what he's talking about? I mean, couldn't he have just pulled my name out at random from the table of contents of *Stupendous*?"

Swinburne leaned forward. "He could have. Recently. The fascinating thing is that he gave me your name almost six months ago—before you had ever published. All we had was a series of rejection letters for weak stories you'd submitted. Didn't it strike you odd that you began to do so well so quickly?"

Now Eddie's smile faded completely. "This is ridiculous," he said quietly.

"Indeed. Imagine paying for it. Which I have." Swinburne smiled again. "Don't feel badly, Mr. Royce. Many great writers have gotten their starts through patronage of one sort or another. We have only to see where you will take your good fortune. I can see from your reaction that you did not know about this. I was suspicious that you and Mr. Blackwood were in collusion somehow, but I could not determine to what end. Now I see that I was wrong."

"How could we have been in collusion?" Eddie asked. "And over what?"

"Over fifty thousand dollars, Mr. Royce. That was what I paid Mr. Blackwood for information about you. With fifty more to come when he followed through with the next groundbreaking novel."

"Why did you believe him?"

"I didn't. Not entirely. But that was when he first told me about traveling in time and that he had gotten information about your career from the future. I realize it was a gamble on my part, but it was one I was willing to partake in once he confessed to me that all his great story ideas had been arrived at through time travel."

Eddie and Roxanne exchanged glances. "I still don't see why you believed him, why you paid him," Roxanne said.

Swinburne smiled. "Yes, I suppose I do have a reputation for holding onto my money. By the way, Miss Blackwood, you'll be interested to know that we found no money in your father's safe once we opened it."

"I'm supposed to believe that?"

Swinburne smiled but did nothing more to respond. The message was clear that Roxanne had no choice but to believe him. After a moment, he said, "Money isn't as great a motivator for me as you would imagine." *No*, thought Eddie. *But power is.* Blackwood had undermined the publisher's power, Eddie knew now, and it had angered him. Swinburne's pursuit of Blackwood, the book, and the Dragon's Tears was as much about putting Blackwood in his place as it was anything else. Swinburne continued. "There are some things worth more than money, and worth risking money on. So your father got his money but not before being compelled to explain the process he had used for his little adventures in time. Miss Blackwood, your father's drug use was no surprise to me, but I was definitely interested when he explained that his penchant for the exotic had led him to a drug that allowed the user to move back and forth in time. He also intimated that he had a book that further aided him in stealing from the future. Looking at how poorly he wrote before he claimed to start time traveling, I saw there was at least the possibility that he was telling the truth. He would not tell me specifically what the drug was, however, and he would never share the book with me."

"And what exactly is in this book?" Eddie said.

Swinburne smiled. "You persist in the charade that you have not seen the book. Very well. I'll play along. Apparently the book explained principles of time travel and the composition of the drug that Mr. Blackwood employed in his journeys to the future. Of course, he would not say what the book was called, specifically, but he did own up to his misdeeds. At that point, I still assumed he had been getting information from the future, not that he was plagiarizing from it."

"Is that what he's been doing?" Eddie asked, trying to sound surprised.

Swinburne grinned and said, "You know very well that that's what he's been doing, Mr. Royce. Don't play games with me. Chester Blackwood is a thief and a scoundrel, and I was foolish enough to be taken in by his machinations. Not that it matters to me that he stole his ideas from others, but since I have known what he has been doing, I have wanted the secret far more than I want to publish another novel."

"And just how did you figure out what he had been doing?"

Swinburne hesitated, seeming to size up the question and Eddie himself. After appearing to weigh his options for a moment, he asked, "What do you know about *Astounding Stories*, Mr. Royce?"

Eddie shrugged, thinking of what he had read about the magazine that would have revolutionized science fiction if Blackwood had not tampered with time. "Good magazine," he said. "Nothing above average, though."

"Would it surprise you to know that I have spies working there?"

"No," Eddie and Roxanne both said without hesitation. Eddie remembered what Roxanne had said about her experience with Whistler and the threat that a network of spies throughout the publishing world would be employed to make sure she did not publish for any company besides Meteor. He was sure she was thinking of the same thing.

"I have people employed at magazines and publishing houses all around the country. And in Great Britain. Everything that comes in over the transom, everything that is accepted or rejected, everything that is slated for publication, I know about. In many cases, before the editors themselves know. When something is truly interesting, I get copies of stories that no one else but the editorial staff gets. This is rather costly, but it is worth it. We all do it. I'm sure that Campbell and Gernsback and others have planted people in the Meteor chain at various times. Over the last few months, I have gotten some very bizarre communiqués from my people at *Astounding*. Come. I want to show you something."

Swinburne pushed himself back from the desk and stood up. Eddie had guessed right. He was a squat little man, probably just over five feet tall, with the pudginess that comes from privilege and lack of movement. There may have been a tennis court and swimming pool on the property, but they did not get much use. Based on the number of books that surrounded them, Eddie assumed Swinburne spent a lot of time reading and very little else when he was not managing his business.

A dozen feet behind Swinburne's desk was the door built into the wall of the room within a room at the center of the ballroom. The door appeared to be metal while everything else in the room was made of expensive and beautifully finished wood. And instead of a handle, there was a small combination lock. Eddie watched in fascination as Swinburne began turning the combination, his back to Eddie and Roxanne so they could not see the numbers he stopped on even if they had been close enough to read them. "Please," he said to them when the lock had finished spinning with a loud click and Swinburne had pulled up on the handle beside the dial to open the door. "I think you will find this interesting, Mr. Royce."

Eddie and Roxanne stood and walked to the door as Swinburne swung it open. Swinburne stepped through, followed by Eddie and Roxanne. Hobart and Luna had also moved from their posts and now stood just outside the door. Eddie and Roxanne found themselves inside of a large room with a low ceiling and a plain wooden table and chairs at its center. The walls were lined floor to ceiling with more shelves except for one wall that was half shelves and the rest filing cabinets and large metal cabinets with locked doors. Wooden ladders on wheels were attached to rails that ran the length of the walls dominated by shelves. "My vault," Swinburne said. "This is where I keep my truly rare items. Completely fireproof with concrete walls and ceiling. Please don't touch anything. Mr. Luna informed me that you are also quite the collector, Mr. Royce."

The thought of his collection handled so roughly and spread so indiscriminately about his apartment made Eddie angry again, but he was so awed by what he looked at now that envy quickly replaced anger.

"Jesus," Roxanne said, looking around the room.

Eddie silently echoed her. He could not tell without pulling books off the shelves, but he was sure that he was looking at the most amazing collection of science fiction anyone had ever put together. On the shelf in front of him were what looked like four extremely early editions of *Frankenstein*. There were more recent books as well. Pristine editions of Wells and Verne, Burroughs and Haggard filled shelf after shelf. Pamphlets and magazines, dime novels from the 1800s, and boys' newspapers bound and labeled on the spines stretched out around the room. One wall was taken up with nothing but boxes of pulps similar to Eddie's collection, but based on the neatly typed labels on the boxes indicating magazines and dates, there were so many more here than he had even conceived of being able to collect.

"I see you're impressed," Swinburne said.

"Very," Eddie said.

"I have been collecting science fiction—or what we're calling science fiction these days—for a long, long time. I have some truly rare pieces. Mr. Luna?" Luna stepped into the vault. "Would you open this cabinet, please?"

Luna pulled out the same ring of keys Eddie had watched him use to open the gates into the estate. He selected a small one and slipped it into the lock on one of the metal cabinets, which was about seven feet high and four feet wide. There was the sound of a pneumatic seal being broken, and Eddie realized that the contents of the cabinet were under pressure.

"Carefully atmospherically controlled to ensure perfect preservation," Swinburne said as Luna stepped away and Swinburne opened the doors. More shelves were inside the cabinet but not nearly as crowded. Swinburne put on a pair of white cotton gloves kept on a metal shelf and picked up a large but slender volume. It looked ancient and extremely fragile. "*L'Histoire comique des états et empires de la lune* by Cyranno de Bergerac. 1656. A very early copy. It tells the story of a man who theorizes that since the sun is powerful enough to draw water into the air through evaporation, he can harness the sun's power to travel through space. So he straps tiny vials of water to his body, goes out into the sunlight, and is whisked into the heavens, traveling through space and eventually reaching the moon. Fascinating, isn't it?" Swinburne was beaming, and Eddie could see that he was incredibly proud of his collection, so much so that he seemed to have forgotten all about Blackwood and time travel for the moment, engrossed in showing off his treasures as he was. "These cabinets are filled with antiquities like this and more modern rarities. If we had the time, I could show you unpublished Weinbaum and Howard manuscripts and early drafts of Wells and others with notes and corrections throughout. I've gathered them from some of the finest collections in the world."

"They belong in a museum," Roxanne said.

Swinburne's smile faded. "Yes. I suppose they do. But they're here instead, aren't they? My private museum you could call it." He put the book back on its shelf without offering to let Eddie or Roxanne see it closely. Before Swinburne shut the doors, though, Eddie noticed a smaller locked case inside the sealed cabinet. It was not much bigger than the safety deposit box he had taken out at the bank to store his contract with *Stupendous*. Swinburne closed the cabinet, and Luna locked it again before stepping back into the doorway of the vault.

Swinburne turned now and moved to a filing cabinet a few feet away. He pulled open the top drawer and quickly flipped through several files before taking out a folder and laying it on the table in the center of the room. "Please," he said, pointing to the plain wooden chairs before the table. Eddie and Roxanne sat side by side, and as Swinburne pushed the file toward them, Eddie felt Roxanne's hand briefly on his knee. She gave it a squeeze and then withdrew it before Swinburne could notice. Eddie felt a rush of chills up and down his body, and it was all he could do not to look at her. Instead, he focused on Swinburne, who said, "Take a moment and look these over. Tell me what you think." He sounded extremely pleased with himself as he said it, gloating almost.

Eddie picked up the thick folder and opened it, sliding it close enough to Roxanne so they could both read the top sheet, a note from one of Swinburne's spies at *Astounding* informing him of some "interesting" stories that the magazine had accepted and then rejected. Eddie glanced at Roxanne when he was done reading it. She just nodded, and he set the cover letter on the table and then felt chills as he began to read what was on the next piece of paper. It was a carbon copy of an acceptance letter written by John Campbell, editor of *Astounding*, to a writer named Robert Heinlein, informing him that his novella "Vine and Fig Tree" had been accepted for publication. It was dated August 25, 1939. Eddie remembered Heinlein's name from

Blackwood's book but not this specific story. He had not yet gotten to the chapter on Heinlein before Hobart and Luna had come to call. The next page in the folder was another letter from Campbell from the following month, withdrawing the offer of publication, citing "unforeseen developments in the marketplace" and wishing the author success with his future endeavors. Eddie had never heard of this type of thing happening and absently flipped to the next page while still trying to figure it out. What followed was a carbon of the actual manuscript of "Vine and Fig Tree" and Eddie felt stunned as he skimmed the first page. It was remarkably similar to the opening of Blackwood's most recent novel, the first scene of which described a disillusioned official in a future theocratic government standing on the battlements of a fortress and contemplating his future before meeting the novel's heroine, whom he would then risk his life and position for. Titled *If This Goes On*, it had appeared as a serial in *Stupendous* in October 1939 and had just been published as his latest book from Meteor a month ago. No doubt, Blackwood's story was the unforeseen development that Campbell had mentioned in his withdrawal letter.

After a few minutes, Eddie slid the manuscript over to Roxanne and let her look at it on her own while he moved on to another set of letters from Campbell, these addressed to Isaac Asimov. The same pattern followed, and Eddie fully realized for the first time that these were real writers whose stories were being published out from under them by Blackwood's manipulation of time. In the world that had been, Heinlein had written "Vine and Fig Tree" and published it in *Astounding*, gaining popularity from it and helping usher in what Blackwood's book had called the Golden Age of Science Fiction. But when Blackwood had gotten a hold of the book and written the stories ahead of time, he had left these writers out in the cold with stories no one would touch because they were too close to what Blackwood had published in *Stupendous*. In most cases, Eddie guessed, the writers would not even have gotten the story ideas since Blackwood had published as much as ten years before the stories and novels were supposed to have been written.

"You look alarmed, Mr. Royce," said Swinburne.

"I'm just trying to understand," Eddie said.

"What's to understand?" Roxanne asked. She had pushed the Asimov story into the middle of the table and looked up at Swinburne, who still stood smiling at them. "He did it. He stole those stories from the future, and now you have proof."

"Indeed I do, Miss Blackwood, and have had for some time. You should have seen the look on your father's face when I confronted him with this evidence of his duplicity. Priceless. Up to that point, he had had me thinking that his forays into the future had merely inspired him. Now I had proof that he was doing nothing more original than going into the future and stealing from other writers."

"But why should that matter to you?" Eddie asked.

"It didn't. I don't care about these people." He waved dismissively at the stacks of papers from his *Astounding* file. "Campbell is suspicious, however, that something is going on. He has no idea about the time travel, of course, but he knows something odd is happening at Meteor, and he's starting to make quiet inquiries. I'm not worried about him, though. All I want at this point is the secret of time travel. I generously offered to let Mr. Blackwood out of his contract in exchange for it. When he refused, I gave him an ultimatum."

"And that was?" Roxanne asked.

"Quite simple. Either a return to his previous productivity or the book and the drug. Failure to provide either would lead to unpleasantness."

"And the deadline for this?" Eddie asked.

Swinburne's smile faded instantly. "His time was up two days ago. Tuesday afternoon. Just before he disappeared. Miss Blackwood, can you tell me if your father mentioned anything about the meeting he and I had on Tuesday afternoon?"

"No," she said, her voice strong and cool. "I haven't seen my father since Tuesday morning in Whistler's office. I told you that already."

"What about before? Did he seem agitated before the meeting or nervous about it?"

Roxanne had told Eddie that her father had seemed bothered about something, but she must have had no inclination to share this with Swinburne. "No," she lied. "Should he have?" Her voice had an icy edge to it.

Swinburne smiled. "Miss Blackwood, your temper is legendary, and I don't want to incur your wrath. I told you earlier that I had nothing to do with your father's disappearance, and I need you to believe me."

"I believed you when you said you were just going to look through his papers. I didn't think you'd have these bastards tear my house apart. Or Eddie's." Her voice did not rise, and its even tone made her anger seem even more intense. It made Eddie uncomfortable. He also caught slight movement from Hobart out of the corner of his eye. Apparently, being called a bastard did not suit him well, and Eddie noted again that Hobart seemed to have a quick temper.

Swinburne waved a hand, probably in a signal to Hobart to stand down. "My apologies to the both of you. I will see that you are compensated for any damage or inconvenience. I am, however, determined almost to the point of desperation to come to an understanding of what your father has done. I don't mind telling you that I presented a threat to your father, one that Mr. Hobart would have made good on given the chance." Swinburne paused. "Unfortunately, he disappeared before we could complete our discussion. It was once I mentioned Mr. Hobart's willingness to convince him of the wisdom of returning my money that he took his leave. Regrettable. I have made mistakes in handling your father, I fear, Miss Blackwood."

"What do you mean, 'disappeared'?" Roxanne asked.

"I mean he disappeared. Before my very eyes. Into thin air. Are there any other cliché's I can employ to get my point across, Miss Blackwood?" Roxanne did not say anything but simply stared. Swinburne met her stare, and for the first time looked away. "As I said, he simply disappeared. It was out there," he pointed out the vault's door. "We were discussing his situation and his inability to meet his deadline. I admit, I may have alarmed him a bit with ultimatums and suggested consequences, but at the same time, I find it hard to believe that a man like Chester Blackwood, having gone through so much already in his dark life, would frighten so easily." Swinburne paused and shrugged. "At any rate, he got up, walked calmly across the room and disappeared. I watched him go. One second here, and the next gone. What did he do, Mr. Royce? Did he go into the future? I am convinced that you know how he did it, and when he came to you later that night, he told you about it. He may have even given you the same power. I want it, Mr. Royce. I intend to have it from you. We could certainly work something out."

Eddie thought about Blackwood making his exit through the time bridge on the other side of the concrete wall. Looking back at Swinburne, he could see that the publisher was growing impatient. His breathing seemed rapid, and his face was red. "I'm sorry," Eddie said. "But I don't know anything else. What makes you so sure I do?"

Swinburne answered with growing malice. "Quite simply because he would not have involved you in this and then left without giving you the secret. He knows you are his literary successor, and he also knows that, like him, you can't write your way out of a paper bag without help. So he gave you the same help he used."

Eddie felt rising anger as he listened to Swinburne's insults, but he stayed calm. He looked at his captor and said, "Mr. Swinburne, I keep telling you that I don't have the book, and I don't have the drug. I don't know what the drug is called. I've told you everything I know. I'm afraid you're just going to have to accept that he's gone, and there's no way you're getting the secret as to how he did it. And it looks like you're not getting your fifty thousand back either. If I'm the next big thing in science fiction, well that's great for me. And I suppose it's great for you, too, but that's where it ends. When I get my groundbreaking idea, I'll be sure to submit the manuscript to you first. Now, Miss Blackwood and I are leaving."

He began to push the chair back. Swinburne sharply and coldly said, "Mr. Hobart, will you please break Mr. Royce's left arm?"

Hobart shot into the vault as though he had been fired from a gun. Roxanne let out a small gasp as he circled behind her chair, grabbed Eddie by the neck with one hand, pushing his head down on the table, and with the other hand grabbed Eddie's left wrist and twisted his arm behind his back. He paused as he held the arm at the breaking point, waiting, it seemed, for final approval from Swinburne. Adrenaline pumping, Eddie noticed that he felt pain differently now that the Dragon's Tears was in his system. It was as though the pain were in a separate body and that he was simply getting notification of it in his brain. It was not something to feel distressed over, but he did know that he needed to end it soon, or it would get far worse. "It'll take me a hell of a long time to type up a manuscript with one hand," he said, grunting the words out with his face pushed against the table.

Swinburne hesitated and then said, "Fine. Break Miss Blackwood's arm then."

The pain and pressure in Eddie's arm were released instantly, and except for the adrenaline, Eddie felt no lingering effects of having been pinned to the table. He sprang up in his seat and turned as Roxanne gasped again. She was half out of her chair and Hobart had moved in close to grab her arm and keep her from having room to swing or kick at him. Eddie could see that she was going to get hurt very quickly in spite of her clear ability to take care of herself. Hobart had her outmatched.

"Wait!" Eddie shouted.

Hobart had succeeded in grabbing Roxanne's wrists and crossing them in front of her as he stood closely behind her, his head just behind hers. At Eddie's shout, they stopped struggling, and Hobart looked at Swinburne for direction. They looked like dancers interrupted in the middle of an intricate move. For the first time since he had met her, Eddie saw that Roxanne looked truly frightened. Hobart, however, wore a sadistic grin, clearly enjoying being close enough to breathe into her ear.

"We're waiting, Mr. Royce," Swinburne said calmly.

Eddie did not know what to say, only that he had to buy some time. The conversation had shifted to violence so suddenly that he had not had time to formulate a plan to get himself and Roxanne out of their predicament. The only thing he knew with certainty was that Swinburne was tired of being told no.

"All right," he finally said after another moment's heavy breathing. "I have the book."

"Eddie!" Roxanne said sharply. Her face registered betrayal, and Eddie felt her anger toward Hobart and Swinburne transfer onto him as he went against everything they had discussed in his apartment.

Eddie tried to ignore her, deciding to keep talking in the hope that he would figure out what to do as he went along and that Roxanne would see he was trying very hard to keep the book out of Swinburne's hands. He had been glad to see that her eyes had not moved to her purse, which was now at her feet beside the chair she had been sitting in. "I've had it since Tuesday, and she hasn't known a thing about it," Eddie said. He turned toward her. "I'm sorry I lied to you. But you can understand that I couldn't trust anybody. Your father warned me that people would try to get it." Still held tightly by

Hobart, Roxanne just nodded at him. Eddie was relieved to see the anger melt away in her eyes. He turned to Swinburne and added, "You may as well just let her go. She has nothing to do with this anymore."

Swinburne said nothing, just stood on the opposite side of the table shifting his gaze from Eddie to Roxanne, no doubt trying to see if he should believe what he was being told. "No," he said after a long silence. "Not just yet. When I have the book in hand, then we'll see. What about the drug?"

"Blackwood told me he had used it all up. When he came to see me Tuesday night, he said he had to make his getaway soon before it wore off and he'd be trapped in 1940 with no way of getting away from you."

Swinburne nodded. "I'm not sure I believe any of this Mr. Royce, but I'm listening. Where is the book? You haven't hidden it at your apartment, and you obviously haven't stuffed it in your shirt. What have you done with it?"

What indeed, Eddie thought. He had to think of something quickly before Swinburne made the leap from stuffed shirts to hiding the book in Roxanne's purse. He was surprised no one had thought to look there yet, but then again Swinburne had been assuming that Roxanne was working for him to find the book, not helping Eddie hide it. Eddie briefly considered saying he had left the book with Pence, but that would be disastrous once Hobart and Luna made the trip back to L.A.

"It's in a safety deposit box," he blurted out quickly.

"I don't believe you," Swinburne snapped back.

"No. It's true. Blackwood gave me the book in Whistler's office and told me to put it somewhere safe, not in my apartment. He told me he would explain to me later why it was so important, so I took him at his word and went straight to the bank. Look." Eddie pulled out his wallet and removed the bank receipt for the safety deposit box he had opened on Tuesday and in which he had placed his signed contract with Swinburne. He handed the receipt across the table. Swinburne had been watching with suspicion and now took the paper as though he were being offered a dead mouse. He clearly did not like what he was being told, did not trust any of it, but it was beginning to look like the truth.

"Fine," he said quietly, folding the receipt and handing it back to Eddie. "In the morning, we'll take a drive to the bank and finish things up. That book does not belong to you, Mr. Royce. It is owed to me, and I will have it."

"You think you'll be able to use the book without the drug?"

"You obviously haven't had time to read it. I am banking on the fact that it will provide me with a means of recouping my losses."

"You may be disappointed."

"I may," Swinburne said, "but I am willing to take the chance."

"I may not be willing to just let you have it, you know. There may still be some negotiating."

"Don't count on it."

"In the mean time," Eddie said, "you can let her go."

Swinburne nodded to Hobart, who instantly released Roxanne's wrists and stepped back. She spun around in a blur and slapped him hard across the face, but the blow did not make his head move in the slightest. He caught her wrist again as she withdrew and pulled her close with his other arm around her waist. "How'd you know I like it rough, baby?" he said quietly and with a grin that pulled his top lip over his teeth.

"Mr. Hobart," Swinburne said.

Hobart let her go but not before whispering, "You and me are just gettin' started, sister." It was said quietly enough for Swinburne to be unable to hear, but Eddie had no problem picking up the sound. He had watched the slap and its aftermath with rising adrenaline, and he longed to step in and smash a fist against Hobart's face, but he restrained himself. He had to focus now on getting them out of the house before the banks opened. What he would do after that, he had no idea.

"Come," Swinburne said. "It's late. We have guest accommodations for the two of you. In the morning, we will go to the bank and be done with our little drama." He looked to Luna and said, "The old servants' quarters."

Eddie glanced at his watch. It was close to three in the morning. He wondered if there would be enough time for him to finish formulating a plan and carry it out before having to show Swinburne a mostly empty safety deposit box. At the very worst, he would have to convince Roxanne to give up the book, but he was as much against it falling into Swinburne's hands as she was, and apparently as much as her father had been. He watched now as Roxanne smoothed her dress and bent elegantly to pick up her purse from the floor, holding it close as she walked out of the vault behind Hobart and in front of Eddie, not bothering to look at him at all. It was just as well, Eddie thought. For the time being, he needed her to believe he knew what he was doing, and if they made eye contact, he doubted he would be able to keep from betraying how helpless he felt at the moment.

CHAPTER TWELVE

With the door to the vault shut behind them, they moved through the house, Luna leading the way. Eddie and Roxanne walked side by side but not too close. Hobart walked behind them with Swinburne beside him. Roxanne wanted nothing more than to hold Eddie's hand or feel him put his arm around her as they walked, and keeping a cool distance from him was almost painful, but she kept it nonetheless. Strangely, she would have sworn that she could feel Swinburne's and Hobart's eyes on her as they trailed behind her and Eddie—Swinburne's on the back of her head as he considered what she was thinking and Hobart's on her hips as she walked one foot in front of the other, conscious of the extra sway she put into each step just to bother him.

From the second she had licked the spoon with the trace of Dragon's Tears in Eddie's apartment, she had felt a strange tingle all through her senses, as though her eyes, ears and nose had taken the equivalent of an electric shock, the effects of which lingered not unpleasantly. She had not been able to see anything unusual during the ride up to Hollywood, no bridges through time as Eddie had explained her father claimed to see. But she had been amazed at how vivid everything looked, at how the neon glowed along Sunset in a way she had never seen before and at how the rumble of Swinburne's Lincoln had made her feel as though a minor earthquake was rolling endlessly through the city. If this was how she was feeling the effects of just a hint of Dragon's Tears, she wondered what Eddie was experiencing and felt almost tortured by not being able to ask.

Luna led them through a door and down a hallway, then through another doorway and into what appeared to be a service corridor. Where the floors everywhere else in the house had been hardwood or elegant tile, here it was industrial looking tile and drab paint on the walls. Roxanne assumed they were somewhere behind the kitchen and that this would have been a route used by cooks and waiters in the days when the mansion had hosted lavish parties in the ballroom that Swinburne had converted into a library and museum.

They stopped at a point in the hallway where two nondescript doors faced each other. The doors opened inward, into each room, and Luna swung one open and then the other. He remained at the second, looking absurdly like the doorman at a fancy hotel. Swinburne pointed at the first door that Luna had opened and said, "This should be fine for Mr. Royce. Miss Blackwood can take the other. You will find a bed and clean linen, and each room has its own facilities."

Hearing this, Roxanne felt her frustration grow tenfold. She did not want to be separated from Eddie, not because she was afraid to be alone but because she wanted desperately to find out what he could tell her about the Dragon's Tears and what his plans were for keeping *The Golden Age of Science Fiction* out of Swinburne's hands. She looked into the room Swinburne had indicated would be Eddie's and then turned toward the room whose door Luna still held open. At first glance, the rooms looked identical. She could see only a corner of each room, but they looked nondescript and drab with dull carpeting and plain furniture and mirrors on each wall near the doors.

Swinburne added, "In case you are entertaining notions of escape, I will post Mr. Hobart in the hallway. He can also assist you with anything you may need."

Roxanne looked questioningly at Eddie and saw that he looked slightly agitated. Unsure of what to do, she took a step toward the door, but Eddie stopped her, gently putting a hand on her forearm as he said, "Wait." His touch gave her the same odd sensation of being lightly shocked, and she found it both pleasurable and unsettling. She looked again at him and saw that he was looking past her and past the door Luna held open, into the room Swinburne had said would be hers. Then, with what looked like some effort, he turned to look at Swinburne and said, "I don't want her out of my sight."

Swinburne smiled at this. "Surely, you don't expect Miss Blackwood to betray you at this point, do you? It hardly seems possible. In fact, I would think she would be more upset at the idea of your being away from her. You have already misled her, after all, regarding her father's book."

"That's not it," Eddie said. "I don't like the way your boy here has been looking at her." He nodded toward Hobart.

Swinburne shook his head. "How valiant of you. I can assure you, however, that Mr. Hobart will be perfectly restrained. My employees are all extremely loyal, Mr. Royce. Like a good dog, he will not bite unless directed by me. And I can assure you I have no intention of issuing such an order. Miss Blackwood's safety is very important to me. Besides, these doors have good locks, and Mr. Hobart does not have the keys."

"But he can get them. Nothing doing. Either I'm in there with Roxanne, or we're all sitting up playing rummy till the bank opens. Or the whole deal's off and we start playing rough again."

Swinburne stood there and weighed his options. "I could force you, of course," he said, to which Eddie simply raised an eyebrow in challenge. Swinburne sighed dramatically and said, "I am not thrilled at the idea of the two of you having such unsupervised access to each other for the rest of the night. But at the same time, I don't see how you could hatch a plot of any kind. There is no getting out of these rooms save through the doors, and we'll move straightaway to the bank in the morning. Go ahead." He nodded his head.

During the entire exchange between them, Roxanne had felt her heart racing in anticipation of being able to be alone with Eddie and out of fear that Swinburne would not relent. Upon hearing Swinburne agree and seeing him nod at them, she had to strain to keep herself from smiling or betraying her relief in any other way.

Eddie did not say a word but took her by the elbow and led her quickly into the room. Once through the door, he glanced quickly around the room and turned to face Swinburne, Hobart and Luna. Hobart looked angry, perhaps at having his plans thwarted but surely not at having his honor questioned. Luna and Swinburne just looked tired. Swinburne said, "Goodnight, Mr. Royce. Miss Blackwood," and Eddie swung the door shut. The latch clicked and Eddie reached out to twist the lock. Roxannne knew it would not hold if Hobart decided to put his shoulder to it, but doubted that anything like that would happen now that Eddie had so publicly brought it up as a possibility.

Roxanne's arms were instantly around Eddie. She held him tightly and rested her head on his shoulder, her face pressed up against his neck. She felt herself tingling all over as his arms encircled her and he held her tightly to him. In an instant, she had gone from feeling unsteady to invulnerable, and the strength of his embrace told her he felt the same. After a while, he brought one hand up to her neck and then caressed her hair; she relaxed her arms and lifted her head to meet his kiss. When she pulled back and opened her eyes, she felt at ease. His smile was the same he had had for her in his apartment before they had known Hobart and Luna were on the street below, before the Dragon's Tears, and she found comfort in knowing nothing had changed between them.

"You okay?" he asked in a whisper, and she nodded her response.

"You?" she whispered back.

164

"I think. The Dragon's Tears . . . feels strange. Have you . . . seen anything?"

She shook her head. "Just strange sensations. Everything's more intense."

He nodded his understanding. Still whispering to keep Hobart from hearing any of their conversation through the door, he said, "I've been able to see a lot of things you probably haven't since we left my apartment."

"Time bridges?"

"I think so. I'm pretty sure I've got a way for us to get out of here, but I'm going to need you to be adventurous."

Roxanne raised an eyebrow. "What are you talking about?"

Eddie took her hand and turned her around so that her back was to him. He pointed into the middle of the room and said, "Do you see anything over there?"

The room was sparsely appointed with a single bed and a cheap chest of drawers. There was a doorless closet that had nothing hanging in it, and another doorway that opened onto a small bathroom with toilet, sink and shower. After looking around the room for a few seconds and seeing nothing out of the ordinary, Roxanne said, "I don't see anything."

"There's a time bridge," he said, whispering even more quietly. "Right there." He pointed.

A look of apprehension spread across Roxanne's face as she looked in the direction Eddie had indicated. "Where is it?" she asked, her voice rising to just above a whisper and trembling slightly in excitement.

"Here." Eddie left her side and walked across the room. He put his hand up and moved it around for a few seconds, as though he were verifying the existence of the time bridge for himself. Looking back at Roxanne for a moment, he then used his hand to trace a shape in the air, its bottom edge about eighteen inches off the ground and its highest point more than six feet in the air. To anyone else, it would have looked like the actions of a lunatic, but Roxanne did not doubt that Eddie really saw something and that he was outlining its boundaries for her.

"What does it look like?" she whispered.

"Just like all the ones I saw on our car ride up here. Narrow at the top and bottom and broad at the center. It has sort of a dancing light at its edges that makes it look almost like fire." He ran his hands around the same shape in the air again. "I don't feel anything when I put my hand in it."

Staring intently, Roxanne began to get the sense of a vague outline in the air. The more Eddie traced his hand around the edges of the time bridge, the more she was able to make out a dim set of boundaries. "My God," she whispered, awed. "I think I see it." She brought a hand involuntarily up to her mouth and just stared. "If you hadn't pointed it out, I wouldn't have noticed it, but now I can tell there's something there. The outline is so faint. Can you see through it?"

"No. I think you have to actually step through it to notice anything."

"You knew it was in here?" She began walking forward to stand next to Eddie, her eyes never straying from the vague outline she was able to make out.

"When we were standing out there in the hallway, I saw a corner of it reflected in the mirror. There are at least three more in the house and a couple outside. Your father used one in the library to escape from Swinburne when he was here last. He told me there were clusters of them, that Hollywood is full of them."

"But how? Why?"

"Who knows? It's just . . ." Eddie shrugged. "There are more things in heaven and earth than are dreamed of in your philosophy, Horatio."

Roxanne shot him a sharp look. "What?"

Eddie smiled. "Nothing. *Hamlet.*"

"I know it's *Hamlet*. Do you think this is time for being cute?"

"I'm not trying to be cute. It's just that this has shown me that there's a lot more to the universe than meets the eye. The things we've been taught are true and constant . . . well, it's looking like they're not."

"I'll say."

"Roxanne, we need to step through."

She raised an eyebrow, shocked. "We?"

"Yes. Come on."

"Why both of us?" She took a few steps back from the time bridge, deeper concern on her face now, and then whispered in an agitated voice, "I don't want to go into the future, Eddie. I told you that."

Eddie sighed and walked to her, taking her hand. "I know," he whispered. "But I have to go through. I need to get information, find out what your father knew before morning so I can figure out what to do about Swinburne. And I'm not leaving you alone here with Hobart sitting outside the door."

"You think he'd come in with you here?"

Eddie nodded. "If he stews in his own juices long enough. I don't think he sees me as much of a threat. Besides, I may need you."

"What did you mean about what to do about Swinburne?"

"Do we just give him the book and be done with it or do we have to figure out another way?"

Roxanne said, "But we already decided that he couldn't have the book."

Eddie nodded. "I know. But we still don't know everything that's in it. Maybe it's harmless. Maybe it's just literary criticism of books that will never be written now. What could that harm?"

"Nothing, I suppose. But what if there's more to it?"

"I need you to read it and find out."

Growing angry now at having to repeat herself, she said, "I told you I don't want to read it."

In response to her words, she saw a look of anger spread across his face, and he sharply whispered, "Well, I'm sorry, Roxanne. If I had time to figure everything out and read the book, I'd do it. As it is, we've got maybe five hours before someone comes to get us for a ride to the bank, and I have no idea what's on the other side of that bridge and how long it's going to take to get the information I need to save both our asses from the mess your father got us into."

Roxanne's nostrils flared, and her gaze turned icy, but after a moment's silence, her features softened and her jaw unclenched. "Do you think it's safe?" she quietly asked.

Eddie's own look of irritation softened as well. "It has to be," he said. "I'll step through first."

She approached the bridge again, her face still expressing awe. "Do you think it's to the past or the future?"

Eddie was silent for a moment. "It's been a bit hard to keep my bearings in here," he said. "Bridges facing west are to the future. And I think this faces west." He paused. "I think."

He had to step around her to get in front of the opening. She grabbed his wrist as he did so, giving it a squeeze and smiling at him. "Come right back."

CHAPTER THIRTEEN

Eddie smiled back and kissed her again. Then he said, "Here we go." He put his foot through the opening and saw that there was a bottom to it. Like a conventional bridge, there was something to walk on even though there appeared to be nothing physically. It was just that the shimmering extended into the opening. Eddie let his foot rest on the base of the bridge. The sensation was unsettling. It felt as though he were standing on solid ground, but his foot was clearly in the air as though he were in the middle of taking a broad step over an obstacle. He put his weight on his foot and stepped through, being careful to get his whole body into the opening, not letting an elbow or hip pass through the shimmering edge and thus keeping him from making the trip. The base was about two feet wide, and he had no problem balancing on it. He wondered what would happen if he stepped off and assumed that he would just be back in the room with Roxanne. In front of him, he could see the other side of the bridge, an opening in the air identical to the one he had just stepped through, but now he could see that it was not the same room as the one he had stepped out of. It might have been the same physically, but not temporally. In the future he was moving toward, the room was darkened.

He turned to look at Roxanne. From his perspective, she was in the same room with him, only he was standing more than a foot off the ground. If she could see him, he must appear to be suspended in midair. From the look on her face, though, he could tell that she could not see him. Her hand had again been brought up to her mouth, which she probably held agape. Her eyes were wide with a mixture of fear and awe at what she had seen. He waved to her, but she gave no indication of being able to see. He spoke her name, but again she did not react. *Better to get this over with and get back to her,* Eddie thought and moved ahead.

In seconds, he was over the small arc of the time bridge and stepped through the other side. He supposed in passing through that there was some risk of appearing to materialize out of thin air if there were anyone watching him coming through. Surely, Blackwood had encountered this type of thing in all his time traveling, but he had not mentioned it to Eddie, so he had no idea how Blackwood had handled it. Seeing that the room he was walking into was darkened, he assumed he would not have that problem right now. Gingerly stepping through the opening and onto actual ground, Eddie looked around and could see nothing save the blue white glow of the time bridge behind him. Now it was a bridge to the past. He held his hands out in front of him and walked in the direction of where the door should be, hoping to find the light switch. When he did, he flicked it on and looked around the room. It was unoccupied, and he felt relieved. "Okay," he said.

Seconds later he was back over the bridge and with Roxanne again. He felt an odd sense of disorientation, something else Blackwood had mentioned about time travel and returning to his own time. It was as though his sense of time and space were slightly compromised for a few seconds. A broad smile spread across Roxanne's face when he came through the opening, and she quickly stepped forward to hug him. "How long was I gone?" he asked, remembering to whisper again.

"Maybe a minute," she replied, stepping back to look at him. "Does that sound right?"

He said it did. "What did it look like when I went through?"

She shook her head in confusion. "It was weird. It was like you stepped up onto a stool or something and then you just faded from sight. It wasn't a now-you-see-it now-you-don't sort of thing. You just . . . dematerialized. And when you came back, you just faded in as you stepped down." She still looked apprehensive but not as intensely so. She nodded toward the time bridge. "What's on the other side?"

"This room," Eddie said. "I don't know when, but I assume sometime in the future. You move in space as well as time. I came out about four feet away, and the bridge seemed to be about four feet long when I was walking on it." He turned to look at the opening again and then glanced at his watch. "We need to get on with it. Make sure you bring your purse and your coat. It might be cold where we end up. The room felt comfortable enough on the other side, but we may not be staying in that time. It could be tomorrow for all I know, and I need to get us further into the future."

After they had both used the toilet, Eddie took her by the hand and led her to the bridge. "Can you see the outline of it well enough to know where your foot's going to go?" he asked her. She stood and stared for a moment and then nodded. "Okay. Be sure. Apparently, you have to believe you're doing it for it to work. If you think you're just taking a big step and your foot's going to come down on the floor, that's probably what will happen." He instructed her to tuck her elbows in and make sure she got her whole body through both openings. Then he gave her hand a squeeze and nodded. She squeezed back and smiled, trying to look brave, Eddie thought, and there did seem to be more resolve and less apprehension in her eyes.

Roxanne nodded and stepped up. She hesitated a moment, as Eddie was sure he had done, and then she was up and fading from sight. It was uncanny, and Eddie could clearly see why she had been frightened when she had watched him go through. He quickly turned the lights off in the room to give Hobart the impression they had gone to bed. The glow of the time bridge in the now darkened room was intense, but rather than stare at it he moved to follow Roxanne through. Stepping through for the third time now felt a bit more natural, and he was relieved when he was all the way into the opening and could see her again about two feet ahead of him on the bridge. She had turned back to watch him come through. "So far, so good," he heard her say, but her voice sounded oddly far away with a slight echo. He just nodded, not wanting her to notice the same thing and be startled by it if he said anything in reply.

Moments later, they were in the now well-lighted room sometime in the future. "We're really in the future?" she asked. Her voice carried a sense of relief as well as amazement. Time travel was a bit mundane, not painful, not frightening. The idea that they could move through time was confounding to Eddie but also exhilarating, and he assumed she was feeling the same things.

Eddie led her to the door and opened it. The hallway was as dark as the servant's room had been when Eddie had first stepped through. He remembered seeing Luna flip on light switches when they had entered the hallway, but he had no idea how far away they were, and he also doubted the wisdom of turning on lights in what was probably the middle of the night. For all he knew, it was ten years later and someone other than Swinburne owned the house. Even if that were not the case, he did not relish the idea of explaining his presence to a future version of Swinburne or Hobart. Keeping things dark and acting like a burglar trying to get out undetected was no doubt the best policy.

He heard Roxanne making a rustling noise, and seconds later the hallway was sparsely illuminated by her Zippo. "Do you know which way to go?" she whispered softly.

Eddie had not noticed any exterior doors during the walk from the ballroom to the servants' quarters, so he assumed that retracing their steps would be a waste of time. He did not like the idea of working their way all the way back through the house to the front door or to one of the time bridges he had seen inside the house. So he pointed in the opposite direction, and they began moving down the hallway. After a few steps, Roxanne stopped and pulled off her shoes. Her heels had been clicking against the tile floor, and even though the noise had not seemed loud, Eddie felt relieved when she began carrying her shoes and they were able to move down the corridor in relative silence.

When they came to a set of double doors, Eddie stopped and tried one. It opened away from him, and he could see now that they were in the house's large kitchen. Windows opened onto the back of the house, and moonlight shone through. With a great sense of relief, Eddie noticed that there was a door leading outside. Roxanne extinguished the lighter and, holding hands, they practically ran for the door. It was locked, and Eddie turned the bolt slowly to keep it from clicking loudly.

With the door closed behind them, Eddie and Roxanne smiled at each other. "You okay?" he asked her. He had made sure to leave the door unlocked.

"I think," she said, looking around as she slipped her shoes back on. "What do you think?"

It was a cool evening and the full moon was about halfway up in the night sky. Eddie looked at it for a moment along with their surroundings. The back of the house was immense and more monolithic than the front. There were trees around the grounds, and off to their left was a building that looked like a garage. At the western end of the mansion was another smaller house, and Eddie remembered seeing the glow of a time bridge in that direction when they had first driven onto the property.

"The weather's no help in figuring when we came through," he said. "It feels about the same as it was the night they brought us here. Do you think?"

"I think so."

He glanced around again. "Let's look in the garage." They made their way to the building, which was clearly very old. There was a window on the side they approached from, and Eddie pressed his face against the glass. "Looks like the Lincoln," he said.

Roxanne nudged him aside and looked as well. "You're right," she said.

"So we're not very far into the future. Maybe not far at all. We have to go further. It's not safe around here yet. Come on."

He led her along the back of the house, walking briskly but carefully over the lawn and using the moonlight to help them find their way. Eddie thought he could still see a blue white glow coming from the other side of the little house that they were approaching. He hoped the next bridge they found would be facing west and would take them further.

They came to the corner of the main house and stopped, peeking around to see what was in front of them. The smaller outbuilding looked like a cottage with a front porch facing the main road. At the back of the building, which Roxanne and Eddie were facing, were two windows, each with light shining from within. From the other side of the cottage, Eddie could clearly detect a blue white glow that he knew would be a time bridge. After they had paused long enough to see there was no one around, Eddie squeezed Roxanne's hand again and nodded in the direction of the cottage. Roxanne did not question him but followed as he began walking cautiously toward it.

As they approached, Eddie could hear music coming from one of the open windows. Staying out of the light for as long as he could, he led Roxanne toward the first window. It was just below eye level as he stood before it. Knowing it was risky but at the same telling himself that he was in the future to get information, he peeked into the window with Roxanne at his side. The room was empty, but the radio playing "Fools Rush In" on the nightstand told him it probably would not be for long. Plain and with a few books scattered around, the room offered nothing concrete to indicate the occupant's personality. The blandness of it caused Eddie to guess Luna. The only things of real interest were the clothes hanging on a hook on the closed bedroom door. These included a pair of pants with the belt still in the loops, and attached by a metal clip to the belt was Luna's large ring of keys. Eddie pointed, and Roxanne, who had been standing on her toes to see in the window, looked where he indicated and nodded. "We may need those," he whispered very softly in her ear. The smell and feel of her hair on his face was a serious distraction, but he made himself pull his head away and led the way to the next window.

"Where do you suppose he is?" Roxanne whispered behind him.

Eddie stood in the space between the two windows. He turned to her, shrugged and shook his head. He had no idea but hoped that Luna was not out making rounds of the grounds. He did not want to bump into him around the corner of the cottage. He doubted Luna would be doing so without his pants, but he would nevertheless have felt much more comfortable knowing where the man was. Thinking about it, he quickly moved on to the second window, and when he peeked inside, he immediately pulled back. Hobart was in the room, lying on the bed. Eddie caught just a glimpse of him before darting away again. He paused, tried to give Roxanne a very serious look while nodding toward the window, and then brought his eyes up to it again with extreme caution. He stood stock-still and observed as Hobart lay sprawled across the bed in a sleeveless undershirt and khaki pants. His head was propped up on pillows, and he was reading a digest-sized magazine. Eddie tried to see the title, but Hobart's hands obscured it. It would not be hard to guess at the type of publication, though. The wall beside Hobart's bed was plastered with pictures of women. Many were nude or partially nude. The rest appeared scantily clad or provocatively posed. Some of the pictures looked like post cards. Others had probably been torn from magazines or books. There were also a few drawings that looked clearly pornographic although Eddie could not make out the details. He raised an eyebrow and backed away from the window. Hobart had not moved his eyes away from what he was reading.

Eddie nodded his head toward the other side of the house and the blue light that was easier to see once they were away from the glow of the windows. Roxanne carefully followed him, minding where she put her feet so as not to make a rustle and alert Hobart to the sound of prowlers. "Looks like he's a collector, too," Eddie whispered when they reached the corner of the house. Roxanne looked at him inquisitively. Eddie smiled and added, "I'll bet he's a fan of your work." Roxanne just rolled her eyes and pushed Eddie along.

Rounding the corner, another time bridge stood before them. As Eddie had hoped, it faced west. "Can you see it?" he asked her. Roxanne squinted into the darkness in the direction Eddie pointed. Finally, she nodded. "Okay," he said. "Let's go. Same as before. Me first this time, though."

Roxanne agreed and followed. Eddie stepped up onto the time bridge and felt the same odd sensation of stepping on something that was not there. He imagined how much more unsettling it must be for Roxanne, who could barely see the bridge or the base they walked on. When he stepped up and through, he was intrigued to see that this was a much longer bridge. It arced a bit higher than the other one had, and the other opening was at least fifteen feet away. He took a few steps in and looked back at Roxanne. She was following him through without hesitation, and he smiled at her once she was firmly on the bridge behind him. He reached a hand out for hers and held it as they walked single file up the arc and down to the other side.

As they approached it, Eddie saw that it was daylight beyond the bridge. This would be more risky than their previous crossing. It was good that they were not still inside the house, but there was no shelter out here, and if someone happened to be outside or looking out the windows of the main house or the cottage, it would be hard to explain materializing out of nowhere. Hoping for the best, Eddie turned to Roxanne and said, "Wait a second." She looked puzzled, and he realized she was experiencing the quirky traits of sound within the time bridge that he had noticed before, perhaps even more so with her lower dose of Dragon's Tears. Still she nodded her understanding and let go of Eddie's hand as he took the step through the opening and onto the dry ground of Swinburne's estate.

Eddie quickly glanced around, intending to make sure no one was in sight, but he stopped short once he looked in the direction of the mansion. It had been destroyed, probably years ago. All that remained were chimneys and other nonflammable portions of the construction. In the center of the desolation was what looked like a concrete bunker—Swinburne's vault. The garage was also gone. The cottage beside him was still intact, but it looked abandoned with broken windows and peeling paint. Undecipherable graffiti had been painted on the walls in large black and green letters. The ground around him was a mixture of overgrown weeds and brown, dry plants. Looking around in a full circle, Eddie saw no signs of inhabitance. The estate looked long abandoned. Turning to the time bridge behind him, he could not see Roxanne in it but knew she was waiting just beyond the opening, and now he nodded toward her and waved her forward. In a moment, he watched as she appeared before him, starting as a faded, transparent blur that made him think he should rub his eyes, and then she grew solid and real.

She, too, looked around and instantly said, "Oh my God." Eddie just nodded and let her take in the devastation. "What do you think happened?" she asked after a moment.

"Probably a fire," he said. "And probably a long time ago. There's not much left. Come on." He took her hand again after she had buttoned her coat. It was mid-afternoon based on the sun's position, but it was quite cool outside.

"You don't think it was the war, do you?" Roxanne asked a bit nervously.

"The war in Europe?"

"Mm-hmm," she said as they made their way through the rubble toward the vault.

Eddie thought about it and then said, "It could be. But I doubt it. Your father told me not much had changed in the future. He mentioned wars, but I think if there had been this kind of destruction in the states, he wouldn't have been so casual about the future."

They heard a rustling noise to their left, and Eddie saw a rabbit scurry through the brush, disappearing behind the cottage. Roxanne said, "How far do you think we came?"

Eddie shook his head. The vault was just ahead, and beside it was another time bridge opening, probably the same one Blackwood had stepped through in 1940 to take him who knew where. "No way to know. It could be 1945. It could be 1990. Your father said fifty years was about the limit for the bridges in either direction." He had been eyeing the nearby time bridge and now stopped walking, taking both her hands, facing her and saying very clearly, "Here's the thing we have to remember. Your father said traveling in these things was like a maze to get to the time you wanted. We can go in and out from past to present and back again. The trick to getting back to where we belong is in retracing our steps exactly. So we have to go back through that time bridge." He turned, and she turned with him. The bridge they had come through was now fifty yards away but clearly visible to Eddie even in the daylight. "And then back into the house and through the first one we came through. Otherwise, we're going to end up who knows where."

"Or when." She gave his hand a squeeze. "Don't worry. I have no intention of getting lost. Are there others around here?" Eddie nodded toward the bridge they were approaching, but Roxanne gave no indication of being able to make it out. "Do you see just the one entrance, or both sides?" she asked.

"Just one. Why?"

"I was just thinking. If these things are always here, and you enter one side from the east in 1940 and go into the past and come out the other side, say five years earlier, then when you turn around and look at it, it's facing west and takes you back the same distance into the future. Right?"

"Right."

"So if the bridges are a constant, then the east facing side should be there in 1935, too. What's to stop you from being in the past, finding the same east facing entrance you just walked through and looping back further and further five years at a time into the past?"

"Sort of like a revolving door for time travel?"

"Mm-hmm."

He looked around. There were other bridges in the distance, but they were difficult to make out even in the dim light of a cloudy day. Still, there were none that he could have looked at and said with certainty were entrances into the same bridge he was looking at. If the bridges worked the way Roxanne said, then all a time traveler needed to do would be to determine the length of time a bridge spanned and then continue entering and exiting it until arriving at the desired time. Knowing this, Chester Blackwood would not have had as much difficulty returning to his proper time after getting lost in the maze. If it would have been possible, Eddie was sure, Blackwood would have done it.

He shook his head. "It's not there," he said. "You're right, though. It makes sense that you should be able to see both sides. But then again, your father did tell me he didn't really know how to use the Dragon's Tears. Maybe at one drop, you get limited perception. Maybe you're supposed to drink the whole vial or inject it or God knows what. As it is . . ." He shrugged. "It's all gone, and all we have to go on is what he told me and what we can see right now."

They had been approaching the vault from the back side and now circled around to the front. The door was gone, but the rest of it was intact, a testament, Eddie supposed, to how well Swinburne had built it to protect his precious collection. With no windows and the concrete ceiling still in place, there was no light inside save what daylight came through the open doorway. Again, Roxanne's Zippo came in handy as she flicked it on and the two stepped inside. They were not the first visitors. Trash was strewn around the floor, and there was a mattress in one corner. It would be a good place for squatters to stay when the weather was not too cold. There was no sign of bookshelves or filing cabinets or any of the other things they had seen in the vault in 1940. All signs of Swinburne were gone. Eddie felt extremely uncomfortable standing here, and based on Roxanne's seeming hesitation to explore any further, he assumed the feeling was mutual.

"Let's get out of here," Eddie said. Roxanne did not need to be convinced. As they turned and walked out again, they were facing the front of what had been the estate. The wall and gate stood about fifty yards in front of them, and beyond that the road Luna had driven them along. Eddie noticed something through the gate and said, "Come here a minute." They walked quickly away from the vault, glad to be away from it, and toward the gate. The closer they got, the slower Roxanne seemed to walk until Eddie was practically an arm's length ahead of her, seeming to pull her along. Clearly, they had seen the same thing, and he guessed that she did not want to get a better look. Still, she did not let go of his hand, and he led her to the gate.

"There's your blighted land," Eddie said when they reached it. A chill breeze blew up sharply from behind them, giving them both goose pimples as they stood before the gate.

"Jesus," Roxanne said quietly.

Beyond the gate and across the road was a sharp drop off the hillside. With no houses to block the view, they could see Hollywood and Los Angeles spread out before them much as they had the day before from Mount Wilson. Now, they were not so high up. Also, the city had changed. It spread out immensely in a haze of gray and white with huge buildings cropping up across the city and tremendous highways crisscrossing it. Where before there had been large greenbelts breaking up the urban landscape, now there was nothing but buildings and roads. The sky along the horizon was also an unnatural shade of brown. Even the small slice of the cityscape they were able to see through the gate gave them a sense of enormity, as though the city went on forever in a completely boundless, characterless way.

"I think it's been a few years," Eddie said, awestruck.

Roxanne was silent. He looked at her and saw that her face had grown pale.

"You okay?" he asked.

She nodded slowly but then said, "Don't you get the feeling we're not supposed to be seeing this?"

"I hadn't thought about it like that. Not yet."

"I mean, if it's 1980, then I might be down there somewhere. And I'm 65. I can't be seeing this. I can't be up here, too."

"Okay," he said, trying to be soothing. He saw that their situation genuinely disturbed her and found it strange that he was not bothered. Perhaps it was the Dragon's Tears, or maybe there was some other quality in him, something Blackwood had spotted, something they shared that made dabbling in time travel seem more an intriguing curiosity than a thing of great weight, as it clearly was for Roxanne. He took her by the hand again and led her away from the gate. Once her back was turned on it, her mood seemed to ease a bit, but she remained quiet as they walked.

He took her back to the cottage. Here, too, the door was missing, and others had been inside since the time of the estate's abandonment. There was more trash and writing on the interior walls. None of it was readable. Eddie wondered if it was a different alphabet that had developed over time or if there had been some influx of immigrants who had brought a new way of writing. He kept reminding himself, though, of Blackwood's words about very little having changed in fifty years. He found comfort in the thought and tried to chase away the nagging memory of Roxanne's warning about her father's propensity for lying.

The cottage was laid out simply with a main room at the front of the house, a small kitchen and bathroom to the left, and the two bedrooms at the back. There was some smashed furniture in the house, but no more kitchen appliances. The tub, toilet and sinks had been removed. Eddie was surprised the place had not been demolished or burned down on its own over the years. In the bedroom that had been Luna's, Eddie found a plastic box that resembled a wooden milk crate. For all he knew, milk crates were now made of plastic. At any rate, it was something to sit on. He turned it over and shoved it against the wall beside the window where, one night many years before, he and Roxanne had peaked in to see Luna's pants hanging from a hook on the door.

"Okay," he said. "I know you're not going to like this, but I need to leave you here for a bit." Roxanne had been looking at the milk crate and the litter that surrounded it. Now she jerked her head up, a look of stunned fear in her eyes as she met Eddie's gaze. "Look. It's the middle of the day. I'm not going to be gone for long. You'll be fine here at least until dusk. I'd have you come with me, but I don't think you want to go down there." He nodded toward the gate and the view of the city they had just left.

"You're right," she said.

"Besides, I have a job for you. I need you to sit here and read that book. As much of it as you can between now and the time I get back."

She nodded slowly, resignedly, and Eddie was relieved that she had dropped her adamant position about not wanting to know what was in the book. He guessed that the shock she was experiencing at having traveled through time and seeing the future had mitigated any untoward feelings she had about reading a book about science fiction stories that would now never be written. "What do you need me to look for in it?" she asked.

Eddie smiled at her. "I need you to find out if there's anything in it, anything at all, that you think Swinburne shouldn't know. Anything you think he might be able to take and use and maybe mess things up even more. Anything political or cultural. The science fiction stuff . . . I don't think that can be damaged any more than what your father's already done to it."

He watched her face as she thought about it. Finally, she nodded her head. "So you think we'll need to give it to Swinburne?"

"Probably. I want to be sure it's not a mistake."

"Okay. But where are you going?" she asked.

"Down into Hollywood. I need to find out what happens to me, what your father knew about me that this book told him. He tore a page out that had something to do with me. If I can figure out what he knew, I'll know how to play it with Swinburne." He paused and looked at his watch. In their own time, it was close to four in the morning. The bank would open at ten, and he guessed that Swinburne would want to leave for the bank by nine. Eddie wanted to make sure they were back in their room by eight at the latest. "Now look. If something happens to me and I'm gone more than three and a half hours, just walk outside and through the time bridge. Do you think you can find it on your own, or should I go outside and mark it?"

"I can find it. Now that I know what I'm looking for."

"Good. Go back in the house, cross over the next bridge, and you'll be back in the room where you're supposed to be. Tell them you fell asleep and I was gone. Give them the book. Say you just found it in the room when I disappeared. Hobart will get canned and Swinburne will leave you alone. He'll have to."

183

Roxanne nodded.

"Do you have any money?" he asked, knowing he only had twelve dollars and some change. He was not planning on needing money, but he also had no real idea of what he would find, and any resource was better than nothing. He did not know if 1940 currency was still good or not in the city below, but in case it was, it would not hurt to have as much with him as possible.

Roxanne opened her purse and dug out *The Golden Age of Science Fiction* and her wallet, from which she pulled two twenty dollar bills. She handed them to Eddie, and he thanked her. "I'll get these back to you with interest," he said, winking. She smiled back at him and said, "I'll hold you to that."

"Hang on a second," Eddie said as he slipped the bills into his wallet. He turned and went back into the main room. Among the debris was a broken dining chair, just the seat and two legs still attached. Eddie flipped it over so the legs stuck up in the air. With his foot on the seat, he pulled on the leg, twisting it a bit until it broke free. He brought it back to Roxanne. "Here. If anyone but me comes in here, go out the window and through the time bridge. Don't try to hide and wait for me. Use this if you have to."

"All right, Eddie." She sounded more confident now, no longer shaken by the sight of future Los Angeles or their situation. Eddie found her strength arousing. Once again, she was the same Roxanne who had stood up to Swinburne and Whistler and struggled with Hobart. He put his arms around her and kissed her hard. With the Dragon's Tears in his system, Eddie could feel Roxanne's heart beating against his and her blood pulsing through her lips and tongue; her breath against his cheek felt like fire. Her arms wrapped around his back and her hand went up his neck just as it had done the day before outside the observatory. He held her close and felt the contours of her body against his with an intensity and completeness he had never known. Pulling his lips away from hers and stepping out of her embrace was one of the hardest things Eddie had ever done, and as he did he saw real regret on her face. It was not that she was about to be left alone, he realized, but that they would not be together for the next couple of hours. The look on her face was enough to draw him back to her, to make him forget all about Swinburne and Hobart and the fact that they were probably forty years away from where they should be. Still, he knew he could not forget any of those things if they wanted to return to anything like a normal life.

After they whispered their goodbyes, Eddie turned and walked out of the house and jogged across the estate to the gate. When he got there, he looked back at the cottage. There was no sign of Roxanne, no sign of anyone having been there, which was what he wanted. He doubted that there was just one person who had been using the house and the vault as a place to hide or get shelter; rather it was more likely a succession of people at different times over the years. He wondered if there were still problems with itinerants as there had been in Los Angeles with the Okies in his own time. If so, the abandoned buildings would make a tempting sight for someone passing by on the road looking for a place to sleep, and even more so if the passerby knew there was a beautiful woman waiting inside the old house. It was unlikely, though, that the Hollywood Hills would be a common place for transients seeking shelter. Even so, Eddie wanted to get back here quickly. Splitting up was awfully risky.

CHAPTER FOURTEEN

Eddie leaped onto the gate and pulled himself up to its top, looking in both directions before climbing over and hopping down. He remembered that Luna had driven them in from the east, so that was the direction he went in, continuing to jog for as far as his lungs could stand it. The cold air and his lack of exercise made the effort a strain, but he was determined to move as quickly as he could. The road followed a ridge, and there were a few other estates along it before it began to wind down into the hills again. The houses were immense along the ridge, but as the road curved down there began to be a mixture of older homes, some quite modest, squeezed into the hillside with larger dwellings that spread upward and into the slope rather than outward as Swinburne's home had done. Eddie did not stop to gawk but kept moving at a quick pace, choosing every road that turned downward in the direction of Sunset Boulevard. At the first intersection he had come to, he paid careful attention to the two names on the street sign so he could find his way back to Swinburne's estate later. He did not know if he was taking the quickest route down the hill, but he was reasonably sure that if he kept to his pattern, he would emerge on level ground again eventually.

Some cars passed him as he swiftly walked down the hill, and he avoided looking at the drivers lest he draw attention to himself through eye contact. He could not help noticing the cars, though. The shape had changed radically. Gone were large fenders and running boards. The cars were generally lower now, sleeker, and they were painted a variety of bright colors. Some were extremely small with only front seats, and Eddie had to wonder if they were some type of toy for the wealthy. As he got lower down the hill, he also noticed a smell that permeated the area. It reminded him of auto exhaust but fainter, and Eddie assumed it was the by-product of so many cars and so many people. He wondered what the population of Los Angeles was now and how many of the people owned cars.

After more than thirty minutes of rapid downhill walking, he came out of the twisting maze of houses and car-lined streets to a straight road that went down the remainder of the hill into a nest of tall buildings. Eddie had passed at least a dozen time bridges on his way down the hill, some in the roads, some in people's yards, some half in and half out of walls. Blackwood had been right about Hollywood being full of holes in time; Eddie wondered where they all went and saw the temptation that Blackwood must have felt to explore opening after opening.

Once he reached Sunset Boulevard, he turned east, walking toward the heart of Hollywood. While he had been the only pedestrian coming down from the hills, he was now one of many others moving on foot along the sidewalk, and he had to make a conscious effort not to stare at some of them. Men generally dressed in denim pants and tennis shoes, which struck Eddie as an odd combination since denim generally was not associated with tennis. Furthermore, he did not see it as possible that so many people would be out for a day of tennis and end up in Hollywood. As Blackwood had told him, most of the men and some of the women wore undershirts with nothing else over them, and they seemed completely without self-consciousness in doing so. And most of the shirts did have slogans or pictures on them. Eddie tried to read a few of them as men walked toward him, but then he caught their eyes and saw that they did not appreciate the obvious scrutiny, so he stopped.

Women, on the other hand, were less predictable. Some also wore denim and undershirts, but others wore skirts or dresses, and the skirts were quite short. Their blouses were also often incredibly low cut. He began to see women who were wearing what looked like lingerie on the outside of their clothes—with dresses or pants covered with a layer of lace. Some wore flimsy lace gloves that looked like they did nothing to keep their hands warm. Many of them had bare legs even in the cold. And their hair was oddly different. Some had hair that seemed to sprout from their heads like spikes. Others had long, straight hair, and still others had their hair teased and piled high on their heads in stiff waves and curls that framed their faces. Regardless of the style, though, he saw women with unnatural colors—purples and bright reds, jet black that obviously came out of a bottle. He could not understand any of it.

After another half hour's walking, he was on Hollywood Boulevard. He stopped for a moment and looked east then west, trying to take it all in. The street was a bustle of pedestrians and traffic, and he immediately knew what time of year it was. Green plastic garland decorated every light pole, and arched across the street at regular intervals were banners and other decorations reading "Merry Christmas." Everyone carried packages and bags and walked slowly, looking in shop windows. From each open door he passed came the sounds of Christmas music. Some of the songs Eddie recognized, though not the versions being played. Most were new to him, though, as was everything else around him.

The people were remarkably different. Eddie had been used to seeing Mexicans and Asians and Negroes in Los Angeles, but always in the Mexican and Asian and Negro parts of town. Here, they were all intermingled, and no one seemed to notice or find anything odd about it. There were no doubt some tourists in the crowd of people who made their way along the boulevard, but Eddie doubted that everyone here was from elsewhere since so few people seemed to be gawking at the scenery or taken aback by the signs, some of which read "Peep Show" or "Live Nudes." Nor did many people stop to read the names on the gold stars along the sidewalk. Eddie recognized a few of the names but not many, and he had to stop looking eventually because he kept having near collisions with people who seemed quite used to the spectacle. If most of these people were locals, then, Hollywood had certainly changed. At least he did not have to worry about not fitting in since there seemed to be no single standard of fashion or behavior.

Sounds were also different. The noise of the cars and buses that ran up and down the street, music that blared from the stores he passed or the enormous radios that some people carried, and just the voices of the people as they walked and talked along the sidewalks all added up to a nearly deafening cacophony. Eddie had to wonder how much of this was caused by his heightened sensitivity from the Dragon's Tears and how much of it was actual terrible noise. He was glad Roxanne had stayed above in the hills. If the sight of the sprawling city had bothered her so much, being down in it would have been far worse.

After walking for a block and trying to get his bearings, Eddie decided that he had better move quickly and decisively if he was going to get the information he needed and get back to Roxanne in time. He walked into a shop with a sign that read "Hollywood Souvenirs and Novelties," guessing that it would be the kind of store frequented by tourists asking questions. He was a bit surprised to see that the woman behind the counter was Asian, maybe Chinese. In 1940, it would have been unusual to find her working outside of Chinatown. Now, however, there seemed to be nothing abnormal about her presence here in Hollywood. No one gawked or made rude comments, and the woman behind the counter appeared entirely lacking in self-consciousness about her ethnicity or employment.

Eddie could not get over the assault to his senses that the store confronted him with. Light came from tubes in the ceiling and was so bright that it illuminated everything in shocking detail and seemed to leave no shadows. Everything in the store was incredibly vivid and brightly colored.

Loud music came from a hidden source, as Eddie saw no radio or speakers anywhere in the store. The song being played had something to do with there being no Christmas in Africa and the need to feed the world. Miniature Oscar statuettes littered the counter along with myriad dolls, most likely caricatures of famous actors and actresses. Eddie picked up one of the Oscars, expecting it to be heavy, and was shocked to find it weighed only a few ounces. He puzzled over how the bronze could be so light and then put the statue back on the shelf. On the large, gaudy posters that lined the walls, he recognized Chaplin and Cagney and a few other actors he had seen recently—Humphrey Something and a much older version of the cowboy actor Eddie had seen in *Stagecoach*. Most of the other pictures were of a buxom blonde and an aloof looking young man in a red jacket. Racks of clothing, mostly undershirts with slogans and pictures on them, filled the rest of the store. Eddie wondered how the place stayed in business selling such junk.

"Excuse me," he asked the woman behind the counter. "Can you tell me where there is a book store or a library near here?" He spoke haltingly, not because the woman was Chinese but because he was worried that his own voice, his 1940 way of speaking, would mark him as odd or different in some way.

The woman seemed unfazed by Eddie's voice or anything else about him. She appeared to think about the question for a moment and then said in a voice completely without accent, "No libraries that I know of. But I think there's a bookstore down that way a few blocks." She pointed in the direction Eddie had been walking. He thanked her and went back to the street.

Outside, he saw a newspaper rack and bent to look at the issue of the *Los Angeles Times* displayed in front. The date read December 14, 1985. Eddie had known that he and Roxanne had traveled far in time, but now he felt awe and a bit of fear to know they had gone forty-five years. He also felt glad that he had come far enough to be able to get the information he needed.

Not far from Hollywood Souvenirs and Novelties, Eddie passed a storefront window that caught his eye. The sign above the door read "Hollywood Coin and Pawn." Below that, painted on the window amidst portrayals of reindeer and elves were messages about jewelry, TVs, guitars, guns and other items. Eddie had been drawn to the display in the window, though, by several coins laid out on black velvet, among which he saw a number of buffalo nickels and mercury dimes similar to the change he had in his pocket. Thinking about the watch Blackwood had pawned somewhere in the future, he tried to walk into the store, but the door was locked. A second after he tried it, he heard a buzz and a click coming from the door. Confused, he tried the door again, and this time it opened. Inside, he found a fat, balding man with a cigar who looked up from behind a newspaper and gruffly said, "Afternoon."

Eddie returned the greeting and got right to the point. "Those coins in the window," he said, reaching into his pocket. "I was wondering what you'd be able to give me for these." He spilled about a dollar in change onto the counter and watched as the man folded his newspaper and chewed his cigar, his eyes intently on the coins. He was trying, Eddie saw, not to betray any real interest, but the way he carefully began to examine each one revealed that a cache like this did not come his way every day. He made rows of quarters, dimes, nickels and pennies.

"These," he said, indicating the pennies, "not much. But the rest I'll give ya five bucks for."

"Okay," Eddie said, reaching for his wallet. "What about this?" He pulled one of Roxanne's twenty-dollar bills out and laid it on the glass countertop. As he did, he noted that it was dated 1928.

"That's a different story," the pawnshop owner said. "Not mint condition, but not bad. Thirty bucks."

Eddie decided he would push his luck. "That's all?" he asked.

The pawnbroker twirled the cigar around between his lips and gave Eddie a look of disgust. "Look," he said, "I got an overhead here. If I want to sell it, I got to make a profit here. You want top dollar, go to a coin show. I'll give ya thirty-three and that's it. Ya got more like that, we can work out a different deal."

With a smile on his face, Eddie left the pawnshop. He had walked in with fifty-two dollars and change and walked out with a hundred. Roxanne would have her interest and more unless he needed to spend it all on information. About ten minutes later, having walked three or four blocks and passed numerous people and businesses that frankly shocked him, Eddie walked past a storefront window with a display of books. He looked up and saw "Book World—Used and New" written high up on the glass in chipped red letters. Immediately, he walked in.

The smell of the bookstore greeted him and his heightened senses. The smell of paper, some of it slightly mildewed, made it like walking into his own apartment, and he loved it. He saw at once that if this store did not have what he was looking for, he would be hard pressed to find his information elsewhere. Shelves ran from floor to ceiling and from the front of the store to the back. Rolling ladders like the ones he had seen in Swinburne's vault could be found around the store to provide access to upper shelves. There was also a stairway with a hand painted sign on the wall that read "More Books" with an arrow pointing up. On the sides of the shelves and scattered around the store, someone had placed numerous bright yellow pieces of paper with little admonishments written on them. They said things like "This is not a research library. If you're going to read the book, please buy it first" and "Don't pull books from the shelves and put them back in the wrong places. You will be asked to leave." *Not very friendly*, Eddie thought, but then again perhaps bookstore patrons had gained a reputation for being ruffians or slobs or cheapskates in the years since 1940. Still, the gruff sounding signs contradicted the good cheer of the Christmas music that played throughout the store.

"Can I help you?" came a voice from behind the counter at the front of the store. Eddie had been standing just inside the entrance, staring at the inventory. Now he turned and saw a tall, thin man of about fifty wearing an undershirt with the store's name on it. Behind the counter, bookcases with glass doors housed shelves of books all facing Eddie. In front of him, the counter was made up of a glass display case. Eddie stared as he approached, stunned to see images of Roxanne throughout the case and on the shelves. Dozens of issues of *Stupendous* and other pulps from the twenties, thirties and forties were displayed on small stands, each issue encased in plastic and with small tags listing their dates and the price of each issue. "Can I help you?" the bookstore employee repeated, sounding a bit annoyed this time.

Startled out of his reverie, Eddie said, "Yes. I'm sorry. I just . . . I just haven't seen magazines like these in . . . a long time."

The man smiled. "Yeah. We have a pretty good collection here."

Eddie stood before the case and looked down at the magazines. The March 1935 issue of *Stupendous* had a price tag of $35 and featured a shrieking Roxanne being carried by a menacing robot toward a waiting spaceship. She was dressed in a costume with a plunging neckline and hems slit to her thighs. Eddie could not believe it. The magazine had cost 25 cents in 1935. "Do you sell a lot of these? Is there a market?"

"Oh yeah, especially for those Frehling covers," the man said, leaning on the counter so his face was inches from Eddie's and seeing which magazine Eddie was looking at. "You interested?"

"No. Not right now, thanks. I'm looking for a copy of *The Golden Age of Science Fiction, 1938-1945* by Marion Rigby. Do you have a copy?"

The man thought about it for a moment, as though he were going over the store's inventory in his mind. "Rigby, huh?" He looked puzzled. "Never heard of her. Do you know when it was published?"

"1978."

He pulled a large book out from under the counter. Eddie saw that it was called *Books in Print*. The man flipped through, ran an index finger down a page and said, "Nope. No such animal." He put the book away and then grabbed another. "This is for out of print," he said, turning pages rapidly. When he got to the page where the book should have been listed, he stopped, scanned it carefully and then snapped the book shut dramatically. He looked up at Eddie and said, "You sure you got the title right?"

Eddie wanted to say yes but hesitated. There was no sense in pushing the issue. Blackwood had changed the future and Rigby had not written her book. Wherever Marion Rigby was and whatever she was doing, she had probably not become interested in writing about science fiction because of the ways Blackwood had changed the genre. Eddie was disappointed. He had been counting on being able to read the missing page torn out by Blackwood in order to know how best to deal with Swinburne when he got back to 1940. Now he did not know what to do. He turned to look at the immense collection of books on the shelves that spread throughout the store and decided that the information he was looking for had to be somewhere in front of him. If not in Rigby's no longer extant book, then he could surely find it between the covers of a different one. Although tempted to go to the History section, Eddie knew he would only be drawn into books that gave him information about what had happened in the forty-five years he had skipped over, so he asked where the science fiction section was instead.

Eddie found it very interesting that the books on the shelves were not what he had expected. Instead of the hardcover books with cloth bindings and dust jackets he was used to finding in book stores, the majority of books here were small enough to fit in his back pocket and had covers made of paper only slightly thicker than the pages inside. He had seen some books in the stores like this and remembered them being called paperbacks, but they were unusual in 1940. Still, they were convenient and economical, and they must have caught on, especially with the science fiction reading public if this one row of shelves was any evidence. Eddie stood in what felt like a long cavern of books reaching to the back of the store and almost to the ceiling. The shelves above eight feet or so were labeled as overstock, so he did not pay much attention to them. Instead, he started with the shelves in front of him, noting thankfully that they were neatly alphabetized by author.

In the V section, he found books by van Vogt but noticed that none of them had copyright dates before 1940. They did span a long period of time, though, stretching up to what would be quite contemporary books in 1985. Good, thought Eddie. If Blackwood had done damage to van Vogt's early career, at least the other writer had been able to recover and begin publishing after what Marion Rigby had called the Golden Age. Eddie found the same in the S section when he came to Sturgeon. There were volumes of books, mostly short story collections, but nothing with copyright dates before 1940.

Eddie moved on to the R section and felt a tingle all over his body when he found books by Edward Royce. There were four of them, all paperbacks, and all with the same title. "Son of a bitch," he whispered. The books all bore the title, *The Blighted Land*. Eddie hesitated to pull one off the shelf. Seeing his name on the spine of a book had been a fantasy of his since he had been twelve years old, and now that the fantasy was being realized—with the help of time travel, of all things—it was not at all what he wanted to see. *What rotten thing did I do*, he thought, *to get my name on the cover of Roxanne's book?* Maybe he had just stolen the title. But what if he had stolen the actual idea, or worse? He thought about his borrowing from Shakespeare to get published in *Stupendous* and the things Blackwood had stolen from Heinlein and the others.

He thought about how Blackwood had insisted he and Eddie were the same. Had Blackwood known that Eddie would steal Roxanne's book? *But I wouldn't do it*, Eddie thought. *I won't.*

Taking a deep breath, he drew one of the copies of *The Blighted Land* from the shelf and looked at the back cover. The synopsis of the plot read just as Roxanne had described her idea for the book earlier this evening as they had lain naked in Eddie's bed: "In this masterpiece of science fiction, the world as we know it is gone, destroyed by war and a plague that the war has fostered. A small band of survivors leaves behind all they know, traveling across the ruins of America in hope of finding a place to call home, free of the new terrors that roam the land in the wake of violence and destruction." The cover was black and white with the silhouettes of four people shown walking toward a rising or setting sun with the title and Eddie's name written in large letters above. He could not believe it.

Opening the book to the first page, he began to read and instantly knew he had not written a word of it:

> The throbbing pain in her wrist awoke Karen Ragsdale, drawing her up from a deep, dreamless sleep. Disoriented, she rubbed at her wrist, her eyes still closed, and then bolted upright when she felt a foreign object protruding from her skin. In a panic, she plucked at a plastic tube inserted into one of her veins, pulling it out with a sudden spurt of blood before even thinking about it. She gasped and held her other hand tightly to the wound to stop the bleeding and then looked around, frantically trying to take in her surroundings as she screamed for help, her voice coming back to her in eerie echoes. Moments later, blood still dripping between her fingers and her chest still heaving in short breaths, she came to the simultaneous realizations that she was in a darkened hospital room and that she was completely, utterly alone. Aside from the lingering echo of her screams in her own ears, she was in the most remote, devastating and unforgiving silence she had ever known in her twenty-two years. Her mounting terror grew more from her utter isolation than from the question of how and why she had woken up in a hospital bed after never having been sick a day in her life.

Eddie closed the book, telling himself that the hack who had had the nerve to recast *Hamlet* as a space opera could never have approached writing like this. It was clear that it was not merely Roxanne's title on this book with his name on it, nor was it just her ideas inside, but rather it was Roxanne's writing altogether. It made the apparent theft that much worse.

Completely baffled, Eddie turned to the copyright page. The first thing he noticed was that there was a long list of printings and that the version of the book he held in his hands had been issued in 1978. It was the forty-third printing, which stunned him. For the first time, he wondered where the other version of Eddie Royce was in this future that he had stumbled into and how much money he had made off of forty-three printings of this book. The thought was almost enough to make him forget that the money had essentially been stolen from Roxanne—almost enough, but not quite. Above the list of printings, the copyright information stated that a serialized version of the book had appeared in *Stupendous* in 1944 followed by a Meteor Press edition in 1945. Subsequent printings were listed only by date, not press, so Eddie could not tell if Swinburne's company still retained control of the publishing. This current edition was published by a company called Avon, which Eddie had never heard of.

So far, this had not helped him much. Rather, it had only made him more confused. He quickly flipped to the back of the book and found a short About the Author paragraph on the last page. "Little is known about Edward Royce," it read, "who rose out of obscurity to produce a single, remarkable novel, *The Blighted Land*, published posthumously in 1945. A native of Iowa, Royce wrote short stories in Los Angeles and Hollywood during science fiction's Golden Age and died mysteriously in 1944. Avon has also made available *The Collected Stories of Edward Royce*." When Eddie saw the word "posthumously," he felt the blood drain out of his face, and a wave of nausea overcame him. "What the hell," he whispered.

He looked at the other copies of *The Blighted Land* on the shelf. All were from the 1970s, all published by Avon, and all included the same information about him, nothing more. He had been squatting as he looked at the books, as the shelf containing them was level with his knees. Now he stood up and almost lost his balance, the circulation in his legs having been cut off. He steadied himself against the shelves, glanced around to be sure no one had noticed, and then he moved on, taking one copy of *The Blighted Land* with him. He wanted to see if there were any books by Roxanne on the shelves, but as he walked there was a steady ringing in his ears, and he could not get out of his head the idea that he would be dead in less than five years. He wondered if this was what Blackwood had known from the missing page of Rigby's book.

In the B section, Eddie found all of Blackwood's books in various formats and editions: *Nelphi, Empire, If This Goes On*, his *Robot* series, collections of short stories, and all the other books Eddie had copies of on his shelves at home. Some were cheap editions from the 1960s, and others looked more recent and classier in their artwork and design. The books that had blurbs about the author simply praised Blackwood as a giant of science fiction who shaped the genre for decades after his death, but none of the blurbs mentioned when or how he died. Eddie supposed that it might be common knowledge with an author as popular and acclaimed as Blackwood. Still, he would have liked to know what the official line was on Blackwood's disappearance.

There were no books by Roxanne Blackwood, and Eddie also thought to check for Archie Dumont, but there was nothing there either. Eddie had no way of knowing whether it was because Roxanne's Dumont stories were doomed to obscurity and never reprinted beyond the pages of *Stupendous* or because something else Blackwood had done to change the future had made Roxanne's literary output disappear. All he knew for sure was that Roxanne had written her book and that Swinburne had published it, but for some reason the book and the fame had been stolen away from her and given to Eddie, who was talentless in comparison, he saw now.

Eddie took his copy of *The Blighted Land* back to the counter and set it down next to the register. The same clerk who had helped him before picked up the book and said, "Third one this week. We can't keep this thing in stock these days. It's like it was Vietnam again or something, so many people are reading it."

Eddie had no idea what that meant and so kept silent. He just nodded, hoping he would not appear too idiotic.

The clerk continued talking as he rang up the sale. "That's when I first read it. Big in the peace movement. Everybody talking about it. Strange for a book that old to have this kind of staying power. Kinda like *1984*, I guess. Two dollars and twelve cents with tax."

Eddie handed him a ten-dollar bill he had gotten from the pawnshop and looked up at the shelves behind the counter as the store employee opened the register and began counting out Eddie's change. On a shelf directly in front of him were familiar copies of Blackwood's books. These were the hardcover, dust-jacketed books he was used to, all Meteor editions just like the ones he had in his apartment. Also on the shelves were other books with titles he had never heard of and from publishers like Gnome Press, Fantasy Press, and Prime Press. Eddie thought about Blackwood walking into a store like this when he had first begun his foray into time travel. It may have been the very store where he had bought his copy of *The Golden Age* in another future that no longer existed. If Blackwood had stood where Eddie was now, there would have been no Blackwoods on the shelf, maybe even nothing from Meteor. There certainly would have been more Heinlein and Asimov and van Vogt than there was now.

Looking at the shelf, at the other old books published after Eddie was supposed to die, he realized that he could do the same thing Blackwood had done. He could buy up books from the mid and late forties and get them published under his own name before their authors had a chance to even think of the plots. He could change his future. And this, he realized, was what Blackwood had wanted—not necessarily for Eddie to do it, but rather for him to have the choice, for him to face the certainty of his impending death and decide whether to let it come or to change the future. Blackwood had shown that the future could be changed, and now Eddie was determined to do the same. However, he was not content to accept the idea that following in Blackwood's steps and stealing from the future was the only way out. The distaste he felt at his seeming culpability in Roxanne's book being published under his name made him balk at the idea of stealing anyone else's work, be it Roxanne, Heinlein or Shakespeare.

"Do you know what happened to him?" Eddie asked as he received his change.

"Royce?" the bookstore worker said, picking up the copy of *The Blighted Land* for a moment and then setting it down and sliding it across the counter to Eddie. "Wasn't he the one . . . yeah, he was the one who went off the road up on Mulholland. Took 'em like four months or something to find his body." Eddie shuddered inside, hoping he was not betraying the horror and revulsion he was feeling. "I think the book came out when he was still a missing person, so it was kind of controversial till everything got sewn up."

If Roxanne had been bothered at the idea of being in two places at once, of being twenty-five in the Hollywood Hills while her normally aged self roamed the city below, Eddie had her beaten. With a bit of investigation, he should have no problem finding the local cemetery where his body had been buried forty years ago. Perhaps it was even a few blocks away in the

Hollywood cemetery, keeping company with Valentino and Fairbanks. Again, he shuddered at the thought.

Eddie thanked the clerk and then nodded toward the copies of Blackwood's books. "How much do those go for? The Blackwoods?"

The clerk turned and looked at the row of books. "You've got good taste, man. They range, depending on condition, I'd say between one and five hundred. We've got a pretty nice collection of them here."

"Are they first editions?"

The clerk scoffed. "You shittin' me? Firsts are pretty much impossible to come by. Collectors have had those hoarded up for a long time now. These are all just early reprints."

"What would a first edition go for?" Eddie asked.

The clerk shook his head and said, "Easily three hundred to a thousand, depending."

"And if it were signed?"

Now the clerk just stared. "Why?" he said, after a moment's pause. "Do you have one?"

Eddie was not expecting the question. He was afraid that if he appeared to know more about the books than the clerk, the other man would stop offering information. He hesitated and then said, "I think I know someone who does."

The clerk shook his head again and smiled at the thought. "I don't know, man. I mean, I remember hearing about an auction maybe five years ago where there was one, and that went for something like three thousand, so who knows? From what I've read, Blackwood was a real son of a bitch to his fans, so he didn't hardly sign anything."

Eddie was picturing the row of books on his shelf at home almost identical to the shelf he looked at now, only every one of his was a first edition and, as of two nights ago, all were inscribed and signed by Chester

Blackwood. There was one book before him, though, among all the other Blackwood books that was not on his shelf at home, and it stood out from the others. Eddie had not noticed it before because he had been so busy looking at the old books by other authors, the Blackwood books being so familiar to him. "What's *Master of the Future?*" he asked now, pointing at the last book in the row. It looked different from the other books and appeared not to have been published by Meteor.

The clerk turned and opened the glass doors, slipping the book out from its space. "Biography of Blackwood. The first one that got published back in the sixties. Very rare in hardcover."

"Can I see it?"

The clerk held the book as though he were afraid Eddie would do something bad to it. "You interested in buying it? It's like eighty bucks."

"No," Eddie said. "I just want to look at it for a minute."

The clerk smiled, clearly satisfied with himself before saying, "Haven't you seen the signs? This ain't a library."

Exasperated, Eddie set his copy of *The Blighted Land* on the countertop and said, "I understand. I just need to get a little information out of that book. Would it be worth another twenty to you?"

The clerk's smile faded. He glanced left and right quickly, then handed the book to Eddie. "Don't leave the counter. And don't make it obvious that you're reading. Just check the condition."

Eddie nodded and slipped a twenty to the clerk. Then he took the book. A plastic cover protected the dust jacket, which had a picture of Blackwood on it from several years before Eddie had met him. It was clearly a publicity photo, a close-up of Blackwood wearing a fedora and looking serious and slightly to the left of the camera. Eddie quickly turned to the index and scanned a finger down the list of alphabetized subjects. There was one listing for Edward Royce on page 410, almost the end of the book. Eddie turned to the page and skimmed quickly to find his name. It stood out to him, following the words "implicated in the death of." He tried to read backwards up the page but got confused and made himself stop. He needed to understand all of this. After looking up at the ceiling and taking a breath, he made himself start reading on page 409, paying no attention to the clerk's glare.

The book read,

> The mystery of Blackwood's disappearance was solved on March 22, 1940 with the discovery of his Packard parked along an access road to the Lake Hollywood Dam. A suicide note left on the front seat referred to his despondency over the stomach cancer that had been diagnosed the month before. Blackwood apologized to his fans and his daughter and signed the note formally, 'Yours Truly, Chester Blackwood.' His body was never found.
>
> The Los Angeles County Coroner's office delayed in having Blackwood declared dead while a thorough search of the reservoir was conducted, and even after the search was called off, there was no forthcoming certification of his death. In the mean time, a legal battle began brewing between his daughter, Roxanne, and his publisher, the Meteor Press, over control of the estate and subsequent publishing rights. Without a death certificate, Roxanne had very little leverage, and Meteor controlled Blackwood's publishing until 1945 when Roxanne finally won her case, had her father declared dead, and severed all ties between Meteor and the Blackwood estate. It was long rumored but never proven that the publisher influenced the Coroner's office to refuse to declare Blackwood dead without a body.
>
> Roxanne Blackwood never enjoyed her victory over Meteor. Almost immediately after winning the case, she was implicated in the death of Edward Royce, author of *The Blighted Land*. Although never charged in the case, which was eventually ruled an accident, she spent enormous amounts of money from her father's estate in fighting to keep herself out of jail. When her legal troubles had ended, she went into seclusion and transferred control of her father's estate to a charitable trust. She died in 1960 of alcohol related illness.

Eddie closed the book. He felt shaken. "Okay," he said, pushing it back across the counter. He turned his back on the counter and stared at the rows of shelves that filled the bookstore.

"Find what you needed?" the clerk said casually, his voice sounding to Eddie like he was hearing it from a distant room. His feet felt numb and another wave of nausea had overtaken him. He had gotten so much more information in the store than he had been expecting, and he wished now that he had never known any of it.

The thought of himself dead by 1945 had upset him, but thinking of Roxanne drinking herself to death fifteen years later, spending the last years of her life in wretched seclusion, was enough to make him want to cry. What was more, he realized, Swinburne no doubt had had a hand in both Eddie's and Roxanne's destruction. The car accident that Eddie would die in seemed like more than an accident, given the location on Mulholland, not far from Swinburne's estate. He also felt certain that Swinburne was behind the theft of *The Blighted Land* and that his own death would be engineered in conjunction with the theft and the fight over Blackwood's estate. How the pieces of the puzzle fit together, Eddie could not be sure of, but he knew that Swinburne was at the heart of it. That Swinburne would fight Roxanne for control of Blackwood's estate did not surprise Eddie, but that he would make things worse by seeing to it that her name was dragged into Eddie's death and that she would be so broken by the events that she would effectively take her own life—the thought made Eddie livid, and he silently promised himself that he would beat Swinburne at his own game.

He had not responded to the clerk's question but had simply stood beside the counter for several seconds waiting for the feeling of nausea to pass. Now the clerk asked, a bit impatiently, "You okay?"

The question startled Eddie, and he realized that he needed to move, needed to get back to Roxanne and move forward with his plan to get them out of the mess they were in. With a deep breath, Eddie turned back toward the counter, muttering, "I'm fine."

His quiet reply was drowned out, however, by the sound of the bell over the door at the end of the counter as another customer came in off the street. The clerk instantly lost interest in Eddie, saying "Hi, can I help you?" as Eddie took his copy of *The Blighted Land* from the glass countertop where he had left it.

Then, before he could turn toward the door, he heard a man asking the clerk, "Do you have a biography of Chester Blackwood?"

For only an instant, Eddie focused on the clerk's face, his eyebrows raised in surprise, and then Eddie turned to face the man who had just walked into the store. It was Will Pence.

"Jesus Christ," Eddie whispered, grabbing the counter to steady himself.

At first, Pence looked as shocked as Eddie felt, but then a calm look of understanding passed over his features. "Eddie," he said with a smile. "Small world."

The clerk, his eyes moving from one to the other, simply said, "Trippy."

CHAPTER FIFTEEN

There was a bustling coffee shop a block away from the bookstore, and Pence had led Eddie to it rather quickly. As soon as they had gotten out of the store, Eddie had sharply asked, "What the hell is going on?"

"Wait," Pence had said, putting a hand on Eddie's shoulder and steering him onto the sidewalk and into the flow of foot traffic. "Let's go someplace where we can talk." They had walked in silence then, Eddie trying to make sense out of everything—not just his and Roxanne's fates and how he was going to undo the future he had learned about in the bookstore, and not just the question of what his neighbor was doing here in 1985. These things weighed on him, but he also had yet to adjust to being in this future, and the surreal confrontation with this new time kept assaulting him: the noise, the traffic, the clothing, the people. He had the strange sensation of knowing exactly where he was but feeling completely lost at the same time.

In the coffee shop, a red-headed waitress with a nametag reading "Sindee" and a startling amount of cleavage pushing its way out of her orange and white uniform had taken their order, poured them two cups of black coffee and left them to talk in a booth near the back. Eddie sipped at his coffee immediately, grateful that it was strong, and then looked expectantly at Pence across the table.

"You look like you've seen a ghost, Eddie," he said. Pence was clean-shaven and clear-eyed, definitely sober, and he was dressed conservatively in slacks and a shirt. Like Eddie's, Pence's clothes did not seem out of style for 1985—there really being no dominant look that men's or women's clothes had here in Hollywood—but Eddie noticed that his own and Pence's clothes looked somewhat heavier than those of the people around them, and he could only guess that garments in 1985 were being made of lighter material. Like the Oscar statuettes he had seen earlier, everything in this time seemed lighter and more cheaply made than items in 1940, and Eddie could only wonder if this was a sign of the culture's progress or degradation.

Now he nodded at Pence. "I can imagine. That's about what I feel like."

Pence smiled. "You took me by surprise, too, you know. Want to explain what you're doing here?"

Eddie shook his head. "You first. I get the feeling you know a bit more about what's going on than I do."

"Fair enough. I just have to ask, though. You got here with something called Dragon's Tears?"

"Yes."

"And you got them from your pal Blackwood?"

Eddie shrugged. "I wouldn't call him a pal exactly. But yes."

Pence leaned forward, putting his elbows on the table and clasping his hands together in front of his face so his chin rested on his thumbs and his index fingers met in a point just below his nose. He sat that way for a few seconds, clearly trying to determine how best to proceed. When he began speaking, he did so quietly, just loud enough for Eddie to hear above the jumble of other voices in the coffee shop, the sounds of plates bumping together, the ring of the cash register at the counter, and the frequent laughs from different tables.

"I was born about 90 years ago," he began. "Came to LA in the early 20s, chasing the fast money." He paused and looked around the diner with a smile. "Christ. If these people only knew what it was like back then. Place was a meat grinder. Anyhow, I got pulled into some shady stuff. Nothing all that bad, mind you. Just muscle for the people who did do the really bad things."

"So all that talk about the movie studios?" Eddie asked.

"Did that, too. Just not in 1940. See, the drug trade here collapsed in the early 20s."

"This story's familiar to me."

"Heard it from Blackwood?"

Eddie nodded.

Shrugging, Pence continued, "I knew him back then. We worked for the same guy. Blackwood handled the dealing. I was what they'd call security these days. Kept everybody honest. Made sure nobody dipped into the profits or the merchandise. There was a whole network based in Chinatown, spread up to Hollywood and Beverly Hills where the money came from, and out to the docks at Long Beach and San Pedro where the supply came from. And when the bottom fell out, I moved on. Did my work as a private contractor for the studios or whoever needed my services. But, you know, you can never really move on, not completely. When the organization wanted me back, I had no choice. They'd have had me floating face down in the harbor in no time if I'd tried to refuse, and no amount of dirty pictures in a secret file would have saved my ass. So I went back to work for them . . . and ended up here. And in 1940. And a few other times as well."

"Why?"

"There's a monastery up in the hills out toward the Pacific Palisades. Back in 1925 it was just a big house that these monks from China or Nepal or Tibet . . . I don't know. Anyhow, they had this place and they were working on building a temple or monastery. You should see it now. Amazing. But back then it was just getting started."

"They're the ones that used the Dragon's Tears?"

Pence nodded. "I guess Hollywood is like a Mecca for them or something. So many holes in time."

"Right," Eddie said, indicating that Blackwood had explained this to him as well.

"So to get their supply of Dragon's Tears from China or wherever, they had to go through the head of the drug ring. I don't know if he was beholden to the monks or trying to buy his salvation or what. I mean, I don't know if their whole system works that way or not, but anyhow they had this shipment of Dragon's Tears coming in, and it got stolen."

"By Johnny Woo."

Pence raised an eyebrow and looked sternly at Eddie. "What do you know about Johnny Woo?"

A bit taken aback by Pence's reaction, Eddie said, "Nothing. I mean, not much. He's the guy who Blackwood got the Dragon's Tears from." He proceeded to relate the story as Blackwood had told it, explaining how the dying Woo had shown up at Blackwood's Hollywood bungalow in 1925 as well as what Blackwood had done with the Dragon's Tears afterward.

Pence grinned and shook his head. "Son of a bitch," he said. "And they never found the body. That explains a lot. Doesn't exactly help me, though."

"Why?"

"Because when the syndicate called me back in, they charged me with finding Woo and bringing him back to 1926 for punishment. That's when he stole it, by the way. So he ends up dying even before he took the stuff." He shook his head again. "Having him dead doesn't help me. I have to bring him back alive."

Eddie found himself amazed at the story. "So they sent you . . . into the future? To find him?"

"That's right. They gave me a supply of Dragon's Tears and sent me on my way."

"To 1940?"

"For starters. See, these monks. They're . . . I don't know how to describe it. They're very in tune with these time bridges. They don't pass through them. They just contemplate . . . reality, I suppose. When someone does pass through, they know about it. It's like they sense a disturbance in the system, kind of like a spider feeling something on the edge of its web. So they knew someone had gone through a bridge from 1926 to 1940."

"But you had no idea where?"

Pence shook his head. "None. Needle in a haystack, right? Now you know why I drink. Every time there's been movement across a time bridge, the monastery's contacted me. Sent me here. Sent me there. All to find Woo. Now it looks like a lot of those leads could just as easily have been Blackwood doing his time traveling."

"So when you disappear from time to time from your apartment?"

Pence smiled. "I'm not out protecting a starlet."

The thought amazed Eddie. "You're in the future."

"Most likely."

"And you haven't found any sign of Woo?"

Pence shook his head. "When I saw you with Blackwood on the stairs, and you told me how successful he's become, I started thinking something might be going on. The Chester Blackwood I knew in 1922 was a cold bastard and a drug addict who could never have had the kind of success you described for me the other night. I started doing some digging the next morning and found he'd disappeared. That clinched it. He'd looked scared when I passed him on the stairs. You think he took off because of me?"

"Maybe." Eddie looked up as the waitress brought him his order, a plate of scrambled eggs and toast. For Eddie, it was the middle of the night. He had not eaten since the sandwich with Roxanne in the mountains, and he had been salivating at the smell of food since entering the diner. He smiled politely at the gum-chewing waitress, who ignored him, asked if he needed anything else and walked away the second Eddie answered in the negative. He began shaking salt and pepper onto the eggs and said, "Blackwood was planning on running beforehand. He told me he was sick, cancer. And he also made it sound like he had some people upset with him that he needed to get away from."

"Swinburne?"

Eddie nodded, taking a bite of the eggs. "So you think he came here?"

"I went to the monastery. They'd felt a couple disturbances the last few weeks. 1985 was a focal point. I've been here for a couple days now seeing if I can track him down, see what he can tell me about Woo."

"You should've asked me. I don't think he knows anything more about what happened to Woo or how he got shot. Have you found anything?"

Pence shook his head and finished his coffee. "Nothing. He probably changed his name. Could already be dead. Now I know about the cancer, I can start checking records for deaths matching his age and description. He could still be around, but it's probably a dead end."

"Why were you looking for the biography?"

"Just hoping." Pence turned his hands, palms up in a signal of surrender. "Figured there might be something about his old haunts, places he might be drawn to now. Time to head back to 1940 and wait for something else to happen."

"And crawl into a bottle while you wait?"

Pence raised an eyebrow. "Maybe." He looked Eddie in the eye. "What about you? Did you find what you were looking for in that bookstore?" Eddie sighed and sipped his coffee. Then he laid out for Pence the things he had discovered about himself, Roxanne and Swinburne, feeling no qualms about revealing everything. "So now what?" Pence asked him.

"I've got some ideas," Eddie said. "It might not work out, though. Swinburne's dangerous. He might be more dangerous than I think. I know he's a blackmailer. I don't know what else he might be."

"A killer?"

Eddie shrugged. "Indirectly maybe."

"You worried?"

Eddie exhaled sharply through his nose in a quiet snort. "Yeah," he said. He leaned forward, his elbows on the table on either side of the now empty plate that the waitress was in no hurry to clear away. "Can you do me a favor, Will?" he asked.

"Name it."

"When I get back to 1940 with Roxanne, I'm going to try something, try to work a deal with Swinburne. It might not take. He might just want to have me killed. . . I might not make it back out of his mansion."

"You want me to come with you?" Eddie thought Pence sounded eager as he asked the question, most likely hoping Eddie would answer in the affirmative. It would likely do Pence some good to have a concrete nemesis, Eddie thought, someone he could actually do combat with rather than the seeming apparition that was Johnny Woo.

For a moment, Eddie thought about it, wondering how Swinburne and Hobart would react if he emerged from the locked bedroom with Pence in tow rather than Roxanne. But as he reconsidered the plan he had already formulated, he shook his head even though he knew he would be disappointing Pence. "No," he said. "It wouldn't work out well for Roxanne. I think I've figured a way to get both of us out of this, but I need to do it a certain way that doesn't involve any . . . security, you called it?"

"Mm-hmm."

"Thing is, though, if it doesn't work, can I leave you something for Roxanne? I'll have her come to you if I don't make it to our rendezvous."

"Of course. You sure, though?"

"Absolutely. I need to find a pen and something to write on."

"And then?"

"Then," said Eddie, "I need to get some food for Roxanne and get back up into the hills." He looked around for the waitress, hoping she would not object to bringing him a pen and some scratch paper from the manager's office. Then he added, "Oh. And I need to find a women's clothing store."

CHAPTER SIXTEEN

After parting with Pence on Hollywood Boulevard, Eddie took a cab back into the hills. The car smelled of cigarettes and more faintly of alcohol. Eddie felt a bit uneasy in the back seat, letting the cabbie take him into the complicated network of narrow streets that twisted their way through the opulent neighborhoods. Still unsure of his bearings, he would have preferred retracing his route back to Roxanne on foot, but since he had taken more time in the city than he had wanted to, he had opted for the taxi to make up for lost time and reunite with Roxanne as quickly as possible. Not wanting to tell the driver to take him all the way to the rusted old gates of Swinburne's estate for fear that he would raise suspicion about trespassing on the property, Eddie had the cabbie let him out at the intersection of two residential streets not far from the burned out ruins. He paid the fare and got out of the back seat of the yellow taxi, taking with him two bags and leaving behind his copy of *The Blighted Land* save one page.

He watched as the driver pulled away and then began walking uphill and toward the part of the road that ran along the ridge. The wall of Swinburne's estate met him soon enough, and when he was at the gate he paused, looked up and down the road to make sure no cars were coming, then lightly tossed the bags over the gate and climbed up and over it. As far as he could tell, everything on the property looked the same as he had left it. He did not know what he might see that would give away signs of other trespassers, but he was nonetheless relieved to see that there were none. He picked up the two bags and jogged across the property toward the cottage.

When he got there, he called out "Roxanne?" quietly so as not to alarm her before he walked in the door. He smelled cigarette smoke in the air and heard sounds of quick movement as Roxanne stood up in the back room and raced into the living room to meet him. She threw her arms around him and they kissed. It was so good to hold her after being so bombarded by the ugliness of what he had read in her father's biography. Roxanne was real, alive. Her embrace, her scent, the sound of her breathing against his ear all erased the images of her that he had been carrying since he had left the bookstore. "You're okay?" he finally asked as they stepped away from each other.

She just nodded. "You?"

"Yeah." He wanted to add that he had not been okay before their embrace, but he knew he should not do anything to indicate that he had been distressed.

Even so, his expression must have given him away, as she put her arms on his shoulders, holding them and looking him intently in the eye. "You found something, didn't you?" she asked. "Something you shouldn't have."

Eddie hesitated. He had already promised himself that Roxanne would know nothing of what he had found. Even though she had come around to cooperating with him in time traveling and reading *The Golden Age of Science Fiction*, she had been so shaken by the experience and been so fearful before about not wanting to know the future that he felt it best that she be kept as much in the dark as possible. For the same reasons, he had also decided not to tell her about his meeting with Pence. "I found some things out. Things I needed to know. And things you said you didn't want to know, so I'm going to keep it to myself."

"But it's bad, isn't it?"

Eddie nodded. "It's bad if we let it be. It's bad if we let Swinburne make it bad. But I'm pretty sure I've got it figured out. Did you get through the book?"

"Yes." She took him by the hand and led him back into the other room where she had been sitting since he left. The book was open face down on the floor beside her purse. On the windowsill were several cigarette butts. "Most of it, anyway. It's like reading literary analysis of my father's whole career without him being mentioned in it. Kind of strange. He really stole all those stories. Anyway, I don't understand all the references to things, but as far as I can tell there's nothing here that Swinburne can use to destroy the world or make it a better one for himself."

"Good. Then we give it to him."

Roxanne looked at him, nodding as she said, "So was all this for nothing? Should we have just given the book to Hobart and Luna when they knocked and then gone back to bed?"

The thought of being in bed with Roxanne made Eddie's heart race for a moment, and he felt his pulse in his ears. After a distracted few seconds, he said, "No. We had to know what was in it. Swinburne thinks it's a manual for time traveling, that it gives away the secret to Dragon's Tears and who knows what else. He'll be disappointed that it's just a long synopsis of things he's already published, but now that I know what's in it, I'll know how to sell him on it. Besides, I needed to get here." He raised his arms to indicate not just the cottage but also the future. "It's what your father wanted me to figure out, and if I hadn't, things would not have gone well."

Roxanne nodded. "You're right. I don't want to know." She nodded toward the two bags in Eddie's hands. "What's that?"

One was small and the other large. Eddie offered her the smaller first and said, "Food. We never had dinner. I was feeling kind of faint down there, so I grabbed a quick bite and got some for you." As he was speaking, Roxanne was tearing open the bag. She found a cooling hamburger wrapped in colorful paper and fried potato wedges in a paper carton. She began eating without saying a word, apparently not mindful of appearing unladylike.

"I see you were hungry, too," Eddie said with a smile. As she continued eating, he said, "There is something I need to explain to you. I'm not going to give you details, but I need to make sure you understand this. After we get back, they're going to find your father's car in a few days. He made it look like a suicide." Roxanne looked at him, her mouth full but her eyes suddenly showing a mixture of sadness and alarm. He continued quickly, "It's okay. There's no body. They'll never find one. I'm convinced he's here in the eighties or somewhere nearby in time. Anyway, the important thing is for you not to fight Swinburne over your father's literary estate. If you do, he'll make your life hell. Don't fight to have your father declared dead. Don't do anything. Just let Swinburne have his way for a year or two. Then quietly move to have your father declared dead if the coroner hasn't done it already. Cut a deal with Swinburne if you need to. Don't try to make him give up everything."

As he spoke, she continued to eat, nodding her head occasionally to show that she understood. When Eddie was finished, she said, "This is really important?"

"Really."

"Okay. I'm not going to like it, but okay."

"Good." He paused a moment and then said, "Roxanne, have you ever told your father about your book?"

"My end of the world story?"

"Right."

"No. Never." She smiled ironically. "You know, it's funny. I never really thought this in so many words, but I guess I never trusted him with my ideas. I knew he had it in him to steal it, so I kept it to myself." She had set the remainder of her hamburger down on the paper and picked up a potato wedge. "Why do you ask?"

"Nothing. You don't want to know." Eddie waited a moment before saying, "There's one more thing. If things go badly for you down the line, don't turn to the bottle."

Roxanne raised an eyebrow but said nothing.

"I'm sorry. That's all I want to say. It's just I don't think you have your father's liver."

Roxanne nodded. Eddie could not tell if she found his advice disturbing or not. She swallowed her last bite of the hamburger and quietly said, "Eddie . . . I've been thinking while you were gone. How is any of this possible?"

"Time traveling?"

"Mm-hmm. I mean, that and just the whole idea of being able to change the future. This book." She nodded toward *The Golden Age of Science Fiction.* "What happened to that future?"

Eddie looked with her at the book. He shrugged. "It doesn't exist anymore."

"But that's what I mean. How did it ever exist? How can something that hasn't happened yet even be there for someone to encounter by going through one of those bridges? How did my father change something that hadn't happened yet? How are you going to change it again?"

Eddie stared at her for a moment. She was asking questions that had crossed his mind as well, but he had not had the time or ability to concentrate on them at all. Part of him had not wanted to think about it. He had been moving automatically for hours now, the need to find answers and to wrest himself and Roxanne from Swinburne's control being the only things he would let himself focus on. Now he let himself consider her questions for a moment and exhaled slowly before saying, "Maybe he didn't change it. Maybe the future . . . maybe it's not just one thing. Like there are multiple futures—

the one we're in now, which seems to be the one your father made, and the future that he walked into where Heinlein and those guys wrote their own books, and maybe more. And we're just on a track heading into the future, or into *a* future. And your father switched the tracks into a different tomorrow."

"So in some other . . . dimension? . . . those books are still on the shelves with the original authors' names on them?"

"Maybe."

"And you're going to try to switch the tracks again."

"Get us into a different tomorrow."

"Where Swinburne isn't holding all the cards," Roxanne said. As they had been speaking, Eddie had watched her eyes widen. Now she said, "Your railroad track metaphor. It makes sense if you think about time differently."

"You think?"

"Mm-hmm. Think about it. You take the train to Chicago; you know Chicago's there the whole time you're traveling. It's not like it doesn't exist yet. It's there and it's waiting for you, independent of you. It's just that we're used to moving through space."

"But we're talking about moving through time."

"Right," she said. "And the future's there in time, not just the idea of it, just the way Chicago is there in space."

"And if you went to New York instead of Chicago, then Chicago would still be there."

"Mm-hmm. So this time, our time, daddy's time, Marion Rigby's time . . . they're all real. We just found a way to switch ourselves onto a different track."

Eddie nodded. "It makes sense. In a way. It's also possible we're completely crazy."

Roxanne smiled. "True enough." She nodded toward the bag he still held. "What's in the other bag? Dessert?"

Eddie smiled. "No," he said, unrolling the top and opening the bag. He moved it so she could see inside. "Clothes."

"What? Did you buy me souvenirs down there?"

They both laughed. Eddie was relieved he had not frightened her too badly with his warnings or his talk of her father's faked suicide. His laughter was tainted by his knowledge of what he was going to have to do to keep himself from getting killed on Mulholland Drive, however, and now he said, "I wish that's what it was." He nodded toward the bag. "This is how I'm going to get you out of Swinburne's."

"It's a disguise?"

"No. I'll explain when we get there."

Now her face grew serious. "Wait a minute," she said. "What do you mean, get *me* out of there. What about you?"

Eddie sighed. "We're going to have to split up. I've got it all figured out. There are things I'm going to have to discuss with Swinburne that you don't want to hear. It's going to be best to get you out of there before I do, and it's not like they're just going to let you waltz out. We've got a bit of work to do when we get back there." He looked at his watch. In 1940, it was almost six in the morning. He should have been exhausted by this point but felt fine. Perhaps the Dragon's Tears also had a stimulant effect, or perhaps it was just adrenaline from everything they had been through. Or maybe it was the fact that where they were now, it was the middle of the afternoon. At any rate, the idea of sleep seemed preposterous. "We need to get going."

Roxanne's expression had fallen from serious to dejected as he had spoken, but she must have seen the wisdom of what he said, as she made no protest but simply wiped her lips with a paper napkin Eddie had stuffed in the bag and then said, "Okay." She gathered her cigarettes and lighter and stuffed them into her purse along with *The Golden Age of Science Fiction.* "Let's go," she said as she slipped on her coat.

Holding hands, they walked out of the cottage and to the time bridge. Now it faced east and would take them into the past. Eddie looked around at 1985 for a moment. There were parts of it he definitely did not like, but it had been a profound experience. He wondered if Blackwood were out there somewhere or if he had already died, as Pence had postulated. Eddie and Roxanne had agreed that he should go through the time bridge first this time, so after a moment's hesitation he let go of Roxanne's hand and stepped in. Their return went as expected with her stepping in after him and following him through. They had been gone a few hours, so when they stepped through to the other side, the night was considerably cooler and the full moon had risen higher. It was disorienting to see the mansion restored and the cottage no longer vandalized. They still needed to get back into the house, into the servants' quarters and through one more time bridge before they would be back in the right time. Roxanne took a step toward the main house, but Eddie stopped her with a hand on her forearm. He nodded toward the cottage.

"I need to go in there," Eddie whispered.

"For what?" came the whispered reply.

"I don't know when we are, but at some future date, Mr. Luna is going to lose his keys. Remember we saw them on the back of his door? Wait here for me."

Roxanne did not listen. She followed Eddie as he moved to the front of the house. The door was not locked, probably because of the security offered by the locked gate and high wall around the estate. Eddie turned the knob and quietly pushed the door open. Before he could take a step inside, Roxanne, put a hand on his shoulder. "Let me go," she whispered.

"No," Eddie replied. "It's not safe."

"Not for you it's not. You're heavier than me. You'll squeak the floorboards," Roxanne said, a mischievous smile on her face. Without giving him a chance to reply, she silently slipped off her shoes and handed them to

Eddie, then pushed past him and went through the door. He stood at the open door and watched as, seconds later, Roxanne's Zippo lit up to illuminate the room for a moment. He could see her walking toward Luna's door cautiously, using the lighter to avoid furniture and other obstacles in her way. When she got to the door, the lighter went out. Eddie held his breath as he listened for the click of the latch or the squeaking of the door on its hinges. Roxanne must have moved incredibly slowly and deliberately because he heard neither, even with his senses heightened from the Dragon's Tears. After what seemed an incredibly long time, he detected movement and then was able to make out Roxanne's shape coming toward him. She flicked on the lighter again when she got close to the door and then was out, proudly placing the keys in Eddie's hands.

They moved quickly away from the cottage, and Roxanne put her shoes back on while standing in the grass next to the main house. "Now will you tell me what you need these for?" she asked hoarsely even though it was probably safe now to speak above a whisper.

"I don't know what I'll need them for. It's mostly just in case. But for you, that's how we're getting you out of here. Come on." He led her to the garage where, with more help from the Zippo, they found the key to the Lincoln. The garage doors themselves were not locked. Eddie took the key off the ring and gave it to Roxanne.

Next, they walked down the private road, completely grown over with weeds in 1985, and to the gate. Here, too, Roxanne held the lighter as Eddie tried various keys, and when he found the one for the gate, he gave it to her as well. She slipped both into her purse. "One more," he said as they started walking back toward the mansion. He pulled his own keys from his pocket and took one off the ring. "My apartment. I want you to go there tomorrow at two. Today, I mean. If I'm not there, let yourself in."

Roxanne took the key but did not say anything for a few steps. Eddie looked at her face in the moonlight and could see she looked upset. "How will you get in?" she finally asked. Her voice sounded strained.

"I've got a spare." He squeezed her hand. "It's going to be all right." She looked up at him and smiled. "One more thing. If I don't show up after a little while, no more than an hour, I want you to go down the hall to Pence's apartment. Tell him I'm late, and he'll know what to do."

She looked confused. "What do you mean, Eddie? What—"

"Shhh." He put a finger to her lips. "Just trust me, okay? And trust Pence. He'll know what to do. Really." After a moment, Roxanne nodded a bit reluctantly, and they walked in silence back to the house and around to the back and the kitchen entrance.

Soon, they were back at the servants' quarters. Eddie closed the door behind them and turned on the light. "You ready?" he asked, nodding toward the remaining time bridge that they needed to cross in order to get back to where they were supposed to be. They had done their time traveling quickly and had plenty of margin for error, and although he did not want to part from Roxanne, Eddie was eager to get the last portion of his plan under way. The sooner he could tell himself that he and Roxanne were free from the future that he had found and free from whatever machinations of Swinburne's had set that future in motion, the better he would feel because it would mean that Roxanne, at least, was safe.

"No," she said, taking Eddie by surprise. She put her hand on his chest and faced him. "Eddie, when we go back through that time bridge, Hobart is going to be on the other side of the door." Eddie nodded. "I need to be able to say goodbye to you without him there."

Feeling compelled to reassure her, Eddie began to say, "Roxanne, I—"

"Shhhh. Eddie, I don't know what you have planned, but I want you to know I trust you. And I know you're trying to keep me safe and keep me from knowing too much. The thing is, though, I need to know if you're really going to be at your apartment tomorrow or if you're just planning on skipping out on me. Following in my father's footsteps."

Eddie sighed. He fully intended to meet her, but he also knew that his plan for freeing both of them from Swinburne could fall through in a dozen ways. He also remembered how swiftly Swinburne had resorted to violence earlier in the evening and that it had been the threat of violence that had driven Roxanne's father to escape through a time bridge. Not wanting to alarm her, he said, "I'm not skipping out on you, Roxanne. But I can't say for sure what's going to happen after you leave. I want to be there tomorrow." He hesitated. "I just don't know if I will be. I haven't seen that future."

"Okay," she said, her voice hushed, just above a whisper. "It's okay." She stepped up to him and raised her lips to give him a brief, gentle kiss him. "If I don't see you tomorrow, you know I'm going to miss you, don't you?"

Eddie nodded. "I know. Me, too. We could be good together."

"Mm-hmm."

"I'm not saying we won't be."

"I know."

"But . . ."

"I know," she said again. They kissed once more and then held each other for a long time.

After a while, he said, "I think it's time" and gave her another light kiss. Then he stepped away from her and opened the bag they had brought from the future. He pulled out a dress with a blue and white pattern and laid it on the bed. "You may as well change now," he said, taking undergarments out of the bag as well. "You should change into these as well. I don't like the idea, but Hobart's going to be able to tell if I hand him things that haven't been worn." For some reason, he felt uncomfortable watching her disrobe completely after having just effectively said their goodbyes. He looked at the floor, the door, his shoes and the bag from the future as she slipped out of her clothes and into the ones he had bought her. As she turned to let him button the back of the dress, he said, "Make sure you take the empty bag with you and destroy it first chance you get."

"Okay," she said, handing Eddie the dress she had been wearing during the time they had been together. He draped it over his arm and then took her underthings from her after she had gathered them. The style of the new dress was odd for 1940, but the fit was reasonably close. "You did good," she said as she looked at herself in the mirror, pulling a bit at the new underwear to adjust it under the dress. "You have a lot of experience buying women clothes?"

"Just lucky," Eddie said with a bittersweet smile.

They gathered their things and were soon stepping into the opening to the time bridge. They passed through and in seconds were back where they belonged, but it did not feel right to Eddie. The mild feeling of disorientation he had experienced before when returning to his time was now much more intense, probably from having been gone longer and from having traveled to more than one time. In a few seconds, though, the feeling passed. "You okay?" he whispered to Roxanne, and she whispered back that she was. The light was off, and a sliver of light came from under the door. Eddie knew that Hobart was on the other side. Roxanne flicked on her lighter, and they looked around the room. There was no sign of Hobart or anyone else having entered while they were gone. Eddie asked her for the book, and she slipped it out of her purse and handed it to him. He looked at it for a moment, and then Roxanne let the lighter go out.

"Okay," Eddie whispered, standing face to face with her as their eyes adjusted to the dark. "I guess this is it. I'll go out for a second and talk to him. Then I'll reach in and grab the clothes. Give us ten minutes and then get out of here. Same way we went before. To the kitchen, out to the garage and then gone. The only money I have won't be good for forty years or so. Otherwise I'd tell you to just dump the car down the hill and take a cab."

"It'll be okay."

"I know. Just go get your car and go home. Leave the Lincoln outside my place. I'll tell them where to find it. When you get home, make sure you check your mail to see if your father didn't send you a little goodbye present like he did me. Try to get some sleep, and then come back to my place."

"I hope you're there, Eddie."

"Me too."

She threw her arms around him and squeezed hard. He buried his face in her hair and breathed her scent in deeply. He lowered his hands to her hips and held her gently as she kissed him. "Be careful," she whispered.

"You too. And don't forget what I told you about what to do about your father's estate."

She nodded her understanding and they separated. Eddie watched her sit on the bed, and he turned to the door. He hung the dress and undergarments on a hook on the door, then turned the lock and twisted the knob. He gave her a little wave that he was not sure she could see. Then he stepped into the hallway.

The lights were on, but Hobart was asleep. He had brought a utilitarian kitchen chair into the hallway and had leaned it back against the wall. He slept in it at an impossible angle, and Eddie found it surprising that Hobart had not fallen to the floor once he had gone on the nod. To his credit, he was a light sleeper and a good guard of Swinburne's captives, as he opened his eyes almost immediately once Eddie gently pulled the door closed behind him with a slight click. He was instantly on his feet, the chair falling to the floor behind him with the crack of wood on tile. Eddie held a hand up palm outward in a signal that all was well. He did not want Hobart to think he was trying to escape.

"I need you to take me to your boss," he said. He waved the book with his other hand. "I've got what he wants."

Hobart looked at the book with considerable confusion. "How'd you get it?" he asked. "You ain't left the room."

"We had it the whole time. Just take me to Swinburne."

Hobart nodded to the door. "Bring her, too. I ain't lettin' her out of my sight."

"She's not going anywhere," Eddie said. "She's fast asleep. I don't want her to know I'm cutting a separate deal with your boss."

Hobart shook his head. "No dice. Wake her. It's my ass if she gets away."

Eddie nodded and held up a finger, indicating that Hobart should wait. He turned and opened the door a few inches, just enough to reach in and pull the clothes off the hook on the back of the door. As he did, he felt Roxanne's hand caress his. She had gotten off the bed and was standing by the door, no doubt listening and waiting for him to reach back in one last time. Eddie smiled as his back was turned to Hobart, rubbed his closed hand against Roxanne's for a second, and then drew his arm back out the door and pulled it shut. He turned to Hobart, holding up the clothing like a hunter displaying his catch. Roxanne's panties and lacy bra were clearly visible in the folds of the dress, and Hobart's eyes widened at the sight.

"She's not going anywhere," Eddie said. "Not stark naked. Even if she did wake up."

Hobart nodded and smiled. "Maybe I should go in and check on her."

Eddie felt a surge of adrenaline. He thought of Roxanne listening on the other side of the door and wondered if she was afraid. He would like nothing more than to punch Hobart in the face, and he wondered if the Dragon's Tears had done anything to enhance his strength. Even if it had, though, his and Roxanne's situations would be much better if he kept his temper.

"Nothing doing," he said sharply. "You take me to Swinburne now or the deal's off, and he'll know it was you who blew it."

"Cool your heels, buddy. The deal's off when Mr. Swinburne says it's off. But just to keep things running smoothly, we'll go see him. You give me those, though."

Eddie made a show of reluctantly handing over the clothes and then watched with satisfaction as Hobart took the clothing and nodded and nodded in the direction he wanted Eddie to walk. Hobart rubbed the lace of the bra with his thumb as he went, and Eddie knew he would have no trouble keeping him convinced that Roxanne lay in the room sleeping in the nude.

When they reached the doorway out of the service area and entered the main part of the house again, Hobart wordlessly led Eddie to a wide staircase with an ornate railing, and they went up to the second floor. After a minute of walking down a portrait-lined hallway, they stopped at a set of double doors, and Hobart knocked. There was no immediate reply, and Eddie stood there with Hobart listening for sounds of Swinburne stirring. He saw another time bridge opening at the end of the hallway.

Hobart knocked again, and now there was an angry sounding "What is it?" from the other side of the door. Hobart looked nervously at Eddie, as if to say this was all Eddie's fault. Then he cleared his throat and said quietly but still loud enough to be heard through the door, "It's Hobart, sir. The Royce guy wants to talk about a deal with you."

There were angry sounding grunts from beyond the door but no words. After a few seconds of silence, they heard Swinburne say, "Well, bring him in, then."

Hobart opened the door and stood aside as Eddie entered. The bedroom was enormous, larger than the whole cottage where Hobart and Luna lived. It was decorated ostentatiously with velvet furniture and red carpeting, a room fit for a king, or Swinburne's notion of what a king's room should be. The bed was immense with a carved wooden frame and four bedposts that reached halfway to the ceiling. There was also an ornate desk along with matching wardrobe and dressers. All of the woodwork in the room was intricately carved. Eddie was sure he could live for years on what the furniture in this room alone had cost.

A bedside lamp had been turned on, and Swinburne stood now beside the bed, pulling a robe on over silk pajamas. "What on earth could this be about, Mr. Royce. You're not content to have ruined my night up to this point?"

Eddie walked halfway across the room before speaking. "I thought we might make a deal," he said, holding up the book.

"Is that . . .?" Swinburne said, his eyes wide.

"Yes."

"Let me see it." He began walking toward Eddie, but Eddie withdrew the book from sight, holding it close to his body. Swinburne stopped. "Where did you have it?"

Eddie smiled. "Roxanne's purse."

Swinburne shook his head and shot Hobart a glare, apparently for having failed to search Roxanne when he and Luna had picked them up at Eddie's apartment. "Where is Miss Blackwood now?" he asked Hobart. "You were supposed to be watching her."

Hobart held up the clothes. "She's not going anywhere."

"Ah. I see." He turned his attention to Eddie. "I knew the safety deposit story was flawed."

"No," Eddie lied. "I actually did have it there. I just got it out yesterday after Roxanne and I found her place destroyed, before we went to my apartment. I'll sell it to you."

"Sell it? It's mine already. Miss Blackwood's father owed me the book or the money."

"That's true. But he gave it to me, not you, didn't he?"

"What do you want for it?"

Eddie shook his head. "Not until you tell me why you want it so badly. What do you think is in it?"

"The future." Swinburne's eyes glazed over for a second as he thought about it. "You've read the stories, Mr. Royce. All the time travel stories from Wells to . . . to Blackwood, I suppose. More so than anyone else I've met in years, I know you've read the books and stories I've read, Mr. Royce. Aren't you elated at the idea that science fiction, the promises and the horrors of science fiction are, instead, more in the realm of science fact? To travel in time . . . I can imagine no greater thing."

It was like Swinburne was having a religious experience. Eddie wondered what the older man would do if he knew that Eddie had just finished traveling in time, both forwards and backwards, in the last few hours right here under Swinburne's nose. Perhaps Roxanne had read Swinburne wrong. Perhaps he did not want to travel in time in order to expand his empire or take advantage of the knowledge it would give him. Certainly, Swinburne seemed like the type who would use time travel to gain power and influence, but what if he was really just an ardent devotee of science fiction enraptured by the idea that his fantasies could be realized? But then Eddie thought of everything Swinburne had done to him and Roxanne in the last twenty-four hours, thought of Hobart almost breaking his arm and manhandling Roxanne, and he knew that, lover of science fiction or not, Swinburne was unscrupulous, conniving, manipulative and ruthless. He had used Roxanne for years and would continue to. He had exploited Chester Blackwood's weaknesses for his own gain. He had destroyed Roxanne's home and Eddie's apartment to satisfy his urges and would doubtless do more damage to anyone who stood in his way if he found out the truth about the Dragon's Tears.

Eddie held the book tightly. "If Blackwood made you think this was a manual for time travel, then he fooled you again, Mr. Swinburne. This book isn't going to tell you how Blackwood did it. The drug was the thing, the only secret, but he didn't give it to me, and I don't know what it was called. The book isn't about the drug at all. So get used to the idea that you're not going to travel in time."

Swinburne sighed. "You disappoint me, Mr. Royce," he said. "If Chester Blackwood was so set on giving you information about what he had done, why would he withhold the final piece of information?"

Eddie shook his head. "I can't say for sure. Maybe he wasn't planning on disappearing again so quickly. Or maybe he knew the kind of man you are, how persistent you'd be in asking. If he didn't want you to know, then he'd probably have just kept it to himself."

Swinburne's eyes looked moist for a moment in his frustration. "But what harm would it have done if I had known?"

"Probably none," Eddie said. "Maybe that's the point. Maybe Blackwood finally just wanted to stick it to you in the end just because he could." Eddie tried not to grin as he thought that his own motivation in keeping Swinburne ignorant of the Dragon's Tears was not far off from the lie he was making up about Blackwood.

"Spite," said Swinburne, shaking his head. "An ugly motivator, Mr. Royce. Not that my own motives haven't been ugly at one time or another. Still, to think of what the man has deprived me of . . . if you're telling the truth."

Eddie did not blink or look away but met Swinburne's gaze directly and said, "I'm telling the truth, Mr. Swinburne. I don't know the secret, and the secret's not in the book." He paused. "But I'm convinced you'll want the book anyway."

Swinburne's voice was icy as he said, "Go on."

Eddie said, nodding, "It's a book that I can imagine you would find very valuable. It's a book that hasn't been written yet. A book from the future. What better place for it to end up than in the best private collection of science fiction ever assembled? Imagine. A book that has been acquired through time travel. If that's not the ultimate science fiction book, I don't know what is."

Swinburne stared silently then said, "What's in it?"

"Blackwood. His whole career. You'll see there's more to his little deception than the things you got from your people at *Astounding*."

Swinburne nodded. "How do I know it's not a hoax? How can you really say what it is?"

"Well," Eddie said with some hesitation. "You do have your manuscripts from Heinlein and Asimov. That verifies something, doesn't it?"

"I suppose it does." Eddie could see that Swinburne was trying hard to keep desire for the book from showing on his face, but he was failing. He kept licking his lips, and his hands twitched as he stared intently at the book. He was like a cat at a window staring at a sparrow flying around outside.

"What are you proposing in exchange for it?"

Without hesitation, Eddie said, "Roxanne. Let her out of the deal you have with her, whatever it is that you and Whistler are holding over her head to keep her posing for Frehling. Let her write. Publish her."

Swinburne was clearly thinking about it, weighing his options. His eyes never left the book in Eddie's hand. Finally, he said, "No deal, Mr. Royce."

"But you told her you'd let her out of the deal if she got the book and the drug from me. You even told her to seduce me to get the job done."

Swinburne smiled. "If that was the impression Miss Blackwood had, so be it. You creative types often hear only what you want to hear. I have no intention of changing the conditions of her employment. Miss Blackwood with her uncanny effect on Mr. Frehling is indispensable to my plans. Much as I would love to have that book, I'm afraid I need Miss Blackwood more."

Eddie had been afraid of this. He had no idea what plans Swinburne was referring to, but the publisher clearly had his goals set, and his desire for

Blackwood's book was not strong enough to override them. More than anything, Eddie wanted to get Roxanne out of the mess she was in, and he had been hoping the book would be the key. *Still, there may be other ways,* he thought. "What plans?" he asked.

Swinburne smiled. "You should know by now that I am a visionary, Mr. Royce. In my own way, I've seen the future, and it is Roxanne Blackwood. Look there on my desk. Turn on the lamp if you like."

Swinburne nodded toward the ornate writing desk along the wall, and Eddie walked cautiously toward it, keeping an eye on both Swinburne and Hobart. The thug had remained at the door. As Eddie reached the desk, he heard the sound of an engine starting outside and looked to the other two men to see if they had noticed. Their unshifting demeanors told him they had not, and Eddie listened as the Dragon's Tears brought him the sound of the Lincoln's engine fading in the distance. *Goodbye, Roxanne,* he thought as he stepped to the desk and switched on the lamp that sat in the middle of it.

On top of the desk was a single sheet of heavy paper; in its center was an image that Eddie assumed was artwork for a book cover. Penciled notations in the margins indicated that the final production would be about the size of the paperback books Eddie had seen in Book World in 1985. The notations aside, however, his eyes were drawn to the image that took up most of the space on the page, an image that was obviously another Roxanne-inspired Frehling painting with the damsel in distress being carried off by a robot in almost the same pose as had been on the cover of the March 1935 *Stupendous* cover he had seen in Book World's display case. This version of the illustration was different, however, because the robot was not leading her toward a space ship or any other menace typical of science fiction. Instead, it was carrying her toward a bed. The title emblazoned above the illustration was *Forbidden Love*. There was no author listed on the cover, but there was a forty-cent price printed in the corner.

Turning to Swinburne, he said, "What is this?"

"The future," Swinburne answered. When Eddie made no reply, he continued. "It's just a dummy I had made up to test the waters."

"I don't get it."

Swinburne smiled condescendingly. "I'm not surprised, Mr. Royce. Paperback books are the next phenomenon in publishing. They can be slipped into a pocket or purse, concealed completely. And they sell just as well as pulps for just a fraction more money."

"Forty cents isn't a fraction."

"No. But that won't be a typical paperback. I expect we'll have a regular run of titles at twenty-five cents or so. But *Forbidden Love* and others like it are aimed at a more adult audience than the typical trash we publish for the teenage set."

"It's smut? Science fiction smut?"

"You could call it that. I prefer erotica."

Eddie looked again at the cover. Frehling had managed to convey lust eerily in the mechanical face looming over its gorgeous victim. "Kind of goes against Blackwood's Three Laws of Robotics, doesn't it?" he asked.

Swinburne smiled. "Isn't the whole point of Blackwood's robot stories that there is always potential for deviation from the rules that govern the robots? This isn't much different."

"You really think there's money in this?"

"Of course. And we have a built in audience, Mr. Royce. Thirteen-year-old boys have been eating up copies of *Stupendous* for years with pictures inspired by Miss Blackwood on the cover. Those thirteen-year-old boys are now turning into twenty year old men, and they're developing twenty-year-old tastes. The titillation of *Stupendous* is fine for boys, but men need a pay off. We've been grooming them for this. A young man who's been fantasizing about the women Miss Blackwood so beautifully brings to life will see a book like that and find it irresistible."

Eddie was shocked, not so much at the marriage of science fiction and pornography but rather at Swinburne's blatantly ruthless understanding of his audience. Looking again at the cover illustration, Eddie could see that Swinburne was right. There would be countless readers of science fiction who would be drawn to a book like this. He also realized that he was going to have to change his bargaining tactics. "Okay," he said. "Okay. So Roxanne's not part of the bargain. Do you still want to negotiate?"

"Very much." Swinburne's eyes had hardly moved from the copy of *The Golden Age of Science Fiction* in Eddie's hand throughout their conversation.

"I want a contract. For a book. It's called *The Blighted Land*. It's top rate science fiction, better than anything Meteor has ever published."

"That's quite a claim. And you've written this book?"

Eddie hesitated, and then said, "Yes. Well, no. Not yet. It's in the works."

"Fine. Finish it. I'll have Mr. Whistler give it a fair assessment, and if it's good, we'll publish it."

"No. I want a contract. An acceptance now. And an advance of five thousand dollars."

Swinburne laughed. "You must be joking, Mr. Royce. You want me to pay you for a book you have not yet written?"

"It's no different than the short story contract you gave me."

"Oh, but it is. For one thing, you won't be paid for those stories until they're written and accepted. For another, stories are much more easily replaced if something should fall through. Mr. Whistler has hundreds of hacks trying to get into *Stupendous*. But if we set up a print run for a novel, do some advance marketing, and so on, and then it turns out to be garbage, well, that's money down the drain."

"This book is different." Eddie reached into his back pocket and pulled out the page he had torn from *The Blighted Land* on his taxi ride up the hill from Hollywood Boulevard. On one side was the book's title and author, and on the other side was the publication history. "Blackwood gave me this along with the other book. He wanted me to see what I would be capable of. When he told you I'd be the next big thing, this must have been what he based it on."

He held the page out and walked toward Swinburne, who accepted it gingerly. Eddie watched as the publisher looked at one side of the page and then the other. His face betrayed nothing as he read. After a while, he looked up at Eddie and said, "Interesting."

"Just interesting?"

Swinburne sighed, rubbing the paper gently between thumb and forefinger. Eddie assumed he was trying to determine if the torn out page were a fake or not. He must have made a decision, as he said, "No. More than that. All right. A five thousand dollar advance."

"In cash. Before I leave here today."

"Done."

"And a contract spelling out exactly what you're buying, including title and author. First North American serial rights and reprint rights for two years. Then full control returns to me or my literary executor."

"Executor?"

"Roxanne."

Swinburne raised an eyebrow. "Are you planning on an untimely end?"

"No, but you never know what can happen. I could get struck by lightning walking out of here. Or I could skid off Mulholland Drive some night. I don't want control to fall to you if anything should happen to me. I suppose that also might make it less attractive for you to engineer a lightning strike or anything."

"Mr. Royce. Such crass methods are beyond me. At any rate, we can certainly incorporate Miss Blackwood into your plans. May I at least examine the book before we finalize our agreement?" He reached out a hand, palm up.

Eddie held the book back. "One more thing." He paused, not entirely sure of himself. He knew he was pushing his luck, but he had to try. "I want an hour in your vault. One box of pulps from your collection to round out my own."

Swinburne's expression drooped. Parting with five thousand dollars was clearly easier than parting with any of his collection. He contemplated Eddie's demand. "You're not being reasonable, Mr. Royce. You ask too much."

Eddie nodded. "Reprint rights for three years. You can see the book's good for it." He indicated the copyright page that Swinburne still held.

"Your collection means that much to you?"

"We're of the same mind on that," Eddie said.

"All right. One hour and one box of material. Nothing from the locked cabinets, no unpublished manuscripts, nothing from before the turn of the century. And I have final approval on the contents of the box. Mr. Hobart will supervise to make sure you don't vandalize anything."

Eddie thought of his own collection at home and said, "Seems to me he's the bigger threat where vandalism is concerned."

Swinburne let the comment go by without remark. He looked at Hobart and said, "Will you fetch Mr. Luna and have him open the vault? Then return to us and escort Mr. Royce downstairs." Hobart left without a word. "You will get your hour, Mr. Royce, during which time I will examine this book of yours. You trust me with it?"

"If you want *The Blighted Land*, you'll hold up your end of the deal. And you'll leave Roxanne alone."

"Why would I do anything else? She's too valuable to me."

237

"Well," Eddie said, "for starters, she stole your Lincoln a few minutes ago."

Swinburne raised his eyebrows.

"She may be wrapped in a blanket, but I told her how to hotwire it, and she should be halfway to Pasadena by now."

"How did she get out the gate?"

"She's good with a bobby pin."

Swinburne looked angry. "You're not telling me the truth, Mr. Royce."

"Roxanne is a resourceful woman. I wanted her out of here. I wanted her away from Hobart. She went. Leave her alone. You'll find your car on the corner of Central and Olympic later today. If you want me to deliver *The Blighted Land*, just forget about it."

Swinburne nodded. He looked disgusted. "I feel you have bested me on this one, Mr. Royce. But the game is not over."

"I think we can both win. What's wrong with that?"

Swinburne said nothing. He sat at his desk and held out a hand for *The Golden Age of Science Fiction*. Eddie gave it to him without another word. Swinburne licked his lips and carefully opened the book. "Remarkable," he whispered.

Behind Eddie, Hobart entered the room again. He was no longer carrying Roxanne's clothes, and Eddie wondered what he had done with them. Hobart cleared his throat, and Swinburne looked up. "The vault's open, sir."

"Good. Take Mr. Royce down and give him one hour to pack a box. There are empty ones in the storage closet. Keep an eye on him. Then bring him and the box back here." Without another word, Eddie turned and followed Hobart out of the bedroom.

CHAPTER SEVENTEEN

"Clock's tickin'," Hobart said as he pulled up a chair at the table inside the vault and sat down. Moments later, he tipped the chair back on two legs and swung his feet up onto the table, completely relaxed and clearly not worried about Swinburne walking in and discovering him in such an unprofessional posture. "When we're done here, you gonna go wake up Roxanne?"

Eddie stood in the middle of the vault and had been looking over the shelves where all the boxes of pulps were stored. He felt like someone had let him into a museum and told him to pick whatever he wanted for himself. Now he shot Hobart an angry glance and said, "She's none of your concern now. Let Swinburne handle things with her. Where are her clothes, by the way?"

Hobart just smiled and did not say anything for a few seconds. "Safe," he finally said. "She can have 'em back if she asks nice."

Eddie decided to drop it. He moved to the shelf and began pulling boxes off, setting them on the table, and carefully flipping through the painstakingly filed issues of magazines. He knew exactly which ones he already had at home, and he was looking in part to complete his collection. He was also quite happy to acquire duplicate copies of some of the more valuable pulps he had already found over his years of collecting. The thought of the issues under glass in Book World kept returning to him as he searched box after box. Soon, his own box was beginning to fill up with old issues of *Stupendous, Amazing Stories, Astounding, Weird Tales, Wonder Stories, Fantastic, Marvel Science*

Stories, Gernsback's *Science Stories,* and others. He found boxes of Munsey's *All Story* from 1912 with first appearances of *Tarzan* and *Under the Moons of Mars.* There were old copies of *Argosy* with Abraham Merritt novels printed in them and several copies of the August 1923 issue of Gernsback's *Science and Invention,* the first magazine devoted entirely to science fiction—although it was still called "scientific fiction" at the time. He carefully slipped these into his box, wondering if Swinburne would balk at their departure from the vault. Eddie doubted it, as he usually found more than one copy of most of the magazines in the collection. Still, he was taking the most pristine copies and was sure it would pain Swinburne considerably to let some of them go.

Eddie was most deliberate in looking through the boxes of *Stupendous,* being sure to get a copy of every issue that had a Roxanne inspired illustration on the cover. This was almost every issue from the last seven years. The only exceptions were when the covers portrayed males fighting monsters or aliens, and there were very few of these. Eddie expected they had not sold well compared to the issues with one beautiful version of Roxanne or another on their covers.

He looked at his watch. It had only been fifteen minutes, and the box was almost full. He had covered only the first three shelves of the six that went up to the ceiling. He would have to be more discerning with the rest of the boxes, many of which were labeled with titles he was not familiar with. Glancing at Hobart, he saw that Swinburne's watchdog was monitoring him with a look of incredible boredom, paying attention to what Eddie was doing, but clearly without interest. Eddie would have preferred not to be watched so closely.

"I expect I'll use the whole hour," Eddie said. "You want something to read?"

Hobart shook his head slowly. "I don't go for this science fiction stuff," he said with disgust. Eddie had the distinct impression that Hobart meant it, that he had tried reading some of it and could not stand it.

"It's not for everyone," Eddie said, hefting a box from the fourth shelf down to the table. "I suppose you go more for the true crime type of thing." He thought of Hobart's collection of pornography on his walls and knew that true crime would come in at a close second.

Hobart nodded. "That type of thing. Sure."

Looking into the box before him, Eddie was surprised to see not science fiction but Westerns. The pulps in this box were titled *Trail Tales*, and Eddie dismissively glanced at a couple of issues, telling himself that these were of no interest. Still, he wondered why they were here in Swinburne's science fiction collection, and his curiosity prompted him to turn to the table of contents. He recognized none of the names of authors or stories, but the fine print below the masthead revealed that this was a Meteor publication, one of the many pulps that Swinburne had launched over the years to build off of the success of *Stupendous*. Sliding the box back onto the shelf, he quickly looked at the titles listed on other boxes on shelves above him. Based on their names, he guessed that he was looking at boxes with more westerns as well as detective stories, true crime, romances and adventure stories. On the top shelf were boxes without titles on the labels, only years. They ranged from last year, 1939, and went back ten years. The question of why they might be untitled prompted Eddie to walk to the rolling ladder affixed to the wall and pull it toward the end of the row.

Hobart watched, still looking bored, as Eddie climbed the ladder and pulled one of the unmarked boxes out from the shelf just far enough for him to look inside. It was not empty. A photograph of a nearly naked woman on the cover of a cheaply made magazine called *Glamour Girls* met his gaze, and he raised an eyebrow. Reaching into the box, he opened the cover of the magazine, but this was not the kind of thing that listed editors and publication information. Still, its presence here among the rest of Swinburne's collection told Eddie that this must also be part of the Meteor empire, and he immediately thought of Roxanne, Whistler and Klaus Frehling and the sordid story Roxanne had told him on their drive to Mount Wilson. Somewhere in the row of boxes was most likely a copy of the magazine that had gotten Roxanne into so much trouble. He tried to remember the title of the magazine that her pictures had been in, but it would not come to him.

Hobart still had an eye on him, and Eddie pulled the 1939 box off the shelf, carefully balancing with it on the ladder, and climbed down. He began to rifle through the box, trying to appear as though he had the same interest in its contents as he had with the other boxes he had looked at. As in those boxes, this one contained multiple copies of each issue, but since these magazines were more flimsy and thin, there were far more copies of each than there were of the fiction magazines. The magazines were not all *Glamour Girls*. Some had no titles at all. Some featured a single model, and others had variety. Some were all pictures, others all erotic stories, and many were a combination. Turning pages of the magazines in the box, he was a bit shocked at what he saw. While the covers showed women in lingerie or wrapped in sheets or in otherwise titillating postures, the interiors left nothing to the imagination. The paper was as cheap and pulpy as most everything else Meteor put out, and the result was that the photographs were often grainy and indistinct. But he was still clearly able to see completely nude women, some of them with men, some by themselves, some with other women. Eddie felt certain that most of what he was seeing was illegal, but he really had no idea about obscenity laws. If they were illegal, he felt sure that Swinburne had paid off enough people to keep from being bothered over it.

At the back of the box, though, Eddie got another surprise. There were two thick folders with black and white eight by ten glossy photos, the original images that had been used to put the magazines together. Eddie did not bother looking at many of them, but he saw enough to be able to tell that what had been grainy and sometimes obscured in the magazine had started out as clear and explicit. He looked up at the top shelf and the box marked 1932, reasonably sure that was the year Roxanne had said her troubles with Whistler had started. It was possible, he realized, that similar folders in that box held the same pictures Whistler had used to coerce Roxanne into her modeling career for *Stupendous*.

After a few minutes, he put one random issue from 1939 into his own box and then acted as though he were about to pick up the box of pornography and climb the ladder again when he stopped, looked at Hobart, and said, "You might like these." He pulled an issue out and slid it across the table. On the cover was a woman in a negligee bending over at the waist and looking seductively at the camera, her breasts all but completely visible.

Hobart immediately took notice. He dropped his feet to the floor and sat up, put one elbow on the table, and just looked at the image for a moment. He looked at Eddie to get a reaction, and Eddie obliged by smiling in a conspiratorial manner. "Hot stuff," he said.

"I'll say. I didn't think the old man went in for this type of thing."

"It takes all kinds," Eddie said. "Here. Feast your eyes." He pushed the 1939 box toward Hobart, slid the ladder down toward the middle of the shelves, and climbed to the top again. Constantly glancing between Hobart and the box in front of him, Eddie began looking in the 1932 box for the issues that had Roxanne's pictures in them. It did not take him long. When he saw the title *Secret Lives* on one issue, he remembered that was the name of the magazine Whistler had shown Roxanne with her picture on the cover. The issue he looked at now featured a different woman, and there were no pictures of Roxanne inside, but two more issues back and he found what he was looking for. She was definitely younger in the photo, just over 18, Eddie calculated. She stood naked next to a window with a lace curtain pulled across her, a look of surprise and allure on her face, the fantasy clearly being that she had just been walked in on. Disturbing as it was, Eddie found himself aroused simply because it was Roxanne. Reminding himself to concentrate, he put the magazine at the front of the stack inside the box and began looking for others with her photos in them. He soon found four more, two of which had Roxanne on the covers. The photos inside the magazines were as poor in quality as the others he had seen, but he could tell they were of Roxanne when he came across them.

At the table, Hobart still focused on the issues in front of him. Eddie was pleased to see that Hobart's predilections were definitely getting to him as he looked at the magazines in the box. Swinburne's thug began moving around in his chair and shuffling his feet, and he was no longer looking at Eddie at all. His restlessness amused Eddie, and he wondered how long Hobart would be able to stand it.

"Sure are a lot of these things to go through," he said, trying to sound more tired than he was.

Hobart looked up from the fourth magazine he had selected, seeming surprised to find himself in the room with anyone else. His pornographic pursuits must normally be so solitary, Eddie thought, that looking through the magazines in someone else's presence must be disconcerting. Hobart closed the magazine and cleared his throat, still moving restlessly in the chair. He glanced at his watch, looked at the door of the vault, and then said, "You gonna be much longer?"

Eddie made a show of looking at his own watch and then said, "I've got another good half an hour here and a lot more boxes to look through. I figure I'll need the whole time. What about you? Find anything good in those?"

Hobart shrugged in response. Eddie could see he was making Swinburne's thug uncomfortable, and it amused him to see how much Hobart wanted to appear unperturbed.

"You know," Eddie said, "pretty much all of these boxes have duplicate issues. Swinburne won't miss one or two extra going missing. If you want some for yourself, that is."

"That's all right."

"I could slip a few extra in my box for you if you like and get them back to you later. Or you could just take them now."

Hobart's eyes narrowed. "You said you need the whole half hour?" Eddie nodded in response. "All right, then." Hobart stood up and gathered the magazines he had just finished looking through and then looked menacingly at Eddie. "I'll just be a minute. If you fuck around with anything here when I'm gone, I'll kill you first chance I get. You got it?"

Eddie felt his mouth go dry. Hobart meant what he said. Eddie was planning on doing exactly what Hobart had told him not to do. Still, he said, "You've got nothing to worry about from me. I just want to fill up my box and get out of here."

Hobart turned and walked out of the vault. Eddie practically slid down the ladder, the 1932 box in his hands. He assumed Hobart was on his way to the cottage where he and Luna had their quarters; no doubt, that was now the same place where Roxanne's dress and underwear had been taken. Eddie knew it would take Hobart a few minutes to get there and back, but the thought of Hobart moving quickly and returning before Eddie could finish the task he had given himself gave him a hollow feeling in his stomach.

He quickly flipped through the remaining issues in the box and found no more pictures of Roxanne, at least none that he could be sure were of her. In the folders at the back of the box, he found the glossy originals of her in various stages of undress. In one she was nude and kissing a man. In another,

245

she and a nude woman embraced. Eddie knew his face was turning red as he looked at the photos. He did not have time to go through all the photos in the folders but was content that all of Roxanne's pictures must be in this box, so he pulled both folders out of the box and laid them on the table next to all the copies of *Secret Lives* that he had found with Roxanne's pictures inside or on the covers.

Getting rid of these would not completely solve her problem. He knew it was possible that Whistler still had copies of the photos he had blackmailed her with, but it was also possible that Swinburne had insisted on their return. It was also likely that there were other copies of the magazines still in existence. Eddie found it hard to believe that anyone would hang onto eight-year-old pornography of such poor quality, but then again he had only to think about the wall in Hobart's room to realize that he was wrong. There would be many people, he told himself, who would be just as surprised to find a grown man hanging onto copies of *Stupendous* that he had bought when he was twelve years old, so it was far from unlikely that there would be pornography collectors with images of Roxanne tucked safely away. Still, other than Swinburne or Whistler, it was doubtful that anyone who still had one of these copies of *Secret Lives* would associate the beautiful woman on the cover with Roxanne Blackwood if she ever did get to write and publish a novel. Even so, given the importance that Swinburne attached to Roxanne and her ability to inspire Klaus Frehling, and the necessity he clearly felt to keep her in his control for as long as that inspiration held out, Eddie knew that Swinburne would not be content to rely on photos and magazines tucked away in a forgotten box in his vault as the only guarantors of his power of her. The photographic negatives had to be somewhere, and without them, none of his pilfering of Swinburne's collection would do Roxanne any real good.

Eddie poked his head out the door of the vault. There was no noise anywhere in the house, no sound of Hobart's returning footsteps. He thought there must be a safe in the house, possibly in Swinburne's room, where he would keep things like the negatives used to blackmail Roxanne. A search of Swinburne's room would be impossible, though. Eddie thought about the time bridge that was just outside the vault and of going forward or backward in time to a point where the house was empty and he could search for the safe, but even then, he did not know how he would open it or how he could accomplish this before Hobart returned. Then he turned back into the vault and gasped involuntarily. Looking around, he felt almost physically struck by the realization that there was, indeed, a safe in Swinburne's house and that he was standing in it right now. The concrete walls were thick enough to withstand the fire that would eventually destroy the house. Where else would Swinburne keep something so valuable as the negatives?

Eddie instantly thought of Pence and what he had described as his insurance file of prurient photos of compromised movie stars. "Jesus," Eddie whispered as he remembered what he had seen inside the locked, pressurized cabinet where Swinburne kept his most valuable pieces. There was a small, locked box within the cabinet, definitely big enough to hold negatives, cash, and other valuables.

Extremely conscious of the noise they could make, Eddie pulled Luna's keys out of his pocket and began looking for one that could open the cabinet. He tried one, then another, then three more before finding one that slipped in and clicked when he turned it. Again, he heard the rush of air as the pressure seal broke. Eddie paid no attention to the manuscripts and rare books that filled the cabinet; all he was concerned with was the little locked box on the middle shelf. It was bolted or welded into place at the back of the cabinet, so Eddie had to reach in with one key, try it, then select another and reach in again. Looking nervously toward the vault door and trusting his enhanced senses to hear if Hobart was coming, he kept trying key after key. At the point of despair and all but having convinced himself that Swinburne must not trust Luna with a key so valuable, Eddie tried another key. It slid into the lock and the little door on the front of the box pulled open on its hinges.

The box was about ten inches square and perhaps five inches deep. There appeared to be no cash in it, but only stacks of envelopes. Eddie pulled out as many as he could in one hand and began examining them. On the front of each was a handwritten word or two, usually a name. He recognized some of the names from news stories he had heard—Hollywood types, prominent businessmen, names from L.A.'s social elite. Some of the envelopes felt heavy and were thick with documents; others felt empty. On one of these thin envelopes was written the word "Blackwood." Eddie put the rest back and opened this one, finding several strips of photographic negatives. He held one up to the light and saw the reverse image of the photo of Roxanne at the window, covered in lace.

Hurrying, he closed the door and locked it, then did the same for the cabinet. He turned to the table, grabbed the stack of *Secret Lives* and the folders with the glossy photos in them, and then briskly walked out of the vault and around the side of it. The time bridge stood before him. He was turned around inside the house and unsure if he was facing east or west, past or future. He could only hope for future and some distance in the future at that. If the bridge only went forward a few days or weeks, his efforts would be useless. If he had to stay in another time long enough to find an appropriate bridge and get rid of the photos, magazines and negatives, it would be a help to Roxanne, but staying gone too long and having his absence discovered by Hobart would jeopardize everything else he had set in place to help himself and Roxanne out of their predicament. He decided before stepping through the entrance that if the bridge were unsatisfactory, he would simply turn around and return the material to the vault and never tell

Roxanne he had seen any of it. She had been surviving the terms of her blackmail and would have to continue to do so without Eddie's help.

By now, crossing over in time was a familiar phenomenon, and Eddie stepped up onto the bridge with the little stack of sleazy photos and magazines in his hands, careful to get his whole body through the opening. It was a bit narrower than others he had passed through. Once inside, he was relieved to see an arc in the bridge and that the exit appeared to be several feet away. If the bridges were consistent, this should put him at a considerable distance from 1940, as the bridge outside the cottage had done. The only question was if it was into the past or the future.

When he stepped through the other side, he felt disoriented for a moment because he was outside again. It was cold and daylight was fading. Dark clouds filled the sky, and the ground was wet. It had just rained, and from the look of the clouds, the storm was not over. He smiled, initially pleased that he had come into the future far enough to be at a point after Swinburne's house had burned to the ground. But then his smile faded as he looked to the side and did not see the concrete walls of the vault. It had still been standing in 1985, so either Eddie had come further into the future or not at all. He looked around and saw absolutely no sign of the mansion or the vault. There were no ruins, no cottage, no wall around the estate, no gate.

He had come into the past, perhaps as far as 1900 or more, long before Hollywood had even been conceived of. Los Angeles would be down the hill, but it was a far different city than he had known, possibly one without movie studios or housing booms or even very many automobiles and roads to accommodate them. In the twilight, he could clearly make out the openings to at least a dozen time bridges around the hilltop that would someday be Swinburne's estate. This was where Blackwood had stepped through on Tuesday when he had needed to get away from Swinburne and Hobart, and

Eddie imagined him standing here in a virtual Grand Central Station of time bridges, wondering which one to choose next.

Thinking of Hobart returning to the vault and finding him gone, Eddie moved quickly, tearing the photographs and magazines one after another into several pieces before tossing them into the air, the breeze catching the bits of paper for a moment and making them look like erotic confetti before they were caught by the weight of moisture in the air and pulled to the ground. Eddie saw flashes of skin, breasts, thighs, and Roxanne's face fly through the air and then land on the dampening soil where Swinburne's mansion would someday stand. His last task would be to destroy the negatives, which he planned on tearing with his teeth and then grinding into the dirt. Before he could begin on them, though, he was overcome by a sense of uneasiness. Something was wrong, and feeling suddenly panicked, he turned around.

The time bridge was gone. All of the time bridges that had only just now been visible all around the hilltop were gone. Eddie's heart raced as adrenaline coursed through his system, and he found himself trembling uncontrollably. Feeling helpless, he looked at his watch. It read 7:20. He had taken the Dragon's Tears not more than eight hours ago in his apartment before leaving with Hobart, Luna and Roxanne. Blackwood had said a drop would last twenty-four hours. "What the hell?" he whispered. Even as he was raising a foot in futility to try stepping into the time bridge where he thought it had been, he was considering several possible explanations for what had just happened.

It could have been that the Dragon's Tears were no longer as potent as they had been fifteen years before when Blackwood had first obtained them from the dead Johnny Woo. And it was also possible that the dose dripping off the tip of the glass medicine dropper had been less than the doses Blackwood had taken in his own time travels. Eddie also had to consider the possibility that Blackwood had lied about the duration of the drug's effects, but as to what purpose the older writer could have had in deceiving him, Eddie could not fathom. All that he knew with certainty was that he was trapped somewhere in the past with no Dragon's Tears left and no way to get back to 1940. Without thinking about it, he thrust the envelope of negatives into his pocket and ran in the direction of Hollywood, the rain that had been threatening now beginning to fall in tiny drops.

CHAPTER EIGHTEEN

By the time Roxanne got home to Pasadena, it was half past eight. She pulled the Cord up to the curb in front of the house and sat there staring at the column of brick that housed her mailbox, telling herself she should get out of the car and check to see if Eddie had been right about her father sending her a goodbye message. At the same time, she was afraid to look. She did not know which would be worse—receiving a final farewell from the man who had made her life so difficult or not receiving it and knowing he had simply abandoned her one more time. The sun shone brightly this morning, the fronds on the Queen Palms that lined her property catching the light and giving off an iridescent glow of greens and yellows. She stared at the trees for a moment and then put on the car's brake.

Earlier that morning, she had done as Eddie had asked, leaving Swinburne's Lincoln parked along the curb on Central Avenue across the street from Eddie's building. The street had been crowded with other cars, and the only space she had been able to find was at the north end of the block, a bit of a walk back to her own car but just across the next street from the Terminal Café, and she had decided to stop there for a minute before retrieving the Cord and going home. After quickly sipping her coffee at the counter and smoking a cigarette, she had gone into the women's room. Looking at herself in the mirror, she put on a bit of lipstick, and then shook her head in resignation. No amount of make-up, she realized, could conceal the weariness she now wore on her face. She had been up for almost twenty-four hours and felt like she had crammed in a week's worth of living. Her hair was disheveled, and dark circles under her eyes made her look ten years older. The dress, she decided, was pretty, but she knew she would not let herself keep it, anomaly that it was. When she left the women's room, she quickly paid for her coffee and walked out the door. It was not that she was in a rush but rather that she was now self-conscious about the oddly styled dress Eddie had bought for her forty-five years in the future. She did not want to stay in one place too long and draw attention to herself.

Once outside again and slightly rejuvenated by the coffee and the smoke, she walked down the block to her Cord. Before getting in, she stopped and looked across the street at the window of Eddie's apartment where she had sat the night before after their lovemaking. She looked at her watch. It was almost eight o'clock, which meant six hours before she would be back here again. She hoped Eddie would be here, too, but her instincts told her he would not be, that he had gone the same way her father had gone and that she was on her own to figure out what to do next about Swinburne, her father's estate, and her own continuing predicament with Whistler and Frehling. With a little sigh, she slid into the seat, the leather cold to the touch, and cranked the engine to life. It felt good to be in her own car again, and she accelerated away from the curb with renewed energy and purpose.

Now with her determination ebbing again, she reached into the mailbox in front of her house and was surprised to find a single piece of mail waiting for her, an envelope with her name and address written on it in her father's hand. There was no return address. Her hands trembled a bit, and she felt a rush of adrenaline as she walked around the front of the car and got behind the wheel again. She did not bother pulling into the driveway but sat at the curb with the engine rumbling and the heater blowing warm air on her legs, opening the envelope and reading what was inside. There were two sheets of paper, both handwritten. She began reading the top sheet: "Dear Roxanne, I'm sorry to have to say this in a letter rather than in person. I am also sorry to have to be leaving you this way. Unfortunately, there really is no other way, as you will discover very soon, I am sure. To this list of apologies, I must add my own parenting of you. As you can doubtless attest, I often did not know what to do, and so often did nothing by default. I have caused you great suffering by my actions and my inactions, and I am sorry. But, Roxanne, you have survived me beautifully—in every sense of the word. I am proud to be your father if not proud of the father I have been. Be strong. All my love." He had not signed it, probably because he had not known what to call himself— Daddy, your father, or even Chester Blackwood.

Roxanne nodded at the letter and smiled. It was more than she had expected and showed that there really was a man of substance in her father, albeit hidden beneath intoxication, profligacy and neglect. In light of what Eddie had told her about her father's exploits and the hints he had dropped to Eddie about where he would be going, she found it interesting that there was no mention of time travel, of meeting in the future, or anything else that might contradict the apparent suicide that would no doubt be discovered soon. He had wanted everyone to think he was gone—including her. The deception should have angered her, she told herself, but it did not. If he had not seen fit to share with her his secrets about cancer and plagiarism and time travel, she should not be surprised that he had opted to leave her uninformed of the true nature of his death. She was glad she knew the truth, thanks to what Eddie had told her. She would be sure to give the note to the police when they came to investigate the apparent suicide.

The second sheet of paper from the envelope was much more brief. "Roxanne, I implore you to destroy this piece of paper after you have read it. Don't give it to the police or to Swinburne or anyone else. Never mention it. There may be a man named Eddie Royce who will be asking around about me. He's a good man. Help him if you can. He comes with my blessing and because I've invited him." This note was not signed either. Roxanne looked at the postmark on the envelope and saw that it was from Tuesday. Her father had most likely mailed it at the same time he sent Eddie the package with the book and the Dragon's Tears in it. For reasons she could not fathom, the thought of her father sneaking back in time to mail the letter and the package, trying to help her and Eddie, brought forth the surge of tears that his goodbye letter had failed to provoke. She sat in the car and sobbed for several minutes before pulling herself together.

After easing the car up to the house, she went inside and stood looking at the mess Hobart and Luna had made. She sighed at how much worse it looked in the light of day, wide bars of sunlight streaming in through the east facing windows. She should start cleaning the mess, she knew, but she did not have the energy. Dropping her coat on the floor in the entryway, she went upstairs and burned her father's brief note about Eddie before taking off the anachronistic dress and falling into bed after first setting her alarm for noon.

She did not sleep. Even though she had not gotten any sleep the night before and would normally have fallen into an oblivious slumber after a full night's carousing, she felt not the least bit tired, perhaps because what she had been through did not count as carousing. Or perhaps she was still processing the surge of adrenaline she had felt when she had gotten her father's note, or maybe there was a lingering stimulant effect of the tiny amount of Dragon's Tears she had taken the night before. More likely, she told herself as she lay calmly in her bed, looking at the ceiling and waiting to feel drowsy, it was simply that the twenty-four hours she had just been through had brought with them so much change. She had lost her father, been threatened by her boss, had had her whole house ripped apart, and had met and made love to and almost certainly fallen in love with a man who she expected was now facing new dangers without her and might be gone from her life for good.

And she had traveled in time.

The thought actually made her smile as she rolled over and hugged a pillow. It seemed like a dream now, but it had been real. The future, she knew, was real—as real as the present, as real as the sheet pulled up to her shoulder. She had been there and come back, and the idea of moving slowly toward it at a natural pace gave her a sense of comfort about the way her life would play out—good or bad—that she had never felt before and knew she would never be able to explain.

By the time she actually drifted off to sleep, she had only twenty minutes before the alarm went off, and she awoke startled and disoriented, feeling worse than if she had not slept at all. She had fallen swiftly into a dream and had been in the middle of it when she woke up. In the dream, she was back in the ruined cottage in the future waiting for Eddie to get back. But instead of reading *The Golden Age of Science Fiction*, it had been a volume of Shakespeare, and she had been looking frantically through it trying to find a play Eddie had written, convinced that Shakespeare had stolen it from him. The floor of the cottage was littered with books, like her own house was and Eddie's, too. Among the books were pictures of herself in the nude, the pictures Whistler had shown her years ago, but the faces were all cut out or inked over and obscured. She kept tearing strips from the photos to use as bookmarks in the Shakespeare, oblivious to the contrast of impersonal, disembodied breasts and thighs against the columns of verse as she laid the strips into the book. When she had awoken, she sat on the edge of the bed, rubbing her eyes and shaking her head, trying to think of something else.

"Stupid dream," she whispered to herself and got up finally to find some clothes among the disarray that Luna and Hobart had left her room in.

****

At precisely two o'clock, the lock clicked in the door of Apartment 5 at 845 1/2 Central Avenue. It was followed by the turning of the knob and the squeak of hinges. Minutes before, there had been knocking at the door, but it had gone unanswered. Now Roxanne stood in the doorway, a silhouette between the light of the hallway and the darkened apartment.

"Eddie?" she called quietly. There was no reply. The shades had been pulled down, so she could not see anything in the room. It was possible Eddie was asleep on the bed across from the door, but she doubted it.

She stepped into the room, clicked on the light and closed the door behind her, turning the knob again to latch it so as not to make much noise. She had not wanted to attract any attention to herself. While Eddie's friend Pence down the hall could probably be trusted, she still did not want to have to explain to anyone her presence here or how she had gotten a key to Eddie's apartment.

The room was empty, as she had been expecting. If Eddie had answered her knock, she would have been elated, but all morning she had been preparing herself for the possibility that he would not. When her light knocking on the door had brought no response, it had only confirmed her expectations. Eddie's apartment was as they had left it the night before when Hobart and Luna had escorted them out. The sheet was still the only thing on the bed where she and Eddie had made love; her spent cigarettes were still on the window sill where she had left them; Eddie's clothes and possessions were still strewn about the room; and the floor was covered by Eddie's magazines and books. Some were in the piles she had been trying to make while he had slept after their lovemaking, but most were still scattered in disarray. Nearest her feet was a copy of *Stupendous* from July 1936, its Frehling cover portraying Roxanne in suggestively torn clothes, driving a laser sword into the thorax of a hairy spider twice her size.

The image made her angry, and Eddie's absence made her angrier still. She whirled on her heels and opened the door, storming down the hallway and toward the stairs. As she went, her heels tapping rapidly on the wooden floor, she passed the door to Will Pence's apartment where she and Eddie had knocked the night before. Remembering Eddie's advice that she look Pence up if anything happened to Eddie, she considered stopping and doing as Eddie had wanted, but her feet kept moving, and by the time she had convinced herself that talking to Pence now would be a good idea, she was already down the stairs and stepping out onto the street.

It was a sunny day but still cool, winter still holding onto Los Angeles in its feeble way. Roxanne wore a green print dress and had left a light coat in her car across the street. She ignored the impulse to go to the car and slip the coat on just as she had kept going past Pence's door even when she knew she should stop. Instead, she walked briskly up the street, cars and trucks rumbling past, mostly to and from the Southern Pacific terminal where Roxanne headed as well. The cool air on her arms, face and shins made her walk that much faster, and in minutes she was entering the Terminal Café for the second time that day.

The little diner had been bustling when she had been there this morning, but it was quiet now with the lunch rush over and dinner still hours away. The same waitress who had worked the counter this morning was still there pouring coffee. Roxanne avoided making eye contact and walked straight back to the phone booth beside the restroom doors, feeling a bit more at ease to be behind the booth's opaque doors.

She dialed the main number for Meteor Publications and asked the operator to put her through to Swinburne. When the operator insisted that Mr. Swinburne was not receiving calls, Roxanne had her put the call through to Whistler, who answered in his usual gruff tone.

"Whistler," he said.

"It's Roxanne."

Before she could say more, the editor spoke quickly. "Roxie! You were supposed to be in here this morning. You take your phone off the hook or something?"

"I didn't call to talk about that. Is Swinburne in there today?"

"Here?"

"Of course there. Don't play dumb with me."

"Sorry kid. No, look, I don't think he's in. Haven't heard from him all day."

"I want you to convince the switchboard operator to put me through to him. If not, you give me his home number."

"What's this about? You in some kind of trouble?"

"Just get me through to him," she said sharply, having no patience for Whistler's sudden attempt at expressing concern for her. Her tone must have carried her meaning. Whistler said nothing else; instead, Roxanne heard a click followed by silence.

The anger she had been feeling since finding Eddie's apartment empty had only intensified as she tried to get Swinburne on the phone, and she had to force herself to calm down as she stood in the phone booth. But she still felt agitated when, after another click, she heard ringing in the receiver. After three rings, Swinburne answered.

"Miss Blackwood," he said calmly.

Either Whistler or the operator had told him who was on the phone, she realized, irritated by the fact that Swinburne once again had more information about things than she did.

"What happened to Eddie after I left?"

"Mr. Royce? You know as well as I do."

"Don't try to stonewall me, goddamnit. What did you do to him?"

Swinburne seemed unfazed by her ire. "Miss Blackwood. Please. You have no reason to be angry with me. I was dealing quite openly and honestly with Mr. Royce. You, on the other hand, were a bit less than honest in your absconding with my automobile."

Roxanne shook her head. "Eddie told you where to find it?"

"Yes, but that still doesn't excuse the theft, does it? I haven't yet decided if I should bring the police into the matter."

Roxanne raised an eyebrow. "Go ahead. I'm sure they'd love to hear about false imprisonment."

"It's your word against mine. Really just a misunderstanding."

"The same goes for the car. You've got no proof I stole it."

Swinburne sighed. "All true. This is all a bit tiresome, though, Miss Blackwood. Was there something I could help you with?"

"Yes!" she fairly barked at the publisher. "What happened to Eddie? Where is he?"

Again, Swinburne exhaled loudly. "As I said, Miss Blackwood, I know as much as you do. Your Mr. Royce and I were engaged in amicable negotiations. He apparently left my house before they could be completed. I have no idea where he went or by what means. And you would like me to believe that you are similarly ignorant?"

Roxanne could not tell if she should believe Swinburne or not. She knew that Eddie would not simply have left before completing whatever negotiations he and Swinburne had been in the middle of, and she was left thinking about her father and how he had disappeared before Swinburne's eyes by stepping through a time bridge when apparently threatened by Hobart. Eddie may have needed to do the same thing, she told herself.

"Don't try to turn this around on me," she said. "You did something to Eddie, or your thugs did. You hurt him or made him think you would, and he had to . . . run."

"I can assure you, Miss Blackwood," Swinburne said, impatience beginning to show itself in his tone, "that neither I nor my associates did anything of the kind. What would it profit me? But this is pointless. If your Mr. Royce should reveal himself to you, kindly give him my regards, and let him know I am still interested in pursuing our arrangement, his unreliability notwithstanding. And in the meantime, my dear, I suggest you watch your tone and hold up your end of your own bargains. I understand Mr. Frehling was without a model this morning. Surely, there is no need to remind you of what you stand to lose if you choose to opt out of our arrangement."

Roxanne's heart was pounding. She felt trapped. Suddenly the comfort and anonymity the phone booth had provided were replaced by a sense of claustrophobia, and she wanted nothing more than to be back outside in the cool March air. If only she had known what Eddie had been negotiating and how far those negotiations had gone, she told herself. Then she would know how to play Swinburne. As it stood, with no real knowledge of what had gone on after she had left the mansion or of what Eddie had discovered when they had gone to the future, she felt as though she was in the same position with Swinburne this morning as she had been when the week started—an employee who was asked to humiliate herself on a regular basis in exchange for a very nice salary, the promise of greater rewards in the future, and the understanding that her past indiscretions would never be exposed.

"I will take your silence to be general agreement," Swinburne said quietly, and Roxanne could see the self-satisfied curve of his thin lips in her mind's eye. "And now, if you don't mind, I have work to do. There was a reason I did not want to take any calls today, Miss Blackwood. Our extra-curricular events of the last few days aside, I do have a business to run—and a little party to plan. I trust you will still grace us tomorrow evening at the celebration for Miss Le Blanc?"

Roxanne closed her eyes tight and fought the urge to scream, tears of frustration welling up. She had all but forgotten about the party for Rebecca Le Blanc and the unsavory appraisal she had received from Vivian Parker just two days ago in Swinburne's office.

Swinburne continued. "We'll be glad to receive you around eight? And, please, feel free to bring an escort. Perhaps Mr. Royce if he should deign to reappear. I'm most curious to continue our conversation."

For a moment, Roxanne said nothing and then barely audibly said, "Fine" before restoring the phone's receiver to its cradle. Before sliding open the phone booth's door, she whispered to herself, "Damn it, Eddie. Where are you?"

She walked slowly back down Central Avenue toward her car and Eddie's building, amazed at how different she felt now from just a few minutes earlier when her ire at Swinburne had driven her up the street and to the phone booth. From the moment she had met Eddie, she had begun to feel different about her predicament, hopeful that there could be a way out of it; and when she had done things like travel in time and work with Eddie to outwit Hobart and Luna, her sense of control over her own life had increased. But now that sense of control was gone. For years, she had gotten by with only herself to count on; in Eddie, she had suddenly found herself with a partner, and having someone to share her thoughts, hopes and fears with had been incredibly liberating. Now, with Eddie gone from her life just as suddenly as he had entered it, she found herself feeling more alone than she had in years. Before, she had grown oblivious to being alone or had made a virtue of it, but now the feeling was intense, and she saw no way around it. It made the walk down the block seem interminable.

Her car was parked at the curb on the southbound side of Central, right in front of Eddie's door, and as she neared it, she thought again of what Eddie had told her about contacting his neighbor if Eddie failed to meet her at his apartment. There really was nothing else she could do, she realized. Swinburne still had her under his control, and all she and Eddie had been through seemed to be for nothing. Talking to Eddie's neighbor certainly could not make her situation any worse. Without giving herself a chance to change her mind, she went back into the building and climbed the stairs, resisting the temptation to check Eddie's apartment one more time and knocking instead on the door of apartment number three.

Remembering how Pence had not answered his door when Eddie had knocked the night before, Roxanne was relieved to hear movement from the apartment now as she stood outside the door. Moments later, Pence opened it and looked at her with a slight smile. She had not known what to expect from a private detective, as Eddie had described him, and while she felt slightly put off by the coldness in his blue eyes, there was something about the confidence in his smile that told her he could take care of himself, and she decided that any friend of Eddie's would have to be a friend of hers.

Before she was able to say a word, Pence spoke quietly. "Miss Blackwood, I assume?"

Roxanne raised her eyebrows and nodded.

"Eddie told me I might expect you."

"When did you talk to him?" she asked immediately, a wave of relief washing over her even as she told herself not to get her hopes up about Pence's ability to help her find Eddie.

"Perhaps we should talk inside," he said, opening the door further and standing aside. "Please. Come in."

Without hesitation, Roxanne said, "Thank you," entering the apartment and waiting while Pence closed the door behind her. When he indicated a wooden chair beside a small desk, she sat down after turning the chair to face the bed where Pence now took a seat. "Did Eddie call you?" she asked.

Pence exhaled sharply in a heavy sigh. "He told me it would be better if I didn't explain how and when he contacted me. It would just confuse things."

Frustrated at this response and a bit taken aback, Roxanne said, "Please. I don't care if it's confusing. Just tell me whatever you can. Do you know where he is?"

"No," he said, shaking his head.

"Did he tell you what . . . we've been involved in?"

"Pretty much all of it. I know about your father, the Dragon's Tears, Swinburne. I know the two of you traveled to the future."

"And you believe it?"

Pence shrugged and raised an eyebrow. "Eddie was pretty convincing."

"He found a way to contact you from the future, didn't he? Was it when he left me and went into Hollywood? Or after we separated again this morning?" Pence's expression did not change; the cold blue eyes looked at her with some sympathy but not enough to prompt him to speak. Roxanne continued. "He went through another time bridge to come back here?"

Perhaps realizing that Roxanne would not give up easily, Pence finally said, "I really shouldn't . . . Eddie was pretty clear that it would be easier on you if you didn't know all the details."

Roxanne shook her head in frustration, regretting how she had gone on about not wanting to know the future. Eddie had taken her seriously, so much so that he had convinced Pence to keep her in the dark about some of what Eddie had done during his time traveling. It could not be undone, she realized, and all she could do was make the best of it. If Pence had even a bit of information about where Eddie was or what had happened to him, it was more than what she had now. And if there was no way of getting the information except on Pence's and Eddie's terms, then so be it, she told herself, at least for now.

"All right," she said. "So what is it he did allow you to tell me?"

"As far as telling you, nothing specific. He told me to look out for you. And to give you these." A large manila envelope was on Pence's desk, and he reached for it now, handing it to Roxanne.

She took it, her fingers trembling slightly. It was the same type of envelope Whistler had given her years before, the one with the nude photographs of her inside it, and she thought for a moment that Eddie had gotten hold of them somehow and was giving them back to her. But when she opened the envelope, she saw several pieces of paper with handwriting on them. *More goodbye notes,* she thought.

As she was pulling the pages from the envelope, Pence said. "Would you like some privacy? I can—"

"No," she said quickly. "It's fine. I'll just . . ."

She started reading the first page. "Dear Roxanne," Eddie had written. "If you've gotten this from Pence, something has gone wrong with my plan. I wish I knew from this end what it was and how you should handle things, but I don't. My plan is to get Swinburne to release you from your contract in exchange for your father's book. If it doesn't work, I'm going to convince him to give me a contract for *The Blighted Land,* written by me but with you as my agent and literary executor in case anything happens to me. You'll write the book. We'll pass it off as written by me. When it becomes the success I know it will become—and, Roxanne, I *know* it is going to be a huge success— then we'll shop it to a different publisher and reveal that it was you all along who wrote it, that Edward Royce is just your pen name. We can even come up with a new pen name if you want to keep me out of the public side of things altogether.

"That's my plan anyway. Like I said, if Pence is giving you this to read, it means something has gone wrong. I don't think Swinburne will try to hurt me. Not yet anyway. But if something goes wrong and I have to get out of there quickly, I'm going to do my best to head into the future and then come find you. So don't be surprised if I show up on your door in a day or a week or a month."

Roxanne smiled as she read this. The thought of him coming back to her gave her a warm feeling. She continued reading.

"But in the meantime, write. Start on your book. I can't explain why, but it needs to be published before 1945. Something's going to happen then that will make the book have a lot more power, but it will only seem that way if it's been published beforehand. It's got something to do with the book seeming more prophetic, and it will make the message stronger.

"The other thing you should do is continue playing ball with Swinburne and Whistler. I know you're going to hate every minute of it, but until you know for sure that I've gotten you out of your bind, you're going to have to play along like you don't know that's what I was trying to do. For all you know right now, I succeeded, but I can't say for sure. So keep on posing and doing whatever Swinburne wants until the book gets published." Roxanne thought again about the party Swinburne expected her to attend tomorrow night. The idea still made her want to wretch, but reading Eddie's note helped her look at it differently. Even in Eddie's absence, there was still a plan, and knowing she was following it would make the humiliation of going to Rebecca Le Blanc's celebration a bit more tolerable.

"But there's one more thing," Eddie's note continued. "The possibility that I don't make it back to you. Maybe Swinburne's done me in. Or maybe I'm going to get hit by a bus somewhere in time and I'll never make it back to 1940. I just don't know. I hope none of it happens and Pence can just give me these pages, and I'll burn them. But if you're reading them. . . you have to plan for the worst. So write the book. You'll find another page here where I designate you as my sole heir and literary executor. On one more page, I'm renouncing any connection to *The Blighted Land*, saying it was all written by you. I'm also leaving a suicide note." Roxanne's arms were instantly covered in goose bumps as she read these words. "Get your book published. Get through whatever contract Swinburne sets up. Feed him some line about how I don't want to deal with him, that I'm negotiating only through you. And then, when it's time to shop the book around to other publishers, have me declared missing. Plant the suicide note in a car by the beach. It will look like I've walked into the waves. Then the book is yours.

"And in the mean time, Roxanne . . . I don't know how to say this. It seems like goodbye, and it's hard to write. I think I've fallen in love with you. I know I haven't said that to you, and I know we've only just met, but I feel like I've known you forever. It's not fair to ask you to wait for me to find you again, especially since I may be dead by the time you're reading this or I may be in a place where I'll never be able to get back to you from. But if you can, just for a little while, wait for me and know that if there's any way I can possibly get back to you, I'm going to do it.

"And if you can't do that, I'll understand. The only other thing I ask is that you try to preserve my collection for as long as you can. The time may come when I'll need it. If I haven't found you in twenty years or so, sell it to the highest bidder.

"And one more thing. Trust Pence. Trust him as you would trust me. He knows more than I can tell you now and more than he'll let on, and he can help you in ways you won't be able to imagine. If I haven't been able to get you out of this mess, Pence will. I know you don't like having to count on anyone but yourself. But if for no other reason, then do it for me, Roxanne. Let him help you."

He had signed it, "Love, Eddie," and Roxanne had to wipe at tears when she was finished with the letter. She had not looked up at Pence once during the time she was reading it, but she did now to find him looking at her with genuine interest.

"Are you all right?" he asked.

Roxanne nodded and swallowed hard, hoping to keep more tears from coming. After several seconds, she asked, "Do you know what's in here?"

He shook his head.

Roxanne looked back at the pages in her hands. Beneath Eddie's two-page letter were his suicide note, his will and power of attorney, and his sworn statement that he had not written a word of *The Blighted Land*. Each was post-dated several years in the future to give her time to get the book written and published. The suicide note referred to Chester Blackwood and Eddie's realization that he could never write as well as his idol, that he was a fraud who needed a ghostwriter to help him and that because of it he was killing himself like Blackwood had.

"God damn it, Eddie," she whispered and then slipped them carefully back into the envelope. Looking at Pence once more, she told herself she would destroy Eddie's note to her as soon as she had the chance. The rest of the papers would go into her father's safe at their house in Pasadena. Smiling ruefully at Pence, she said, "Well, I guess he's gone. He says he'll try to get back, but . . ." She shrugged. "Swinburne may have killed him."

Now Pence leaned forward and said, "Your guy Swinburne. You know much about him?"

Roxanne shook her head. "Just that he's rich, that he's made his fortune in publishing and who knows what else. He lives all alone in a great big mansion in the Hollywood Hills, and he's not one to be taken lightly."

Pence nodded. "I've done a little digging at Eddie's request. You're right about all that. Not to mention he's got a nasty reputation in some circles. He's always moved in high society, but he doesn't come from old money. He also doesn't seem to have any real friends. There's been more than one allegation that he started out as a blackmailer before he got into publishing."

"That doesn't surprise me."

"I would guess he's at least as dangerous as he seems. Maybe more so."

Roxanne exhaled, noticed an ashtray on Pence's desk, and asked, "Do you mind if I smoke?" When he waved his hand toward her in a welcoming gesture, she dug into her purse for her cigarettes, offering one to Pence, which he accepted. She held the first drag in her lungs for a few seconds and then let the smoke out, pleased at the quick sense of satisfaction it gave her. "Eddie says I can trust you," she said, pointing with her index finger and her cigarette at the envelope with Eddie's note in it.

"He's right."

"Do you think he's dead?"

Pence shrugged. "I hope not. I doubt it, actually. Swinburne doesn't seem the type to take it that far. Still, accidents happen. I can keep digging if it would make you feel better."

Roxanne nodded her head. She took another drag, tapped her ashes into the ashtray, and said, "How can you get more information than you already have?"

Pence followed her to the ashtray with his cigarette. "If I could access Swinburne's house, I could look for any sign of Eddie, or any sign that something bad happened there."

Involuntarily, Roxanne shot him a quick look.

"What is it?" he asked.

"Do you really think you could find something in his house?"

Again, Pence shrugged. "Depends on if there's anything there to find. If there is . . . then probably."

"I can get you in."

Pence leaned forward. "How?"

They smoked their cigarettes as Roxanne explained about the party she was expected to attend the following evening. At Pence's prompting, she told him more about the layout of the house and grounds and everything else that had transpired while she and Eddie had been held there. When she described Hobart and Luna and the way Hobart had manhandled her and Eddie, she saw Pence's expression grow cold.

"I'm coming with you," he said when she was finished, both of their cigarette butts smashed into the ashtray. "Even if I can't find out anything about what happened to Eddie. You shouldn't go up there alone. Not now."

Roxanne raised an eyebrow. "I think I can take care of myself," she said, but even as the words came out of her mouth, she realized that she welcomed the prospect of having someone whom she could consider an ally with her when she went to Swinburne's. So she added, "But at the same time, some company might be nice."

Pence smiled and then offered one of his cigarettes. He did not use a lighter but rather struck a wooden match and lit both cigarettes from it.

"I have a lot of things to think about," Roxanne said. Pence's cigarettes were stronger than hers and had no filters. She began to feel a bit light headed as she added, "A lot to get used to."

Pence nodded. "You've had some big changes in the last couple of days."

"I'll say. Any advice?"

He was silent for a moment and then said, "Do what Eddie said you should do—whatever it was."

"I can tell you what he said."

"If you like. I'd also suggest you not make any big changes right away. Lay low. When everything gets tossed up in the air, most people make the mistake of trying to pick up the pieces before they've all hit the ground."

Roxanne nodded. "When will I know that's happened?"

Pence shrugged. "Hard to say. Just try not to let your emotions run away with you in the meantime, and you'll know when it's safe to make a move."

"Against Swinburne?"

"Mm-hmm."

"And until then, just play it safe."

"That's right," Pence said. "Just do what he'd expect you to do."

"Unpleasant as it may be."

Pence nodded in response and blew smoke toward the ceiling.

"All right then," Roxanne said, sounding as though she did not quite believe herself. Then, putting out her cigarette before it was half finished, she said, "Can I call you Will?"

"Of course."

"All right, Will. Shall I pick you up at seven tomorrow?"

CHAPTER NINETEEN

Even with Pence as her escort, Roxanne felt extremely uncomfortable turning off the main road and driving her car through the gates of Swinburne's estate. Just two nights before, she and Eddie had been driven through the same gates as Swinburne's virtual prisoners, and she had only escaped through Eddie's cleverness and their use of time travel. The further she got from that night, the more surreal the whole experience seemed in her memory, and she had sometimes found herself thinking it had all been imagined or dreamed. But now as she turned the wheels of her Cord onto the winding driveway now lined with other shiny, expensive cars, she knew how real the whole experience had been. She thought of how the estate would look in 1985, how it felt to look past these gates to the incredibly developed city below, and how the stolen key had sounded in the lock as she had snuck her way out in the chilly morning after saying goodbye to Eddie for what was beginning to seem like the last time.

She had spent the rest of the previous day and all of this one putting her house back together, a task that had been physically and emotionally exhausting. With the job far from completed, she had let herself lie down on a sofa in the main downstairs room to nap just before noon but had been awoken by the doorbell. Two uniformed police officers at the door had come to inform her that her father's car had been found near the Hollywood Reservoir and that there was evidence he had committed suicide, possibly drowning himself. Having been forewarned by Eddie, she affected grief for the policemen, getting choked up and then asking for some time alone. The

272

police had been obliging and sympathetic but had left her with a business card and requested that she contact their office as soon as possible.

Once they were gone, she had closed the door, put her back to it, and slid to the floor. It was going to be incredibly difficult, she realized, to play the mourning daughter for the police and the dutiful employee for Swinburne—while actually grieving Eddie's apparent loss the whole time. She told herself there was nothing for it, though; if she was going to get through the next few days and make worthwhile whatever sacrifice Eddie seemed to have made, she had no choice but to pull herself together and put on the show that everyone around her was expecting. And the first step in any of this was to finish making her house look as though Hobart and Luna had never been there. If the police should decide to inspect the house in response to her father's apparent death, it would not do to make them suspect Swinburne of any foul play. After a few more minutes on the floor, she had gotten up and gone back to work, her need for a nap forgotten.

She had eventually picked Pence up at his apartment after having spent too much time at home trying to decide what to wear. She wanted nothing too revealing so as to keep from giving Pence the wrong idea about her purpose in having him with her and to keep from looking too much like the women on the covers of *Stupendous* in a house full of people who would doubtless know the magazine and Meteor's other publications quite well. And at the same time, she had not wanted to appear too dowdy, too uncharacteristically conservative and thus give Swinburne a sense that she was acting in any way independently or against his expectations. Distasteful as it was, she wanted Swinburne happy with her performance tonight and hoped that, as a result, he would be a bit more forthcoming about any deal he had made with Eddie about *The Blighted Land*. She had opted for a black dress with an open back, a high neckline and a scattering of sequins that accentuated her curves; with it, she wore a short jacket that would help her feel more modest if the evening grew uncomfortable.

Driving up to the doors of the mansion, she let a parking attendant open her door. She and Pence exited, and she smoothed her dress while watching the Cord be driven away toward the gates again. Turning to Pence, who was underdressed in a simple suit and tie, she said, "Shall we?" He took her arm, and they went inside.

Where the house had been dark and silent on Wednesday night and Thursday morning when Hobart and Luna had led her and Eddie through it, the place now bustled. Guests roamed the entryway and the gallery that led off it in either direction, music played from a distant room, and every lamp was blazing. Roxanne recognized some of the more successful writers she had seen around the Meteor building as well as some actors and actresses; most of the people at the party, though, were unfamiliar to her. They looked classier than the actors and writers, more moneyed, and they all seemed to know each other.

When she and Eddie had been brought into the house, Hobart and Luna had steered them into Swinburne's library. Now Roxanne could see that the double doors leading into that room were closed. The party flowed through the gallery and entryway and to the right of the front doors into another large room identical in size and shape to the library. The house was laid out in a horseshoe shape with the two great rooms at either extreme end. As she and Pence made their way toward the ballroom, the sound of chamber music grew louder, and Roxanne kept an eye out for Swinburne among all the partygoers.

After taking a glass of champagne from a tray, she offered one to Pence, who declined with a subtle shake of the head. This pleased her, as Pence's seriousness reminded her that he was essentially here as her bodyguard. Not knowing what to do with the second glass of champagne, she quickly gulped the first one down, smiled a bit embarrassedly at Pence, and then walked with him through the ballroom, holding the second glass and sipping from it occasionally. It was good champagne, and it warmed her throat as she drank it.

The ballroom was immense. Large paintings lined the walls—expensive looking portraits and landscapes—and an audacious fireplace dominated the far side of the room. Leather sofas and armchairs lined the perimeter of the room, and in its center was a marble dance floor on which no one was dancing. The four-piece chamber group played lilting music for the partygoers who milled around, drinking, smoking and talking loudly.

Swinburne was holding court near a bronze sculpture of a ballerina in one corner of the room. When he saw Roxanne, he broke away from the group of people he had been talking with and met her and Pence as they approached him.

"Miss Blackwood," he said effusively. "I'm so pleased you've decided to join us."

It was difficult for Roxanne to keep a smile on her face. From the instant she had seen Swinburne from halfway across the ballroom she had had the impulse to run. Hoping he did not notice the goose bumps his presence had inspired on her forearms, she said, "Thank you for inviting me." Turning to Pence, she said, "This is my good friend, Will Pence."

The two men shook hands, and Roxanne watched as Swinburne silently appraised her escort, clearly trying to determine if there was more to Pence than met the eye while no doubt wondering just why Roxanne had chosen this man above others to escort her to the party. She was glad to see that Pence played it cool, shaking Swinburne's hand but making eye contact with him only for a polite moment before turning his gaze back toward Roxanne.

"Miss Blackwood, you'll want to see Miss Parker and Miss Le Blanc as soon as I can round them up. They'll both be pleased to see that you've joined us."

"Certainly," Roxanne said, still smiling and nodding.

Then she saw his expression shift to one of deadly seriousness, and he leaned in close to her. Speaking quietly so that she could barely hear, he said, "We had a strange theft last night. Would you care to explain it?"

"I don't know what you're talking about," she said, making no effort to match his discreet tone.

He smiled coldly. "Mr. Luna's keys mysteriously disappeared. And a night *after* you had such an easy time with my garage and gate locks and the ignition to my car. One would think you had managed to travel through time."

He let the words hang between them, and Roxanne did not respond but simply stared at him until he looked away and took a step back. Without saying anything else to her, Swinburne drifted off into the party.

"Bastard," Roxanne whispered as he walked away.

"Easy," Pence said.

She finished the glass of champagne and gave him a look that said she could tolerate only so much. "When do you want to do your snooping around? I want to get out of here as soon as I possibly can."

Pence nodded and quietly said, "I can go now. He had you and Eddie on the other side of the house?"

"Yes."

"All right. You going to be okay alone for a bit?"

"I'll be fine."

"Okay. If I don't come find you in an hour from now, leave without me."

Roxanne nodded her agreement, and he gave her hand a light, reassuring squeeze as he turned and made his way back out of the ballroom. She stood and watched him go, his cheap suit not hard to pick out from among the tuxedoes and other formal wear of the people he maneuvered past. Although a bit rough around the edges and no doubt dangerous when provoked, he was essentially a good man, she had decided after their talk the previous afternoon, and she knew intuitively that Eddie had been right about being able to trust him. Now she felt a bit sorry to see him go, knowing that his absence meant she would have to begin socializing with the rest of Swinburne's guests, none of whom interested her in the least.

About ten minutes after Pence had gone, Roxanne was standing near the quartet, listening to them play and trying not to glance at her wristwatch, when she saw another man who looked out of place making his way through the ballroom. It was Hobart, and she cringed at the sight of him. Part of her wanted to get his attention, making it obvious that she was here and completely unafraid of him, but another part of her wanted to stay as far away from him as possible. When the thought occurred to her that something might have gone badly with Pence's plans to explore the house undetected, her need to hide from Hobart vanished, and she began working her way toward him.

By the time Hobart found Swinburne, Roxanne had maneuvered to within six feet of him, and she watched as he bent slightly to whisper into his boss's ear. Swinburne turned sharply to look at him and barked, "Now?" incredulously before remembering himself and turning his head to whisper something back to Hobart. To Roxanne, Swinburne looked agitated and caught off guard, but he did not seem angry, and she doubted that any discovery of Pence had prompted Hobart's arrival at the party.

As Swinburne finished his whispered message, he leaned back from the other man's ear, and Hobart simply nodded and took a step back. As he was turning to go, Roxanne heard Swinburne call after him, saying, "Tell him not now. Tomorrow." Then he turned back to the people he was talking with, his fake smile back on his face in an instant.

Burning with curiosity, Roxanne began moving in the same direction as Hobart, hopeful that she might have the chance to determine what was going on. Before she could take five steps, though, she felt a hand on her upper arm, commandingly grasping her triceps. She turned in surprise to find Vivian Parker looking at her with a smug smile.

"Miss Blackwood," she said, letting go of Roxanne's arm and shifting her weight so that one of her hips jutted out a bit provocatively. "I'm so pleased you could make it. Rebecca will be just thrilled that you've come out as well." The woman was dressed very similarly to the outfit she had worn in Swinburne's office when Roxanne had first met her three days earlier—a mannish suit of clothes including a loosely fastened necktie and vest. Her short, dark hair was plastered closely to her scalp with a spiral curl on each side of her head spreading onto her cheeks like feminine sideburns. The sight of her made Roxanne feel more bothered than she had been at seeing Hobart.

Even so, she smiled and said, "I wouldn't have missed it for the world." Hoping to get away, she half turned and said, "I need to find my escort. He seems to have gotten himself a bit lost in all this."

Vivian stopped her short with the return of her hand to Roxanne's upper arm. Her grip was firm but not tight. "Please don't go so soon, Miss Blackwood. May I call you Roxanne?" She continued without giving Roxanne a chance to answer. "In anticipation of your arrival tonight, I brought along something I thought you might find interesting. I have it just through there." She released Roxanne's arm again and pointed now at a door near the ballroom's blazing fireplace.

It sounded to Roxanne like a come on, the sort of line that men had been trying on her for years in one situation and another. But at the same time as she was repelled by Vivian's advances, she was also curious to see where this would lead. She had known from the moment Swinburne had invited her to the party that there was something more to it than just the expectation that she extend a professional courtesy to the newest author in Meteor's stable. Now it looked as though she would find out what else Swinburne and Vivian had in store for her. Forcing herself to smile but not wanting to appear too eager, she said, "All right. But only for a minute."

After threading their way among the small clusters of people who talked, laughed and drank in this corner of the ballroom, Roxanne watched as Vivian opened the door she had pointed toward and stood aside to let Roxanne enter first. Inside, she looked around a small sitting room with a blue divan in its center and several leather upholstered chairs with antique tables in between them. Like in the ballroom, there were paintings on the walls, but now she saw that there were two windows. As a last resort, the windows offered an escape and made her feel a bit more comfortable to be alone here with Vivian Parker, especially after the other woman closed the door behind her, shutting out the noise of the party and cutting Roxanne off from the safety of the crowd.

"So," Roxanne said, glancing around the room and trying to appear nonchalant but cheerful. "What's in here that's so wonderful?"

"Why don't you have a seat?" Vivian said, indicating the divan.

"I thought this was going to be quick," Roxanne said, still trying to sound cheerful while making no move toward the divan.

"That's up to you." Vivian crossed the room to stand close to Roxanne, looking her in the eye as she continued. "I know your secrets, Roxanne."

Roxanne raised an eyebrow, trying not to let the other woman see the alarm she was beginning to feel. She had managed to maintain her composure when Swinburne had all but accused her of time traveling, but she feared that she would not be able to hide the anxiety Vivian Parker was making her feel. "Really?" she finally managed to say with what she hoped was convincing incredulity.

"Really." Vivian smiled. It was the same predatory look she had given Roxanne in Swinburne's office when they had first met. "I know all about your naughty past, your dirty pictures, and the deal Augustus struck with you to keep them hush hush." She tilted her head downward and looked up at Roxanne with mock coyness. "And I know all about your little science fiction stories and your pathetic *nom de plume*. And I know about your father, and all his little peccadillos. And I know all about this boyfriend of yours who's gone missing."

The more Vivian spoke, the worse Roxanne felt. Initially angry with Swinburne for divulging the secrets of her past, she had begun to grow more and more fearful. It was as though a venomous snake had just wriggled its way into the room and had slithered up to her ankle before she had even had a chance to see it for what it really was.

But then, after a moment's hesitation, Vivian added, "And I know a little something about moving back and forth through time."

Roxanne was powerless to hide her feelings of shock and fear. It was as though the snake had struck, and she could do nothing but wait for its poison to spread throughout her body.

"You're surprised, I see," Vivian continued, beginning to pace back and forth in front of Roxanne, never getting more than an arm's length away. "Do you suppose your boyfriend ran out on you because he was trying to protect your father? That must make you feel just awful." She paused and smiled. "You might be more surprised to find your father's secret doesn't matter so much anymore. Your boyfriend sold you out for that silly book and then hid himself away for nothing." She stopped pacing directly in front of Roxanne and said. "Curious?" The icy smile came out again. "Augustus and I have found our own means of getting to the future. Let your father and boyfriend think they've kept their secret. We've found another way."

Roxanne felt herself grow cold as she listened. At the same time, the muscles in her arms and neck tensed involuntarily, her jaw tightened, and she had to fight the urge to bolt from the room. "I don't know what you're talking about," she finally managed, but she knew as she spoke that her words were not convincing; she had lost the sense of amused disinterest she had managed to convey when she had first entered the room.

"Please, Roxanne. You can't fool me. I know too much. Maybe even more than Augustus."

"How?"

Now it was Vivian who raised an eyebrow even as she smiled. "Much better. Curiosity is so much more pleasant than phony denials." She paused and then resumed her pacing as she spoke. "I don't suppose you know anything about my family. We've been here for generations. My father owned most of what is now Hollywood. Worthless land when he bought it. Then he began to sell it off bit by bit as the movies came in. This very hilltop and most of what's around was in my family before this mansion was here. These hills were my stomping grounds. I used to come riding through here. I had a few little bowers tucked in among the groves here and there—wicked little places where I would sneak liquor and bring girls from school and corrupt them."

She paused to look at Roxanne, seemingly awaiting a response. When none came, she went on. "So . . . late one rainy afternoon in 1920, I had hiked up into the hills with a flask of whiskey and found a nice spot to drink it between downpours. I was just getting up from my little sheltered spot when I saw a man across the glade. He hadn't been there a second before, and then he just appeared. I thought I was hallucinating."

Listening, Roxanne felt her heart begin to race, and she hoped her face did not betray her feelings. Her first thoughts were of Eddie, but then she realized that Vivian might also be describing Roxanne's father. She tried to keep her eyes focused on Vivian's face as the other woman continued pacing back and forth in front of her.

"But it was real," Vivian continued. "As real as the rain on my face. I was hidden there among the bushes, and I crouched there, peeking through them. The man had something in his hands, and I saw after a minute that it was papers of some kind. He started tearing them into pieces and throwing them into the air, into the mud. And then, when he was done, he turned around suddenly. He looked agitated and started stepping up into the air. I thought he looked like a horse pawing the ground. And then he ran away—bolted like a rabbit down the hill. Can you imagine?"

Roxanne shook her head. Trying to sound cool, she said, "It's an interesting story, but I don't see what it has to do with me."

Vivian smiled self-assuredly. "You shall, my dear. You shall." She turned and walked across the room. A small portrait hung on the room's west wall, and Vivian went to it now. Reaching up to the frame, she pulled it toward her, and Roxanne saw that the painting was mounted on hinges and that it concealed a small safe. "Knowing you would be here tonight, I asked Augustus if there was somewhere safe where I could keep these for tonight so I could show you. They're my most prized possessions." She began turning the combination lock, glancing over her shoulder at Roxanne momentarily and then looking back at the safe. "When I saw that the man was gone, I ran out to the spot where he'd been and picked up the scraps of paper he'd torn up and thrown into the mud." With a click, the safe door opened, and Vivian pulled out a small leather folder. She turned toward Roxanne, holding the folder in front of her. "It was like a jigsaw puzzle, the most wonderful jigsaw puzzle imaginable. It took me days to put it all back together, but here it is."

Vivian flipped the folder open, and Roxanne saw an eight-by-ten print of one of the nude photos Klaus Frehling had taken of her. The picture had been torn into pieces and glued back together on another thicker sheet of paper. The photo was stained and water damaged, but Roxanne could clearly see that the woman in the picture was herself as she had looked at eighteen. In it, she stood in front of a bed and absurdly held a large fan over one of her breasts. She remembered the night she had posed for it along with dozens of others but felt neither embarrassment nor shame nor even irritation at seeing it here and now in the middle of all of Swinburne's wealth and held up before her by this cold, frightening woman. Instead, all she could think about was Eddie. She knew now that he was not dead, that Swinburne had done nothing to harm him. If Vivian Parker had truthfully described the way she had acquired the picture and others just like it that she now began flipping like the pages of a book, it meant that Eddie had snuck the pictures through a time bridge to the past in order to destroy them and free her from Swinburne. And then, apparently, the Dragon's Tears had worn off; the way Vivian described Eddie trying to step up into the air made Roxanne think of how awkward it had felt to try to step up onto the time bridges that she had barely been able to see. Eddie had not made his escape into the future but rather was trapped in the past.

Roxanne shook her head. "I don't need to see any more," she said as Vivian continued to turn the pages of her pornographic portfolio. When the other woman cruelly continued flipping from one image to the next, Roxanne turned away. Behind her, she heard Vivian close the folder, and then she felt a hand on her shoulder. It repulsed her, but she held still, knowing she needed to hear the rest of what Vivian had to say.

"These photos were my constant companions," Vivian said. "For years. I had no explanation for them, for how I'd gotten them, for who that man was. But it didn't matter. I was in love with the woman in these pictures. Can you imagine?" She laughed sharply. "Do you have any idea, Roxanne, how . . . beautiful you are? My God. You could have anything you want. Anyone you want. And you get yourself stuck in this stupid arrangement with Augustus so you can . . . write a book someday? Roxanne. Set your sights a little higher."

Roxanne turned back to face Vivian. She looked at her venomously and said, "I don't want the things you want. My sights are just fine."

"So you say. You're happy this way, posing for those stupid magazines?"

Roxanne exhaled sharply. "Happy enough."

Vivian smiled, ignoring Roxanne's ire. "That's how I found you, you know. Your work for Augustus's artist. When I saw the sketches for the cover of Rebecca's book, I couldn't believe my eyes. It was you. The woman from my pictures."

"So Swinburne knows about these?" Roxanne nodded toward the folder.

"Oh, yes."

"And the man on the hill?"

Vivian shook her head. "I told him I found them. I told him where and when but nothing else. He started telling me about Chester Blackwood and his suspicions that your father had somehow found a way to travel through time. If I hadn't seen the man on the hill just . . . appearing the way he did, I would have laughed Augustus out of the room. But I didn't. I believed it was possible. How else could pictures taken in 1932 show up on a rainy hillside in 1920?"

Roxanne shook her head in response.

"So Augustus and I started a little quest. He pursued your father, pressured him. I sought out other avenues . . . through Rebecca."

Curious, Roxanne simply said, "Rebecca?"

Vivian smiled. "My little darling has a torrid past. We all do, don't we? Have you ever smoked opium, Roxanne?"

"No."

"It's glorious. Drank absinthe?"

Roxanne shook her head.

"So many things I can introduce you to. Wonderful. Dear Rebecca hasn't been so sheltered. She knows people, has always moved in those circles. We made inquiries. And we finally found what we were looking for. As I was saying earlier, your boyfriend protected your father's secret for nothing. It's called Dragon's Tears."

Vivian said it with flare and clearly watched for a reaction. Roxanne could feel her heartbeat in her ears but betrayed nothing. She smiled and repeated, "Dragon's Tears."

"Quaint, isn't it? It's taken months of dealing with the most unsavory people, but yesterday morning a man made contact with us. And soon we'll have it."

"And you think it's real?" Roxanne asked, trying to find out more. "It sounds like someone's playing a joke on you."

"We'll know soon enough."

"And Swinburne is in on this?"

"Of course."

"And what are you planning on doing if this turns out to be real? Bestsellers for your girlfriend?"

"Don't be stupid," Vivian said, her voice cold now. "My aspirations run circles around those of your father and Augustus. It's not about selling books or making money. How short sighted."

"That's what Swinburne wants? Money?"

"And knowledge. He doesn't like the idea that your father outsmarted him. Let it go, I say. My God. Roxanne, if I could go back in time, do you know what I'd do?"

"Not into the future?"

"No. Not yet. I would stop my father from selling off all this land at a pittance to the developers. I would own it, control it. All of it and more. With enough control and influence, coupled with absolute certainty of what lies ahead politically, culturally . . . Roxanne, I tell you, I could get a man elected President if I chose to. Any man I wanted. Maybe even a woman. How would that be?"

Roxanne smiled. "You're thinking big."

"And why not?" Vivian dropped the leather folder onto the divan spine first so that it opened onto the cover of *Secret Lives* as it fell. She stepped forward, taking Roxanne by the hand. "No one ever got anywhere by thinking small. And, Roxanne, I want you with me." Roxanne tried to pull her hand away, but the other woman's grip on her was strong, and she immediately grabbed Roxanne's other hand, holding both of them tightly. As Roxanne began to struggle and walk backwards, Vivian's grasp strengthened. Veins on her neck and forehead began to bulge, and Roxanne saw her expression shift from excitement to angry desire.

Vivian had Roxanne within a foot of being backed up against the wall when the door to the ballroom opened, and Rebecca Le Blanc walked in. Appearing quite agitated, she began speaking without really seeing what was happening. "Vivian, Mr. Swinburne wants—" She stopped, her face a sudden blank, her red hair still swaying from the momentum of her footsteps as she had quickly entered the room.

Vivian let go of Roxanne's wrists and turned on Rebecca. "What is it?" she barked.

Rebecca stood still for another moment, her mouth agape. Then she repeated herself and went on, her voice so quiet that Roxanne could barely hear over the sounds from the party coming through the open door. "Mr. Swinburne wants you right away. He says . . . our friend's here now. He wants to negotiate right away and be done with it. He won't take no for an answer."

"Christ!" said Vivian. She turned back to Roxanne and forced a smile. "I'm sorry I lost my temper with you, my dear. I want to finish our conversation still." Then, turning to Rebecca, she said, "Don't let her leave. I swear to God, I'll kill you if you let her out of this room." With that, she rushed out, closing the door behind her.

The instant Vivian was gone, Rebecca transformed from quiet and cowed to a woman enraged. "You bitch!" she shouted at Roxanne and began advancing toward her.

Roxanne saw that Rebecca would settle for nothing less than violence, and she readied herself. The redhead was a bit younger than Roxanne and a bit smaller, and Roxanne did not feel physically intimidated by her. But the other woman's rage was something to be reckoned with, and Roxanne took a few steps backward, getting the divan between herself and Rebecca and hoping to talk her way out of the situation. "I think you've got the wrong idea about me," she said.

Rebecca shook her head. The semi-nude photo of Roxanne in the folder on the divan caught her eye, and she rushed toward Roxanne, coming at her between the wall and the foot of the divan. Without thinking about it, Roxanne rushed around the head of the divan, pushing it toward Rebecca as she did, and then she scrambled to the door that Vivian had gone out of moments before. She swung it open and got two strides into the ballroom when she felt her hair being pulled viciously from behind, pulling her off balance and down onto the floor.

Gasps went up among the partygoers as people scattered from the commotion; the chamber musicians continued playing even though all four had a clear view of the disturbance. Momentarily overwhelmed, Roxanne lay on her back, and before she could begin to roll onto her side, Rebecca was on top of her, straddling Roxanne's stomach and tearing her own dress in the process as her knees bent the fabric beyond its breaking point. She would have been smarter to sit on Roxanne's chest, using her shins to pin Roxanne's arms to the floor. As it was, Roxanne saw the first fist coming toward her face, and she instinctively raised an arm to block it. She began bucking her hips and half rolling under Rebecca to dislodge her assailant but had to raise her arms again to fend off more blows. Tears streamed down Rebecca's face, and she was shouting unintelligibly.

To Roxanne, the attack seemed to go on forever, but it was less than a minute before someone physically pulled Rebecca off of her. Roxanne could only see that it was a man and that he literally picked up Rebecca and tossed her away so that she landed on her knees on the hardwood floor. As Roxanne began trying to sit up, the man turned, knelt, and offered her his hand. It was Pence.

"Will!" she said, taking his hand and letting him help her to her feet.

"Jesus, Roxanne," he said, sounding a bit winded from his sudden exertion in breaking up the fight.

"Bitch!" Rebecca shouted from the floor.

At the same instant, another voice shouted from the middle of the ballroom, "What the hell is going on?" Roxanne recognized Swinburne's voice. Raised in anger, it was high pitched and whiny, but it was commanding enough to cause the music to stop and the crowd to part. A corridor lined with partygoers opened with Roxanne and Pence at one end beside the immense fireplace and Swinburne in the middle of the room. He was flanked by Vivian Parker on one side and an Asian man with a thin mustache and an inexpensive suit on the other. In his right hand, he held a briefcase that he immediately dropped to the floor as soon as he saw who stood by the fire.

"Woo," Pence said, and in one fluid motion he shoved Roxanne away from him and reached into his breast pocket. Roxanne stumbled, almost losing her footing, and turned to see Pence pull a gun from inside his jacket. At the same time, she saw that Johnny Woo had a gun in his hand as well, and amidst screams and shouts from the crowd, both men fired.

Her ears ringing, Roxanne saw Woo double over and fall to the floor at Swinburne's feet, and then the ballroom erupted with people running and shouting as they tried to get out of the line of fire. Roxanne could no longer see what was happening around Swinburne but no longer cared, as she saw that Pence had also been shot. He stood where he had pulled the trigger, but his posture was all wrong. From the waist down, he appeared to be standing straight, but his upper body was twisted, and he had a growing spot of blood seeping into the material of his jacket. His expression was one of utter confusion.

Roxanne rushed toward him, calling his name, but when she got beside him she stopped herself from touching him. He stood so strangely, and the blood stain was spreading so quickly that she was afraid she might hurt him worse. Tears streamed down her face, but when Pence looked at her, it was with the same cold smile she had first seen when they had met.

Seconds later, his expression shifted to one of alarm, and Roxanne heard more commotion and shouting behind her. Before she could turn, Pence grabbed her by the shoulders with both hands, a look of incredible pain on his face, and spun her around so that her back was to the fireplace and his was to the rest of the ballroom. Over Pence's shoulder, she glimpsed Rebecca Le Blanc standing ten feet away; Johnny Woo's gun was in her hand, aimed at the spot where Roxanne had just been standing. Before Pence had even stopped spinning Roxanne around, another gunshot sounded, and Pence's body slammed against her, toppling her over backward with Pence coming down on top of her. Her head hit the hearth with Pence's full weight on her body. She felt like her skull was going to split open, and the floor seemed to be spinning under her. Knowing she should get out from under Pence, she felt strangely calm at the fact that her arms had no strength. With a buzzing in her ears and the light in the room seeming to fade, the one thing she could clearly see was Rebecca Le Blanc slowly approaching, the gun at the end of her outstretched arm. "Oh my God," Roxanne said, completely involuntarily. Then, as Rebecca moved her arm to point the gun at Roxanne's head, another figure burst from the chaotic mass of partygoers. The last thing Roxanne saw before losing consciousness was Vivian Parker tackling her lover from behind, both women tumbling into the blazing fireplace.

CHAPTER TWENTY

Roxanne regained consciousness in the midst of an inferno, Pence's body still on top of her. She heard the popping and crackling of flames, distant screams and the crashing of beams. Heavy smoke filled the room, and she could see only a few feet in any direction. Her head still pounding, she had regained some of her strength, and began pushing Pence off of her. As she did, she saw a person approaching her through the smoke, a man crawling slowly toward her and looking as though he would fall on his face with every movement of his arms and legs. At first, Roxanne thought the man was coming to rescue her, but when she saw how weakly he moved, she realized that he was another forgotten partygoer and now a victim of the fire.

It was not difficult for her to imagine what had happened—Vivian and Rebecca plunging into the fireplace and then no doubt rushing back out with their clothes on fire, spreading flames throughout the house. Confusion and panic must have followed, and it was not surprising that Roxanne and Pence had been left behind in the ballroom. She could not guess why this other man was still amid the flames, but she would not have been surprised to learn that there were others trapped as well.

Then, as Roxanne was managing to get her legs out from under Pence's, she saw that the man now crawling past her was the one called Woo whom Pence had shot and who had put the first bullet into Pence. Alarmed, she prepared to defend herself against another attack, but then she watched, dumbfounded, as Woo crawled a foot past her and then seemed to raise himself up into the air and fade from sight. He did not disappear into the smoke; he had simply disappeared.

Dragon's Tears, Roxanne thought, realizing that Woo was the man Vivian had referred to who was going to supply her and Swinburne with Dragon's Tears. Then she remembered the details Eddie had given her about how her father had first obtained the drug from a dying Chinaman, and she knew that it must have been this same Johnny Woo, an apparent time traveler himself who was peddling Dragon's Tears to the wealthy.

Faced with the more immediate problem of getting herself and Pence out of the fire, she put Woo and time bridges out of her mind and started pushing at Pence as hard as she could. She no longer cared about hurting him and was able to get him over onto his side and then his back. With her face close to his, she shouted, "Will! Will! Wake up!" There was no response.

Beginning to panic, she screamed his name again, barely able to hear her own voice over the sounds of the fire. Then she pulled his jacket open and tore furiously at his shirt, popping off the buttons and revealing a bullet hole in his shoulder, the first wound he had sustained from Woo. It had bled copiously, his shirt having soaked up much of the blood, but more of it soaked the skin around the wound. She knew that if she turned him over, there would be another gunshot wound where Rebecca had hit him with the bullet meant for her. She also knew that he was dead even before she put her ear to his chest, trying to hear or feel his heartbeat.

She sat up coughing, her legs bent under her and tears streaming down her face as she looked at the dead man. There was no time now for goodbyes, regrets or apologies. Smoke hung close to the floor in the high-ceilinged room, and she saw flames working their way across the walls near her. Looking across the ballroom in the direction of the doorway into the gallery and safety, she saw nothing but smoke and flames; some burning piece of the house had fallen across her path to the exit and was setting the furniture on fire. To get out of the house that way, she would need to work her way around the burning obstacles. Behind her was the room where Vivian Parker had taken her, and she remembered the windows she had seen there, but the doorway was completely blocked by flames.

Resolving to crawl her way through the ballroom and get as far as she could, she bent down, putting her face as close to the floor as she could and beginning to pull herself along on her elbows and knees. But before she had gotten even two feet away from where she started, she stopped. In front of her was Pence's outstretched left arm; when Roxanne had torn open his shirt, something had fallen from his shirt pocket and rolled across the floor until his arm had stopped it. Now she stared at it in disbelief—a small vial filled with amber liquid. She did not stop to think about whether it could be anything other than Dragon's Tears or how it had gotten into Pence's shirt. Instead, she thought only of how Woo had disappeared into a time bridge near the fireplace.

In her panic, she quickly twisted off the cap with its glass dropper attached, brought the vial to her lips, and took a short sip. Immediately, the pain in the back of her head faded away, and the sound of the fire intensified; she could distinctly hear what must have been a thousand creaks and pops as the flames consumed parts of the walls and weakened others. Turning toward the fireplace, she saw the time bridge but was astounded at its appearance. Rather than the faded outline she had seen with Eddie or the shimmering opening Eddie had described, the time bridge that Roxanne saw looked like an oval of blue flame with rainbows of light shooting out from it in every direction.

She did not question the wisdom of entering the bridge, even given the intensity of its appearance, but crawled to it, coughing. Without glancing back at the burning ballroom or Pence's body behind her, she crawled up into the opening, hands first and knees and feet after. Once inside the time bridge, the sound of the inferno behind her faded immediately, but she barely noticed the change. Dumbfounded, she looked at the bridge ahead of her and trembled. When she had walked over the bridges with Eddie after having only licked the spoon with the Dragon's Tears residue on it, they had been barely visible straight lines from one opening to next. Now, after having impulsively sipped an unknown quantity of the substance, the bridge before her was far more complex. As she had expected, the bridge did extend straight across from one end to the other, but it also branched off into several other bridges, each with a different opening in the distance. "Train tracks," she whispered, remembering the analogy she and Eddie had come up with to explain traveling in time and Eddie's desire to switch the track they were on for a better one just as her father had done.

Staying perfectly still, she crouched at the entrance to the bridge, willing herself to move but too frightened to advance even an inch. She was terrified of taking the wrong path, reasoning that the alternate paths led not to different times but rather to different versions of the same time. On one path could be the future that her father had altered, and along another could be an entirely different one where her father had used Dragon's Tears to gain the kind of power that Vivian Parker had aspired to. She could not fathom the possibilities that the different paths represented, and choosing the wrong one would put her into a future or past more alien than anything she could imagine.

Telling herself that following the straight path with Eddie had led to their leaving and returning to the right time, Roxanne began crawling forward. As she passed each alternate path, she hesitated, wondering what she would find on the other side if she took it. But she avoided veering to the left or right, as she knew that going into an alternate time would prevent her from ever getting back to the version of 1940 that she knew. It would be too difficult to retrace her steps, so she stayed on the straight path and in a few minutes arrived at the other end of the time bridge.

Beyond the opening, she could see that it was dark and that there was no fire burning. She also saw that she would be outdoors when she passed through the opening; the hilltop on the other side of the bridge was lit by the moon, and there appeared to be no sign of Swinburne's mansion. Holding her breath, she crawled through, putting her hands down onto dirt and clumps of dry grass. A cool breeze blew across the hilltop, and she stopped moving forward, looking carefully for signs of anyone else around. She did not want anyone to see her the way Vivian Parker had spotted Eddie's arrival in her time. Several yards away from her, she saw Johnny Woo lying prone among the chaparral and tufts of wild grass. There was no one else around.

The intensity of her every sensation left her a bit bewildered, and she sat still for a minute. It was as though she could feel every one of the fine hairs on her forearms individually as it was stirred by the breeze. Her fingertips could trace the intricacies of the miniscule ribs in the blades of wild grass she sat in, and the smells of all the plants and animals on the hilltop made her wonder how she had ever failed to catch even a fraction of all these scents. Her vision was also intensified, the moonlight on the hilltop illuminating everything around her as with the clarity of the sun.

When she had passed through the second time bridge with Eddie, they had found the burned out ruins of Swinburne's mansion with his vault and the small cottage still standing. Now she knew how the house had burned, but as she stood up and looked around the hilltop, she saw no sign that there had ever been a building here. She doubted that she and Woo had traveled far enough into the future to obliterate all signs of Swinburne's estate, so she was reasonably sure that they had come into the past, into a time long before the house had been built, maybe even before Vivian's father had sold the land. And while there were neither other people nor buildings on the hilltop with her and Woo, there were countless time bridges. They appeared to her as tall shimmering lights with darkness at their centers, waves of colors radiating out to the edges and undulating like water.

Still standing beside the bridge she had just crawled out of, she looked around and found several fist-sized rocks. She gathered these and made a small pyramid at the base of the time bridge to mark it lest she become confused when the time came to return to her own time. Then she went to the man lying in the dirt. If he was alive, she told herself, she would do what she could to help him. If he was dead, she would sit here on the hilltop for as along as she felt it was necessary to allow the fire in 1940 to be put out so she could return to the ruins and get back to her life.

Woo was conscious but disoriented. He was lying on his belly, and when Roxanne gingerly pushed against his shoulder, he turned on his side and pulled himself into a ball and groaned. His hands grasped his knees.

"It's okay," she said. "I'm not going to hurt you. I want to help." She crouched down beside him, hesitant to touch him again. "Where were you shot?"

Woo did not move, nor did he respond to her question. Roxanne simply stayed beside him, neither speaking nor moving, and just waited. After a few minutes, Woo's arm came off his knees, and he started making an effort to sit up. Roxanne put her hands on his shoulders to help steady him, and he muttered something in what she assumed was Chinese. She stood up and reached down for his hands, which he slowly extended upward. When she gently began trying to pull him to his feet, he let out a cry of pain, but he did not let go of her hands. She saw that he was still trying to stand, so she continued pulling even though she could see the effort was hurting him tremendously.

Once she had him on his feet, she put one of his arms behind her neck and held onto it with her right hand so that he was held against her left side.

296

She switched hands quickly and bent her neck, using her right hand to pull open the front of Woo's jacket. His shirtfront was covered in blood, and she carefully let the jacket close again. Woo was panting, and she could smell his perspiration.

"It looks pretty bad," she said to him. "But I'll try to get you to some help." With one of her hands behind his back and the other holding his right arm around her neck, she took a tentative step with him, and his feet moved forward, matching hers. "You're Johnny Woo, right?" she asked.

Woo muttered in Chinese again, but she did hear him say the word "Woo." Whether he was answering in the negative or affirmative, however, she could not tell.

"Well," she said, "for what it's worth, I'm Roxanne." She added "Blackwood" as an awkward afterthought.

"Blackwood," he said in a hoarse whisper. "Chester Blackwood."

Roxanne nodded, sure now that this was the same man who had given her father the original dose of Dragon's Tears. "My father," she said.

"Son of a bitch," Woo said.

Roxanne let a little laugh escape her. "This is too much," she said and continued slowly leading him toward the ridge where she knew a road would someday run connecting Swinburne's estate with the rest of Hollywood. She could see a faint glow in that direction, the lights of the city, and when she and Woo reached the point where Swinburne's gate would someday be, she saw below her a far less bustling Hollywood than she was used to seeing in 1940 and nowhere near the almost frightening size and activity she had seen in 1985.

Woo occasionally groaned and sometimes mumbled in Chinese, but he did not stumble, nor did he give any indication that he wanted to rest or stop altogether. Not sure of the best way to go, Roxanne followed the ridge that the road would one day be built on. Once on the other side of the ridge, she saw that there was a trail ahead of her, and she turned onto it and began following it down. Woo could not move quickly, and so their progress along the path and down the hill was extremely slow. Roxanne feared that moving him too fast and making him exert himself would cause his blood loss to quicken, but she also knew that if they moved too slowly, he would bleed to death before she could find help for him.

After almost an hour, the trail broadened, and she saw that it opened onto a paved road. "Won't be long," she said with relief. At the same time, clouds passed in front of the moon, taking away much of Roxanne's ability to see as clearly as she had at the top of the hill. Covered in sweat, she was breathing hard now and with her heightened awareness from the Dragon's Tears could feel blisters developing on her feet.

The road twisted through a canyon, and it was not long before Roxanne noticed driveways branching off of it and little houses tucked into the hillside. At the first of these, she stopped walking and looked to see if any lights were on. The house was dark, and she prodded Woo to move ahead. The next house had a light on, and she hoped that whoever lived here had a telephone and could call for help. But then she stopped where she stood.

"Oh my God," she said.

Woo grunted.

Roxanne stood staring at the house she had lived in as a child, and she knew that if she knocked on the door she would find her father as he had looked when she was little, and that she herself was asleep in the back room. By the light of the moon, she could see the window at the back of the house that opened onto her tiny bedroom. She had lived here with her father from the time her mother had left them until Chester Blackwood had sold his first novel. It was his little Chevrolet that was parked in the driveway next to the house.

She knew now where and when she was. It was 1925, and if she were to search Johnny Woo's pockets, she would find a vial of Dragon's Tears, the same vial that her father would find in an hour or so after he let Woo into his house. The man she was helping would be dead by then, and her father would wrap him in a rug and take his body into the mountains, the nine-year-old version of herself asleep in the backseat of the little Chevrolet.

Roxanne had tears in her eyes at the thought of her father here in the house, and she was tempted to go to the door and knock. But she also feared that her father would recognize her, even on an unconscious level, and so she knew she would have to stay where she was.

Gently swinging Woo's arm over her head, she turned to face him. Keeping one hand on his shoulder to steady him, she spoke slowly and just above a whisper. "You knew my father. Chester Blackwood." She paused and was relieved to see the glazed look in Woo's eyes lessen for a moment, and she knew she was getting through to him on some level. "He's here, inside this house. He'll help you." She spoke the words although she knew there was no saving Woo. The only good that could from his death would be for her father to get the Dragon's Tears. If he did not, she realized, this version of the past would be changed and the version of herself asleep inside the house would grow up into an entirely different woman. Knowing that Woo was as good as dead, Roxanne wanted nothing more than to keep this version of time from jumping onto a different track and possibly altering the future that waited for her on the other side of the time bridge she had marked with rocks high in the hills above her.

Turning Woo to face the house, she positioned herself behind him and pushed him forward toward the front porch. She trembled as she remembered sitting on the porch swing and walking on the rails, her arms stretched out for balance. At the porch steps, she feared Woo would fall forward, but she held him firmly and waited as he lifted one foot and then the next. When she had gotten him to the front door, she held him steady for several seconds and then released him, relieved that he did not fall over. Then she stepped to the side, thought about how Woo might knock on the door in his state, and pounded heavily on it before stepping farther away from it to hide in the shadows.

Seconds later the door opened, and light from inside the small house illuminated a small portion of the porch. "What the hell?" she heard her father say. Then Woo fell into Chester Blackwood's arms. Roxanne heard her father swear, and then he pulled Woo into the house and laid him on the floor before closing the door. Paralyzed, she waited several seconds before moving and then, realizing that her father might come back onto the porch to see how Woo had gotten there, she bolted down the steps and out to the street where she stopped and turned.

No sounds came from the house. She imagined her father dealing with the bleeding man and wondered what would happen now. Before she could bring herself to turn away and begin walking back up the hill, she heard a noise from behind her, and as she turned, she heard a man say, "Hi Roxanne."

She gasped as she turned. A man stood in the shadows beside a tree, but even before he moved toward her, she knew who it was, having recognized his voice.

"Eddie," she said, his name almost choked off in her throat by the emotion she felt.

And then she was in his arms, and she knew that everything was going to be all right. Everything about him felt as it should—his hands on the small of her back, his scent, the slight burn of his whiskers on her chin as she turned to kiss him—and she felt as though she would melt into him as they stood embracing in the street, all thoughts of her father and Johnny Woo gone from her mind.

"My God, Eddie," she said as they ended their kiss. "How did you get here? I was so worried when you weren't at your place."

"I know," he said. "I'm sorry."

"Did Swinburne do something to—"

He cut her off abruptly. "It was the Dragon's Tears. It wore off when I wasn't expecting it to. I've been trapped here."

"Thank God it's only been two days."

Now he stepped back from her, holding her hands in front of her. He looked at the ground for a moment, and then she saw him look back at her face. "For you," he said.

"What do you mean?"

"It's 1925, Roxanne. When I went through the time bridge and got stuck, it was 1920."

Understanding dawned on her immediately, and she was horrified. "Eddie!" She reached up and put both hands on either side of his face, her fingertips at his temples. "What have you . . ." she tried to ask and then was speechless.

"Does Woo have the Dragon's Tears?" he asked, ignoring the question she seemed unable to answer.

She nodded and then, realizing why he asked, said, "But I do, too." She had slipped Pence's vial into an inner pocket on her jacket and took it out now, holding it up for Eddie to see. When Eddie reached up slowly to touch the vial and then gently closed his hand over hers, the Dragon's Tears safely in her grasp, Roxanne felt herself tingle all over.

"Good," he said. "Otherwise I'd have had to have broken into your father's place to get at it." He sighed heavily, clearly relieved. "Come on," he said. "Let's walk down this way." He began leading her down the hill and away from her father's house as she put the Dragon's Tears securely back in her pocket.

As they walked down the hill, Eddie described what had happened between him and Swinburne after he and Roxanne had had their last goodbye. They held hands as they went, and when Eddie explained how he had been trapped in 1920, she squeezed his hand harder.

"I knew there was no way to get back to 1940," he told her. "But that was the only thing I wanted. So I started thinking about how I could get some Dragon's Tears. The only thing I could think of was how your father had gotten the first batch. He told me Johnny Woo had shown up at his door late one night in 1925. So I got a job and laid low for five years. It wasn't too hard to find out where your father lived." They had stopped walking in front of a small house a few doors down from Blackwood's modest home. Eddie nodded toward it. "I rented this place late in 1924, and every night I've been hiding in the bushes outside your father's place waiting for Johnny Woo to come stumbling along. I figured if he was in the bad shape your father described, I'd be able to wrestle the Dragon's Tears away from him, take a dose, and give it back so he could go up to the house and fulfill his destiny. When I saw he was with someone, I held back. I'm glad it was you he was with, but I've got to tell you, that was about the last thing I expected to see."

She was amazed at what he told her but even more amazed that she had found him again after having thought he had gone out of her life forever. The moon had come out from behind the clouds, and its light shone fully on Eddie's face now. She could see that there was very little difference in the way he looked. The five years he had spent in the 1920s must not have been too hard on him. Without either of them saying another word, they turned and went into Eddie's house, still holding each other's hands.

CHAPTER TWENTY-ONE

The morning sunlight streamed brightly into Roxanne's bedroom making her white sheets and pillowcases fairly glow. She and Eddie had slept with the window open, and now they could hear sparrows chirping from their perches among the fronds high in the palm trees in the front yard. Eddie had a pillow propped against the dark oak of Roxanne's headboard, and he half sat up against it, Roxanne's head on his chest and his hand toying with her hair. On the windowsill sat the now empty vial of Dragon's Tears, a glint of sunlight reflecting off its curves, the contents of the vial having been washed out as soon as Eddie and Roxanne had made it back to her house.

They had been back in 1940 for three days now and had separated only long enough for Roxanne to deal with the police investigation into her father's apparent suicide and to be looked at by a doctor to make sure she had not fractured her skull on Swinburne's hearth. When not dealing with the press or the police or Roxanne's lawyer, they had spent almost all of their time in bed, unable to keep from touching one another.

Not wanting to do anything that could upset the path of the future, Eddie had resisted the urge to write or publish anything in the 1920s and had gotten a job as a copy editor for the *Los Angeles Record*, the newspaper that Chester Blackwood had written for. Eddie had been careful never to bump into Blackwood during his time at the paper and had been relieved when the future science fiction writer had been fired for drunkenness.

As they had held each other in the single bed in that small house in 1925, so different from the comfort they enjoyed now in Roxanne's Pasadena home, Roxanne had told him all about Pence, Vivian Parker and Rebecca Le Blanc, the gunshots and the fire. They had agreed it was best to wait a few hours before crossing back to 1940 to be sure the danger was over. Even so, Roxanne had been anxious to get the final crossing over with, explaining to Eddie how she had taken a larger dose of Dragon's Tears and what must have been the significance of the divergent paths on the time bridge.

"I don't want to end up in the wrong 1940," she had said. "Not now. Not after everything we've been through to get out of the mess my father got us into."

Eventually, Eddie had gathered the few things he needed, left a note and some cash for his landlord, and the pair had walked up into the Hollywood hills just before dawn. It had been no problem for Roxanne to find the right time bridge with the little pyramid she had built in front of it, and she had given Eddie a drop of Dragon's Tears, insisting he take no more.

On the other side of the bridge, what remained of Swinburne's mansion was still smoldering in an early morning rain. Fire crews had left, and though Roxanne had found her car among the eight or ten still parked on the grounds of the estate, she had lost her purse in the fire and had no keys, so she and Eddie had made the long walk down from the hills once more. Picking up a *Los Angeles Times* on Sunset Boulevard, they read with awe that Swinburne was dead, last heard shouting about saving his books as the mansion had burned. The list of the dozen others dead included people from the film and publishing industries as well as socialite Vivian Parker. There was no mention of Rebecca Le Blanc.

Now Roxanne traced her finger up and down the line of hair on Eddie's stomach and asked, "What would you have done if Johnny Woo hadn't shown up during all of 1925?"

"I thought about that," he said. "I suppose the only thing to do would have been to bide my time and then show up in my apartment at two o'clock on the day I was supposed to meet you. What would you have done if you had shown up and found me waiting there but twenty years older than when you'd seen me the night before?"

She smiled. "Probably screamed," she said teasingly. "And then do what we've been doing the last three days."

Eddie chuckled and continued playing with her hair.

"There are things I don't understand," he said.

"Like?"

"Like Swinburne. The book I read in 1985 made it very clear that he lived long past your father's disappearance, long enough to make your life hell. We saw that the mansion was burned then, too, but he didn't die in it. And now he did."

Roxanne did not say anything for several seconds. "Eddie," she began hesitantly, "all those different paths in the time bridges I saw . . . there are a lot of different futures, more than we can imagine."

"In some, Swinburne lived, and in some he died? Is that what you mean?"

"Mm-hmm."

"And in some your father never got the Dragon's Tears, and in some he did."

"That's right."

"But how did he get them originally? In the 1940 where Asimov and Heinlein were publishing their stories, Pence and you wouldn't have been at that party. Pence wouldn't have shot Johnny Woo, and you couldn't have helped him get to your father."

Roxanne thought about it. "You're right. But who knows what else happened in that version of 1940? If my father had never been a famous writer, I might still have ended up posing for Klaus. Swinburne might still have blackmailed me with those photos. Vivian Parker could still have fallen in love with me just based on the cover for Rebecca's book."

Eddie picked up the thread of her thought. "Makes sense. And somehow I would have been involved with Swinburne, or my name would never have ended up in *The Golden Age of Science Fiction*."

"Having written my book," Roxanne added with mock severity.

"Having written your book," Eddie said with a smile. "So it makes sense that you and I both would have been at that party."

"And Woo? And Will?"

Eddie shook his head. He was still deeply bothered by Pence's death. "Swinburne was in deep with Vivian Parker, and Rebecca definitely moved in rough circles. If Woo had been trying to peddle the Dragon's Tears in 1940 while he hid out from the drug smugglers from the twenties, maybe Rebecca would have gotten wind of it."

"Once Swinburne and Vivian heard about it . . ."

"They would have wanted it. They wouldn't have needed your father to spark their interest."

"So Woo would have still gone to the party," Roxanne said.

"He could have. Someone other than Pence could have shot him. Hobart, maybe, if the deal went sour. And if he had gone through the time bridge after being shot, there's a chance he could have found his way to your father's place on his own without your help. Chester told me Woo had been there once earlier in the twenties."

Roxanne sat up, pulling the sheet up over herself, and looked at Eddie. In the bright light of the morning, she looked at Eddie's face. She had already gotten used to the little changes in him during the five years he had been gone, but it still felt strange to her that those five years had passed for Eddie when only two days had passed for her. He had put on a bit of weight, filled out a bit more. All traces of boyishness were gone from his face, and he was beginning to get lines around his eyes and on his forehead. She actually found him more attractive now than she had before he disappeared.

"You hungry?" she asked. When he said that he was, she offered to go downstairs and make breakfast.

"Let me do it," he said.

She raised an eyebrow. "Really?"

"Really. It's about time I stopped eating all my meals at the café. I need some practice if I'm going to get a place with a kitchen."

Without hesitating, she said, "You could just stay here, you know."

Eddie smiled at the thought, a look of mild surprise on his face. "Be your kept man?"

"Why not?"

"What would the neighbors say?"

She laughed. "Nothing more than they would have said about my father's wicked ways. And who cares what they think?"

"I like the way you think," he said and got out of the bed.

At the foot of the bed were two of Roxanne's robes, one white and the other green. She watched him put on the white one and said, "Seriously, Eddie, what are you going to do?"

He let out a thoughtful sigh. "I've been thinking about it." He crossed around the front of the bed and sat down on the other edge next to Roxanne. "I had a lot of time to think when I was . . . gone. You know? I'm not a writer, Roxanne. Not like you. I love science fiction, but I'm no good at writing it." She began to protest, but he stopped her. "I mean it. I got lucky with those stories I published in *Stupendous*, but there's no career in that. At first, I thought I'd open a bookstore like the one I saw in 1985, but it's too soon. The market's not there yet for all the things I've collected. I'll hang onto it—maybe open a store in thirty years."

"And in the meantime?"

He shrugged. "With Swinburne gone, Meteor's going to be foundering a bit until his estate gets settled. The company's probably going to get sold, parceled out."

"We could buy *Stupendous*."

"Maybe. Or I could start my own magazine."

"You think?" she said, excited.

"There's going to be a gap in the market. And I know how to fill it."

"How?"

He smiled. "You want to bet if I get a hold of those guys Asimov and Heinlein that they've got some more stories up their sleeves, things they thought up after your father stole their other ideas? It's about time science fiction got its golden age."

Roxanne leaned forward and hugged him, nuzzling against his neck and the terry cloth robe. Eddie held her as she said, "You're going to be great."

"With you," he said. As she leaned back, the sheet fell away from her body, and he looked eagerly at her for a moment before forcing himself up from the bed. "You've got your own work to do, you know," he said as he walked to the bedroom door. "That book of yours won't write itself." Then he added, "Eggs over easy?"

"Over hard," she said a bit mischievously and then listened to him chuckle as he walked toward the stairs. She dropped back onto the bed for a moment, her head on the pillow he had just been leaning against, and she turned her face into it, breathing in his scent. She stretched her arms out luxuriously after a few minutes and then sat up. The green robe was still at the foot of the bed, and she reached for it, slipping it on as she got out of bed.

Her writing desk was beside one of the windows—stationery and pens arranged neatly on it and her portable typewriter in its case on the floor beneath. She considered the desk for a moment and then walked out of the room and down the hallway toward the stairs and beyond them. From downstairs, she could hear the sounds of pans being rattled in the kitchen as Eddie gathered materials for breakfast.

The door beyond the top of the stairs opened onto her father's office, and she went inside. Most of the mess from Hobart and Luna's ransacking of the room had been cleaned up, and now the office looked much the same as it had when her father had written his stolen books here. It was not a room she had spent much time in when her father had lived here with her; she had never felt entirely comfortable in the office. Now, she felt differently about it and walked in, going straight to the large antique desk with the big Smith Corona typewriter sitting on it and a pile of blank paper beside it. Tentatively, she touched the keys and then tapped the spacebar. The carriage moved heavily, and she smiled.

Downstairs, Eddie had four eggs sizzling in a frying pan and bread in the toaster. He was looking for coffee in the cupboards when he thought he heard a noise from upstairs, and he quickly turned the knob on the stovetop to kill the flame under the frying pan. The sharp, crisp clack of a typewriter's letters hitting a sheet of paper carried down the stairs, a staccato rhythm punctuated by infrequent pauses and the regular ringing of the bell. Eddie smiled broadly and re-lit the burner on the stove.

ABOUT THE AUTHOR

Richard Levesque was born in Canada and grew up in Southern California. By day, he teaches composition and literature—including Science Fiction—at Fullerton College, and by night he works on his novels and short stories. He joined the ranks of independent novelists in 2012 with the release of *Take Back Tomorrow* and followed that with *Strictly Analog* and the first Ace Stubble novella, *Dead Man's Hand.* In 2013, he published a second Ace Stubble novella, *Unfinished Business* as well as *The Girl at the End of the World,* a post-apocalyptic YA novel. His most recent novels are *The Devil You Know* and *Foundlings.* When not writing or grading papers, he spends time with his wife and daughter, works on his collection of old pulp magazines, and tries to be better than a mediocre guitar player.

You can learn more about Richard at http://www.richardlevesqueauthor.com

Strictly Analog

*"...fast-paced futuristic thriller..."-**Publishers Weekly***

What's a private detective to do in a future where nothing is private any more?

For Ted Lomax, the answer is to find clients who need their info kept off the grid, and that's what Ted has done for years, skirting the high tech that runs the new California and living on the fringes of society. But when his daughter is accused of murdering her boyfriend—an agent in the Secret Police—Ted has to dig himself out of the hole he's been in for years in order to save her.

Before long, he's pulled into a shadow world of underground hackers, high-end programmers, and renegade gear-heads, all of whom seem to have a stake in California's future. The further he digs into the case, the clearer it becomes that it's about more than one dead agent. Solving it might save his daughter. And it might get him killed. And it just might open the door to secrets that reach back to the attack that almost killed him eighteen years before. At any rate, Ted Lomax will never be the same.

"Levesque brings the goods. I really enjoyed reading "Strictly Analog". It's a story that should appeal to fans of early Gibson or Sterling. And now that our world is much closer to the cyberpunk vision of tomorrow that was forecast decades ago, the story should appeal to contemporary detective fiction fans too. "Strictly Analog" is highly recommended."--*The New Podler Review of Books*

*This review was of the manuscript version submitted to Amazon's Breakout Novel Awards competition in 2013.

The Girl at the End of the World

Her fight begins the day the world ends.

Scarlett Fisher is an average California teenager. She likes hanging out with her friends and talking on the phone. She does all right at school, and she's made the best of her parents' divorce. But in one way, she's special: on her fifteenth birthday, a fast-moving plague wipes out everyone she's ever known, yet somehow it passes her by.

Her family dead, alone in a corpse-strewn metropolis, she has no choice but to survive. She needs food, shelter, a safe place to sleep. She discovers that an ordinary girl is capable of extraordinary things, and that she's more resilient than she imagined. Even so, she wishes more than anything that she could just find another survivor.

Unfortunately for Scarlett, not everyone who survived the plague is looking for companionship. And she's about to find out just how difficult survival really is.

Foundlings

Derek Chandler had it all—the education, the promising future, the beautiful wife—but a tragic accident changed everything and his life now stands in ruins. Haunted by the ghosts of what might have been, Derek tries to lose himself in his new job, but what begins as a minor academic mystery soon unravels, leaving him with the burden of a second truncated life: that of long-vanished science fiction writer, Kichiro Nakamura.

Convinced that finding Kichiro is somehow the key to finding his own peace, Derek is drawn into a frantic search of modern and post-war Los Angeles as he tries to reconstruct the shattered kaleidoscope of American and Japanese cultures. And the key to everything just might be the beautiful—and very suspicious—tattoo artist, Yuki Kamikaze.

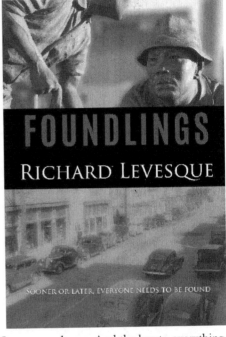

FOUNDLINGS

RICHARD LEVESQUE

SOONER OR LATER, EVERYONE NEEDS TO BE FOUND

creative writing
articles

music — guitar
piano

surfing / weight dirt
exercise

Spanish

family (michelle/girls/...)

— santiago
— online saddleback
— ?